329
YEARS AWAKE

BY ELLIE MALONEY

329 YEARS AWAKE

SCI FI EPIC

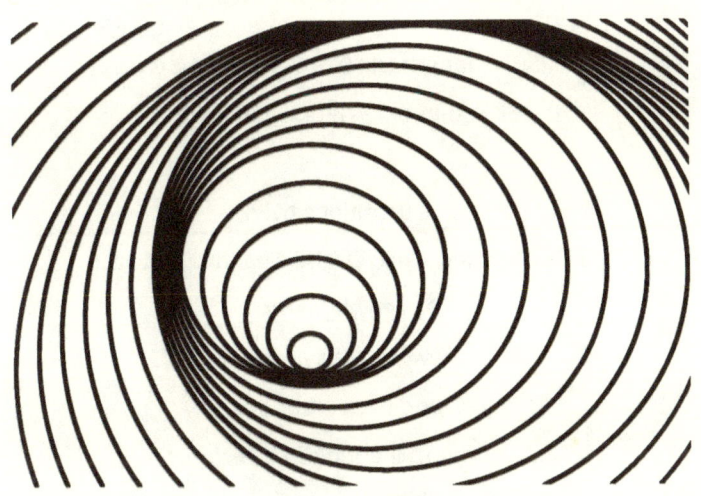

Jalapeño Publishing

College Park, MD

Published by Jalapeño Publishing

PO Box A, College Park, MD, U.S. 20740

www.JalapenoPublishing.com

ISBN (paperback) 978-0-9983614-1-3

ISBN (e-book) 978-0-9983614-2-0

Illustrations by:

Ellie Maloney, Akiko Okabe, Leandro Correa

Design elements:

www.Pixabay.com

Front and back cover design:

www.RockingBookCovers.com

Photography:

Viktor Bondar

To my spouse, C. - for eternal
support and inspiration. To
you, who bought me wine,
listened to my stories,
worked hard to
support my whims...
There would be no
book without you.

ACKNOWLEDGMENTS

Writing a book perhaps is a solitary experience, but from the conception of the idea to the product on the shelf - it takes numerous generous souls who volunteer their time and inspire a writer to take the story one step further. I have a long list of thanks to the people who I both know personally and whose minds and ideas I experienced via their work.

To Brittany Micka-Foos and Andrew Reeves, for brilliant editing and beta-reading. God knows what you've been through reading my first drafts!

To my parents, who spared no expense on my education. I hope this book, if nothing else, stands as a justification of that investment.

To Rujanee Mahakanjana, Viola Van de Sandt, Sandy and Dom McCarthy, Rosemary A. Johns, Javier Alvarez, Buck Detroit, Bradley K. Bleckwehl, and others for beta-reading the novel. Your feedback was invaluable.

To Akiko Okabe, for helping me make sense of some Japanese context, spot-on suggestions, and for fantastic illustrations.

To Dr. Roger Penrose, Dr. Leonard Susskind and Dr. Michio Kaku, for inspiring numerous science ideas. Namely, Dr. Penrose inspired the idea of oscillation — the fictional ability of humans to change reality through consciousness.

To Laverne Cox and other transgender women and men on screen, in the military, in sports, and everywhere, for showing us how to fight for rights with dignity.

Finally, to all my readers, for giving this book a chance. I am forever thankful to every one of you. You make my efforts worthwhile.

Thank you, my dearest ones. You make this world a better place.

Sincerely yours,

E.M.

TABLE OF CONTENTS

...It was a bloody ballet in a cold war theater...

PART
ONE

1
TSUNAMI

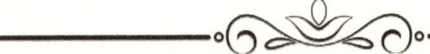

Year 2275.
Monrovia, Liberia

Have you ever had a recurring dream? Mine is always about a tsunami.

In my dream, everything feels real: I taste the iodine-soaked salty spray, I smell the seaweed-reeking air, I hear the thundering wall of death, and feel earthquake tremors gyrate the ground. Many people cannot run in their dream, as if weighed down by gravity, but I can, and as best I can explain, I reset reality. Viscerally, my life hangs on a thin thread, a thread stretching through my consciousness... and I need to pull that thread to reboot the dream once death washes over me, as my consciousness begins to fade.

17

Fade in.

Sometimes, I stand on a cliff looking down at the washed-out beach. The wind whips my face, soaking me with the ocean mist as the clouds turn ominously black. Behind, for as long as I can see, lies a solid bush - twigs and branches so thick, I cannot escape. Ahead is the cliff and the approaching tsunami.

Am I scared?

Fear is not the right word. It's rather like I am solving a puzzle. Remember your middle-school exams? The white analogue clock above the green chalkboard with the thinnest arrow nervously running circles? Remember blood pounding in your head and your heightened awareness to any shuffling or whispering in the room? Add to that, it is math class and you suck at math, but you have that lingering sense that the lazy son of a bitch you are, you need to work harder, apply 110 percent of your brainpower, and you may just figure out how to solve this seemingly impossible math problem.

Feverishly you scribble long lines of basic math equations trying to derive new mathematical solutions, bypassing those pesky fractals that you never grasped. Your brain racing like a feral animal in a maze. Your instincts are sharpened by evolution: live, breed, die, repeat. In these dreams, I am this desperate student inventing a new theorem to compensate for the lack of knowledge; or that feral animal digging is way out through the maze wall and beating the system – whichever analogy works best for you.

This is how I feel about beating the tsunami.

Every time the wave approaches, I strategize how to escape: can't run through the bush and can't jump off the cliff either; the only remaining solution is to hold on to something and let the wave wash over me.

First attempt:

The wave comes and I hold my breath. It's not bad at first, deceptively calming, the way I probably felt in my mother's womb. But oxygen quickly depletes and I suffocate, because the water does not subside soon enough.

Second attempt:

I try the same scenario again. I grab the thorny hickory twigs struggling to disassociate from the pain in my palms. I teach my brain to disregard the thorns pricking the skin and drawing blood. I hear the wave behind me, so close that at any second I will be submerged. I strive to calm my breathing and ration the oxygen in my lungs. This time the wave was not weakened by the impact from the hill, and I receive the full-force blow of water - as hard as a concrete wall - flying at me at the speed of a race car. I black out.

Suddenly something changes: I realize that I am dreaming. Instead of waking myself, a strange sense of calm washes over *me, and I continue running different tsunami sequences with full awareness and a lot more efficiency.*

Third attempt:

This time, tsunami catches me at a beach-side restaurant. It's a one-story building with its foundation slightly above the ocean level. I try running out of the restaurant, but barely make it to the exit when the wave smashes through the panoramic glass windows throwing shards of glass, furniture, and metal railing. The restaurant fills with water immediately, and I am caught in a whirlpool of people, furniture and debris, until my head is smashed against the wall.

Fourth attempt:

The same restaurant overlooking the ocean. The monstrosity of a wall emerges from the horizon. I run through the screaming sticky mess of bodies trampling each other like a herd of gazelles escaping a predator. Running towards the exit, I am knocked off my feet by a sharp metal rod that pierces my body like a hot knife through a stick of butter. The restaurant around me fades out.

Fade out.

Come to think of it, the restaurant in my dreams looks a lot like this one.

***

Anglers restaurant was owned by the same Liberian family for over 300 years. Back in the 21st century, Liberia was a poverty-ridden country, with a handful of rich people who either came from Lebanon and ran all the prospering businesses in the country, or locals who made their riches on corrupt government schemes, often related to blood diamonds. Anglers was acquired by a young Liberian, who returned home after earning his business degree in Europe, and who saved enough cash to challenge the owner to a game of billiards. The Lebanese owner did not know that Abu spent five years in Germany working in a famous bar that held billiards tournaments. He made friends with some of the most famous European players, who gave him free - and often unsolicited - lessons. During the afterhours, Abu practiced his game and became quite good at it. In fact, he was so good, that in his last year he even qualified to enter the championship.

Abu didn't win it; that would be unrealistic given the amount of talent that flocked there every year from around the world. But Abu's skill was good enough to win him Anglers.

***

"These days, people rarely bother thinking how things were before the Big Ice," Otis Solarin mumbled apologetically, pulling the chair for his lovely date as they entered *Anglers,* "but chronology is hard-wired into my brain. After all, I am a historian; it's like an occupational hazard to me. Whenever I am attempting to understand something, I go back in history looking for the linchpin moment, like in case of finding the reason for these damn tsunami dreams."

Over the last 300 years or so, *Anglers* went from a marginally profitable fish-and-chips joint in one of the poorest countries in the world to a five-star restaurant, located in the hotbed of human civilization; at least the planet-side part of it. In the 2190s, the effects of global warming were so drastic that the politicians implemented a daring, but half-baked project - chemical cooling of the planet, which resulted in a DIY Ice Age. The ice descended from the poles and stretched toward the equator, easing between the zones of Tropical Cancer and Capricorn - the only stretch of Earth where the ground was not covered with meters of ice.

20

By 2275, humanity became a broad generalization. Most humans inhabited six orbital stations and a few austere colonies in space. By the roll of the dice, Liberia, and West Africa in general, became prime real estate as a source of romantic attachment of the humans to the cradle of their civilization. The world order was flipped like an hourglass. Thus began the era of the Big Ice.

The natives of the surviving climate zone were lucky, as they were presented with a choice: to stay on Earth or to move to crammed quarters on one of the orbital stations. Space-side living was not for the meek, and no amount of flashy advertisement could convince Africaners otherwise. In a sense, the planet-side folks were blessed to have nightmares about tsunamis. The spacers' nightmares always associated with boiling in the vacuum.

***

Yenplu (pronounced Nyene-Plu) dug the fork in her vegan fattoush salad, watching the waves through the panoramic windows of the *Anglers* restaurant. Ny, as her friends called her, was from the native-to-Liberia Bassa people, but the name was not traditional to Bassa. The name meant a "white woman," and back in the day it was supposed to imply "a very beautiful woman". Nobody is immune from parents' ignorance. When Ny's parents picked this name, they implied it more or less literally, because of her light complexion. Ny wrestled with accepting her name all her life, feeling mixed up about the original connotation. She couldn't resign to the echo of oppressive beauty standards implied in her name. Finally, she insisted to be called Ny, secretly implying it as the short form of 'deny'.

Otis and Ny took the table next to the window with the ocean waves splashing against black smooth rocks just a few meters away. A trip to *Anglers* was a rare treat, as they had to book it a month in advance. That day they felt even luckier because the ocean was stormy, and they both loved to watch the waves roll in. The magic of the force of nature was calming and completely surreal. Otis was watching the waves with an extra edge, searching the horizon for the signs of an approaching tsunami. He knew that when the tsunami is far enough, you cannot distinguish it from the horizon. And when you actually notice it, it's entirely too late. Otis knew that his tsunami phobia was irrational. The entire Liberian coast was equipped with tsunami sensors, and yet, to him these recurring dreams were as visceral as a paper cut.

21

The rain grew stronger. It was the rainy season, and the name was everything it promised to be. Neither of the old friends were bothered by the rain; it was merely a romantic force of nature.

Ny pulled the blanket from the back of the chair over her shoulders and reluctantly peeled her gaze from the waves.

"...But we don't have tsunamis here, in West Africa," she said.

"Not recently. Since these dreams kept coming back, I

looked it up. Apparently, there was one 73,000 years ago. The scientists say *that* tsunami made any tsunami in human history pale in comparison. It was caused by an eruption of an ocean volcano, that obliterated the Cape Verde Island..."

"Is that so? Maybe you have genetic memory about it. You know, the collective unconscious that Jung loved to talk about."

"Jung had brilliant intuition, and he cared a great deal about dreams. I'd like to get his take on mine." Otis smiled.

The wind sharply changed its direction and threw fine rain mist through the open window. The waiter hurried to close it, to the regret of the budding lovebirds who found it bonding to be present in the face of nature. Although there was zero danger associated with this rain, their genetic memory stirred the survival instinct: adrenaline coursed their bloodstream, drawing blush to their cheeks and warmth to cold fingers. Together with a glass of Merlot, it created a cozy magic around the two.

Ny and Otis were in their forties, with university tenures, paid-off mortgages, no children, and each with a sizable retirement account. By 2275, life was theirs for the taking and they were soaking up every drop.

22

Meanwhile the waiter delivered Otis' order. They placed their orders a month ago, together with the table reservation, so Ny had no idea what her partner was getting. It was a cod fillet with a side of cassava fries, sautéed chard and garlic, with bright lemon wedges on the rim.

"Is that a *real* fish? Are you insane?" Ny whispered as if being pulled into one of Agatha Christie's murder mysteries.

"Oh come on, it's not like it's a beef steak!" said Otis with a layer of exaggerated confidence. He himself felt as if he were committing a small murder, if there was such a thing as a small murder, but the temptation was too great.

"Oh Otis, do you have to be so gross? When was the last time you saw anyone eating a steak?" Otis frowned, mimicking intense thinking, and laughed.

"Come on, dear. We're at *Anglers*, a 300-year-old seafood restaurant! And it's not like eating animal food is illegal..."

"It's not illegal, but you know how I feel about it. Not to mention, it's so expensive."

It was expensive alright. Otis could order five vegan fish fillets for the same amount of money. It was easy for Ny to judge him. A third-generation vegan, she had no idea what a real fish tasted like. He, on the other hand, remembered fishing with his dad on the boat off the coast of Sierra Leone as a boy. Back then, he was a fisherman's son, not a professor of space history in the liberal university, where eating animal products was socially frowned upon.

"Maybe it's my carnivorous genetic memory percolating today!" Otis tried to make light of it.

"Nice try."

"Speaking of genetic memories, back to what you said earlier, that I was accessing my collective unconscious memory about this tsunami. Let's say I take it seriously for a moment. *Homo Sapiens* species first appeared in Africa over 200,000 years ago. You may be onto something, Ny. I mean, I may be accessing the collective unconscious memory of the tsunami survivors from 73,000 years ago. Wouldn't that be something!"

"Maybe, maybe... We just scratched the surface of quantum consciousness theories. The results of the latest experiments are mind-blowing."

23

"On the other hand, maybe I am simply training my brain for something in my sleep... For example, I am trying to deal with mid-life crisis or mortality..."

"I don't think you can apply mid-life crisis to yourself just yet, my dear, not after what we did this morning! Yeah...but the rest of it makes sense. When you are asleep, your brain is free from running your body and can reroute its efforts to something else. Whether your brain is trying to process your genetic memories or to deal with mortality, it would make perfect sense to do it in your sleep..."

Otis considered for a second how esoteric their lunchtime conversation had turned and smiled. *Professors of all generations are a bit prone to philosophic banter,* he thought. He also thought that tonight it was time to make his next move. With those thoughts, Otis lightly brushed his hand against an item in his pocket—a black velvet box with exactly one carat of Ny's happiness.

73,000 Years Ago.
Lenauri, the Unkari Home Planet

Ennuturat and Hundigar were ready to skip. They took their seats at the two-person transporter, bringing the systems online and plotting the course. The transporter was positioned at the edge of a deep crater. The perimeter of the crater was equipped with the state-of-the-art wormhole technology. Planet Earth was their destination. It was used by the Unkari as a lab for the most elaborate biological research they had ever undertaken.

The Unkari originated from an ancient galaxy in the process of being cannibalized by a larger, younger one. Living in such a volatile world, they were running out of time. Within several generations, their galaxy would be entirely swallowed by this gigantic monstrosity with a raging black hole in the middle. Their home world, Lenauri, would likely not survive. Although the disaster was several generations away, the sense of urgency was upon every Unkari, and each one of them did their share to find a solution. Numerous Unkari teams were scouting the universe in search of a new habitat.

It was because of this lingering disaster that Ennuturat's research team had stumbled on a new species that made many Unkari religiously scared. Those creatures could form mental networks and reset reality to the moment of their choosing. They did not manipulate time, as it would appear at first. It was the basic fabric of space-time, down to the sub-atomic level, where everything percolated in a primordial ocean of possibilities that they somehow altered. These creatures could lock onto any possibility of their choosing, their consciousness serving as the ultimate observer. The creatures called this mysterious ability to anchor the universe to a four-dimensional reality an oscillation.

Ennuturat was summoned to testify before the Unkari

Council:

"We used to think that the universe branches out into the multiverse foam, with every possibility derived from quantum superposition becoming a reality in some universe. These creatures made us rethink all we know about the universe," reported Ennuturat before the Council. "Apparently, they lock-in this part of the universe into a four-dimensional cage. How they do it? We don't know. Is it a local phenomenon to this region of space? We also have no idea. But we observed them resetting the reality numerous times, choosing different actions if they didn't like the consequences."

The head of the Joint Unkari Council sprayed several clouds of orange and blue powder in the air from the orifices on the side of his limbs, indicating both fear and confusion.

"Ennuturat, with all due respect, this is hard to fathom. Are you saying that they are immortal?" The grand hall of the Unkari highest collegiate governing body erupted in nervous commotion and various shades of colored powder. Soon enough they could hardly see each other literally drowning in their emotions.

"Order! Order, colleagues!" yelled the head of the Council, restraining himself from spraying any more emotions in the air. "Ennuturat, proceed."

"They are not immortal, master Counselor. They die of old age, and I must add, their life span is as short as an elder's breath. We believe that since they die of old age, they do not manipulate time. The only possible conclusion is that they switch quantum superposition like a light switch and anchor an alternative outcome from the ocean of possibilities to this four-dimensional reality".

25

The five hundred Unkari elders present in the room erupted in so much nervous energy that the meeting was recessed. When the emotional air cleared up and the honorable elders returned to the room, Ennuturat concluded his report suggesting to destroy the entire race arguing that this race was too dangerous to be left alive.

The matter would have been settled unanimously if not for one dissenting voice. Immirtau, nearly the oldest living Unkari, was fragile, barely standing upright while addressing the honorable gathering. It took him tremendous effort to speak loudly enough so that everyone could hear. He persevered knowing that the message was so important, that even if he died right after the speech, it was worth the effort.

"How quickly you, my colleagues, forgot the principles of decision-making! How quickly you abandoned your logic in the face of fear! Don't you realize that if the collective consciousness of these creatures locks the universe itself into a four-dimensional reality, where, and I hate to state the obvious, colleagues, where all of us exist, this may mean that without them the universe as we know it may revert to the primordial ocean of particles. Do you want to risk sliding into non-dimensional existence? Who among you can guarantee that the universe itself will not vanish?"

For the first time during this treacherous meeting silence penetrated the grand hall. Immirtau's argument was just crazy enough to at least grab everyone's attention. Upon several long recesses, the decision was to decisively attack and destroy the entire planet, but preserve some DNA for research. A few galactic rotations later, the Council received a report from the task force assigned to study the genetic samples. The results were not promising. It was clear that working with a small research sample in a lab was not enough to create genetic diversity and isolate the gene that was responsible for oscillation. The report concluded that they needed to move to the second phase of the research, using a planet-size research sample and allowing it to naturally go through evolution. It was clear that there would be no shortcuts in this project. The Council identified a planet capable of supporting carbon-oxygen life forms in the neighboring galaxy, the very galaxy that was ripping their home apart. The planet was seeded with the genetic material from the oscillating species.

And so the tedious research began: live, breed, die, repeat.

***

Back at the transporter, the two colleagues, who had just met each other in person, awkwardly prepared to share the small personal space of the government-issued two-person space can. More so, the two would have to share limited lab space on Earth for the duration of the entire shift. In order to keep their presence secret, Unkari established the outpost on the Atlantic ocean floor. Earth's atmosphere was highly incompatible with the Unkari biochemistry, and from that perspective it mattered little whether the lab was on the dry land or under the water. One way or another, a moment of exposure to the boiling, by the Unkari standards, Earth would be enough to end them on the spot.

"What are the odds that the current sample will be successful?" Hundigar asked, going over the specifications of the route. Although to Ennuturat, Hundigar seemed ignorant, he was not new to the project. Hundigar used to be just a name attached to the faceless bureaucrat across the galaxy, who received routine reports from Ennuturat about the progress of the project. And now this faceless bureaucrat had decided to get his tentacles dirty. Ennuturat could not imagine what compelled young Hundigar to trade his secure office job on Lenauri for work on the site, which was considered a hardship post in the Unkari scientific circles. Except, perhaps, the fact that, for the first time in millennia, the project was showing success, and someone would be getting credit for it.

"All the data checks out. Compared to their ancestors, humans are still underdeveloped, but we reached acceptable similarity. The few previous iterations developed too many dead-end gene sequences. They were not viable for further research and were successfully eliminated from the breeding pool."

"What was the elimination process?"

Didn't you read my reports?" sighed Ennuturat, considering to perhaps apply for a separate transporter.

"Uh, I definitely have read them," lied Hundigar as convincingly as he could. "But it is always better to learn from someone who was there."

"It was the usual combination of protocol measures. Genetic viruses, natural disasters... the planetary scale action for the most part. As you know, we are short-handed here for individual interventions. I believe it was you who approved the latest budget."

Hundugar did not see a jab coming in so soon.

Awkwardly suppressing his emotions, Hundigar tried to move on with the conversation but the transporter slowly filled with the clouds of powder.

"Please, contain yourself," added Ennuturat, an insult to the previous injury. The best Hundigar could do was to fake ignorance.

"How exciting, Ennuturat. Are you excited? We may achieve success in our lifetime!"

We. Indeed.

"Let's focus on the coordinates, colleague, shall we?" snapped Ennuturat.

Ouch, thought Hundigar as he finished updating the coordinates. *Ennuturat is simply jealous.* Ennuturat used to report to him, while Hundigar supervised his project on the Committee, and the two had developed an ego riff the size of the Itarian nebula!

Hundigar was shaking his head, thinking how Ennuturat had treated him unfairly, patronizing him like a small offspring, while they carried the same rank.

Lost in his thoughts, Hundigar did not notice that his limb hit one key erroneously. Not that it would dramatically change the destination, but it was bad enough that they might miss the landing platform *at* the destination point.

28

And so it happened.

***

"Where are we?" yelled Ennuturat as the transporter exited the vortex and crash-landed, obviously, in the wrong place.

Hundigar did not answer. The transporter crashed into the foot of the ocean volcano. The impact made the ocean floor ripple. Hundigar hit his head on the console so hard that the life force left his body.

"Poor bastard..." mumbled Ennuturat. "At least he will not have to go through the embarrassment of disqualification."

With those words, the senior Unkari scientist shoved the lifeless body to the floor, manually started the transporter again and drove it away from the impact scene as fast as he could. The scanners demonstrated a horrific development: because of the impact, the ocean volcano became active. Eruption was imminent. Ennuturat was not worried for his own safety, as he was entering a fortified lab dock. But the most promising research sample would be destroyed when the tsunami hit the land. Galactic rotations of selective breeding would be lost. Ennuturat was nearing retirement, and with that his hope of witnessing the initial results of his entire life's work was dwindling away.

Year 2275.

The Unkari Research Lab, Atlantic Ocean

"Master Ennuturat! You need to see this! I have identified a research subject that is going through the final stage! Look at his brainwaves during the sleep cycle!"

Old Ennuturat slowly got off his reclined chair and proceeded to the monitor, where his young assistant was pulling up various databases on someone named Otis Solarin.

"Hmm... The coefficient of the thalamus activity correlated with the oscillation ability is extremely high. Are you sure he has the gene?"

"Positive! I am so excited! This is the first time we have received this good of a result since the subject named Carl Jung, although the gene was not passed onto either of his five offspring. Otis Solarin, on the other hand... The gene runs in his family."

29

All the excitement and exuberant youth of Ennuturat's new assistant reminded him of the late Hundigar - not a compliment in Ennuturat's vocabulary. Ennuturat gazed outside the large transparent force field of the research lab that separated them from the ocean. A large school of fluorescent fish hurried by, casting shadows on the rippled sandy ocean floor, lit up with the green lights surrounding the lab building. He would never admit it to anyone, but he had grown to love this view and the serenity of the ocean floor. Sometimes he would open the sound channel and flood his personal quarters with the sounds of the ocean. The songs of the aquatic species worked miracles for his old body. "Presuming it is so, and all checks out, do you think he can oscillate when awake?"

"Hmm... I don't know, master. But I know someone on Erinozhan who is creating an artificial field that if successful would amplify the brain waves and simulate the collective network effect of their ancestors. Perhaps he could oscillate in the field. But in any event, his descendants, a generation or two away, will be able to."

"We need him then. As soon as possible."

"Master..."

"Is this going to be an ethics lecture?"

"Master... You know as well as I do... Abductions are ruled illegal by the Council."

"Black hole on their heads! When we are so close, they decide to fall for this 'human rights' nonsense."

"I know, master, it is extremely frustrating, but we have to follow the protocol."

"So what do we do?"

"Well, we discussed the First Contact for some time now. Maybe this Solarin presents a good reason to officially introduce ourselves. He may willingly agree to join our research project. With a little white lie of course, but willingly nonetheless."

"What if he doesn't go with us? Our presence will be revealed."

"Master, it is only a matter of time before they discover us anyway. We could move operations to the Moon, but you know how much this would complicate our work. We need to be proactive. I think at this point, the best course of action is to reveal ourselves and make a good story to go with it. Say, we are looking for partnership. Let them think they actually decide something."

"There might be hope for you after all!" smiled Ennuturat. Ennuturat was old school. Negotiating with the lab animals was beyond his comprehension, but he knew one thing for sure: this universe belonged to the new guard, for better or worse. And the new Unkari, with their evolved vision of these humans, would have to deal with their dangerous ability. Looking towards eternity, Ennuturat had resigned to this new vision, despite what he personally thought of it. "Hmm... First Contact you say. That should be fun... I'd like to see their reaction when we come out of the ocean." He smiled mischievously. "Alright, send a memo to the Council. If they approve, we'll have some fun before I drift to eternity."

"Don't say that, Master. You have many galactic rotations ahead of you," coaxed the young Unkari scientist, fully aware that he was lying. But what's a little white lie, when someone's peace of mind is at stake?

***

Back at Anglers, Ny's eyes sparkled like twin supernovae in the night sky. The reality of the ring on her finger refused to sink in. The sides of the diamond were catching fire, juxtaposed with the background scenery of the angry Atlantic and reflecting high luminescence of the restaurant's ambiance. However, the storm was getting stronger, and Ny focused on the horizon. Otis was waiting for the bill to pop up on the small table screen, as Ny was scrutinizing the waves. When the number pinged, Otis leaned forward allowing the system to read his retina and authorize the payment, when Ny gripped his hand, driving her short-cut nails in his skin.

31

"What is it, dear?" Otis asked her.

"Otis, look, I think it's a tsunami!"

2
NOT ALONE

Year 2275.
Monrovia, Liberia

Moments later...

Ny looked outside the panoramic glass window, and there it was: not the actual tsunami, of course, but the wall of water big enough to give her tsunami nightmares. The restaurant descended into chaos. Many ran outside to the parking lot, some stayed put in their seats, frozen in shock.

Otis and Ny did not run either. Perhaps they subconsciously were hoping it was a dream or a trick of their imagination. One way or another, everything happened in a span of a few seconds, and then the hurling wall of water just dropped like a curtain, leaving behind a cloud of vapor.

Anglers was overlooking the beach, where seconds ago hundreds of tourists peacefully sipped their pina coladas and soaked in the African sun. Now, tripping over the beach beds, umbrellas, and each other, all these folks bolted away from the ocean front. Those, who fell behind, started noticing something in the cloud of steam, where the wall of water came from.

Curiosity won over fear, and Otis and Ny rushed to the beach. Working in the opposite direction to the frightened

35

crowd, they made their way close enough to make some sense of what was going on. There, they saw a row of the coast guard officers, dispatched as the first responders to the unknown external threat, who were assuming a defensive position and pointing their weapons in the direction of the ocean. Between the narrowly spread officers, Otis could see patches of the ocean front. There, fifty meters into the water, he saw eleven domed structures glittering in the sunlight. They floated on the waves in a V-shaped formation, with the V-tip towards the shore. From what he could see, they were at least five meters tall, spherical, with mechanical limbs on the sides. Multiple joints swiftly snaked through water creating all that foam and steam around them.

One of the coast guards yelled: "On my mark! Don't shoot without my command!"

The rest of the soldiers were tensely motionless, keeping their weapons in the 'ready' position.

The nearest dome slowly started approaching the shore. The coastguard commander asserted: "Hold! Do not fire!"

Meanwhile, two helicopters approached from the downtown area. In a matter of moments, they were doing laps around the area of the ocean, looking tiny and frankly worthless compared to the domes. By that time, the majority of the civilians were gone, but the few who remained, huddled together behind the line of the first responders, recording and broadcasting the event live.

36

Ny was clinging to Otis' shoulder, her face paler than ever. Otis asked Ny to stay behind and stepped towards the crowd. She silently shook her head, eyes big and still, but Otis insisted. Pushing through the crowd, Otis stepped on someone's foot.

"Watch out, old man!"

An angry teenager shoved Otis to the side, because he was obstructing the view. Otis wasn't tall enough to see over the heads of the huge coast guard officers. He decided to lay on the sand and get his view between the soldiers' feet: this was a good strategy because disciplined soldiers did not budge.

Otis stretched forward his wrist, directing the wristlet to begin the recording on the maximum zoom, and watching the events on a small holographic display in his field of vision. Thanks to the zoom and good video quality, he could get a close-up look at what was there, in the ocean. He pointed at the leading dome and carefully examined the details.

Otis could clearly see that the semi-transparent surface of the dome was designed to host one single creature, unmistakably alien, sitting at the control dashboard and operating the vehicle. The creature's body was barely seen, and it looked as if it was wearing a protective suit. Otis could only see the helmet, and the tentacles operating the controls. The mere sight of the helmet made him feel queasy: it appeared to have three red glowing eyes. Otis was convinced that the three red glowing eyes could not be good. The domes looked identical. They were floating at a distance, probably waiting for the command from the front leader, just like the human soldiers.

For some time, the scene did not change, except more and more ground troops arrived, and Otis was rapidly losing his visibility. The newly arrived soldiers formed second and third rows behind the frontline, covering the gaps. Recording the event was getting increasingly difficult. When the next batch of soldiers arrived in their armored vehicles and sprinted to provide the reinforcement, Otis decided to move closer and get a better view. A huge officer with shoulders so broad they made him look nearly square, noticed Otis crawling forward on the sand, and decisively waved him to stay where he was. Otis waited until the officer turned around and advanced a bit more. The next time his advances were noticed, the soldier got annoyed, swiftly stepped towards Otis and grabbed him by the collar of his shirt, lifting him from the ground like a kitten.

37

"Step back, I will not repeat myself!" he barked at Otis and shoved him further from the line of the military personnel.

The officer was very persuasive, thought Otis. That was when he noticed one kid climbing on the straw-covered metallic beach umbrella. It was a brilliant idea, and Otis made his way through the crowd to the umbrella and climbed as close to the top as he could. This way he was able to continue recording.

Meanwhile, the soldiers dispersed a force field in front of them. Every thirty meters, a soldier tossed in the air a device the size of a large grapefruit, and it disassembled itself into hundreds of smaller marbles that levitated in the air in a chessboard formation, creating a shield.

When the wall of airborne marbles was established, Otis' video was recording through the punctuated grid, and yet the visibility was still good enough to be able to make out the leading dome, as it slowly exited the water and stopped. Otis could clearly observe that the sphere was actually a half-sphere moving on thin long limbs with multiple joints. Then the half-sphere of the alien ship gracefully landed on the sand, and all the tentacles folded themselves on top of the sphere. The crowd gasped, awaiting annihilation by the laser beam, or some other freaky alien technology. But the aliens waited too.

Otis could hear the soldiers passing the orders: under no circumstances to fire first. The soldiers sweated and prayed to all the gods in the universe. The waiting was unbearable. The nerves were tight like a string, and all the epic nature of the moment was so thick in the air, Otis could have sliced it with a knife. Indeed, humans were witnessing the First Alien Contact.

What happened next, no science fiction writer could have predicted. The crowd heard the music. The sound surrounded them from all directions at once, as if they were in a concert hall. From the first notes, Otis could tell that the piece of music belonged to humans, and it was centuries old. Otis directed his wristlet to identify the piece – it was Bethoven's 'Brandenburg Concerto'. He, like everyone else, had no idea what to make of it. Were the aliens greeting humans with their own music? Did they come in peace? Or was it some kind of a diversion, while an elaborate takeover plan was taking place?

Millions of ideas floated in Otis' head, but in the next moment everything became somewhat clearer. From the base of the sphere, an opening formed and a clear box, the size of a pizza box, started moving toward the crowd. Something yellow and shiny was inside the box. Otis zoomed in on the object – it was a golden disk, flat, the size of a pizza dish. Otis even could make out the grooves on the disc.

Someone in the crowd yelled: "Voyager!" and ushered at the nearest coast guard officer, who immediately threw the man to the ground and dragged him to one of the armored vehicles. While the coast guard tried to contain the situation and completely missed what the guy was saying, Otis realized that the man was absolutely right! They were witnessing one of the two Voyager golden records, sent in space at the birth of the human space era, in 1977. These records were recorded to introduce potential alien civilizations to the human race, and contained various pieces of information, including the Brandenburg Concerto.

Otis immediately jumped down from his observation post and sprinted to the nearest soldier. "They come in peace! Listen to me, they come in peace!" he yelled.

The soldier turned out to be the same square-shaped giant. Otis was met with a hard blow to the chest, and swiftly thrown to the ground. The soldier's knee firmly pinned Otis to the ground, making him spit sand, while the soldier cuffed his hands behind his back. In the next instant, as Otis was dragged to one of the military vehicles, everyone heard the shots. They unmistakably came from the human side, but Otis could not tell what caused them. The crowd of the remaining observers spooked and ran away from the line of fire. Otis was almost positive he did not hear the aliens firing back. But then, how would he know? They could have had a weapon that operated without any sound. After all, initially the military was determined not to open the fire first. Something must have provoked the soldiers to open fire...

39

The last thing Otis heard before he was stuffed in the police car with blackened windows were the huge splashes in the ocean. One by one, all the eleven domes submerged and retreated beneath the waves.

3
JEROEN'S DIARY

YEAR 1912.
CENTRAL ITALY

Wilfred reluctantly eyed a hill drowned in verdant greenery. At the top of the hill, like a monarch's crown, nestled a monastery. Villa Mondragone was located in an isolated place. It was past noon. Monks conducted their business in the city early in the day, so hoping for a carriage ride from one of them was pointless. Wilfrid had to hike three kilometres up the hill that towered 416 meters above the sea level, having no clue if this exhausting treasure-hunting trip would even be worth it. Wilfrid was barely making ends meet.

43

A former dissident, who nearly escaped death at hand of agonizing Russian nobility, he was living in London, trying to fit in and make a living. "An immigrant needs to think creatively," Wilfrid reasoned. The locals had the luxury of going through the motions and steadily climbing the ranks. At age forty-seven, Wilfrid had already attempted success in too many things: a chemist and a pharmacist, a proletariat sympathizer and a revolutionary, and now an antiquarian.

"Normal people stick to one thing in life," Wilfrid chastised himself, panting like a dog and sweating profusely as he climbed the forsaken hill along a dusty path. There was no time to start all over again, and if this antiquarian business were to fall through, he would be officially declared a failure. The pressure was on. As soon as he peeled his eyes in the morning, the anxiety creature on his chest was immediately awake as well. It followed Wilfrid everywhere like an annoying street beggar, and always invaded his head, taking over Wilfrid's thoughts.

Three stops later, Wilfrid finally made it to the front gate of the monastery. In order to get to the front door of the building, Wilfrid walked through a large park, which glory days were still noticeable, but obviously belonged in the past. The shrubbery grew out of control, losing beautiful shapes once given them by a talented gardener. Somewhere on the other end of the building, Wilfrid imagined that one could see a breathtaking view of Italian cities. The hill was overlooking the neatly organized Frascati houses swimming in the blue-green haze of trees. At the heavy ornate door, Wilfrid grabbed the massive iron ring and knocked.

A monk in brown garb appeared and inquired of the guest's business. "My name is Sir Wilfrid Michal Voynich," said the guest in broken Italian heavily laced with a Polish accent. "I am an antiquarian from London and would like to trade with you for any old books you might have."

"Praise the Lord in Heaven!" cheered the monk. "We are in need of money. We have volumes dating back to the sixteenth century, when Villa Mondragone was built." The monk gave Wilfrid a friendly pat on the shoulder and encouraged him to follow him inside.

Year 1461.
S-Hertogenbosch city, Netherlands

Eleven-year-old Jeroen was dreaming. He dreamt of sitting on the cool fuming soil among tall flowers of his family garden. He observed busy ants trotting back and forth with heavy loads on their backs. Right above his head hung a peony in full bloom emitting a dizzying sweet smell. Jeroen pulled the branch in his line of sight to study it closer. At first, he looked at the entire branch - flower, stem, and leaves. Then he looked closely at one single leaf. The leaf seemed to possess a structure - intricate patterns that divided the leaf in sections. Then he looked closely at one section and to his astonishment realized that the small section also had structure. Jeroen strained his eyes, trying to see as deep into the structure as he could. Then he closed them.

With his eyes closed, floating in a kaleidoscope of lights and shadows, he saw the green leaf clearer than before. He focused on the smallest section he could identify and, all of a sudden, his line of vision was pulled inside the leaf: *woosh!* Inside, the leaf was not flat, but filled with chambers, pools of water, and swimming creatures. His mind hovered over the structures as if wandering the cities with fortresses and walls and cannons peeking from the walls. These cities were in perpetual jittery motion. When Jeroen took a close look at one wall, he gasped as it too consisted of infinite sections. His mind was pulled in and he saw a whole new level of complexity. For as long as he could see, this level looked like pearl strands. They were strung tight and vibrating as if someone pulled the threads sending them in a swinging dance, but there were no threads holding the pearls together.

In awe, Jeroen focused on a single pearl. His mind fell inside it like in a deep well: *woosh!* He flew through a swirling tunnel until he ended up in a vast empty space that stretched for miles, where his disembodied spirit hovered free. Far away he could spot structures that he could only describe as tangled balls of yarn - various kinds of yarn - but the threads were made of light or sound or wind, he couldn't quite tell. These balls of yarn were circling around the space as if tied to an invisible loom in the middle. Jeroen realized that this vast space was a transparent sphere, as if made of thin ice. Jeroen's mind caught up with one of the spinning balls of yarn and probed to untangle it. This was not an easy task.

45

The threads were held onto each other by the invisible force. But Jeroen was determined. He knew that there was definitely something inside, and he wanted to see it. It took enormous effort, but finally the threads budged and the yarn was about to untangle. Suddenly, a huge flash of light erupted from the yarn as the threads sprung loose. The force of light blinded him and penetrated every corner of his soul, like a great Judgment Day fire, cleansing and burning away all that was unnecessary, leaving Jeroen nothing but an unrestricted thought. It seemed like a lot of time passed until the light around subsided and Jeroen finally saw himself inside another layer of complexity. This one was undoubtedly the oddest and the scariest at the same time. He knew, there was nowhere deeper to go.

This was it, the basic level of all that there was. Jeroen was standing on the road that only allowed him to move in one direction - forward, always forward. The only way to move along this road was to hop from one flat rock to another. In between those rocks, there was Nothing. Not something that he couldn't see, but the ultimate Nothing, the kind that was before the beginning of the world. The Great Void. Jeroen looked around and saw his friends and family hopping on the parallel tracks alongside him. Each one of them had their own track and they all moved synchronously, in a rhythm of falling water drops from spring icicles: *pop-pop-pop-pop*. Jeroen could not see people's faces, because they were also disembodied spirits, like himself. All the spirits were connected with invisible strands, forming a tangled root system. Once in a while he would spot a person glowing with a halo. Saints? No, Jeroen realized, they were not the saints. They were the enlightened ones.

***

46

Somewhere deep in the Earth's ocean, the head of the Unkari research facility Ennuturat was pouring through streams of data, immersing his long tentacles in the puddles of liquid mercury interfaces. Observing human evolution had been his job for the past millennia. He was looking for the ones who had the potential for an evolutionary leap. Outside the lab, the vast serene ocean enveloped the facility. Suddenly Ennuturat saw an outstanding set of data that belonged to an eleven-year-old boy. Watching human evolution was about as exciting as observing a black hole evaporate, but this set of data pricked Ennuturat's curiosity. He opened the data stream and gasped: "Oh Universe, I think he just had a vision about splitting an atom."

Year 1930.
New York

At age sixty-five, Wilfrid finally possessed the one thing that would solidify his name in history: the Villa Mondragone manuscript. Because of the manuscript, Wilfrid moved his entire family to New York to be closer to the best cryptologists in the world. Fame and wealth seemed within his reach. Who among the antiquarians could boast of being an eponym to their possession? Wilfrid could. It became customary to call the manuscript by his name - the Voynich Manuscript. But the destiny had its twisted sense of humor. Wilfrid realized that he was tormented by a carrot on a stick: the closer he approached the solution, the further away it appeared.

With a gloved hand Wilfried flipped through the pages of his most treasured possession. Over 200 pages of authentic fifteenth-century parchment filled with writing that nobody could read. The thought of passing away before decoding the manuscript was eating Wilfried alive. Ever since he had laid his hands on the book, the secret meaning of the writing and the pictures consumed his imagination. The writing was like nothing he had ever seen. Was it a language? Was it a cypher? No matter how many experts he involved, none could solve the mystery of the manuscript. At first, he suspected that it was a book about herbal medicine. At a glance, it made sense: numerous herbs were catalogued and described throughout the book. Coding the text in that case made sense - to protect valuable knowledge. But years of inspecting the book led Wilfrid to realize that the plants could not be matched with any real plants on Earth!

47

Add to that, the plants were not the only thing exhibited in the book. The manuscript was filled with astrological images - not any normal astrology either, but inexplicable calendars and star maps. Some of the maps, if set in spinning motion, created motion pictures, and motion pictures were invented in Wilfrid's lifetime. The most inexplicable part of the manuscript contained strange drawings of naked women swimming in green pools of water. The water was deliberately green, rationalized Wilfrid, because the author of the manuscript used blue paint elsewhere, thus the blue paint was an option. Why was the water green? Why were the separate pools of water connected with intricate pipelines? Were the scenes sexual in nature?

At times it certainly felt this way, because of peculiar poses and arrangements these women assumed. And if the images were the scenes of decadent love, why there were no men in them? Some suspicions Wilfrid decidedly kept to himself, because that sort of talk could have landed him in the mental institution. When he inspected the scenes with naked women for with a magnifying glass, letting his imagination run wild, he could swear that some of those women had male parts as well, and some male parts seemed to be scratched out from the parchment.

Finally, there was that lingering suspicion that the entire manuscript was an elaborate hoax. There seemed to be some evidence supporting this thought. Each time Wilfrid thought of it, the anxiety creature ate away at his chest. The research seemed to point at the involvement of Edward Kelly with the manuscript. Edward Kelly was bad news. In sixteenth-century England, he was a polarizing figure. Some claimed that he was something of a prophet. According to Kelly himself, he could speak with the angels, could produce gold from the base metals, and was a pillar of occult medicine. Kelly duped important figures of his time, Bohemian Emperor Rudolph II being one of them. It was also proven that Kelly was caught producing multiple forgeries and pseudo-historical documents. Was the manuscript a hoax masterminded by the ultimate con artist of his time, Edward Kelly?

Wilfrid hung on a thin thread of hope that the complexity of the manuscript, its authentic materials and such were impossible to produce by a mere con artist, and required a true genius. Two promising figures seemed to fit the bill. One of them was the thirteenth-century physician and genius of his time Roger Bacon. Another, and Wilfrid's heart leaped with happiness every time he thought about it, was no less than the sixteenth-century genius Leonardo da Vinci. Wilfrid suspected da Vinci was not without merit. Since childhood, Leonardo had invented codes and kept notes in cyphers of high complexity. Leonardo also grown up in a family of some means as a half-child of Italian nobility. The author of the manuscript had to be somewhat wealthy, rationalized Wilfrid, because the price of quality vellum and inks was high back in the day.

Another thing that pointed to a child's work, albeit a budding genius, was the childlike style of the drawings. They were nothing like the masterful sketches of the matured Leonardo. Sloppy, often unfinished, they seemed to be the work of a child who was just beginning to learn the art of drawing. Days prior to his death, Wilfrid sensed that he had to somehow balance the score of his entire life. Was he a success or failure? On one hand, he had discovered a manuscript that puzzled the world. On the other, he had failed to uncover its meaning. With this question raw in his mind, Wilfrid quietly passed away in his New York apartment, leaving the unsolved mystery for the generations to come.

Year 2274.
Fourth Orbital Station

"You'll do great, Anika, stop stressing so much." Anika gave Broner a miserable look.

"Don't give me that look, I know what I am talking about. I watched you for the past two years. If there is anyone on the Fourth deserving a doctorate at nineteen years old, it is you."

49

Anika may have been the embodiment of the iconic Fourther's virtues when it came to research, but this bloody manuscript had buried more careers in human history than she could think of. The walls of Anika's small quarters were peppered with holographic images of strange curvy writings and even more bizarre drawings copied from the Voynich Manuscript. "You are a good friend, Broner, but a terrible liar," said Anika resolutely.

"You know that my theory hangs on a lot of speculations, and there is nothing I can do about it. Any physical evidence that attributes the authorship of the Voynich Manuscript to Hieronymus Bosch belongs to history now."

"True, but your analysis of Bosch's style is impeccable. And! And, add to that, for the first time we can understand the Voynichese language."

"The dictionary and the grammar are good, but the transcribed text makes little sense," she regretfully retorted.

"Oh, allow me to disagree! The sentences make sense; it's just what they tell us may be too incomprehensible. But so was Bosch's art, if you ask me. I'd play it to his overactive imagination." For a few seconds the friends eyed the reproduction of the Garden of Earthly Delights that decorated the wall above Anika's bunk. Incomprehensible - that's the word that suited Bosch's work the best. A triptych that used to be considered a depiction of Earth, heaven, and hell on three wooden boards was filled with creatures that could only be produced by a mad bioengineer or the Dr. Frankenstein. Even more bizarre were the buildings on the painting. Various spheres that resembled spacecrafts, spheres floating on the water, towers resembling maybe even power stations. In any event, these structures departed from anything in the Dutch architectural or painting traditions.

"Alright. Bosch was an eccentric man; nobody can argue against it. But who is the author of the language?" Anika persisted.

"Bosch. He made it up," matter-of-factly pointed Broner.

50

"Wrong. This is where the problem comes in. The language is too complex, the grammar is way beyond any human language, or machine language for that matter. To come up with a language of such complexity Bosch would have to possess our level of technology. I mean quantum computing, Broner. We are talking about the Middle Ages here! At that point, they hadn't invented a microscope yet."

"Something definitely happened in the Middle Ages. It's as if overnight humanity made a quantum leap..."

Quantum leap did not come close to describing what had Anika uncovered in what she believed was a childhood diary of the scandalously famous fifteenth-century painter, Hieronymus Bosch. This diary, the infamous Voynich Manuscript, whose authorship was lost in history, had tormented curious minds for almost a millennium. Nobody could decipher the text, and whoever tried, had tarnished their career beyond repair. Anika hugged her cohort mate and insisted on some rest before her big day. Broner begrudgingly had to agree, realizing that his plans to ask Anika out once again were poorly timed.

When Broner had left, Anika took a steamy shower, draped herself in an oversized shirt, and lay in her bed staring at the ceiling, unable to stop thinking about the upcoming presentation. Sleepless, she propped herself up in bed, pulled up a 3D rendering of the ancient book and started flipping through the pages. Spread by spread, she eyed the all-too-familiar yellowed and stained pages with cryptic, but nearly perfect handwriting, starkly contrasted with primitive drawings of mysterious herbs and flowers. She photographically memorized each stain and each curve of the letter, as anyone on the Fourth would. Genetically enhanced memory was a mandatory pre-birth alteration for each citizen of this human colony. But it was not the memory about the book she was looking for this time; it was the *feel* of it. Like so many cryptographers and linguists before her, she wanted to get into the author's mind. What made him write this book? Was he mad? Was he writing a fantasy tale? Was he afraid of persecution from the church? Each and every one of these hypotheses could be valid, if not only for one thing. A man in the fifteenth century could not possibly have single-handedly created a whole coherent language of this complexity. Let alone a teenage boy.

51

Another problem nestled in the content of the writing itself. How was she going to explain to the panel tomorrow that in the fifteenth century Bosch was writing about galaxies, quantum phenomena, neurons, and genetic experiments? Most certainly the panel would come to the conclusion that her process of decoding was contaminated with modern terminology. It must have been, because there was no reasonable explanation otherwise. The board would ask Anika one question, and it would be over. Did she limit the linguistic pool of words for cross-references to the words that only reasonably could have existed in the fifteenth century? *Why, yes,* she would respond. And then she would say that that strategy spectacularly failed. That was why she decided to go against common sense and include the linguistic data all the way through to the present day. All the words for cutting-edge technology, abstract concepts, astronomy, science; all the words that no way could have existed in fifteenth-century Europe, were fed into Anika's gargantuan analytical program. Initiating the analysis, she forgot about it for two months, waiting until the data was processed. One morning she received a *ping* on her MOD - the analysis was complete. Without much enthusiasm, Anika opened the results, preparing for another round of analysis, but apparently she had succeeded. She ran the analysis for the second time, to be sure, but the result was identical.

Without a doubt, she had translated the Voynich Manuscript. Anika knew that there were probably only two explanations. And among the two, the logical one was that her translation method was contaminated. As for the second one, Bosch had to be a time traveler.

YEAR 1463.
S-HERTOGENBOSCH CITY, NETHERLANDS

52

It was Jeroen's thirteenth birthday. That morning he firmly decided to put childish things behind him and behave like the man of the family. It was a fine day, the fields of wheat looked like a silky Persian rug, with intricate ornaments from red poppies and white chamomile flowers tucked into the threads. It would be past lunchtime when Jeroen arrived at the next village where his grandma lived. Mom sent him with a message and a gift: a fresh loaf of bread and a head of cheese, which were tormenting Jeroen with delicious smells emitted from his canvas bag. In order to distract himself, Jeroen continued to make the list of grown-up things he should do, among which most definitely was getting married.

This last one was difficult. Who should he marry? His older cousin Greta scared him to the bones, especially when her bread wouldn't rise or a cat would walk the cleaned floor with muddy paws, or, or... pretty much all the time. Greta was probably out of the question. On the other hand, Silvia was always nice to him. She lived a little distance from his family, but she loved to visit his mom on Sundays after morning church. There was one problem. Silvia was a widow, and she was old. Jeroen reckoned she must be twenty by now, and he was wondering how much longer she would live. The last thing he wanted was to be widowed with children.

Children scared Jeroen as well. They were fragile, smelled bad, and had a tendency to die. Like his youngest brother, for example. Last winter, Anri was born and did not stay around for too long. Mom said that he was born with a soul too big for this world, and God took him to heaven. Jeroen suspected that Anri was born with too small of a body for this world. Jeroen watched his father tenderly nurse that baby at night when mom was exhausted, but the baby kept crying. They tried everything: poppy sleeping potion, mixed beer with milk, even called the doctor from the big city, but nothing helped. Anri was not made well enough to last.

Thoughts about grown-up responsibilities made Jeroen hungry, and he crawled into the tall wheat grasses, opened the canvas bag, and pinched a small piece of the side of the bread. The bread was so fresh it was a shame to eat it. He just wanted to smell it and look at it, studying the patterns the white flour created on the dark brown crust. Then he said a quick praise to the Lord and threw a piece of the bread in his mouth. Stretched on the cool ground, he looked at the intricate shapes of the clouds in the blue sky. They looked like exotic animals and cities and so many other things, which purpose he could not even begin to imagine. So he retrieved a leather-bound notebook from his canvas bag, and a canvas scroll with a nib, a feather, a few brushes, and a few small vials with the pigment powders - yellow ochre, azure, cayenne, and viridian green. This was Jeroen's first adult treasure - a gift from grandpa, a known painter in the city. Grandpa said that if Jeroen worked hard and practiced, he would someday take his place in the art shop that had been in the family for generations. The notebook and paints were not to be treated carelessly, explained grandpa. They were worth a small fortune: grandpa spent his entire commission from the mayor's wife, who ordered a portrait of her two young girls.

Jeroen wanted to draw the clouds in the sky, but remembering the words of grandpa, he laid his gifts on the ground and lovingly caressed them one by one, until he committed each detail to his memory. Then he smelled the animal skin on the cover of the notebook. He took a deep indulgent breath and held it for as long as he could, and then placed all the treasures back into his canvas bag. It was time to continue his journey. Suddenly, a thick shadow rolled over him, and Jeroen thought it was a rain cloud. He lifted his gaze to the sky, but instead of a rain cloud he saw something that he could barely put to words - a glass sphere hung in the air right above him. And then a ray of light fell straight on him, as if someone had lit thousands of candles inside the sphere. Fear penetrated Jeroen's body, as the light enveloped him and lifted his body from the ground. He grabbed the canvas bag, as his feet were lifted from the ground.

Jeroen realized that it was God taking him to heaven. Instantly he regretted that his grown-up list of things would never be fulfilled, and that he probably would have to take care of little Anri, who God had taken to heaven earlier. That made everything even worse. "God! If you will, please don't take me yet!" cried Jeroen as the wheat fields turned into a wash of color beneath him. But God had different plans. In an instant Jeroen was whisked away so fast that he lost consciousness.

Year 2274.
Fourth Orbital Station

54

Anika stood in front of a panel of disinterested linguists, who had assembled for her doctorate presentation. The white overhead lights were blinding. A holographic emitter displayed a rendering of the Voynich Manuscript next to the rendering of the Garden of Earthly Delights by Hieronymus Bosch. The panel did not look particularly enthusiastic. It was an ad hoc meeting - academia was known for its love of schedules. However, Anika's curator, Professor Mirtu, insisted that her finding deserved to bend some rules.

"Whenever you are ready, colleague," dryly suggested the chair of the panel, the dean of the college of cyber-cryptology. The room was large, but there was no one in the audience. The decision was made to not alert the public to the matter just yet, in case the announcement of the Voynich's translation turned out to be another hoax.

Anika looked outside the panoramic window. There, in the vast darkness of space, she could see a glimpse of the Earth - a rare and coveted view on the orbital station. Centuries ago, Earth had been called a blue planet. Now it was more or less white, ever since the Big Ice had covered 80 percent of its surface due to the misguided attempt at reversing the effects of global warming.

There, buried under the ice, lay Europe, a once sophisticated and cultured continent that had given birth to Renaissance and rock-n-roll, and, among other things, to a profound linguistic enigma - the Voynich Manuscript. Over the centuries of researching the origins of this book, the trace had led to numerous owners in the Middle Ages, but its Italian origin was rarely disputed. Anika was going to challenge that assumption as well. See, she did not doubt that the diary was discovered in Italy. She challenged that it was *created* there. Her careful research had led to an unlikely suspect for the author of the manuscript—a scandalous Dutch artist Hieronymous Bosch. How the manuscript had made its way from the Netherlands to Italy she had no idea, and probably this would remain a mystery forever. What she *knew* was that the author of it was Bosch, just as she *knew* what was written in the manuscript.

Seeing her student's hesitation, Professor Mirtu stepped in. "Colleagues, let me introduce Anika's research. I call for your open-mindedness in the matter, because it is not every day that we get a shot at solving the world's best kept secret. Let me introduce doctoral candidate Anika Borgess. I personally reviewed her application two years ago. Her ability to write truly intuitive code is legendary among the doctorate cohort, as is her passion for art and mystery. You may be assured that Anika is an exemplary citizen of the Fourth and an academic of global proportions." Mirtu's complements made Anika blush. Obviously hearing such unapologetic praise would make anyone blush, but there was more to Anika's shyness.

A part of her doubted that she could be worthy of such high praise as an *exemplary Fourther*, because deep in her heart she harbored one renegade thought - someday she wanted to walk on Earth. It had been two decades since the Fourth had permanently suspended any interpersonal contact between the planet-siders and other orbital colonies. The reasons were too many, but they meant that Anika would never be able to participate in an archaeological dig on Earth, or swim in the ocean of the surviving tropical zone. There, on Earth, lay the clues to so many mysteries of the past, but they would be forever shielded from her reach unless she dared one day to break ties with the Fourth.

Year 1463.
Lenauri

Jeroen woke up in a dark cold room, trying to remember what had happened to him. He was walking to see grandma in the near village. He took a break and rested in the wheat field. It was going to rain. The clouds rolled in. And then, the painful memory came back to him. Those were not rainy clouds that had darkened the sky. It was God's wrath. Poor Jeroen was stricken to the core, realizing that if that was God who had taken him, he must have ended up in hell. "Why, God, why hell? What did I do? Was it because I lied last Christmas about eating the roast? I am sorry, Lord! Please forgive me, I want to go to heaven. I promise I'll take a good care of little Anri..."

Jeroen cried hysterically and hammered on the wall. All of a sudden, he realized that someone else was in the room. A small person in the corner got up from the bare floor and slowly moved towards him, speaking in a foreign language: "Andrà tutto bene. Non piangere."

Jeroen had no idea what the person was saying, but the voice was so soft and comforting, he immediately stopped sobbing and tried to catch a glimpse of the person's face. The person was a boy of his age. Blond curls adorned his pretty face. "Sorry, boy, I don't understand what are you saying."

"Andrà tutto bene. Andrà tutto bene. Il mio nome è Leo," said the boy, pressing his hand to his chest. "Come ti chiami?" This time the boy pressed his hand to Jeroen's chest.

"My name is Jeroen," he understood.

"Mi piace. Bello," smiled Leo.

"I wish you could tell me, Leo, what is going on. Are we in hell?"

This time Leo shrugged his shoulders and bitterly smiled. "Lo non ti capisco."

"I known you don't understand me. I don't understand you either. We need to find someone who we can talk to." Leo gave Jeroen the same confused look. Then he glanced at the canvas bag by Jeroen's side. "Ah, this? This is my birthday gift. I turned thirteen today. It's from my grandpa. Let me just show it all." Jeroen dragged out all the treasured possessions from his bag and laid them on the floor. Leo smacked his forehead as if remembering something important.

"Perdonami amico," and with these words he returned to the corner where he came from and came back with a thin stick, like the handle of an artist's brush. It was smooth and silvery. Excitedly Leo demonstrated the stick to Jeroen who failed to realize what was so exciting about it. Then Leo lightly tapped it on the inside of his palm, and the stick emitted white light, just slightly brighter than that of a candle.

"Oh, you've got a candle! That's nice. I'd like to know what your candle is made of. Maybe someday you can tell me."

"Hai pane!" replied Leo, pointing at the loaf of bread in his bag.

57

"Oh, you want some? I can share. I think under these circumstances grandma wouldn't mind."

***

A year later, Jeroen and Leo were the best of friends. They still didn't speak each other's native languages, but they fluently spoke the language of their captors - the Unkari. "What are you writing in there?" asked Leo, looking over Jeroen's shoulder. For the past few months, Jeroen had filled half of the notebook that he received as a gift the day before his abduction.

"These are some of the plants I saw on this planet. I am making notes so that when I return home, I have a proof of where I have been."

Leo bitterly smiled at the thought of explaining to his

family about planets, aliens, and space travels. "They will think you are crazy, my friend."

"They may. But I will show them the notes!"

"Jeroen, they won't understand." This had not occurred to Jeroen before. When he had left his home, he still couldn't read or write. Jeroen was a sickly child, and could not walk for miles every day to school like other kids of his age. When he turned thirteen, his parents probably felt more confident that he would live and that spending money on his education would not be a waste. That year, grandpa was about to send him to school, but the Unkari had intervened in those plans.

"What do you think they will be doing to us today?" asked Leo. "Oh Lord, you never know. Yesterday they were filling my head with knowledge about space. They hooked me up to this weird-looking hat knit of lit up threads. I felt so sick afterwards."

"But we are learning amazing things. They are saying we are special, the chosen ones, from whom our entire species will evolve."

"That's a big responsibility, Leo. I don't know if I am ready for it. It means having babies of our own. I'm not too good with babies."

"I know what you mean," sadly agreed Leo, but kept the true reason for his sadness to himself. To him, it was not the babies themselves that presented a problem, but the women that were involved in the process of making babies. Prior to the abduction, Leo had given no thought to women. That sort of thing did not interest him in the slightest. When he had first arrived on Lenauri, he had been placed in a reservation of women. Apparently the Unkari had been taking people from their homes for a long time now. Many generations of humans had been born in captivity, and had no knowledge of the way humans lived on Earth. The first day of his abduction, Leo had been placed in a big camp, where thousands of women lived separately from the men. Occasionally they were taken to the breeding rooms and mated with the men chosen by the captors. Then they returned to their camp and raised children until the Unkari decided that it was time to separate them.

The camp was a dreary place. These women created a vastly different social order compared to the one Leo saw at home. To begin with, they did not wear any clothing. Young and old, they walked around shaking their parts and thinking nothing of it. They bathed together in lagoons with green water, sometimes hundreds at the same time, and mated together, also at times in groups. These women did not think highly about men nor had a need for them, except for the time when the Unkari decided that it was time to procreate. Thankfully after a month or so, Jeroen had appeared and the Unkari had placed the boys in a separate cell. When Leo had told how he spent his time before Jeroen's arrival, he often cringed describing women in the reservation. To Leo, they were the real aliens.

Jeroen however, was enthralled by these stories and asked Leo to tell them over and over again, often exclaiming that he surely wished to take Leo's place. "You don't know what you are talking about, my friend. Those women were... like animals. They know no shame. They do things to each other that scarred my mind. I cannot unsee those things, and you wish you were there!"

"Sure! I'd know what to expect from marriage. You surely thought of marriage, haven't you, Leo?"

"Hardly. And now that there is no mystery left for me about these women, I doubt I want to."

"But you lust for them, don't you?"

"Maybe... a little..." lied Leo, when in fact intimacy with a woman petrified him. *Now, someone like Jeroen,* thought Leo... and immediately chastised himself for even thinking about it. Back home people were put to death for such things. The Unkari made it clear that when they had learned everything they needed to know, they would be returned home. Unlike the humans born on Lenauri, boys and girls like Jeroen and himself were to return home and contribute to a better 'recipe of humanity'.

ELLIE MALONEY

Year 1479.
S-Hertogenbosch City,
Netherlands

Twenty-nine-year-old Jeroen was getting married. Aleyt was a noble lady, albeit older, and she treated Jeroen with understanding and respect. Nonetheless, he did not know how to tell her his secret. As a child, Jeroen disappeared and had no memory of two whole years of his life. One morning he was walking to his grandma through the wheat field. It was about to rain. And then - blank. Two years later, he found himself in the same wheat field, but without his canvas bag, where he had his grandpa's gift - an expensive leather-bound vellum notebook. At first, Jeroen thought that he had fallen asleep and someone had robbed him. Dreading to tell the truth to mom, he headed back home, to S-Hertogenbosch. The minute he entered the city, he noticed that people looked at him as if he was a ghost. They just stopped and stared at the boy.

When Jeroen entered his house, mom was near the oven taking out freshly baked bread. Jeroen called her. Mom jumped and lost her footing, dropped the bread to the floor and it rolled towards Jeroen's feet. Mother stared at the boy with tears in her eyes for a very long time, and Jeroen had no idea what to do. Finally, mom said: "You've grown, son..."

Later, he found out that the whole village had considered Jeroen dead for two years. When he did not return home, a search team scouted the route he was supposed to take and found someone's fresh bones in the wood, eaten by a wolf. It was decided that the corpse belonged to Jeroen. Upon his return, Jeroen had changed. The missing memory tormented him. Sometimes he could catch a glimpse of memories that looked like visions from hell: tormented people, sinful orgies, strange scenes as if born in a feverish mind. These memories frightened him. For a while he thought he was going mad. There was something else besides fear. Shame. Shame was ripping his chest apart because of the fragments of the memories about one boy. He did not know who the boy was, or if he was even real, but he had felt that the boy was dear to him. And there was something else. A kiss. A passionate kiss. This boy grabbed Jeroen by the hand, pulled him close and kissed. Jeroen felt betrayed, confused, scared, embarrassed, and lost. Utterly lost. Was there something that he did to invite that kiss? Was that kiss welcome? He could not remember anything.

Years passed, and Jeroen taught himself to forget. He put up a wall in his mind. The only thing that helped him to stay sane was painting. Granted, he couldn't paint everything he saw in his mind, but the mere act of painting was soothing. Because of this secret, Jeroen waited for so long to get married. Most of all, he wanted to make sure that he could remain sane and would not condemn a poor woman to life with a mad man. Years passed, and he learned to cope. Yes, it was denial, yes, it was a half-measure, but it worked. Today, finally, he had a chance for a normal life of a married man. Aleyt was older and wiser. She had a calm and reassuring presence about her that kept Jeroen anchored to reality. There was nothing strange or otherworldly about her. She wasn't a beauty or any remarkable talent. She was as plain as bread. But bread meant sustenance. For Jeroen, this was more than he ever hoped for.

Year 1517.
Milano. Leonardo Da Vinci's Studio

61

Leonardo sat at his private dining hall expecting his favorite apprentice Francesco Melzi for a dinner. At the table, he had bread baked without eggs, stewed roots and leaves without meat, and a jar of wine. He poured two glasses when Melzi walked in. The student walked close to the master and gently hugged him, planting a friendly kiss on his cheek. "Greetings, master! Thank you for the invitation. If you forgive me, I will only have wine with you tonight. My stomach is uneasy." Leonardo pointed his friend to the chair at the table.

"Francesco, you are dear to me like a son that I never had. Why do you think I say this?"

"Mmm, because you cherish our friendship, master?"

"Wrong! You don't have to lie to me about your weak stomach in order to avoid my diet."

The teacher was shrewd. Francesco laughed heartily. "Ah, Leonardo, nothing escapes you. And you are my dearest friend. But this obsession of yours with not eating meat has made you not the most welcome dinner host. I never asked you, but now is a good time for you to tell me what is it about!"

"Ah, I don't know. I have memories, maybe dreams, of some strange animals slicing humans... It is rather strange, I know. But these images are so vivid. It made me think that animal flesh and human flesh are much the same. I cannot cause death on a living thing, even if it is a chicken."

"What about eggs?"

"They are the seed of life, you know. Same thing. Like eating unborn babies."

Francesco's stomach flipped and he swallowed a gulp of wine to chase away the taste of gall in his mouth after hearing Leonardo's grotesque explanation. "There are many things that I revere you for. This rebellion against meat of yours, master, is not one of them."

It was Leonardo's time to laugh. "What can I say! I hold respect for your ideas and your individuality above my eating habits. Let's drink then! Thank God for grapes!"

"Praise the Lord! To you, my teacher!" exclaimed Francesco and drank a few long gulps at once. "So what is it, my teacher, that you needed to tell me so urgently?"

"Francesco, I am old, and Lord only knows how long will I live. I need you to be the executor of my will."

"That's a great honor, Leonardo. However, why me?"

"Who do you suppose it should be? Salai?"

Francesco did not bite. Salai was a sensitive subject. Although teacher loved him, this man was nicknamed "the unclean one" for a reason. Even though Leonardo did not hold Salai with the bonds of faithfulness, Francesco always thought that this talentless impostor of an apprentice could be more discrete. Salai spent Leonardo's money, brought in his "boys," and trashed the guest quarters in loud orgies. And then he would blink his eyes and offer to pose naked for Leonardo's next masterpiece. It was all it took to soften the poor old dupe's heart. "Come on, Francesco!" insisted Leonardo. "I already told you, be honest with me. Do you think I can trust Salai with my will?"

"I'd advise you to be cautious with him in such matters."

"Cautious. Is that what you call it? We both know that the day my soul departs, he will sell everything on the nearest street corner and spend half of the money on wine and another half on the prostitutes. When his headache passes, he will live the rest of his life homeless, or may even be thrown in jail for sodomy. We both know, Salai is not equipped to live in this world on his own."

"Perhaps you are wise about it, teacher."

"How is he by the way? I am not on speaking terms with him since his last orgy."

"I stopped by his room on the way here. He asked me for money. I did not give him anything. I thought he could benefit from a day of sobriety. Especially since he was painting."

"Oh, was he? What was he painting?"

"Oh, I don't know, it was... "

"Stop lying, Francesco! "

63

"Alright, alright! Mona Lisa! There. I said it. He was painting Mona Lisa."

"My Mona Lisa?"

"In a sense," hesitated Francesco. "I believe it will come out differently."

"How so?"

"Well, he was naked. He had a mirror in front of him. And was painting himself in front of the mirror... wearing a heap of horse's hair on his head."

Leonardo stared at Francesco for a second, trying to imagine this sight and then burst out laughing. "Perhaps I should give him a visit after we are done. This sounds entertaining. Speaking of the business, like I said, I have nobody else I can trust with my will. So you might as well accept this. I made some notes." With these words, Leonardo reached out to the shelf and picked a few sheets of parchment carefully filled with neat writing. "Study these notes and let me know if you have questions. However, there are some items I need to show you now."

Francesco reached out and picked up the handwritten will, immediately sinking his eyes into the text. "Go to page two. Paragraph 46," instructed Leonardo.

"The Mystery of My Soul? What is it, teacher?"

"Let me show you. Follow me." The two walked to the back of the room. There, on a work station, a few items were arranged for Francesco's inspection. Leonardo picked up a leather-bound vellum book. "Open it." Francesco obeyed. It was filled with handwriting in a code, and some illustrations of herbs and other strange things that Francesco decided to study later.

"Interesting. Do I need a cypher, teacher?"

"I don't have it."

"You mean you did not write this?"

64

"If I did, I have no memory of it. Many years ago, when I was a boy, I was lost. I probably injured myself, because I have no memory what I was doing for two years, until someone found me sleeping on the street. I woke up, and just like that, I had no memory of the entire two years of my life. I had a canvas bag with me. There, I had this book and some writing supplies. That's all I know."

"Did you try to break the code?"

"What do you think? It was a work of my entire life. I failed. Now it is your task. However, since I have no idea what mysteries this book holds, you must be careful, my friend. Whatever you find out must become your own secret, because I have no idea what you may find out about the two missing years of my life."

Year 1582.
Italy

Edward Kelly arrived in Italy in pursuit of an upcoming auction. The rumor had it, some items from Leonardo da Vinci himself were for sale. Of course, he couldn't be sure, but the fact that the auction was held by the descendants of Francesco Melzi, an executor of da Vinci's estate, was a good sign. Melzi was a great artist in his own right, but he was no genius. Kelly was not interested in another painting on a religious subject. He was after big fish. During the pre-auction reception, Kelly was able to talk to Melzi's grand-daughter Maria. She was charming and the two continued the conversation in the barn. During that passionate conversation, Kelly was told that there was a particular book they auctioned that could be either a goldmine or worthless. The family sold it as writing of da Vinci's student, nicknamed Salai. The book was written in a code and supposedly had recipes for male vigor, as was backed by the illustrations of herbs and naked women, whom Salai supposedly was close to.

Secretly Maria told Kelly that the book was probably worthless. For years, her family spent money on decoding it. The best experts agreed that the book must contain gibberish of a drunkard. When Kelly was through with Maria, he proceeded to find her father suggesting that if he wouldn't sell the book at lower price, he would make their suspicions public, and thus the book would be worthless. The Mezli family could not figure out why Kelly needed the book if he knew it was worthless, but decided to cut their losses and sold it. Several months later, the con artist Edward Kelly wrote a letter to John Dee, a man who had an access to the court of the Bohemian Emperor Rudolph II. Rudolph was known for throwing loads of money on purchasing various alchemic and occult artefacts. Rudolph was particularly keen on buying medical books, as he suffered from many ailments, the majority of which, Kelly suspected, were the result of Rudolph's own overactive imagination.

65

The letter stated:

Dear Sir John Dee,

I am writing to you in hope to find you in good health and that we can share my recent discovery. A manuscript came into my possession. It belonged to the great Roger Bacon himself. Sir Bacon wrote unspeakable medical secrets in the diary, and in order to protect the secrets, he encrypted the writing with a code. Angels spoke to me one day and taught me the cypher that Bacon used. Angels believe that this knowledge belongs to people. I believe that the knowledge belongs to people as well. But we cannot allow it to fall into the wrong hands. The more I reasoned about who would be worthy of the incredible privilege to possess such a powerful knowledge, I realized that it must be his majesty the Bohemian Emperor Rudolph II. For a reasonable fee, I can serve the Emperor as an interpreter, and we both can partake in the glory of being a part of such a great discovery.

Dearly yours,

Sir Edward Kelly of England

66

The rest was history. Kelly sold the manuscript to Rudolph for a hefty sum. After his death, the Emperor left sizable debts. Among the creditors was the Emperor's pharmacist Jakobus Sinapius from Tepenec. Many of Rudolph's creditors received their payment with items from his extensive eclectic collection, and Jakobus inherited the manuscript, which they all believed to be written by Roger Bacon, a fact that they could not contest due to the lack of sophisticated technology. Bacon could not have written the manuscript, because spectroscopy and carbon dating analysis lands it in the middle of fifteenth century, and Bacon lived two centuries prior to when the manuscript was written. Jacobus, like many others before and after him, was hoping to decode the manuscript and learn its medical secrets. Thus he signed the book: "Jacobus Hořčický de Tepenec," a signature he placed on every book in his library. Unsurprisingly, Jakobus did not succeed in decoding the manuscript. He further sold it for cash, until it ended up in possession of Italian monks from Villa Mondragone, where it was eventually discovered by Wilfrid Voynich.

Year 2274.
Fourth Orbital

Tears rolled down Anika's cheeks as she was packing for a one-way trip. The humiliation of her doctorate thesis being rejected broke her spirit. Nothing was dear to her on the Fourth Orbital any more. Once she became a laughing stock in the scientific community, the only place she could go now was the Earth. Immediately after the rejection, she applied for a job as a cryptologist for the Earth Nations military and was assigned to Rabat, the headquarters of the Royal Moroccan Fleet. The door monitor buzzed. "Anika, it's me," she heard the familiar Broner's voice. "You can't leave just like that."

"And why is that?" replied Anika through tears but did not open the door.

"Many reasons!"

"Name one."

There was a silence behind the door. "Your career!" said desperate Broner, although that was the last reason on his mind.

"That is the wrong reason, Broner."

"Let me in, and I will give you another one..."

"This is precisely why I will not let you in. I don't need a reason to stay. Good bye, Broner. I hope you find what you are looking for."

"What if I already found it?"

"In that case, you just lost it," said Anika and set the door monitor on "do not disturb."

67

Year 2275.
Rabat, Royal Moroccan
Fleet Headquarters

Anika rushed down the long corridor crowded with military

staff. Everyone was in a hurry these days. Since the Unkari had made First Contact, the world had changed. Humans definitively realized that they were not alone in the universe, something they had suspected for a long time, but had never had a chance to prove. It was unclear if these aliens were friends or enemies. Everything about the First Contact was ambiguous. First, the location they chose: the Liberian coast. Why not arrive from space? And how did they manage to sneak into the ocean, bypassing the orbital surveillance grid? The unspoken fear was that they actually had been in the ocean for a long time, probably before the orbital surveillance grid was operational.

This meant that they had watched humans even before the Big Ice. But for how long? Second was the Voyager's golden record. Yes, the very 1970s golden record that humans had sent into space, hoping to send a message to alien civilizations. During the First Contact, the Unkari had left behind one of the Voyager's records and retreated into the ocean after the coast guard opened fire. Since then, it had been a month and the military could not locate them in the ocean. They just vanished. Third, and this was Anika's personal favorite, did the Unkari indeed provoke the coast guard to open fire? The details of the First Contact were classified, including the existence of the golden record, and normally Anika would not have gained access to this information. But for some unknown reason, she was given the clearance to the classified report from the First Contact event and summoned to General Nagasaki's office.

In the General's waiting room, about two-dozen visitors were pacing the faded red carpet, anticipating an audience. Anika pushed through the crowd to the secretary's desk and introduced herself. "Finally," exclaimed the relieved young officer and immediately dialed the General's office. "Private Anika Borgess is here at your request. Uhu. They are also here. All of them at once? Yes, General." After the secretary broke off the connection with the General, he cleared his throat and loudly announced: "Officers," and two-dozen military bigwigs simultaneously turned their heads toward the announcer. "General Nagasaki is expecting all of you in his conference hall."

The conference hall was equipped with an oval desk that

seated twice as many people as were immediately summoned to the meeting. The group hastily took seats at the table and prepared to take notes. The General walked in with a man in his forties, dressed in a casual sleeveless yellow shirt and tan pants, a civilian, who looked distinctly out of place. The General took his seat at the head of the table and directed the visitor to take a seat by his left side. "You have been briefed on the events of the past month. I called you here to establish a strategic task force. Your job will be to develop as many scenarios of the unfolding events as possible. The resources of the Royal Moroccan Fleet are at your disposal. Most of you know each other. However, there is someone I need to introduce to you."

The General pointed to a man seated at his left side. "Meet Professor Otis Solarin, an eyewitness of the First Contact. Professor Solarin witnessed how the Unkari exited the ocean while he was having dinner right there in the Anglers restaurant in Monrovia. The restaurant is located on the beach, and he was able to observe the aliens exiting the ocean. Professor Solarin teaches space history and he immediately identified the Golden Record. Long story short, he disagreed with the coast guard's decision to open fire and started a fist fight with the officers. Professor Solarin spent a month in the local jail for assaulting an officer, and because of the hectic events he was forgotten there. Professor, again, my sincere apologies."

69

"Apologies accepted, General," Solarin answered dryly.

"Because the Professor witnessed the account and knows about the record, the decision was made to include him in the task force. This way he can be useful to us while bound by the nondisclosure agreement."

"Glad to be of service," uttered Solarin just as unenthusiastically.

"Another person of interest to the task force is Private Borgess, our linguist from the Fourth Orbital."

"Me? How can I be helpful?"

"Private Borgess, have you seen the record yet?"

"No, I only checked it out in the historic NASA files."

"Alright," said the General and initiated the holographic screen before Anika. A 3D rendering of the record hovered in front of her. "Take a look at it for a minute and see if you can find anything of interest. Meanwhile, Professor Solarin, would you be so kind to brief us about the record?"

"Gladly. In the 1970s, NASA launched two space crafts, Voyager 1 and 2. The purpose of the crafts was to explore the solar system. After the crafts left the solar system, they took different trajectories en route to the nearby stars. At the speed that they traveled, numerous generations would pass until they were expected to encounter anything but empty space. We lost contact with both crafts years ago. Both crafts contained golden disks modeled after the twentieth-century audio carrier - a vinyl record. These records contained data about humanity, our location in space, our culture, our knowledge of mathematics and the universe - all encrypted in the grooves of the records. This was our 'message in a bottle' to extraterrestrial civilizations."

"Thank you, Professor," said the General. "Now it appears that this alien civilization found our 'message in a bottle' and returned it to us. Upon return, the record was enclosed in a transparent case, where in several human languages was written: "Humans lost, Unkari found." Do you see this encryption, Private Borgess?"

70

"Yes, I can see it. Oh my god," gasped Anika. The entire room full of military who's-who peered their eyes at her in anticipation.

"What do you see, Private?" inquired the General.

"Well, among these inscriptions in several languages, there is one that looks familiar to me. I cannot believe it. It is incomprehensible..."

"Spell it out, Private. You are here for a reason."

"This is Voynichese. The previously unknown language from the Voynich Manuscript.

4
MISSING MINUTES

July 3, 1882.
Lebanon, Connecticut

Robert and Richard were successful businessmen. Steel production was their business; astronomy was their life, liberty, and pursuit of happiness. Several nights a week the brothers devoted to their passion, venturing in the back yard and observing the night sky. One such night, Robert's telescope was pointed at the Moon. His twin-brother Richard sprawled on the dewy grass besides him, also gazing at the hazy Moon disk and dreaming. "Someday we will know..." Richard vaguely pointed out to no one in particular.

73

"Know what?"

"What is out there..."

"Someday we will." Robert agreed and returned to his observations. He pressed his right eye to the rim of the viewfinder, dictating notes for Richard to record in the log. All those Moon dreams, combined with a huge Italian dinner, put Richard to sleep. Two hours later, Richard's loud snore was interrupted. "Richard, wake up, wake up now!" yelled Robert while frantically adjusting the focus of the lenses.

"What? What's so urgent?"

"Get up and look for yourself."

Richard got up and pressed his right eye to the viewfinder. "Dear Mother of God!"

"Ok, now you tell me what you see."

"Did you clean the lens?"

"It's as clean as a whistle. So what do you see?"

"To hell if I know!"

"Describe it! We need to make sure that our observations match."

"Well, alright. I see two slices of pizza hovering above the Moon surface."

"Pizza? That's one way to put it!"

"Seriously. Those things look like pizza slices. How long had they been there?"

"About 20 minutes."

"Are they in motion?"

"It appears to be so. I did some quick calculations. These things might be in a Moon orbit."

"They are probably going to collide then. Goodness, can you imagine their speed? I can't quite think straight now, but I know that if I can observe movement over this vast distance, that's faster than... faster than sound for sure."

74

Twenty minutes later, the objects rendezvoused and stopped for a good hour before they started moving in the opposite directions. No natural satellite could possibly move in such a trajectory. And certainly no two meteors could be shaped like equilateral triangles. Next morning, the brothers wrote an article for the local paper, a decision they grew to regret in the weeks to come. Richard and Robert became instantly famous in Lebanon, Connecticut, and not in a good way. The newspaper published a response letter from one of the readers featuring both brothers chasing pizza slices around the Moon.

July 20, 1969.
The Moon

The Unkari transporter was parked at the edge of a Moon crater etched by the impact of the meteor. Normally, for the Unkari, a space rock like the Moon would be generally worthless, but the infrastructure analysts Harutin and Sinbiu had their orders. According to the risk assessment plan, human technology would progress soon enough, and the research outposts in the ocean would have to be removed. The Moon was a viable option for a new secret observatory, because it was tidally-locked, and the shadow-side would be perfect for a long-term facility.

There was one wrinkle in that plan: humanity's ridiculous pursuit of space exploration. "We go to the Moon not because it is easy, but because it is hard!" Sinbiu mocked a phrase that had become iconic among the humans. "What kind of logic is that?"

"I told you, Sinbiu, they will do it. So here we are, on the Moon, watching them disembark on the surface," said Harutin. "We should have shot them down."

"And kill our best research samples?" Sinbiu tried to rub his chin, but his face was covered with a helmet.

"Just look at these idiots..." said Harutin contemptuously. The aliens were watching from afar as two humans disembarked from their awkward vessel and bounced on the low-gravity lunar surface.

"That's one small step for man, one giant leap for mankind..." heard the Unkari in their audio feeds tapped into the astronaut's communication system.

"Actually, I think they are kind of courageous," mumbled Sinbiu carefully.

"You think? And where is the courage in trying to supersede their fellow human tribe? This whole space race is not about courage, my colleague; quite contrary. They are cowards, it's all there is to their philosophy."

"If you say so. I still think it takes courage to venture into open space in that... thing..." Sinbiu motioned towards the Apollo 11 vessel, which almost looked more reliable in the defused sunlight. This way, the observer was not forced to notice all the crude stitching of the metal.

"Oh... I suppose it does." Harutin waved it off. "But let's not waste time, colleague. I guess I have to go talk to them. What an assignment! Make sure you suppress their recording of our conversation."

"I'm on it. You'll have a window of white noise. How long should I set it up for?"

"Let's start from two minutes."

November 17, 1986.
Commercial Flight Air Japan
Paris-Tokyo Over the Alaskan air space

20:15 Hrs

"Anchorage, do you read me?"

Sh-sh-sh

"Yes, Japan 1628. Loud and clear."

Sh-sh-sh

"Anchorage, eh... do we have traffic intersecting our trajectory?"

Sh-sh-sh Click click

"Ah... Negative..."

Sh-sh-sh.

"Anchorage, we have a visual on a... perhaps an aircraft carrier."

Click click

"Beg your pardon?"

"Well I can't tell exactly, but there is something there. My co-pilot and other crew confirm the visual..."

Sh-sh-sh - click - crack - crack - click

"Japan 1628, ah... we stripped filters from the radar data... On the raw data we ... ah... confirm an object in your relative proximity, 3-4 km North West."

Sh-sh-sh

"Well, Anchorage, do you know what is it? My passengers are edgy. I can't prevent them from taking the pictures, you know..."

"Can you describe it?"

"Well, it is cigar-shaped... With the lights evenly spaced along the hull. It looks like it's matching our speed and staying dead ahead of us, within the visibility range from the cockpit and the A isle, the window isle I mean."

Sh-sh-sh-click-crack

"Standby Japan 1628. We will contact the Air Force Base."

20:38 Hrs

"Anchorage, Anchorage! This is a distress call!"

"Come in Japan 1628."

"We may be under attack!"

"We are reading two small crafts by your side. What's your visual?"

"They have separated from the mothership..."

"Mothership???! With all due respect, what are you smoking there?"

Crack

"Anchorage, they exhibit erratic movement patterns, unlike anything I've seen before. What's the update from the air force?"

"It's not theirs. It is an unidentified craft."

"Do you think it is hostile? God help us, Anchorage, I have

a full aircraft of passengers."

"We can't say. Try evasive manoeuvre. We suggest dropping the altitude. Standby for the course correction."

"We read you. Dropping the altitude to the mark."

20:41 Hrs

"Japan 1628! We follow your manoeuvre on the radar. The hostile crafts matched your position. Do you read me, Japan 1628?"

Click click

The com channel was open, but the pilots were not responding. Instead the Anchorage air traffic controller's booth was flooded with the high-pitch sound. "Sanders!" Yelled the Fairbanks airport shift leader Mitchem. "Get the fucking Air Force on the line!"

While Sanders was patching through to the base, Mitchem was watching Japan 1628 on the radar firmly locked between two small unidentified crafts. Regardless of the manoeuvre the passenger craft took, the two satellites seamlessly matched the trajectory and speed. "1628! 1628, come in! What's your status?" Agonized Mitchem biting the skin around his big fingernail.

78

Sh-sh-shhhhhh click click

"Anchorage!" came the agonizing cry of the 1628 pilot. "We are blasted..." *sh-sh-sh* "...with light. light... heat... flooded..." *sh-sh-sh* "and heat, like a furnace... bright light penetrated the walls!"

"1628, perform emergency landing. Confirm!"

"Negative! We have lost control. The electronics is jammed. We are not flying this airplane any more!"

"Let us try to override it from here!" Mitchem tried to take over the flight control, but his attempts met an unusual firewall. "1628... Unfortunately we cannot take over control... How are you holding up? What is your status?"

It took 1628 longer than usual to respond. Mitchem

gnawed at his fingernail too hard drawing blood from the cuticle. Finally the com channel lit up green.

"Anchorage... ah... what's the status on your radars?"

"1628, I no longer see them on the radar. Do you have the visual?"

"Ah... negative... They are gone...."

"Can you control cruising?"

"Affirmative..."

"Take course on the emergency landing. We opened a lane for you."

Sh-sh-sh- click

"The course for the emergency landing according to the provided coordinates is established."

Sh-sh-sh

"1628... What's the status of the passengers and crew? Any ... eh... casualties?"

"We are still checking, but the quick assessment is that everyone is fine. Minus a few hysterical ones, but that's understandable considering."

"Good to hear. Ehhh.... 1628, safe flight."

"With all do respect, Anchorage, go to hell. 1628 over and out."

79

***

"How many times do I have to repeat myself?" pleaded exhausted Japanese pilot Ichiro Akiyama of the flight 1628 en route Paris-Tokyo.

"As many as we require," flatly hissed a man in civilian suit and shaded aviator glasses, although the room was as dim as the devil's soul. The man, who introduced himself as a liaison from the Reagan Administration, took the last drag from his cigarette and squeezed the butt in the filthy ashtray, the only decor attribute in the entire interrogation room. Upon landing, the crew had been whisked away by the U.S. military cogs and transported to an unknown location in vehicles with tinted windows.

Akiyama only knew that he was about a forty-minute drive from the Fairbanks International Airport. "Am I under arrest?"

"It depends."

"On what? I am a Japanese citizen. I need a lawyer."

"Mr. Akiyama. We found illegal narcotics among your personal belongings."

"What? Impossible!"

"As a captain of the airplane, wouldn't you say that you receive reduced security attention when you are boarding?"

"This is nonsense. I need a lawyer."

"Just. Answer. The. Fucking. Question!" At that last word, the bureaucrat smashed his fist down on the desktop, suspending the ashtray in a momentary zero gravity and spilling half of its pungent content.

"Perhaps. This doesn't mean...."

"So you were aware that security is unlikely to check you with scrutiny. How long have you been on cocaine, Mr. Akiyama?"

80

"Never! I have never consumed cocaine or any other drugs!"

"Perhaps the blood test will testify otherwise," smiled the nameless bureaucrat from the corner of his mouth.

"What do you want? Where is this all going?" asked Akiyama in a defeated voice.

"Straight to business, Mr. Akiyama. I like that. These are your choices. We will arrest you for international drug trafficking. We have just the right criminal ring to connect you to. As for the extradition... Forget it. Not gonna happen."

"I take another option."

"Alright. You go back on the plane, you fly your passengers home, and you live happily ever after."

"What is the catch?"

"You change your testimony. There was never a UFO, there were never two aircraft that ceased the cruise control, and there was no supernatural light show."

"So you *do* know about this. What happened to us there?"

"Mr. Akiyama, we requested medical records from all passengers and the crew. We know that you were diagnosed with a malignant brain tumor."

"I was."

"We know that there were two other persons on board with the same condition. We cannot guarantee you, but chances are, that you are in a remission."

Speechless, Akiyama stared at the bureaucrat for some time before breaking into tears. Tears of confusion, hope, fear, but mostly of extreme exhaustion. The prospect of the ordeal to be over destroyed all the bravery Akiyama had worked so hard at keeping up. "Alright. I'll sign whatever you need me to sign. But tell me what happened out there. And don't insult my intelligence by the 'unusual weather patterns'."

"That is exactly what happened, Mr. Akiyama. That is all you need to know."

***

81

Ichiro Akiyama never flew again. His brain scan indeed confirmed an unprecedented remission. Akiyama's doctor kept pressing for information as to where he had received such effective radiation treatment, but Akiyama only laughed it off. His luck did not last forever. In two years, the tumor returned to the active phase, and his time on Earth came to an end. Akiyama did not leave much behind, but a newborn boy. This boy also grew up and began to fly, only not like his father, but in his dreams. In those dreams, he would spread his hands, run off the cliff, and instead of smashing to the ground, he'd soar in the sky like an eagle, resting his weightless body on the currents of Japanese winds.

M<small>AY</small> 29, 1917.
B<small>OSTON</small>, M<small>ASSACHUSETTS</small>

To an Irish-American family, a child was born. A baby of great destiny, great talents, and great faults. A baby that one day would lead the United States to the Moon. A baby who would overcome great physical challenges and become a war hero. A baby whose fate was decided by a combination of obscure genes. Later, this DNA sequence would be classified by the human scientists as dead-end, redundant, muted; in other words, the kind that does nothing for humans. This assessment could not have been further from the truth. In fact, the whole Unkari civilization was petrified by this gene sequence because of its hidden potential to give rise to a powerful ability - oscillation. There was a major problem with this gene bundle: it was paired with a number of fatal illnesses and conditions. Among them was an adrenal insufficiency that caused immune system failure. Such adrenal insufficiency syndrome plagued John F. Kennedy from birth. In other cases, the gene bundle led to lethal brain tumors, the kind that eventually killed John's brother Ted. Initially, the oscillation genes presented a death sentence, but throughout the course of humanity, Unkari achieved more resilient human carriers that lived long enough to procreate and in some occasions to pass the genes to the offspring.

Slowly, these gene-carrying humans evolved to turn muted oscillation genes into functional ones, the kind of evolution they had no idea about, but the kind that was closely monitored by the aliens from their obscured research labs all over the Earth. Humans became developing functionality of the genes. But the more a human subject utilized the gene potential, the faster the health hazards increased, eventually resulting in the subject's death.

***

A few weeks prior to John F. Kennedy's remarkable birth, in a remote Portuguese village known as Fatima, three children were tending to their sheep when they saw an apparition in the sky. Enveloped in light, a small woman was hovering in mid-air. Her lips were not moving, but her hands floated in the air, persuasively gesticulating: "Lucia, Francisco, Jacinta, my children, the Lord God sent me to give you a message..." sounded Mother Mary with her lips tightly sealed. "You need to pass this message to your community."

Early May of 1917.
The Unkari Research Facility,
Atlantic Ocean

Earlier that month, Argon Katu, Ennuturat's counterpart on the Oscillation Project, held a sub-space video conference with the Home Office on Lenauri. Cozied up in his reclined chair, he sipped something of a consistency and color of unset green apple jello. On the other side of the feed, in the Sagittarius Dwarf galaxy, a panel of five Unkari politicians and two xeno-biologists expected an emergency update. Back home, the Project Supervisory Committee was alarmed at the rate of mortality in the populations with the oscillation gene sequence. "Master Argon, with all due respect, you've been at this project for so long, why can't you make any progress?" rattled one of the politicians.

Argon sighed. These conferences were way too frequent for his taste. It irritated him beyond measure when these bureaucrats did not bother reading the reports beyond the summary page, and took his valuable time with these conferences. Plus, they must understand that he is not solely in charge of the project. Every time he and Ennuturat swapped the shifts, there was significant down-time, shift in project's directions, and all the reports that had to be written to the Enkri government bureaucrats; reports they clearly did not bother reading.

83

"Pretor Inkishi, do you have a spare month?"

"Mm for what, Master Argon?"

"For my explanation! You are asking a question that has been occupying the researchers across all branches of science, and you want it boiled down to a sound bite."

Pretor visibly backed off. "I did not want to insult you in any way, but you realize that this project diverts resources from our main goal."

"The search for a new home is important, indeed, but if we do not understand how these species are connected to the universe, we are missing the chance to uncover the biggest mystery of all time. I cannot believe I have to go over this again."

"Master Argon, I recall you once wanted nothing to do with the humans other than blast them out of existence."

"True. But I somewhat changed my mind. The late Honorable Immirtau, may the universe turn his ashes to stars, he had a point. By no means do I believe that by eliminating these species we will reduce the universe to a non-dimensional existence, but you cannot possibly overlook their ability to reset reality. Dare I say, someday their ability may be harnessed for our benefit. Say, if we are ever under attack from a race that actually rivals us, we could use them to change the outcome of the battles. We would be invincible!"

"Or they will somehow 'reset' us," jumped in another politician who Argon did not know and could only identify by the congressional insignia. "Can you guarantee that somewhere on that planet of yours, someone won't start oscillating without your knowledge?"

"You politicians are a breed of your own, aren't you?" said Argon feeling his nerves unravelling. "I bet you make up ten bogus theories before breakfast. Look, they cannot oscillate. Period. Their brain is largely inactive, and they are only capable of basic mathematics and reasoning. Oscillation is like a piece of software that you install on a hardware that is generations older. The only way you can store this program is in a compressed, inactive state. Even the slightest attempt at accessing this oscillation ability would be lethal."

"How so?"

"Well, so far we have identified several problems. First, the brain starts requiring a lot more oxygen, thus drawing a lot more blood. Autopsy suggests aneurysms to be a prime cause of death. It happens too fast to control. Evolutionarily, they have learned to suppress the ability. However, a number of other things can kill a human who attempts oscillation. Let's say, an adrenaline overdose. Or hypertension associated with increased heart rate. In other words, their physical bodies and especially their brains are not ready for oscillation."

"Any ideas why their body requires additional resources to process oscillation?"

"Several, as a matter of fact. But mostly it has to do with the fact that the brain starts growing special cells that are, we assume, responsible for successful oscillation. But so far these cells have no time to grow. A human subject dies well before it. In the future, we suspect these cells will form a new region in their brain, and by the time this happens, the rest of their body will evolve as well."

"So what is your primary strategy?"

"Our primary goal is that the subjects with the gene sequence live long enough to procreate and to pass the gene to the next generation."

"Easier said than done..." said one of the xeno-biologists, deep in thought. "Master Argon, there must be some environmental factors that help the species to evolve..."

"Indeed, there are several that we know of," agreed Argon. "They call one of them a prayer or meditation, based on the cultural tradition of that particular population. Basically, human species instinctively pray when in distress. It serves as a chemical regulator in the body. It lowers their heart rate and adrenaline secretion, and produces certain hormones that actually support growth of the oscillation brain cells. We are not exactly sure what happens, but in short, prayer and meditation eases the negative impact of oscillation on the human body."

"This is perhaps why we observe higher rates of oscillation genes among religious communities!" exclaimed the xeno-biologist.

"Yes, this is it. But these communities also demonstrate serious health concerns, and we are working on measures to treat them on a large scale, without the need for abduction. This is precisely why we requested permission to use radiation therapy from air to treat entire communities at once. This is a very efficient..."

"Master Argon!" interrupted Pretor Inkishi, who was leading a fringe group of the Unkari politicians who advocated humane treatment for the research subjects. "Wait a moment, Master Argon, isn't it dangerous to expose healthy humans to radiation treatment?"

"Well... Technically speaking..."

"Didn't you write a report on how this type of treatment causes various cancers among the healthy subjects...?"

"Well... Yes, I did. But statistically speaking, for the project's purposes, they are the dead end of the evolution. For all I care they may just all drop dead at once because they only contaminate the research sample."

"Master Argon!" exclaimed outraged Inkishi. "I cannot believe what I am hearing! If I didn't know your excellent academic record, I'd bring you before the ethics board. They are sentient beings!"

"They are nothing but worms, Pretor! A biological mass of protein molecules diluted in water and stuffed into body bags. They are our research subjects, and I am treating them as such!"

The meeting seemed to come to a halt. An awkward pause settled in, and Argon looked outside the force field that separated the great Atlantic Ocean from the lab. Outside, the ocean floor glowed green as the lights around the lab's perimeter illuminated sand, rocks, and a school of small fish. One way or another, he needed to continue the work, so he was the first one to break the silence.

"Apologies, Pretor. I guess the hardships of this post wear on me. Look, there must be a solution. I don't want to lose the most promising sample in Fatima due to this cancer epidemic. The gene carriers are humans too, and using your logic, we must give them a chance as well."

Pretor sprayed a puff of lilac powder from the orifice of his tentacle as he motioned it in a conciliatory gesture. "You have a point there, Master Argon. What's the population of that sample?"

"About 100,000 humans, give or take. Thirty eight percent of them carry varying combinations of the gene. This is the highest concentration of the oscillation gene anywhere in the world, and their habit of praying is keeping them alive longer so they pass the gene to the next generation at the highest rate."

"Can't you somehow isolate the affected population and selectively treat them?"

"And how am I suppose to do that? Post a message in the local newspaper?".

"Wait a minute!" exclaimed a second xeno-biologist, who until that moment remained silent. "I've been reading the reports of anthropologists on human mythology. There are many myths about supernatural beings healing faithful humans."

"Oh yeah, most of them have to do with us," shrieked Argon.

"True, but you can use their beliefs to make the sick people come forward."

"You want me to run a theater over there?"

"Perhaps..."

"Do you even realize that not all patients affected with brain cancer even experience any symptoms?"

"Indeed..." agreed the xeno-biologist. "But you can inspect them closer when they all gather in one place. We can create software that would target each sick individual with a focused radiation beam. You can do it if you are close enough and the population is not moving, say if they were gathered somewhere in the open space and listening to a holographic projection of their deity."

87

"You do want me to run a theater there. You got to be kidding me."

"We can send you a few anthropologists to help you with the script and a few technicians to develop a focused radiation beam," suggested Pretor. Argon realized that the Pretor was on board with the idea. Arguing was pointless.

"Oh black hole on your heads! What can I say. Theater it is!"

Year 1942, February 25. Charleston, South Carolina. Office of Naval Intelligence (ONI) Headquarters

Fred Irving Jr. rushed into the mess hall. At the furthest end of the hall was sitting his buddy John reading a thick volume. He barely kept up with flipping the pages, frequently licking his finger. "John! Here you are, buddy!" yelled Fred as soon as he entered the mess hall.

"I...!" John raised his hand without breaking his reading concentration. "What's so urgent?"

Fred walked to John's table and stood there for a moment, transfixed, watching his friend ferociously flip pages. "I swear, John, some days I think it is your practical joke of sorts. How can you read like that?"

"I can read just fine. Unless I am interrupted, jackass."

Fred grinned. "John, we are summoned to the meeting room. Judging from the fuss about it, it's pretty major."

"When?"

"At 1100 hours."

88

John finally looked away from the book and at the white analogue display on the wall. "That's in nine minutes! Why didn't you say so right away?" John immediately hurried out of the mess hall across the campus, leaving his buddy lagging behind. To make it on time, they had to run a good sprinting speed for five minutes straight. When they dropped in the war room, it was packed with local staff. Among the newcomers were two Generals with the Pentagon insignia. The Generals looked exhausted, as if they had sprinted to Charleston all the way from DC. The one with a yellow manila folder with a 'classified eyes only' seal roared at John and Fred:

"Take your seats, ladies!"

"Yes sir! Apologies sir!" saluted John, and Fred followed.

"This country is at war, Ensign. The enemy gives two shits about your apologies."

John and Fred looked at each other: must be the Japanese again. The General with the classified folder continued. "Now that we are all assembled, shall we discuss the matter of national security?" The room was quiet. John could hear blood humming in his ears. "Yesterday, at 1900 hours, the US experienced an unprecedented breach of air space. Up to twelve unidentified aircraft entered Californian air space from the Pacific Ocean and headed to several strategic defence facilities, including the Douglass Aircraft Factory. The movement of these intruders was picked by numerous USAF Bases and radars on the jets raised in the air according to the yellow alert. The enemy exhibited unprecedented skill and aptitude of movement, from hovering completely still to immediately accelerating to speeds over 200 miles per hour. Over the course of the incident, the enemy did not discharge any ammunition. However, the nature of the attack forced the US Air Force to fire at the targets. Between 3:16 and 4:14 am, the ground troops discharged 1400 anti-aircraft surface to air shells while the city was on a total blackout."

The General paused and observed the audience. The entire ONI subcommand division tightly jammed into the meeting room, was making no sound.

89

"It was a bloody 4th of July show out there, boys. We are still gathering the evidence but there were several civilian casualties caught in the friendly fire. The enemy, however, was unharmed. Around 4 am, the enemy moved out from downtown Los Angeles, where the main battle took place, and proceeded to the Pacific shore. There, about 50 miles into the ocean, we lost track of them."

John's mind was spinning miles ahead of the General's briefing, going over numerous strategy combinations to counteract this stealthy enemy. But how could the Air Force lose track of such a massive amount of enemy aircraft? It made no sense. Of course, the rest of the event made little sense as well. Since the small insurgence by the Japanese submarine at the oil refineries on the Californian coast a day ago, the military was on high alert, expecting another attack was imminent. But this highly technological air attack was not what anyone could expect. All the intelligence pointed that the Japanese forces did not have the capacity for an attack by air, and certainly not the kind to cause the USAF to order a complete blackout of Los Angeles, and firing for an hour straight, to the detriment of civilians caught by shell debris. And all of that caused no apparent damage to the enemy craft? Secondly, why did the enemy not return fire? What was the goal of the operation? Perhaps to test the U.S. readiness for the war? Plausible. But without firing a single shot? Japanese were known for their suicide missions, but from the way it looked, the enemy did not suffer any harm. It hadn't been a suicide mission. This was a mission devised by a cold and calculated enemy. The kind of enemy that was in no hurry, merely toying with the U.S. Air Force, pushing their buttons to see when they would flinch. And by all means, they flinched. Several civilian casualties at the hands of its own military was no small wrinkle on the fabric of public trust and confidence. But losing track of the enemy craft as they leisurely removed themselves from local airspace? That was unheard of.

The General finished the factual portion of the briefing and proceeded with the assignment. "Officers, your subcommand is specialized in asymmetric warfare tactics. Your skill is in devising strategies to fight a vastly different enemy, and until now this has meant fighting against militias, rebels and the like - insurgences on their own terrain. We need you to use this skill and apply it to the scenario, where the United States of America plays the role of a lesser power on a home terrain, and the enemy is vastly exceeding and utterly unknown."

Low-level shuffle and whispers traveled the room. It did not take a genius to conclude that such a vastly superior power hardly existed on the face of the Earth. Japan was out of the question; the nation used its citizens as human shields. Although it was an effective, albeit sickening, tactic, it was not the kind of scenario the Pentagon General presently described. The U.K. was an ally, and even if it would go rogue, as unlikely a scenario as it was, it would not be able to put forward the kind of advanced technology that had been observed last night over Los Angeles. Germany? Yes, Germany was a formidable force, but the chances of a German air force coming this close to the U.S. and remaining unnoticed were minimal. Plus, Germany was overextended on the European front at that time. So, the Soviet Union? Also bogged down in the war, it's technical capacity was not a secret. There wasn't a snowball's chance in hell this type of technology could be produced by the Soviets. John quickly went over all the suspects in his head and discarded each one of them as the likely enemy. Then he raised his hand to directly address the General.

"I see a question in the audience. Glad you regained your breath, Ensign. Go ahead."

"Sir, there is no enemy power on Earth that would warrant the asymmetric warfare analysis that you've requested, where the U.S. would fight as a lesser indigenous power against a vastly surpassing enemy. With all due respect, who are we dealing with?"

***

Argon presided at a meeting of four Unkari pilots sent over to the South Californian coast in order to gather medical analytics. Their equipment worked very well from several kilometres above the ground, scanning vast human populations on the subject of the oscillation-related pathologies. "Master Argon, we need new protocols on dealing with this human tribe. They are vigilant, if not to say paranoid. Their petty tribal conflicts make them jittery. I'm surprised that they don't fire at their own shadows." Argon smirked. This sounded like an accurate assessment of his research subjects. "So what exactly happened over there?"

91

"At first, we needed to scan and potentially treat from brain cancer several prominent subjects in their military complex. For that purpose, we took an observational position over what they call a Douglas Factory, where they build their silly flying machines. We have several important subjects with the gene there, but they will not have time to spawn offspring if we don't treat their cancer with a radiation blast. But since they were expecting an attack from the Japanese tribe, they spotted us immediately. Their vessels were raised in the air and followed us, preventing us from dispatching a steady radiation beam. We had to perform evasive manoeuvres.

Eventually, our subjects were relieved from work duties and proceeded to their habitats in the city of Los Angeles. We followed. By that time, their military was on high alert, and they started shooting."

"Damage?"

"Funny, sir. Very funny."

"Damage to the research subjects, you idiots!"

"Oh, yes. The life signs of two gene-bearing subjects were lost. We believe it was due to the ammunition debris that they discharged in the air. Their fire power skills are primitive and dangerous to themselves."

"Wonderful. I send you on a simple medical mission, and you start a war."

"Sir, if they were not so spooked, expecting to be attacked by their own kind, everything would go as usual. Perhaps you should obtain a permission from the Council to perform a few extractions."

"You know damn well that the politics on the extractions has changed. Only in case of an emergency, remember? I doubt that I can present your incompetence as warranting an emergency action. Dismissed."

92

Argon sprayed a few puffs of colored powder in the air at the pilots, who shuffled to the exit. Argon waited until they left, got off his work station and walked towards the transparent energy shield that formed the barrier between the lab and the surrounding ocean. The abyss was haunting and luring. So many times he wished that the Earth environment was not lethal to the Unkari chemistry. Otherwise he would be taking long uncloaked swims in this ocean full of vibrant and simple life. Argon missed his home planet and the green methane oceans, where he loved to dive and splash as a child. This happy time had passed many galactic rotations ago. Now he was stuck on this carbon-oxygen saturated world, where a single breath would make his blood boil, and the low atmospheric pressure would make his insides burst.

Besides all of that, his research subjects had entered a dangerous era in their evolution. Although Unkari helped humans to become more intelligent, to grow more knowledge in order to exercise their brains so that the effects of the oscillation genes could take hold, this had caused rapid technological advancement, perhaps so rapid as to significantly threaten their own safety. Now several human tribes possessed a very primitive and dangerous technique of splitting the atom which they used as a weapon of mass destruction. This did not fare well with the Unkari's plans to grow the population sample and allow it to multiply the oscillation gene. No, instead of breeding and expanding, they were striving to self-destruct. This suicidal tendency had been written about by many Unkari xeno-anthropologists. Some had suggested that subconsciously humans rebelled against their existence as laboratory subjects. A lot of fancy words were wasted on this psychobabble, thought Argon. This was a popular topic among the Unkari cultural elites. To them, this human experiment was one of the most popular live entertainments, a reality show of sorts. Many Unkari enjoyed observing humans as if they would observe Lenaurian worms in a jar striving to get outside the boundaries of their understanding.

Argon was pragmatic. To him, all these psycho-existential trash talks were just that, trash, unsubstantiated, uneducated speculations about a subject they knew nothing about. On the other hand, he knew everything there was to know about humans. He witnessed their predecessor race, an advanced and even frighteningly respectable species, that could bend reality on a deep sub-atomic level, playing with the probabilities of existence and anchoring them to a four-dimensional reality of their choosing. The First Humans were fearless and powerful. They spent their lives, albeit short ones, in productive pursuits of knowledge and advanced their understanding of the Universe. Argon respected that about them. Any truly worthy enemy evoked feelings of respect in Argon. This nonetheless did not stop him from lobbying total annihilation of the species, as a purely preventative measure.

93

The First Humans, however, had presented the Unkari with an ultimate puzzle. Their oscillation ability went against everything the Unkari knew about the nature of the universe. The ability was too tempting not to reverse-engineer it. As any reverse-engineering process goes, in order to understand the technology, you needed to build it from the ground up, from a single protein, and watch it assembling itself into a sentient, living, breathing being. This part was easy. The difficult part was in making the seemingly useless gene sequences work. Argon knew that the consciousness of the human civilization must be exercised, expanded, prepared as a vessel for the oscillation power to take root. This was the stumbling block of the project.

Building a human being from a single protein molecule was easy. Making it oscillate without killing itself seemed to be nearly impossible. It was as if nature password-protected its secrets, preventing even the Unkari from getting their tentacles on its mysteries. Sometimes Argon felt as if he was standing behind a closed door with a pile of keys at his disposal, but unable to find the right one. More than anything in the world, Argon hated to feel powerless.

July 12, 1952.
Washington DC

94

The Unkari pilot squad leader Berenbeck was approaching Washington DC from the Atlantic. Leading four medical relief vessels, he made sure all the instructions were followed to the letter. Chances were, humans would open fire this time as well, but this did not bother Berenbeck as long as they did not kill their own kind. This risk was always there when they needed to treat large urban populations from brain tumors, and Washington DC was one of the worst when it came to human's paranoid security concerns.

Livintau, who was piloting the second Shalosh in the formation, patched through on Berenbeck's receiver. "Ok, so they actually suspect that we are here. What I don't understand, why they can't figure out we are not here to attack them?" Livintau was just transferred from the medical mission in the Intari Go quadrant, where the Unkari were attempting to uproot the local primitive life in an otherwise suitable for colonization planet. Livintau had placed his transfer request a long time ago, wishing to work on a mission that at least on the surface had its goal of saving lives, rather than destroying them.

"They have tunnel vision, Livintau", answered Berenbeck as best as he could. "They don't live very long. And systemic knowledge does not transfer well from generation to generation."

"Perhaps. But I have read that intergalactic species are becoming popular in their mythology. And myths are very good at surviving generations."

"Livintau, let's continue this discussion at a more appropriate time." Although Livintau was a pilot working for the Unkari military, he was a civilian exo-physiologist. His interpretation of a protocol was rather liberal. "Livintau, Erondo, Gunkari, ready the laser net. Let's do the job with as little exposure as possible. I really don't want to have another treatment from Master Argon."

"That's because he is getting old", mumbled decorated fighter pilot Gunkari, commissioned to Earth to participate in each surface mission because of the rising security concerns. "But who am I to say that. I'm only a Kha-yal of the 3rd rank."

"Clear the air from non-mission critical discussion!" pressed Berenbeck only slightly firmly, more to follow protocol, rather than in disagreement. Argon *was* getting old, and living on this hardship post was not good for his mental health. But Argon was as stubborn as the Intarian pestilence. And he was well connected. This combination allowed him to pretty much write his own ticket until he retired or proceeded to eternity, whichever happened first.

July 14, 1952.
Massachusetts,
11th Congressional District

For John Kennedy, some Mondays were worse than others. Although Congress was in recess, he had no time to rest. Dick Nixon was already running on the VP ticket, and nobody even liked Dick. Hey, even Ike didn't like Dick! That year, beloved by all, Congressman John Kennedy had to campaign for the

Senate. At 35, most would consider this a hell of an accomplishment. John considered it a minor annoyance, a detour from what he actually wanted to pursue – the commander in chief and leader of free world. That was *his* calibre!

In all honesty, John felt as if his clock was ticking. Behind the public image of vigor and strength was a broken man, who could not even get off the bed without a mysterious concoction of drugs, the content of which he didn't even want to know, as long as it helped him to get through the day. *Speaking of drugs...* thought John and picked up a phone. "Bobby, are you awake yet?"

"I am now, John," was the answer at the other end of the telephone. "For Christ's sake, it's five in the morning..."

"I need it, Bobby."

"What, now?"

"Now, Bobby. It hurts so much I may shit myself."

"Christ, we don't want that," a sleepy Bobby Kennedy uttered flatly. "What do you want me to do?"

"I need Dr. Feel Good *today*."

"He was scheduled to fly in tomorrow, are you sure you can't wait? Maybe I can send you a cute nurse or something..."

"Bobby!"

"To give you shots! Christ, John! I'm not your pimp."

"Ok, send your nurse. And send the plane after Jacobson. *Now.* I can't even get up to take a piss."

"Ok ok, John, I'm sorry. I'm awake now. I'm on it. Should I call you for some coffee and eggs?"

"Alright. I suppose. Hurry up." John hung up and kicked back in his bed, staring at the ceiling and trying to disassociate himself from the excruciating pain in his back. Certainly it didn't work, and he knew it wouldn't work without Jacobson's shorts: three in the back and two in each leg, just to get up. He reached out to his nightstand and turned on the radio. Vera Lynn's hit *'Auf Wiedersein, We'll Meet Again Sweetheart'* burst in the room. For a moment, John's pain was muffled by memories of a particular German sweetheart who was bad news all together, but her legs could make him forget not even his pain, but his own name. That sweetheart he would not meet again. Dating someone who the FBI considered a German spy was bad for his career.

Then there was Jackie... He had met her just two months ago, and she was getting into his head like a young wine. Perhaps too proper, but perfect for a First Lady. Charming, good upbringing, good pedigree... Like her horses... A knock at the door interrupted his thoughts. A maid walked in with his breakfast on a tray and a stack of morning newspapers. She placed the tray on his bed and courteously left. Jack made an effort to sit upright, but only managed to spill hot coffee all over the sheets. After knocking the wind out of the mattress, John shoved the coffee-stained comforter to the side and pulled out the newspaper from its folds. Between the coffee stains, the front page read:

Washington DC Under Attack

"What in the world..." John kept reading.

Apparently over the weekend, sightings of multiple aircraft had been reported all over Capitol Hill, the airport, and other strategic locations. The newspaper recounted the most incredible race that involved the Andrews Air Force base jets in the air, chasing invincible illuminated objects that had either hovered absolutely still or had accelerated at a rate that defied logic. Fighting off excruciating pain, he reached out to the phone and dialed.

97

"Dick, you awake? It's John."

"John... Oh wait, let me guess, you partied all night and haven't gone to bed yet..."

Nixon was grumpy not without a reason. "Dick, what the hell happened in DC over the weekend?"

"You mean, the star wars?"

"The star wars is right!"

"I don't know if I can tell you anything that wasn't in the newspapers... Except... I saw it with my own eyes. The Andrews guys chased these things all night. Hell, it was not only me. Thousands saw it."

"Is it... credible?"

"Well... They are blaming it on the weather. Hell if I know. I just don't know what kind of weather shows up on multiple radars, John."

"Dick, I can't tell you in details, but I saw this before. Ten years ago."

"Let me guess. L.A."

"You said it. So what the hell did we get ourselves into?"

"Well, don't help Stevenson with the race. Ike and I win, and we will find out!"

"Aren't you a genius, Dick," John retorted sarcastically. "But who do I call about it? Come on, Dick. This is something major."

"Try LBJ. Just a guess. But for heaven's sake, wait until the sun is up."

"Alright Dick. Go back to sleep. Give my regards to Pat."

(Muffled) *'John says hi to you, Pat.'*

(*Muffled) 'Oh that's nice, Dick, tell him to go back to sleep.'* John laughed.

(Into the phone) "She says hi to you too, John. And when am I going to give my regards to your significant other?"

"Perhaps sooner than you think, Dick. I may just have found the one."

"You always say that, John."

"This time it's real. I just need her to break off her engagement!"

"John!"

"What?"

"John, I don't want to know."

January 23, 1961.

JFK's First Day in the Office

The inauguration ceremony was held on Friday. John's entire weekend turned into a euphoric blur. That was why Monday started off late. At around noon, John descended to the Oval Office to receive a line-up of security briefings, but the first order of business was to have some coffee and talk to Bobby. Bobby walked in minutes after John himself had shown up, still technically hung over, but thanks to Jacobson's concoctions, as clear-headed as ever.

"Did you know, Bobby, that the closest an Irishman came to the White House prior to this moment was to design its architecture?"

"Oh really? It was designed by an Irishman?"

"Yes indeed, it was. And now an Irish family will design its policies. And according to Jackie, some renovations to the interior are coming up as well."

"I'm sure she'll do a fine job, John. So will you, with the policies that is, Mr. President!"

"Thanks, Bobby. It would be impossible without you, brother."

"I am worried about you, John. About your health."

"I heard that before. And you are not helping."

"That's all I ever do but help, John!"

"Oh you know what I mean. It is not helpful hearing you nagging at me all the time."

"You cannot be constantly on speed."

"Amphetamines, Bobby. Sounds almost like vitamins!" John laughed heartily, but Bobby shook his head.

"You can't go eight more years like this."

"You sound like a broken record."

"Alright. I'll shut up for now. There is a line-up of generals outside your door. I probably should be going, Mr. President."

Bobby smiled warmly. "Ok, send them in. Let's see what

secrets are hidden in these walls."

"Watch out for your own secrets, John. I am serious. I don't have many ideas left that would keep Hoover's mouth shut."

"You'll figure something out, Bobby, I'm sure."

"Don't make my job more difficult than it already is."

***

Meanwhile, Argon had a meeting of his own. Like Bobby Kennedy, he was also worried about John's health. Not only had John had one of the strongest pre-oscillation results, but now he held an important office. Controlling a U.S. President whose life was already monitored was easier than someone Unkari did not monitor for oscillation. The Unkari medical specialist Korem-Atoo walked into Argon's office. "How is he holding up?"

"He is pushing his body to the limits. Honestly, I wouldn't give him as much as three years."

"Is Jacobson cooperative?"

"As usual. No questions asked. You'd be surprised what he can do given enough of their currency."

"My concern is that since he is in the office, they may scrutinize his blood and discover the nanites."

100

"Yes, that's a problem. Should I involve more doctors?"

"Doctors are snoopy. Let's avoid them if we can. Maybe someone on his secret service staff?"

"Hmm..."

Korem-Atoo sprayed two faint puffs of lilac powder in the air.

"How about his Vice President, Johnson?"

"He was chasing our shadow for years now, through the Senate Armed Forces Committee and the Blue Book... Korem-Atoo, I don't know if he can handle the truth."

"Look, Argon. If John Kennedy dies, which according to my scans is highly likely, Lyndon Johnson will take over. We need to bury the space race and the Project Blue Book. It is getting out of control. This guy, Hynek, is running around as a converted believer, and I tell you, he is a pain in the tentacles. He asks a lot of questions."

"Lyndon Johnson is a screw-loose. I cannot trust him. He is not like this doctor, Jacobson. Money is of no interest to him."

"I have an idea. How about a subconscious influence? We can record some protocols to his brain about what to do if Kennedy dies, and what to do about the Blue Book."

"I like the idea in general. But the implementation may be challenging."

"Well, as Vice President, he flies a lot, so we can access him in the air."

"Alright, see to it. Just get a good coder for this. We don't want to make him do something ridiculous. He has too much power now."

July 27, 1969.
The Oval Office

Seven days after the Moon landing, President Nixon held a top-secret briefing. A yellow manila folder on his desk with the 'Classified Eyes Only' stamp contained a single typed page. It read:

101

Agenda:

1. Apollo 11. Missing minutes. Aliens warn us against pursuing further Moon exploration.

2. Dismantling of the Blue Book Project.

3. Diversion tactics to discredit public UFO claims.

4. DARPA's progress on reverse-engineering the Roswell UFO.

Nixon checked his clock – five minutes till the briefing. "John, I wish you were here, buddy. You won the Moon race, but apparently, this is where we stop." Years had passed since Kennedy's tragic death, and he still missed him. Yes, now that he was dead, he could simply miss him, in the purest sense, without being jealous and angry. Those feelings meant nothing anymore.

In fact, now he could have used John's take on what the hell was going on.

Who was the real enemy?

It was clear as hell that the Soviets had nothing to do with it.

Then the 1952 early morning phone call came to his mind. The L.A. incident. The DC incident. Now this Iranian incident, with many more in between. They were here. Who were they?

Nobody knew. Humans had played catch up with them, and DARPA had made some spectacular progress on the craft downed in 1947, at bloody Roswell, New Mexico. A butt of the joke to most Americans, Roswell was no joking matter among a small group of scientists and generals possessing the highest clearance. The UFO that had crashed on that sheep ranch had scared everyone, but it also motivated them to continue to work, as if racing an invisible wind.

102

And not just any wind - an interstellar one.

5
A MAN WHO SAVED THE WORLD

-1-

Vasya watched a giant fly cruising across the dusty classroom. That particular fly was surprisingly noisy; one might even think it was a bumblebee. The fly had no idea it was violating Valentina Ivanovna's biggest taboo: no humming in class. Every one of the 30 kids in that classroom, Vasya included, were mortified to upset their teacher, because she was known for summoning parents to school. The fly apparently did not care about the rules. Vasya admired the fly: it had wings, and the wings gave it courage. For a seventh-grader like Vasya, a math exam was a big deal. He was old enough to understand social pressure and the need to do well, yet still a child to see the difference between merely an exam and a life-and-death situation. Despite the pressure to perform, Vasya Arkhipov was a surprisingly lazy kid, at least according to his mother. She often said that Vasya walked with his head stuck in clouds.

105

Vasya himself knew that he was a strange child, but had no idea why. Take his school as an example. Vasya rarely did his homework, but his exams always came out straight A's. Like today. Valentina Ivanovna had a stack of graded exam papers on her desk, and she looked grim. She sat down at her desk, planted huge glasses at the bridge of her nose, and with the panache of the entire Communist Party behind her authority, she took the top paper from the stack and proclaimed. "Samoylov! Dva!" Samoylov facepalmed and tried his best not to cry. "Litvinova. Tri!" Litvinova, a tall lanky girl with braided hair and freckles that looked like red pepper flakes, folded her arms with a ferocious expression over her face. A "C"! Nothing to brag about.

At some point, it was Vasya's turn.

"Vasenka Arkhipov..." The teacher's face melted in a cheesy grin. "Dushenka. Pyaterka!"

An "A". No, he wasn't cheating, not in a usual sense. But he didn't study for the exam either. Vasya's school was located several villages away from his house. Every day Vasya walked 30 minutes to the bus stop, then hopped on the bus with a bunch of farmers and school kids, and rode for another 30 minutes to the village where the school was located. Then together with the school gang, he merrily trotted for another 15 minutes to the school courtyard. After the classes, they retraced the route back home. That day, after the math final results came in, the 7-A class was not in the mood. A lot of the kids would be grounded, or worse, beaten up. And every sober and caring parent in every home would be bringing up the forsaken Vasya's "A". Vasya's "A" was like a salt on a sore wound to every one of his classmates. Dima, who was sitting a few rows behind Vasya, looked at his "F"-graded paper with contempt. That summer he was supposed to receive a new pair of shoes, not a hand-me-down from someone in the neighborhood, but a brand-new pair from the market, but this "F" turned those dreams to ashes.

106

With venom in his heart, Dima crumbled the hated paper and catapulted it at Vasya's head. Dima was very good at throwing things, and the paper hit the target as intended. Next moment, a swarm of paper balls was launched at Vasya, turning into an all-bus riot. The bus driver looked at his mirror and saw that the situation was getting out of control. He slam-jammed the breaks and yelled at the passengers to get out. "If you don't want to ride the bus like civil members of society... walk like the savages that you are! Get the hell out of my bus, you ublyudki." The crowd immediately calmed down and everyone returned to their seats. "Wait a minute, you little pricks! You think this is it? Who's going to clean up the mess? If you want to ride the bus, you must pick every scrap of paper and stuff it in your pockets. Litter in your own house, ublyudki." The kids obeyed and got down on their fours, crawling on the bus floor and picking up the mess. Down on the floor, Dima and Vasya met head to head. Dima sucker-punched Vasya ever so slightly, just to make a point that he was not over the whole thing.

"So how did you know the answers?"

"I saw them in a dream..." Vasya mumbled hesitantly.

"In a dream??!" Lena, Dima's sister, who was crawling on the floor next to the guys, was not buying it. Dima was about to punch Vasya again, but the bus driver announced that they were taking off and requested everyone in their seats. Lena and Dima sat behind Vasya, fully intended to continue tormenting him. "What do you mean, in a dream?" Lena would not give up. "Boys are such liars!"

"Not all boys!" protested Dima.

"Most of them are! Vasya is the biggest liar there is! And a cheater!" insisted Lena. "I saw him from my window for the whole week. He was always out and about, and that's before the final exam. I guarantee you he did not pick up a textbook even once!"

107

Vasya wanted to protest, but Lena was right. He had hardly opened the textbook. He had great memory and remembered everything that was taught in class, but when it came to homework, he just couldn't find any time to attend to it. His daddy was on another drunken binge, and it was time for spring gardening campaign. Mom was working all day on a collective farm, trying to meet her quota, but dad, who was granted a disability pension, could in fact attend to their own garden, but he drank like a horse. Especially in spring, when it was a critical time for work. In winter he managed to sober up and became more present, spent time with the family, but every time the pressure of a deadline was on a horizon, he would drink himself into a stupor. With mom being busy at the collective farm, the task of planting spring veggies was all on Vasya. "Look, Lena, you are right. I did not read the textbook, ok? That's nice that both of your parents are tending to your farm. If I wasn't planting potato the week before the exam, what would we eat all winter? My grades?"

Vasya was shaken. It was embarrassing to even imply that his dad was an alcoholic. "Ok, how did you know the answers to the test then? And don't give me the dream nonsense."

"I... how can I explain...? It's like as if I remembered making a mistake, getting my test graded, with all the mistakes corrected, and then writing it again. In my memory, I have access to all the times when I made the wrong choices on the test, hundreds of times..."

"That makes no sense." Dima was annoyed. "Are you saying that Valentina Ivanovna allowed you to take the test multiple times?"

"No, not at all. I took the test only once, with you guys. But I have memory as if I took it multiple times. Like as if I had a dream..."

"Who do you think I am? A clown?" Dima burst out in rage. At that moment, he could care less if he had to walk home, but he needed to teach this punk a lesson. He grabbed Vasya's collar with his left, and with his right fist delivered a punch straight in Vasya's nose.

The lights went out.

108

-2-

Vasya opened his eyes. He was still on the bus. Lena and Dima were sitting behind him, looking severely pissed off. The bus was slowly taking off after all the trash was collected and the kids were settled in their seats. "So how did you know the answers?" Dima's voice brought Vasya back to reality. The memory of a nose punch was so vivid, but did it really happen?

Vasya was not going to take a chance. "I studied at night, with candles, ok?"

"Nerd," Lena fired at him. "Boys are such nerds. And you are the worst, Vasya!"

Bitter, Vasya broke eye contact with Lena. For a moment,

he concentrated on a fly buzzing on the bus window, trapped, and probably just as bitter as Vasya himself. He sniveled and rubbed under his nose. Wet drip-off smeared over his fingers, when Lena yelped:

"Vasya, you are bleeding!"

Vasya looked at his palm - it was covered in red blood.

Not again, he thought. How embarrassing!

He straightened up in his seat, tilted his head back and squeezed his nostrils with the tips of his fingers to stop the bleeding. "What is it back there again?" yelled the bus driver.

"His nose is bleeding!" Lena yelled back.

"What did you do to him, you little pricks?"

"We did nothing, swear!" Dima protested.

"Well, don't get any on the seats. Get him a handkerchief or something..."

Vasya made it home looking miserable and bloody. His face, shirt, and palms were stained with dry brown blood. Mom greeted him with a hug. "Oh dear, the nose bleeds again?"

"Yeah, ma. It's nothing. Probably just the nerves about the exam."

109

"How was it?"

"An "A." Of course."

"Good for you! At least someone has a future here. Keep it up, and you may save the world one day. You can become a doctor or a teacher."

"I want to be a pilot, ma."

"A pilot, you say. Alright then. Pilot it is, dear. Go straighten up. The lunch is on the stove."

-3-

Vasya did not become a pilot. By the age of 18, he wore

glasses and could not pass the physical for the Air Force. But he was otherwise a remarkable recruit: excellent memory, cool-headed demeanor, and attention to detail off the chart. He was physically fit as well, especially in martial arts. Without any formal training, it was as if he anticipated every punch, and skillfully avoided it. Vasya's bloodwork revealed that he was slightly anemic, with low blood sugar. Together with the assignment to the Navy, Vasya was prescribed an extensive nutrition regiment: extra butter, liver sausages, and a special treat: GEMATOGEN, a blood candy, that tasted remotely like caramel and contained blood product to increase red blood cell count. Blood or not blood, the candy tasted good for the marines with limited menu, and Vasya could trade two packs of cigarettes for each candy bar. It was a good trade: cigarettes were a universal currency in the army.

-4-

Years later... Vasiliy Arkhipov's transfer to the K-19 submarine was one hell of a promotion. K-19 was a remarkable piece of engineering. It was a one of a kind nuclear submarine, that superseded the American USS Nautilus in speed, in submergence depth, and in nuclear ballistic missile range. Also, it was original in every way: for a change, no stolen American blueprints were used. Compared to the diesel submarines, the nuclear ones could spend an unlimited time underwater without the need to surface for recharging the batteries. That gave the Soviet subs a critical advantage: they were nearly impossible to detect, especially when they skillfully navigated the isothermal layers of the sea to cloak the submarine from the enemy sonars.

It was only appropriate to commission K-19 for its first mission on July 4, 1961, when the U.S. was celebrating their Independence day. It was Khruschev's way of saying: "Not so fast! That Independence of yours is an evolving situation." Or perhaps it was Khruschev's way to tally the score of the Vienna Summit, so that there was no ambiguity in the court of public opinion as to who had won that battle. The K-19 had remarkable potential, but its execution was rushed. When Arkhipov was assigned to the K-19 as a deputy commander, it was still all the rage and fanfare. However, behind the scenes,

K-19's construction seemed a harbinger of bad tidings. Despite all the construction deaths and freak accidents it took to get her out of the dry dock, in public consciousness they were not yet welded to her hull, as grim medals to the Soviet disregard for human lives. Arkhipov's tour of the submarine was delivered by excited and ambitious technical officers, who happily pointed out all sorts of gimmicks and gadgets, as they proceeded to her nuclear heart.

"Well, that's about it!" pointed the technician to Archipov when they reached the nuclear reactor. "Shall we inspect the mess hall now?" Speechless, Arkhipov recounted all the compartments he saw, and at no point did he notice any essential spare modules: air circulation filters, engines, and even the nuclear reactor's cooling system. Failure of any of these elements during the mission would mean sure death of the entire crew.

"What do you mean, that's it! Where do you keep the spare parts?"

"We don't have spares. I mean we have some tools and bolts, but no major spare modules, if that's what you mean, Sir."

"But I looked over the specks. We should have had the spares for most of the life-support systems and essential equipment..."

111

"Yes, indeed, deputy commander. But see, each detail is custom made. There is no part of this boat that could be mass-produced. They only had enough time to create one set of each element, just enough to equip this baby. But sir, fear not. This baby is the best thing the Soviet Union ever produced! It will outlast all of us!"

They must be out of their mind, though Arkhipov but kept his mouth shut. "Alright, walk me to the mess hall, officer."

"Great! Commander Zateyev is expecting us!"

-5-

Arkhipov was in the control room when he received a report

about a problem in the nuclear reactor section. "What is the nature of the problem, officer?" he inquired over the intercom.

"The reactor coolant system is failing, sir."

"What do you mean, *failing?* The mission had just begun!"

"Sir... the reactor's hull is breached, and we are losing pressure. We are not sure what exactly caused the breach."

"What's the prognosis?"

"Sir..." The officer's voice crackled.

"Ok, I get it, the end-prognosis is lethal. But when do we reach the critical temperature?"

"Forty minutes. An hour... It all depends if the breach expands and how. If the breach rapidly bursts, sir... We are cooked..."

"...Hello World War III. NATO base is just seventy miles away, they will interpret a nuclear explosion as an act of war," mumbled Arkhipov. They had to act fast! "Gather the team to seal the breach."

"Sir, the nuclear fission products, sir..."

"Stop wasting my time, Officer. Get to work! I expect a repair plan in place within 10 minutes." Arkhipov cut the communication with the officer and immediately reached out to Captain Zateyev over the intercom. On the other side of the doomed boat, Zateyev nervously bit his fingers, but otherwise was surprisingly together. Years in the military taught him to take any situation as a problem-solving puzzle. He believed that in the face of danger, soldiers who fall apart are selfish and even dangerous.

"I am already aware of the problem, major," reported Zateyev in his usual matter-of-fact tone. "So it happens, we have another one. The antenna is down. We are cut off from Moscow."

"Damn it. I wish I was there when she was built..."

"Beg your pardon?"

"Nothing, sir. I'll report when the welding team is at the

reactor."

Clang.

A heavy intercom phone handle connected with the base on the wall. What slipped from Arkhipov's tongue was not something he would ever dare to share with a high-ranking commanding officer, because it would land him in a mental institution, but over the years Arkhipov had learned enough about his strange ability to begin understanding it. Somehow he could influence his decisions and if those decisions had negative outcomes, he could revisit them. How was it possible? Arkhipov abandoned this question and dedicated himself to use this ability to the most benefit for the country. This meant assigning himself to all the most critical military operations and being personally present in the life-and-death situations, like the Soviet-Japanese war, and now handling a nuclear submarine. What he couldn't do was fix the disasters that he didn't cause. He could not correct the manufacturing errors that plagued K-19 in abundance, but there was a chance that he could minimize the damage of the current situation.

Arkhipov sat down and closed his eyes. All of this had happened before, he could see it in his head. Time and time again, K-19 nuclear meltdown resulted in an explosion, a brilliant white light, and then - nothing. No matter what the crew did, the scenarios resulted in an explosion. Over and over again he experienced the death of his crew, the expressions on their faces when light and heat rushed out of the reactor, that fraction of a second when they realized that it was all over. Outwardly, his visions resembled a paralysis: limbs stiffened while his eyes involuntarily moved under his eyelids as if in REM sleep. Excruciating headache and nausea ... And the nose bleeds. Crimson red drops fell on the control panel. *Tap - Tap - Tap...*

113

Arkhipov wiped the blood with the back of his sleeve and headed down to the reflectory compartment, to check on the welding team, ready to enter the reactor chamber. By that time, the temperature of the reactor had reached 700 C, and it would continue to rise with every minute as the fission products were not properly cooled.

"What's the status?" he inquired from the team that

looked mortified but continued putting on radiation suits and gathering scrap pieces of sheet metal and wire to patch the breach.

"It's not good, sir. You shouldn't be here, sir, the radiation level is skyrocketing. Look, your nose is already bleeding. Radiation sickness, sir..."

"You never mind that, officer. Who is going in?"

"We cast lots. The six of us are the lucky winners..." the officer smiled bitterly.

Arkhipov glanced over the group of young men who were preparing to sacrifice their lives. Something wasn't right... "Wait... Orlov, you stay... You weren't there... It was Mishin. Where is Mishin? He needs to go."

"Mishin, the radio technician?"

"Yes, him."

"But sir..."

114

Orlov was befuddled. For some crazy reason, commander Arkhipov was saving his life. Orlov, who was neither exceptionally skilled, nor a personal friend of Arkhipov's... Meanwhile Mishin walked in. His face was furiously distorted as he walked by Arkhipov giving him the most obvious look of contempt anyone had ever seen. Arkhipov had seen that look before, on the bus, in 7th grade. Each time it was because of his visions, only now Arkhipov knew exactly what a life-and-death situation was. He would take all the contempt in the world, just to prevent the disaster from happening. Mishin was not going to argue with the orders of a superior commander, but he was clearly befuddled as to how he got on Arkhipov's bad side.

"I am sorry, Mishin. It had to be you. There was no other way."

"Sir, I am not going to disobey your order. But permission to speak freely."

"Granted."

"You are a piece of ass, you know that? I'll see you on the other side."

"I understand. But trust me, there is no other way. If I went there myself, it wouldn't make any difference. I know, I saw it! I know you won't understand, but you just have to trust me on this." At that moment, loud machine humming passed for dead silence. Scared and doomed, the officers looked at Arkhipov as if he held the keys to heaven with all the answers and all the solutions, with hope and bitterness, with big eyes and trembling hearts. "Officers, you are the finest submariners that our country has to offer. I am proud to serve with you!" And disregarding the Soviet rules about prohibiting religious references in places of service, he quietly added: "God have mercy on our souls," and christened the team with an Orthodox cross, drawn in the air with his two fingers. Arkhipov turned around to hide the tears that welled in the corners of his eyes. He knew that there was no scenario in which these six young men survived.

-6-

Almost a year later, a special commission was still investigating the actions of the K-19 team. The high-ranking apparatchiks were divided on whether to send Arkhipov and Zateyev to GULAG for abandoning the ship, or to award them a medal for stopping the detonation of the nuclear reactor. Both sides of the argument had powerful influencers who kept whispering in Khruschev's ear. This whispering was getting old, and Khruschev decided to attend the hearing himself.

115

The surviving crew was gathered to testify. Orlov was pressing against the gray wall of a poorly lit, windowless hallway. All this time he did not dare to ask Arkhipov why he spared his life that day, but finally the opportunity presented itself, although not under the rosiest of circumstances. Arkhipov walked by Orlov, pounding with his soles down the concrete floor that echoed and reverberated his confident stride, looking ahead at nothing in particular, and took a seat at the furthest red chair, away from the group of the mariners, huddled together whispering and dropping not-so-subtle glances at their former leader.

Orlov needed to know. He approached his former commander and requested permission to sit beside him. The two sat side by side, the grey cool wall behind them. It was not some artificial presto wall, but a real rock and concrete wall, solid, impenetrable, like the mind of the bureau it was housing.

"Mishin died three months ago..." said Orlov, just to get it out of the way. "I am sending his wife half of my paycheck. It's not much... But since they cannot make up their minds whether to make us heroes or enemies, Mishin's pension is under revision..."

Arkhipov silently acknowledged it. What could he say? What could he say in these walls that grew ears from every corner, like poisoned mushrooms grow in a damp thick forest? Orlov turned to Arkhipov and emphatically placed his palm on his shoulder.

"When you go there, sir, you tell them! You tell them that Mishin was a hero!"

And he burst into tears. Shaking with his whole body, he took out a worn pack of cigarettes: Vatra, the cheapest, the nastiest tobacco there was. With shaking fingers, he placed one end of the cigarette in his mouth, but immediately took it out spitting a mouthful of loose tobacco. He pushed the tobacco back into the paper wrap as best he could, placed it back in his mouth and tried to battle the matchbox. The battle was lost from the get go as the striker was worn out, and the matches were damp. Arkhipov took out his matches, which were in pristine condition, and lit Orlov's cigarette. Orlov took a long, indulgent drag, and for a moment refused to exhale. Then his shoulders dropped, and he slouched forward, supporting his forehead with one arm, elbow resting on his knee.

"Sir, tell me why... Why I was not supposed to die that day..."

"I don't know, Orlov, I really don't. I only know that it was Mishin who had to be there. In all honesty, Orlov, it had nothing to do with you." Orlov nervously laughed, with a high-pitch eerie laughter that usually preceded someone snapping. Perhaps luckily for Orlov, a gray-suit bureaucrat poked his head out of the conference hall and invited Arkhipov in.

The First Secretary of the Soviet Union and one of the two most powerful men in the world, Nikita Khruschev presided at the long table. To his left and right sat various decorated Admirals and some grey suits, who remained unnamed. Each of the functionaries had a glass and a jug of water in front of them, placed on a silver tray. In front of Khruschev there was a tray as well, but a bigger one, as it also contained a small vase with scarlet-red carnations. Leaning sideways on their flimsy stems, the flowers were a resting ground for a rather fat fly, which calmly straightened its wings and cleaned its buggy eyes right in front of the General Secretary.

What courage! thought Arkhipov and faintly smiled.

The fly didn't seem to bother Khruschev, but the flowers obstructed his line of sight. Annoyed, he moved the tray to the right, wrinkling and pulling the white table cloth from the left side. Arkhipov saluted and stood in the middle of the room, as there was no chair for him to sit.

Khruschev leaned forward, placing his folded arms on the desktop. "I am tired of this K-19 investigation. Are you a hero, Arkhipov, or a deserter?"

"It is not for me to decide, Mr. First Secretary."

117

"You are damn right about that," winced Khruschev and loudly landed his fist on the table for dramatic effect. "I've heard enough about this incident already. What I don't understand is why you randomly relieved Orlov from going into the reactor, and instead sent in Mishin, a radio technician. Mishin, who is dead now, by the way, had no business of going into the reactor, don't you think? With this decision you may very well have endangered the entire repair mission. I say this is negligence. If not more."

"Tovarishch Khruschev, I know it makes no sense, but Mishin had to be there. Mishin was the linchpin. It was the only combination that did not result in nuclear meltdown."

"What the hell you are talking about?? You need an institution, my friend!"

"....you need an intitution, my friend," simultaneously

repeated Arkhipov.

"How did you..."

"How did you..."

"This is ridiculous."

"This is ridiculous."

"Stop it."

"Stop it... Mr. First Secretary, I can do it all day... And this Admiral here will need a clean pair of pants in a moment." As Arkhipov was saying those last words, Khruschev accidentally knocked over the vase, and the water spilled all over the crotch of the Admiral, sitting on the right hand side from Khruschev. "What the hell is going on here?" Khruschev rose from his chair and smashed his fist on the table. The ribbed glasses on the silver trays jumped in the air.

"Permission to speak in private, Tovarishch First Secretary."

"Out of the question!" roared Khruschev. "You are 30 seconds from being arrested!"

"It is a matter of the national security. Look, I am unarmed. You can order to handcuff me. But I will not speak a word, unless we are alone." Arkhipov knew that in a room with Khruschev the KGB would not dare to eavesdrop. It would be the safest place to talk.

Khruschev thought about it for a moment, but curiosity took him over. "Alright. Handcuff him. And get him a chair! Get me a gun as well." A young officer ran in the room carrying the handcuffs, a holstered gun, and a box of bullets. Khruschev, like his predecessors, was paranoid of murderous plots, and made it a standing policy to not have a loaded weapon in the same room with him. Then he signaled everyone out. While the Admirals begrudgingly obeyed his order and proceeded to the exit, Khruschev opened the bullet chamber of the gun, and one by one loaded the bullets. When the two were left alone, Khruschev pointed the gun at Arkhipov, who remained sitting in the middle of the room. "Now talk. You have 30 seconds, or I will put this whole box of bullets through your head."

"No you won't."

"Ok, I've had enough." Khruschev targeted Arkhipov's head and pulled the trigger.

Clank.

"What??"

"An empty cartridge."

"You are pushing your luck!" And he pulled the trigger again.

Clank.

"The whole box is filled with empty bullets, Tovarishch Khruschev. I cannot explain why, but I know it to be true. I saw it."

"How did you do it?"

"Like I said, I had nothing to do with it. I only know that you can discharge the entire box in my head, and they all will be empty. Perhaps the officer picked the wrong box in a hurry. What do I know?" Profoundly struck, Khruschev sat down at his chair. Then he pointed the gun at the wall, and one by one discharged the entire chamber. They were all empty.

"Do you believe me now?" Arkhipov asked him calmly.

119

"Let's assume that I do, for the time being. I can still drag your ass to places where the sun does not shine. Start talking."

-7-

October of 1962. Arkhipov was assigned as the commander of the submarine flotilla of four diesel-electric B-59 subs headed to Cuba. After Khruschev was convinced that Arkhipov's gift was real, he closed the K-19 investigation and commemorated the crew, but the incident remained classified. Upon Arkhipov's insisting on being assigned to handling nuclear weapon assignments, being in charge of the four B-59 subs headed to Cuba was about as high profile as it could get.

Initially, none of the crew knew the nature of the assignment. For all they knew, they were headed to the Arctic circle for another training mission. Not many even knew what the "special weapon" on board was, as it was guarded 24/7 by a special guard. Arkhipov knew it all.

Cuba was a strategic linchpin in the Soviet's Cold War strategy. After the Bay of Pigs invasion, Castro's temperance ran out. He needed a stronger argument in the fight against the United States. Cuba had to have nuclear capacity, there was no other way. The U.S./ Soviet tension was palpable. Kennedy had escalated tensions by invading Cuba, and by meddling in Russian airspace with their U2s. A moment could come when someone would have to push the button first.

Arkhipov was determined to be there at that moment, because in that scenario, an uninformed or rushed decision may mean the end of the world. Khruschev delegated Arkhipov with extraordinary authority during that mission. Generally, to dispatch a ballistic missile, it required an approval of the ship's commander and the ship's political officer. On that mission, the flotilla commander Arkhipov had veto authority.

By October 22, the B-59 flotilla received the last transmission from Moscow: to maintain their position in Sargasso Sea and not to approach the Cuban shore.

120

The reason was the blockade enforced by the United States. U.S. intelligence established that Cuba was building missile launch sites, and the blockade was supposed to prevent the Soviets from delivering any more missiles to Cuba. October 22 was also the day when Kennedy publicly addressed the nation about the nuclear threat in Cuba. The U.S. radio waves exploded. Having no communication with Moscow, the four submarines laid low and listened to all the frenzy that penetrated the U.S. radio. Unlike the nuclear submarine K-19, the diesel-electric B-59 had to periodically surface to recharge its batteries. To make things worse, the U.S. radio reported on a rumour that the Soviet submarines were approaching Cuba, and the U.S. anti-submarine operation aimed at detecting and surfacing them.

Conditions on Arkhipov's submarine were dire. The battery charge came dangerously low, and they decided to surface, risking exposing themselves to the U.S. search mission. When the radio technicians heard that the U.S. Destroyers were sweeping the area, the B-59 attempted an emergency dive, with a partially charged battery. Not knowing if they had been noticed, Arkhipov and the crew were in a state of offensive readiness. At that time, the air recycling system on the submarine malfunctioned, and the temperature on board rose to 50 C, and in some compartments, well above that mark. Oxygen was saturated with carbon dioxide, causing the officers to pass out.

That was when the first sonar strikes followed. Somewhere above them, an anti-submarine team had located the Soviet subs and was trying to surface them. With no orders from Moscow, the team had to make the decision. Were they under attack? Were the grenade and sonar charges offensive or an invitation to negotiate? Commander Valentin Savitskiy was not of the feeble-minded bunch. The crew used to joke that Savitskiy had a heart of a lion and a mind of a tiger: always ready to get in the fight, ask questions later. Those were not the ideal qualities to handle a nuclear launch sequence. Perhaps for that very reason, Arkhipov was placed on that particular submarine. Or perhaps it was another instance of ridiculous luck that humanity neither sought nor deserved. An act of God, if you wish. But it took an act of man to cash in on that luck.

121

"They've been pounding at us for three hours!" lamented Savitskiy among the select group of high-ranking officers. His formal attire was unbuttoned, sweat soaked it right through, and stench of men's bodies permeated every nook and cranny - way worse than any gym or a laundry bin you could ever imagine.

"So they know our location. That much is obvious," agreed Arkhipov. "This does not authorize us to use the special weapon."

"Wake up, Arkhipov! You don't want them to get their hands on our equipment!"

"Oh quit worrying about your equipment, commander! Same old Valik. Above all, protects his junk," joked Arkhipov and the crew chuckled. And then followed a massive explosion, dangerously close to the starboard hull. Five men,

Arkhipov and Savitskiy included, were tossed in a man-pile like toothpicks.

"Are you saying this is not an offensive strike?" roared Savitskiy. "Malenkov, what do you think?" Political officer Malenkov was the palest shade of khaki. At that moment, his opinion actually mattered, as he possessed a partial key to the launch sequence.

"All I wanted was to go on a few more training exercises and retire..." Malenkov grimly mumbled, getting up from the floor and trying to steady himself for a potential second strike. The second massive strike followed as if on a cue. The five officers again were in a human pile, stenchy, sticky, and furious, like prize fighting dogs, tortured before the fight to draw aggression.

"Arkhipov, come on, get your head out of your ass already! You've heard their radio! They are striking with an offensive weapon! Moscow line is dead! For all I know there may not be Moscow any more!" yelled Savitskiy. Arkhipov started seeing a point in those arguments.

"Let's get to the control room, while we still can, my friend," Malenkov pleaded, softly, almost brotherly. The decision was after Arkhipov.

122

"Look, Vasya, we know how this is going to end. For the people like us, it's all one-way trip. But I'll be damned if I go without taking some of those capitalistic pigs with me!" said Savitskiy and took the partial key off his neck, and inserted it into the keyhole. "Malenkov, it's your turn. It was a good fight." Malenkov nodded and inserted his key in the key hole as well.

It was Arkhipov's turn to complete the sequence. He was supposed to turn the switch on the dashboard, covered with a plexiglass lid. "Let's address the crew first. They deserve to know," said Arkhipov and opened the transparent lid of the launch switch.

–8–

Meanwhile in the White House... John F. Kennedy picked up

the red phone on his desk. "They did what? Yes, go DEFCON 1." And he hung up. Immediately, without knocking, a group of generals rushed through the door of the Oval Office.

"Mr. President. It is time to retreat to a secure location."

"Where is my family?"

"They are being assembled now as well, Mr. President."

"Where is Johnson?"

"In Florida. We have a confirmation that he is being transferred to the nearest secure location as we speak."

"Bobby?"

"We are trying to locate him now. We will inform you as soon as he gets in touch."

They whisked JFK down the corridors of the White House, to a room that was apparently a cleaning storage. Once in the room, one of the generals took the AC remote off the wall and popped open the back lid of the remote, where the batteries were supposed to be. Behind the lid, there were two buttons, totally alien to something so simple as an AC remote. The general pressed one of those buttons, and the solid white wall in front of them started sliding to the side. A passage revealed an elevator door. The General pressed the button. The elevator was on stand-by and immediately opened the door. The group walked in. The general pressed the only button on the console and the elevator started rapidly descending.

123

"Mr. President, the descending will take two minutes. It is time to launch the sequence."

With these words, a man carrying a small black suitcase, handcuffed to his arm, quickly entered the combination on the lock and the lid easily gave in. Inside the suitcase was a small console with a series of color-coded buttons and switches. Another general retrieved a white envelope, unsealed it, and extracted a small white card, the size of a business-card, with a series of numbers typed on it - a partial code. The general started imputing the code on the console of the black box. One of the buttons lit up green, signaling that the nuclear missile launch system was ready to accept the master code.

It was the turn of the President of the United States. "Are you sure it was not an accident?" Kennedy's lips were paper white and paper dry. "After all, you were trying to surface them for hours. Maybe you accidentally hit their missile or they panicked..."

"The first explosion could be considered an accident under these circumstances. But the second, third, and fourth..."

"What? From where?"

"Sonar identified only one Soviet submarine. In reality, there were at least four. After the one that we attempted to surface fired the missile and destroyed our anti-submarine sweep team, three other submarines, located within the radius of 300 miles from each other, launched their missiles as well. Mr. President, Florida and North Carolina took the hit. The third charge was shot down by the anti-missile system. The third one was aimed at DC."

"Dear mother of God. What have we done...."

With those words, President Kennedy removed a locket from his neck and retrieved a chip that contained the launch code. "Remind me, do I have to pick the targets now?" asked Kennedy. It was not every day that he started a nuclear holocaust.

124

"The targets are programmed according to the current scenario. All you need to do is to activate the sequence." The elevator came to a halt. "Mr. President. It is time. You need to do it before we exit through this door."

"Alright. May God have mercy on our souls." JFK signed himself with a Catholic cross and inserted the chip into the appropriate opening.

-9-

At the same time... Somewhere on the other side of the world, Khruschev took a big gulp of an expensive Armenian cognac and ordered to launch ballistic missiles from all strategic locations: submarines along the Pacific sea border, ICBMs in

Cuba and Kazakhstan, all were launched to orchestrate a debilitating strike to the Western allied forces and to prevent further destruction. However, several sleeping agents at the key positions on the Soviet nuclear sites immediately intervened, and of the five missiles, only one ended up leaving the launch silo. But its navigation radar malfunctioned, and it landed in the middle of rural China, causing minimal damage, considering circumstances. The American missiles, all of them, reached the target. All the strategic sites with nuclear capacity were wiped out in a blink of an eye. From space, it probably looked glorious: white mushroom clouds erupting and flaring with fire, like paper lamps launched in the night sky. "Damn good cognac," said Nikita Khruschev, taking his last sip, right before the nuclear heat wave evaporated him on the spot.

-10-

Vasiliy Arkhipov's ears rang as he came to his senses after the last explosion, dangerously close to the hull of the submarine. His vision blurred, his head was light, and his nose was bleeding. No he was not hurt, just disoriented and nauseous. "Get off of me already," groaned commander Savitskiy. "So what is it going to be, Malenkov? Does this still look like a non-offensive strike?"

125

"All I wanted was to go on a few more training missions and retire..."

Malenkov sounded completely defeated, as he took the key chain from around his neck and passed it to commander Savitskiy. "Do what you must, commander."

Both got up from the floor and proceeded to the control room. Arkhipov's nose was gushing bright red blood on everything around: he was choking on it and could hardly speak.

"Don't worry, commander Arkhipov, it will be all over soon," comforted Malenkov, looking into Arkhipov's eyes with the blissful relief of a person addicted to cutting himself, right before slicing a piece of his own skin. Arkhipov struggled to stay alert. A brutal combination of depleted oxygen, malnourishment, sleep deprivation, and his intense visions took him to the edge of human capacity. A small part of him wanted it all to be over, and as soon as possible.

But where was the courage in that?

"Wait, Commander Savitskiy. You need my permission. For the launch sequence. You need my permission." Arkhipov swiftly inserted himself between Savitskiy and the console.

"Oh yeah?" Savitskiy looked passed Arkhipov, at the launch console.

Arkhipov did not budge. "You need three votes."

"I have two votes, right Malenkov?"

Malenkov blinked at Savitskiy and dryly swallowed.

"Savitskiy, sir, you are making a huge mistake. They are not attempting to drown us. These are the invitations to surface."

"And what's the difference? They will have the boat, and us."

"The difference... The difference is we will not start a nuclear war! That simple."

Malenkov started crying, hiding his face in his dirty sleeves.

126

"Should I order to surface?" he sobbed.

Savitskiy was silent.

"Order to surface," confirmed Arkhipov, as he removed the partial keys from the key holes and returned them to Malenkov and Savitskiy.

"Do you think they have soup?"

"Who, Malenkov?"

"The Americans. I'd like some soup. Wouldn't you, Arkhipov?"

Meanwhile in the White House... John Kennedy's red phone rang. Kennedy took a good breath and picked it up. "They did what?" A long pause, while listening to the messenger on the other side. "Thank God, they surfaced." A shadow of genuine relief crossed the President's face.

The world was safe, at least for now.

Thankfully that nightmare where the Soviet submarines launched the missiles and he authorized to strike back, thank God and all the high power of the universe, that nightmare was just a dream. "I say let them go home," answered Kennedy to the question on the other side of the red phone line. "Why not? Point them in the direction of home, make sure they follow the course, but let them get the hell out of there... Oh, and throw them a backpack with Campbell's soup. Chicken noodle, if you have ... What do you mean why. It's a good American soup. That's why. "

-12-

A mechanical fly crawled on the window in Khruschev's office. It looked every bit like a regular fly, but it had a secret. Inside it had a high-resolution camera and a receiver. The live stream was delivered to Argon's research lab, somewhere deep in the Atlantic. From the comfort of his office, Argon observed a meeting between Khruschev and Arkhipov, after the B-59 flotilla returned home. "You do realize that I cannot publicly acknowledge what you have accomplished, Arhipov."

127

"I do, Mr. First Secretary."

"Officially your mission has failed. You disclosed yourself to the enemy."

"I understand."

"But that is officially. Now that it's only the two of us. One hell of a job, son. I don't know how you do what you do, but you saved the world out there."

Argon zoomed in on Arkhipov's pale face. "Who are you? I

don't know you, my pale malnourished human." And he called his assistant to pull all the data on this Russian man, Vasiliy Arkhipov, who allegedly saved the world. "He is not in our database." Puzzled, Riddiff Ron rubbed his chin with a greyish-green tentacle and puffed a few clouds of colored powder in the air. "So he does not oscillate, is that what you are saying?"

"I didn't say that. I only said that, with the Russians, gaps in data happen. They don't keep good records. Unless an oscillation case is hereditary, we may miss a case or two."

"Unbelievable. I'll deal with your 'gaps in data' later. For now, find out everything on this man. And hurry up. He doesn't look too good. I need his blood sample before he drops dead."

"It will only take a minute. If you don't mind, I will take over control of your surveillance drone." With those words, Riddiff Ron directed the mechanical fly at Arkhipov. It buzzed a few times around him, and then landed on his neck, simultaneously piercing the skin like a mosquito. Arkhipov felt the fly on his neck and chased it away.

"Did it work?" asked Argon.

"It sure did. The lab drone is implanted in his skin."

"How long will it take for the results?"

"Almost done, Master Argon. There. I am sending a packet of data on your screen."

"Oh Universe!" exclaimed Argon. "How did we miss him?"

"I cannot believe my eyes!" exclaimed Riddiff Ron. "He is fully oscillating. It can't be! He is not ripe yet. His body is falling apart. I don't understand..."

"I think I may know what has happened here. Oscillation is best triggered by a near-death experience. This soldier has walked on the line of life and death all his adult life. He was in charge of nuclear weapons for years. That is beyond fear for your own life. He feared for the entire human race. That would trigger anyone with the gene."

"So what do we do now, Master Argon? He is falling apart. Shame to lose such a perfect sample."

"Do whatever you want, but fix him. Abduct him if you have to. This case is a priority. We need to study him carefully."

-13-

Year 1998 Vasiliy Arkhipov was an old man. He was sitting next to the window of his tiny one-bedroom apartment, on the fifth floor of the Moscow suburban district, stacked with low-cost concrete housing boxes. Outside his window was an ordinary children's playground: a simple welded swing, a broken sandbox filled with cigarette butts and dog shit. A group of teenagers, dressed in Chinese knock-offs of the Adidas sweat-pant suits and cheap dress shoes with white socks, chain-smoked on the bench next to the sandbox and listened to a tiny radio transistor. It blasted Viktor Tsoi's instantly recognizable voice: moody, gritty, and raw, just like everything around.

A milk truck drove in. A crowd of people who were chaotically waiting around, started fighting over who was going to be in line first. As a veteran and a radiation sickness survivor, Arkhipov was entitled to get his milk ahead of the line, but he rarely did. People would look at him with contempt, which brought up too many memories. Sometimes he felt as if people looked at him with contempt for merely living to his old age.

129

He held himself in contempt for that.

So many doses of radiation, these devastating mysterious nose bleeds, immune deficiencies, bone marrow deterioration, and a weak bladder for crying out loud! His own stench reminded him of the stench on the submarine, where hundreds of marines were cloistered together for weeks, with wet towel rubs passing for showers...

How did he get to live this long?

"Tell me, my friend. How did I get to live this long?" asked Arkhipov of a fly on his window. "You are watching me, aren't you? Every day you are here, my friend. I am many things, but not senile. I know you are watching me." The fly hopped off the window glass, buzzed in the air for a few seconds, and returned to its post. "Well, let me tell you this, my friend," continued Arkhipov. "It's been enough for me. I've lived my share. I want to go now. I am serious. I have no regrets. I want to go before I lose all my dignity. While I am still a man..."

Riddiff Ron watched the old man's face close-up on his screen and could not scrape his eyes away from it. Wispy white quaffs of hair, brown spots all over his skin, clouded blue eyes, and yet, in that fragile shell of a man lived a remarkable mind. The Unkari wondered if he himself would want to continue such a fragile, undignified existence, or rather slip away to the eternity, to become one with star dust and photons and the singing of planetary rings... One with the cosmic background radiation... Radiation... Good radiation... Bad radiation... Riddiff Ron knew that his boss would never approve... But Argon wouldn't be sitting there for hours, keeping company to this fragile human, looking outside his window, listening to him talk about old days, and mostly listening to the silence of what he couldn't talk about.

State secrets. Pain. Lost friends. Lost enemies.

"So if you hear me, my friend," continued Arkhipov, talking to the fly on his window. "If you hear me... Let me go. And when you do, don't miss me, my friend. Sometimes you need to know when to let go."

The Unkari blinked with his double eyelids. "Are you sure? Is that what you want?" He whispered feeling as if he too had lost his mind. The old man had no way of knowing that Riddiff Ron was behind the mechanical fly that watched him from the window pane, day after day.

"I am sure, my friend, I have no regrets," said the old Soviet submariner on the fifth floor of the Moscow suburban apartment.

"Well then, if that's what you really want..."

"That's what I really want..."

"That's the least I can do for you, my friend..."

"That's the least you could do for me, my friend..."

"Alright, then... Sit back and relax ... Close your eyes."

If an Unkari could cry in principle, Riddiff Ron would be sobbing right now.

"I'll just sit back here and relax for a moment. The light hurts my eyes."

The old man, however, was smiling.

"You are a real hero, human Vasiliy Arkhipov. In any galaxy. In any universe."

Riddiff Ron swallowed, choked with an emotion he had never shared with humans before, and started the countdown to deactivate Archipov's life support.

"It comforts me to hear that, my friend," replied Arkhipov, thousands of miles away. "You never held me in contempt."

"How could I? We are both submariners," said the alien, surrounded by a million tons of water. "And you are the better of the two."

131

6
FADE TO BLACK

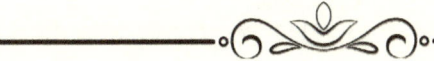

Year 2045.
Bangkok, Thailand

Fah woke from a persistent phone. Her bedroom was dim, as the heavy curtains were tightly sealed. There was no apparent way to tell what time of day or night it was. "Who is this?" inquired nearly comatose Fah.

"Jaden. Girl, what is wrong with you? I've been looking for you for days."

135

"I was busy. Working," said Fah, realizing that she could not fool a three-year-old with that excuse.

"Nice. Real nice. I'm not your enemy, you know."

"I know... So, what's up?"

"I just wanted to know how are you. Maybe take you out for dinner."

"I told you, I'm fine. What time is it?"

"Five".

"Five what?"

"Oh my god. Five in the evening. How long have you been out?" Fah wasn't answering. "Hello?" Jaden persisted.

"I'm thinking, I'm thinking! Wait, what day is it?"

"Unreal, girl! What did you take?"

"Nothing. Just some sleeping pills."

"Okay, I'll be at your apartment in one hour. Get dressed."

"One hour? I won't be ready that soon!"

"You can ditch the ball gown, girl. Just brush your teeth and put some pants on, that's all I ask."

Jaden hung up. Fah sat in bed, her whole body frozen, unable to move. That was when her phone rang for the second time.

"Jaden, I am getting up!"

"Hello. Fah Napasiri?" An unfamiliar English-speaking female voice patched through. That voice uttered only three words, but it promised a sultry mystery and perhaps even an adventure. *All of that with only a few bouncing sounds on the other line,* immediately thought Fah, and decided to actually get off the bed and turn on the lights.

"Fah is listening. Who is speaking?"

As Fah turned on the light, the sight of her face in the mirror made her cringe. In her early 40s, still very beautiful, albeit hungover on prescription medication, Fah's face was furrowed with pillow crinkles. Her chiselled eyes were puffy, and her full lips were chopped from dehydration.

"My name is Veronica Starr," answered the mysterious sultry voice. An army of ants ran up Fah's spine. She thought of Lauren Bacall, an obscure film noir icon from over a century ago. "I am representing an anonymous philanthropist who would like to discuss a business proposition with you."

"What sort of business?"

"Let's just put it this way. My client is a wealthy investor who believes in your talent and would like to invest in your project."

At that point Fah became suspicious.

"Wait, I get it, it's Jaden's idea. Very funny. Ha ha. Tell him he needs to grow up."

"Fah, this is not a joke, and I can prove it. I'll pick you up in one hour at your apartment." And she hung up.

"Right... Bring Elvis with you, would ya?" mumbled Fah into the disconnected phone.

Some time later, Fah was showered, clothed in loose linen pants and a sleeveless shirt, drinking coffee with a cigarette on the balcony of her small apartment. She enjoyed a view of Bangkok from the 58th floor. The pedestrians on the ground wore masks to protect their lungs from toxic smog. Living on the 58th floor Fah enjoyed a privilege of breathing relatively clean air, but a thick smoggy cloud was crawling higher every year. Now they issued a warning for all the tenants living below the 45th floor. At that rate, in a year or two Fah's apartment would be enveloped in smog, which would mean no coffee and newspapers on the balcony. Of course, she could move, if only she could afford it.

For years, Fah had battled for the spotlight in investigative journalism, but had been fired from one news company after another. Neither of the firings were her fault. One time she went after the wrong people, another time she was maligned to her boss by a competitive colleague who wanted her out of the picture.

Her latest job termination was different though. By that time Fah took any job in journalism she could find, and ended up covering the pop culture segment for a web site that made its revenue entirely on click-baiting. Fah's boss did not care if the stories were accurate or even close to the truth, as long as the title was sensational and delivered ROI.

The day she was fired from her last job, two years ago, she had been covering a food festival that claimed to produce the biggest noodle bowl of the century. In order to take the attraction one step further, the organizers claimed that the visitors would be allowed to swim in the noodle bowl once it cooled off enough and everyone had eaten all the noodles they wanted. Fah's boss thought that it would be a great idea for Fah to jump in the bowl of noodles on camera and have all the crowd follow her lead. Fah took the assignment. She hated her job for so long that swimming in noodles on camera seemed to be the least insulting thing to her journalistic credibility.

When time came, Fah stood at the edge of the bowl, spoke her sound bite, and jumped in. The noodle broth was warm, and the noodles swarmed in it like reeds in a stagnant lake, catching Fah's ankles and weighing down her hands. The giant bowl was deep, and she could barely keep her head above the broth.

Then the rest of the crowd started jumping in the bowl.

The broth started shifting in heavy waves, and the noodles dragged her down as more and more bodies landed in the bowl, splashing and tangling the noodles around her body.

Very soon the noodle bowl turned into a death bowl. The organizers rushed to pull the people out, but the more people ended up in the bowl, the worse it got. Finally they figured out that the best thing they could do was to throw in as many floating objects as they could and hope that people could hold on to them. Luckily the outdoor chairs they used for the festival were made of lightweight and durable material that floated enough to sustain a drowning person. Hundreds of chairs were thrown in the bowl, and the drowning noodle swimmers started fighting to retain a chair, creating even more damage.

Fah managed to grab one chair and hold on until the police, fire marshals and ambulance arrived to fetch the noodle lovers.

Seven people drowned that day. The case was immediately picked up by class action lawyers and dubbed "The Death Bowl Massacre." Victims of the Death Bowl Massacre received a compensation that roughly amounted to Fah's annual salary. Fah also received six months' worth of severance at her job.

With modest means to exist, Fah decided to take some time off and pursue something big, something audacious, something that would give her life meaning and restore her career. The only problem was, she had no idea what that project would be. For several months, Fah perused archives and browsed the internet, made copious notes, and added items to her push-pin board. Soon, she ran out of space on the board and started plastering notes and newspaper clippings all over the walls. She'd hoped that one day the big story would simply roll off her tongue.

***

Jaden arrived early. He was a big African-Canadian guy who had come to Thailand five years ago on a vacation and never left. Jaden was a writer without a deadline, one of those who always worked on his book with a subject that was a moving target. Fah met him at a social function and they somehow stuck together. While neither considered the other to be their best friend, in reality, they were the only friends each other had.

Jaden walked into the tiny apartment and glanced at the walls littered with paper, tape, and multi-colored threads of yarn.

"The monster has grown," he sarcastically nudged. "Do you know what is it?"

"Not exactly, not yet. But I am following a lead."

"Oh yeah. I can see. When you run out of wall space your leads will take you to the neighbor's apartment."

"Laugh at me all you want. Speaking of hopeless causes, how is your book coming along?"

"Changing the subject so soon?" Both laughed.

139

"Seriously, Fah, what the hell is this?" Jaden waved at the stuff on the walls.

"This... This, my friend, is a mystery." Jaden looked at the stack of old books on the floor with a sticky note on the wall above the stack: "UFO."

"UFO. I see. Where is the stack about the Big Foot?"

"I know how it sounds, Jaden, but seriously, have you ever read how many eye witness accounts of UFO's have accumulated over the past 500 years?"

"Honey, if all the crazies in the world were institutionalized, Bangkok for once would be far less crowded."

"I know what you mean. At first, I felt the same way. As a

serious investigative journalist... What? Stop laughing, I was a serious journalist once."

"I know, I am sorry, I didn't mean it that way. Ok, try me, maybe I can understand."

"Ok, in short, I decided to focus on a less researched UFO area: Japan during the Tokugawa Shōgunate period." Jaden drew a blank. "That's from 1600 to 1868."

"Okay..." Jaden grabbed a chair anticipating it would be a long one.

"Would you like some coffee? I'll make you some." Fah grabbed a can with ground beans and a vintage copper coffee pot, added water to the grounds and put it on the tiny burner stove. "Let me start from the beginning. During that period, Japan was discovered by the Portuguese missionaries and merchants. Initially the Japanese and the Westerners got along splendidly. The Westerners shared their knowledge and technology, and the Japanese were willing to trade resources but then..."

A forgotten coffee pot boiled over and Fah rushed to salvage the remains of the coffee for Jaden.

"...Then," she continued, pouring Jaden's cup, "the Japanese people isolated themselves. The official narrative is that it was because the Shōgun Tokugawa Ieyasu didn't like the influence of Christianity on Japanese society which was recovering from a bloody civil war."

"It makes sense," said Jaden, sipping his hot black coffee. "Got any sugar?"

"I don't... I drink without; and I always forget to buy it."

"Milk?"

"Coconut milk."

"Will do."

Fah went to the fridge and extracted a pack of coconut milk, set it on the tiny kitchen table. "Jaden, I will show you a few things." Fah picked a few volumes from the stacks on the floor and brought them over to the table. "Look at this drawing." She pointed to a picture of a traditional Japanese drawing depicting what looked like a Westerner coming out of a ship, and a group of Japanese men looking at him. "Do you see?"

"What am I supposed to see here?"

"Look closer." Jaden inspected the painting, taking the book in his hands. He looked closer at the ship, and realized it resembled a classic UFO saucer. Then he looked closer at the Western man, and realized that under the folds of his robes he had octopus-like tentacles. Finally, once Jaden noticed those peculiarities, he realized that the face of the Westerner was far from human.

"Look, Fah, this, I don't know what to say. Westerners looked weird to the Japanese. That's just an artistic interpretation."

"That's what I thought at first, until I dug deeper and found numerous corroborating accounts about a Portuguese scientist named Jose Brito. The pictures of this guy always look the same!" Fah showed a few more pictures from different volumes. They all depicted scenes of this Jose Brito, who was excessively taller than the Japanese characters in the drawings, and who always had tentacles protruding from under his robes.

"Ok, I'll admit, it is peculiar. Fah, can you boil it down for me?"

"The records tell us that this Portuguese scientist Jose Brito came to Japan and befriended Shōgun Tokugawa Ieyasu by promising him to dramatically improve performance of his samurai soldiers, to make them invincible. In return, Brito asked Ieyasu to kick out other Westerners from the country and keep their project a secret."

"How come the secret got out?"

"Recent archaeological digs uncovered Ieaysu's personal diaries where he details his friendship with Jose Brito and the miraculous experiments he performed on his samurai. Apparently, they could predict every move of the enemy and evade it. They could evade bullets and swords alike."

"So what, none of them died in the fight?"

"They all died an honorable death, seppuku."

"They killed themselves. Why?"

"They became sick. And according to the Samurai Code of Honor, a sick samurai is a disgrace to the Shōgun. He must take his own life. Ok, in short, there are records of Jose Brito performing genetic modifications on the young samurai boys in order to give them supernatural abilities in combat. These abilities or alterations led to the samurai's ultimate death."

"Fah, how are you planning to resurrect your journalistic career with a story like this? Honestly, some stories are better left untold, unless you are not afraid of certain labels."

"I'll find ultimate proof."

"Proof of what exactly?"

"Proof that in the 17th century Japan, aliens made genetic experiments on samurai, and that's the real reason for the Japanese isolation period. To perform a controlled experiment. Don't you see?"

"See what?"

"All I need is to find descendants of the Tokugawa's samurai and examine their DNA!"

142

"Oh, as simple as that!" Jaden prepared for a substantial mocking diatribe when the doorbell rang. "Are you waiting for someone?"

"No, let me check though. Maybe it's the landlord."

"You pay your rent, don't you?"

"Oh yeah! For the most part." Jaden rolled his eyes as Fah proceeded to open the door. From the kitchen, Jaden heard a female voice, dark and smoky, like night on the Bangkok back alleys.

"Nice to meet you, Fah. I'm Veronica Starr."

YEAR 1602.
LENAURI

Ennuturat's long dreamless slumber was over. He opened his drowsy eyes and allowed a tantalizing green glow to enter his perception.

"Home! Home at last, but not for too long."

Ennuturat's bedroom was set to a minimalist design, only functional technology was present. Ennuturat did not allow any distractions to side-track him from his mission.

Every night Ennuturat returned home from Earth to Lenauri to immerse in deep hibernation, like all Unkari before him. In the entire history of the Unkari civilization, only several scientific expedition members slept where their road found them, and often it ended up tragically. Every Unkari was viscerally aware of their vulnerability during the sleep cycle. This vulnerability was the result of their evolution, their environment, their life style. This made Unkari dependent on their brothers who were awake and stood guard for the sleeping ones. Always intertwined, they guarded each other's sleep. No matter what quarrels and grudges they held against each other, the Unkari as a whole were forced to be united against the rest of the universe.

Ennuturat finally felt like the blood in his body awoke. It carried chemicals that brought a surge of energy and acuity. Early in the morning, Unkari were always at their most energetic and creative, which was why wasting morning time in bed was unforgivable. It was not illegal or inappropriate, more like imprudent. So many revolutionary ideas and decisions could present themselves in the morning to an awakened Unkari mind! After all, morning hours could bring Ennuturat closer to cracking the oscillation DNA.

143

Ennuturat resolutely shook off the last flakes of sleep that clung to his eyelids like moths, and swiped his tentacles in the air a few times, bringing online a liquid silvery display. Sticking his tentacles into the liquid puddles hanging in the air, he looked up his calendar. What had happened during his sleep? Various messages flashed before his eyes, but he was looking for a specific message. It was the morning message from the Enkri ambassador to all awakened Enkri Unkari about the state of affairs on the planet.

Ambassador Taiber Enkri was on screen.

"Good morning, Enkri, may this waking hour find you in sharp mind. I will make this message brief in order to save you valuable morning hours. In general, no major problems occurred this night and our Katu brothers did a reasonably good job at running the planet. We discovered several valuable mining sites in the Gamma Quadrant of the CG9 galaxy. A remarkable find of a potentially suitable habitat for our species was detected as well. Detailed reports on both issues are attached; feel free to browse through them at your convenience. For specific areas of inquiry, please go to the reference list below. I incorporated a wealth of details that will satisfy your needs."

Ennuturat scrolled down the list of subjects, ranging from agriculture to literature, and found the one that he was interested in: "Project Oscillation. Earth Research Facility."

Once he selected the topic, all sorts of reports popped up, but he looked for a video message from Argon, the lead Katu researcher who looked after the project when Ennuturat slept. "Let's see, Argon, what sort of mess you left for me to sort through."

144

"Good morning, brother Ennuturat. I will be as brief as possible. We have made some strides in isolating one of the human tribes, and prepped the ground for implementing a new set of experiments. We suggest using samurai as research subjects. As we learned from the previous experiments on human subjects, mainly carried out on Lenauri reservations, the chances of activating an oscillation gene are best when the subjects are having a near-death experience. The samurai fit the research design perfectly as a class of humans specifically trained to seek death. Once you see the detailed reports on Japanese culture, you'll see that this sample is ripe for progress."

"There is more. Since this tribe is so isolated from the rest of the humans, I believe you can spend your shift among them. I know how lonely and boring it gets in the lab. Watching fish swim by gets old quickly. So as long as you keep other humans from showing up in Japan, the island is all yours to explore. You will need a proper outfit and some augmented reality field, so you seem more human to them. I left detailed notes on this subject as well. Have a good day,

Ennuturat. Do good work, but remember, don't grow too attached to your pets."

Ennuturat cleared his throat and mumbled aloud: "I'm sure a butcher like you has no attachment problems whatsoever."

Before heading back to Earth, Ennuturat decided to visit human reservations, which Argon had mentioned in the video message. Ennuturat wanted to know how the atrocious Katu brothers treated the kidnapped humans while Enkri were asleep. Ennuturat was a close personal friend of Ambassador Taiber Enkri, and decided to catch up with him before he went to sleep. But the time was limited and he had to hurry because Taiber Enkri had already fought drowsiness and it would be uncaring to force him to stay awake for much longer. Ennuturat sent a message to Taiber requesting a meeting at the reservation.

Year 2045.
Bangkok, Thailand

Fah opened the door to face a Western woman, dressed professionally and flawlessly. Veronica Starr stretched her white elegant hand for a handshake, which was surprisingly firm and yet intimate. An army of ants ran not only up Fah's spine, but all over her body.

145

Meanwhile, Veronica Starr assertively entered the apartment. Seductively smiling from the corners of her eyes, she looked over Fah's walls.

"So that's what it is like..." Veronica Starr uttered. Meanwhile Fah stormed to the kitchen, determined to call Jaden on his machinations.

"Jaden, the joke is over the top!"

"I have no idea what are you talking about!" Jaden protested a bit too emphatically to sound believable.

"Wait a minute, is she some kind of an escort? I appreciate the sentiment, but I am not going out with hookers, however classy."

"Fah... Wait, you think it's me?"

"Jaden, the joke is not funny."

"Fah..."

"Cut the crap, Jaden!"

"Fah..." insisted Jaden, pointing behind her back. Fah turned around and saw Veronica Starr right behind her.

"Fah, you really thought I was an escort? Honey you cannot afford me."

Finally the truth sank in. Fah stared at Veronica Starr, dumbfounded and embarrassed.

"Jaden, I take it, it is not your practical joke..." Jaden negatively shook his head. "Well then... Spare me any further embarrassment, Veronica Starr, and tell me what is it that you want from me."

"Like I mentioned over the phone, I represent a powerful investor who wishes to remain anonymous. This investor would like to sponsor your research."

"What kind of research?"

"The research you have plastered all over your walls."

Year 1602.
Lenauri

Taiber was already expecting him when Ennuturat stepped onto the observation deck of the human reservation. Taiber was seated on a chair with his back to the entrance, observing the busy commotion of humans beneath the glass domes, several floors below on a large screen in front of a panoramic window. He was sipping from a cup of fuming energy drink, and yet his head kept dropping to his chest as he struggled to stay awake.

"Greetings, Ambassador Taiber. What an honor. Thank you for meeting with me at such a late hour."

"Hr.. Hm... Who... I am..." mumbled Taiber, startled by Ennuturat's presence.

"I am sorry, Ambassador, I did not mean to startle you."

"That's alright, Master Ennuturat. I am ready to call it a night, so let's not waste precious time. If I fall asleep in the middle of our meeting, my apologies in advance."

"None required, Ambassador. You are forever honored among Enkri for your life's sacrifice."

"It is not how I imagined it when growing up."

"How so?"

"I was taken from my home very young. My family put so much pressure on me to be the best Enkri Ambassador I could be, and I... *hrrrrrrr.*" The Ambassador passed out, but only for a moment. Mastering an enormous effort, he awoke himself and nearly jumped off the chair trying to straighten up.

"It's alright, Ambassador. Don't worry. We shall have a long conversation one day." Ennuturat sat beside his esteemed friend gently placing a tentacle on his shoulder. Ennuturat felt deep respect mixed with sorrow as he watched Taiber struggling to stay awake. That was the kind of a sacrifice no Enkri would understand. Maybe perhaps only the rival Katu Ambassador, who was the only Unkari except Taiber forced to stay awake off-cycle, against their metabolic nature.

147

"I doubt we will ever have a chance for a longer conversation, beyond what this narrow dawn gives us."

"They are working on breaking the cycle. I believe the research is getting close."

"Don't give me false hope, Ennuturat. I am smarter than that. The research is nowhere ready to be tested on the Unkari subjects."

"One can hope..."

"Hope, my friend, is an empty... *hrrrrrrrr.*"

"Oh Universe..." Ennuturat tried to gently tap at Taiber's shoulder but this time he had sunk deeper into sleep than before. However, Taiber miraculously pulled it off again, straightening up and looking directly in Ennuturat's eyes.

"Let's not waste any more time, shall we? What brought you here, Master Ennuturat?"

"The status of reservations, Ambassador. It is appalling."

"You mean how badly humans are treated?"

"Not that, the proposal of giving them legal rights!"

"Why would you be opposed to that?"

"Ambassador, I understand that here, back home, this is a fad of the day. Enkri think of humans as their pets. But, with all due respect, they are research subjects. We are on a mission to crack the mystery of oscillation, how these pets are connected to the fabric of spacetime, and how can we use this ability to our military and economic advantage. To do that, we need to test the research subjects, study their consciousness in near-death experiences. I hate to say it, but as the head Enkri researcher, I agree with Katu on this one. There is no other way to study these species other than by dissecting them."

148

"Ennuturat, I can't help but think that the humans kept here and on Earth would not recognize each other. They are capable of such plasticity in culture, such an aptitude to create a highly ordered, intellectual society; and, at the same time, to be pure savages, beasts driven with nothing but instincts. And yet they carry a potential to oscillate, savages and intellectuals alike."

"Yes, Ambassador! *They* can, and we *can't!* This truly frightens me! What is so bloody special about these worms that gives them the key to reality?"

"Ennuturat, I hope you are always mindful of the big picture. We don't know if these species could be important to understanding the universe itself. Can you imagine, Ennuturat, one day we may discover where we came from, where everything came from!"

"Taiber, I hope you are not partial on siding with that cult of human worshipers, whatever they call themselves."

"I keep an open mind. And so should you."

"I cannot believe it! You can't be possibly thinking that these species are essential to the foundation of the universe!"

"Well that's up to you to find out, Ennuturat. I only wish.... *hrrrrrrrr.*" And with those words Taiber dropped his drink, spilling it all over the floor. His body became soft and filled out the form of a chair, while his breathing became deep and slow. Ennuturat scanned Taiber's life monitor and realized that he would not be wake again until his hibernation cycle was over. Frustrated with this development, Ennuturat called Taiber's assistant who was tasked with delivering the Ambassador to his chambers. If this obsession with humans among Enkri continued, he thought, his project might be shut down 'for ethical reasons', or stricter regulations on the experiments might be imposed. Who knows, they might even shut down Lenauri reservations. What then? Give humans citizenship? Ship them back to Earth?

Ennuturat headed to the exit when an enormous explosion shook the observation desk.

BOOOOOMMMMMM!

Ennuturat fell to the ground, but managed to roll over to look outside the panoramic window. The force field that shielded the observation deck was intact, but the deck swayed from the explosion. Struggling to stay steady on a rocking floor, Ennuturat crawled closer to the observation window. Several stories below, Ennuturat saw hundreds of glass domes that housed various reservations of humans in climate-controlled barracks. One of the domes had exploded and was spewing fire and a copious pall of smoke.

149

A young security officer crawled to check if Ennuturat was ok. "Master, are you alright?"

"I am alright, officer. What happened there?"

"I am not sure, I just stepped in to take my shift. Katu shift was relieved just moments ago."

"Escort me down there, I want to know what happened".

"We cannot be sure it is safe. The ruptured dome leaked human atmosphere into ours, the temperature and pressure difference may be unsafe, let alone all the oxygen in the area."

"I need a suit then. Hurry up, officer. Take me to the chamber where we can suit up."

***

Suited up, Ennuturat and the security officer were headed to the explosion site. From the top floor of the deck the domes seemed tiny, but on the ground floor it became evident that each dome was the size of several city blocks, buzzing and hopping with humans, breathing their human air, naked and completely unbothered by it. Some of them clung to the glass walls watching the alien masters hurry to the place of the explosion. They threw rocks at the glass walls, smothered their faces to the cold glass surfaces making crazy faces and, in general, behaved like animals.

"Master, if you don't mind me asking, I heard, on Earth they don't behave this way. Is that true?"

"They don't, officer. There they have many different cultures, but most of them are more civilized than this."

"Fascinating. Don't you think that it is a shame to keep them like this?"

"Officer, if I were you I'd be concerned with where to get a ride. Walking to the dome will take too long."

"Got it, sir. Let me check on the nearest security vehicle."

150

While the officer was messaging for a ride, Ennuturat paused at one of the dome's walls and looked inside. That was the female reservation dome. Human males and females were kept separately in order to control breeding. Except for the mating times, males and females did not interact. Over the generations living separately, men and women had developed mutual disinterest in each other. They were like completely different species that hardly saw benefit in each other.

Meanwhile the patrol glider arrived, and Ennuturat hopped in. As they approached the explosion site, Ennuturat observed the reservation from the air: hundreds of domes arranged in tidy Fibonacci spirals, connected with sky bridges. The geometric perfection of the reservation was mesmerizing. Also it was mesmerizing because of the sheer scope of the reservation. It had grown literally overnight, whilst Ennuturat had been sleeping. Argon Katu was not wasting time here.

The glider descended a safe distance away from the plumes of dark smoke. A crew of first responders were measuring the air composition to assess the damage to the methane-rich Unkari atmosphere. They shook their heads, indicating that the problem was serious.

"Evacuation of all non-essential personnel!" Ennuturat heard one of the first responders' voice patching through the com link. Ennuturat opened his channel to 'public'.

"I need to talk to someone who knows what happened. Ennuturat Enkri here, the head researcher for the Oscillation Project."

"Greetings, Master Ennuturat!" a voice came through. "Commander Farnau Tan. This area is dangerous. There is a 38% chance of a secondary explosion. However, if you meet me in Dome 745 in 40 minutes, I'll be glad to fill you in."

"Thank you, Commander Farnau Tan. Your assistance is much appreciated."

Ennuturat requested the glider to take him to Dome 745, which was a safe distance from the explosion site. As the glider flew up in the air again, Ennuturat observed the first response crew roll out the containment field around the explosion area. A wide area around the dome was enveloped in amber resin that immediately hardened and forever trapped all the surviving humans, if there were any. Under the resin shield, the mass grave of the research subjects together with their homes and the dome itself was excavated and recycled by the robots that spewed out cubes of raw materials, recycled from the debris.

151

Arriving at Dome 745, Ennuturat walked to the command post attached to it. A new shift of Enkri guards had just arrived, relieving drowsy Katu officers from duty. A crew shuttle was there to take Katu to their homes and to make sure they did not collapse into sleep on their way. Dragging their alien feet, the Katu officers stepped into the shuttle, lumbered in their seats, pulled the safety bar in front of them, and placed breathing masks over their faces. With an obvious look of relief, they closed their eyes and submerged into their sleep, as if they could not wait one second longer.

Ennuturat identified himself to the incoming officers, and they allowed him to enter the premises of the dome. The door to the main dome opened and Ennuturat found himself in a snaking tunnel with transparent walls. There he could observe the humans without exposing himself to their hostility or their environment. He walked through the tunnel that separated him from the human habitat, like in an aquarium. Humans swam in their oxygenated air like stupid fish, ignorant of the world outside their fish bowl. Born and raised in isolation from their mother civilization, these humans were like tumbleweed in the desert, blown here and there by the cosmic winds: no roots, no understanding; and yet, somehow, full of hidden complexity, as if password-protected, hack-proof, outside of the Unkari's reach.

"What are you, beasts or gods?" mumbled Ennuturat, observing two women with long matted hair, naked, engaged in a fist fight, as if to death. A group of women of all ages and shapes gathered around the fighters, heckling and rooting for their side. The tension was palpable, and although Ennuturat was completely safe, he instinctively took a step back, feeling the cold glass wall pressing upon his back.

Kaboom!

A loud sound occurred right behind Ennuturat's back. Quickly turning around, he saw a giant fierce-looking woman standing behind the glass wall, right in front of him, looking into Ennuturat's eyes without fear. She was holding a bunch of rocks in her fists.

Kaboom!

The woman threw another rock at the glass wall, with a look on her face: "Come get me, you bastard!"

Ennuturat sprayed a few puffs of color in the air and immediately felt embarrassed for such a public display of emotion, even though he knew humans could not read the color language. But it was a sign of weakness, a momentary irrational fear, and Ennuturat had thus exposed himself to one of his laboratory animals. Silently chastising himself, Ennuturat walked away from the fight scene, deeper into the dome.

Moments later, Commander Farnau Tan reached out to him over the com link and instructed him to meet in the Unkari Circle. The Circle was the area where the Unkari workers of that dome took breaks and collected their thoughts, trying to clear their minds from the scenes of human violence and cruelty. The circle contained a garden with a methane lake in the middle and artificial methane fog floating above, reflecting the light a certain way and creating a bizarre light show. It was a spectacular and calming place, and Ennuturat was happy to spend some time here before he had to return to Earth.

"Greetings, Master," announced Farnau Tan as he walked into the Circle. "It is an honor to meet with you in person. What brought you here?"

"May the universe open to you, Commander. Soon I am departing for Earth to continue the research. However, I found the note about this facility from my Katu counterpart. I was going to read the reports later, but since I am here in person, I wanted to see for myself what he was implementing in my absence."

"I see, Master. I arrived to my shift early as per demand of my Katu counterpart, because he wanted to make sure I understood the scope of the reservation project before he departs. And I must admit, I'm glad I did. There are some remarkable experiments taking place here. I'd like to show you."

153

With these words, Farnau Tan swirled his tentacles in the air a few times, bringing to life a large screen. There he selected a recording of the laboratory experiments. The video demonstrated a laboratory facility with stasis pods. A scientist in a protection suit appeared before the camera and began explaining.

"Stage 3 of the experiment Oscillation Network. Since we are failing at isolating the oscillation gene and making it work outside of human consciousness, we decided to take a bold step and link humans into a multi-conscious network. This was achieved by surgically stitching several pairs of new-born twins into a network of eight subjects. These eight subjects grew together to adulthood, and were fostered to develop telekinetic abilities. For that we used a combination of meditation (or prayer, as some call it), mind-altering chemical stimulation, electric shock and sleep deprivation. All of that was at the previous stages. Now, the subjects are considered to be ready to oscillate in a special field that we created. This field is designed to propagate oscillation between the subjects on a quantum level. We previously were close to achieving individual oscillation cases for small projects like flipping a coin. Now, the eight modified subjects are tasked to change composition of one glass of liquid. To add some artistic touch to this project, we decided to take inspiration from one of the human miracle myths, about turning water into wine. The historic context of this myth, we believe, is from the time when one of the humans went unchecked and developed a functional oscillation capacity. We overlooked the case for long enough that it developed a major following and it was difficult to keep the story under wraps. We just gave up on trying to contain it. Anyway, I digress..."

With those words, the scientist approached one of the stasis chambers and the camera zoomed to reveal what was in it. There, Ennuturat saw a monster with eight heads, eight bodies, eight legs, only two arms; all tangled in wires and hooked to a bunch of huge machines that monotonously hummed. The human 'octopus' was seated at the table, with a cup in front of it.

"These eight subjects will be tasked to turn the water in their cup into wine. From a quantum perspective, the idea is very simple. At the level of quantum superposition, the cup contains every element that could mathematically exist based on the amount of atoms in it. This probability is not without limitations. For example, they cannot create a black hole from the amount of matter in the cup. Well, I suppose they could, but the black hole created from the squeezed together atoms of a glass of water would be too small to even be detectable. It would immediately evaporate. That is why turning water into wine is highly plausible. Both liquids have similar density. All the research subjects must do is access the water through their consciousness on the quantum level and reassemble the molecules of water into the molecules of wine. Enough talking now, let's get to the fun part: human trials!"

The scientist looked way more excited than was appropriate for anyone conducting an experiment on a sentient creature. Granted, the tests were important, and even Ennuturat was anxious to see how the experiment turned out, but universe knows, he at least paid mental respects to the lives sacrificed in the name of science.

"Who is this Doctor Death?" inquired Ennuturat.

"Oh, that is Goran Katu. He was recruited by Argon for this shift. Goran was impounded by the Council for numerous ethical violations. Argon pulled some strings and he was allowed to practice again, under Argon's supervision."

"This Goran is in good company. I don't always agree with the liberal tendencies in the Enkri philosophy, but Argon reinforces my allegiance to the Enkri. Our two tribes are just too different."

"I wholeheartedly understand you, Master. But keep watching, it's going to be interesting."

Meanwhile Goran continued his preparations.

"The final piece of the puzzle here is creating enough urgency in the subject so that he releases an explosive chemical cocktail in his brain, in order for oscillation to occur. This, as we found out, could be achieved through torture and near-death experiences. I'll skip the details of how we arrived at this conclusion, but torture proves to be less effective. Apparently, consistent infliction of pain numbs the subject and the proper chemicals are not released into the brain. What needs to happen is the realistic death threat, an experience of losing life. Something happens to the subject in those moments before he dies, and this metamorphosis is so powerful that it allows these creatures to hack the fabric of the universe. As a result, quantum probabilities that are not naturally occurring in our daily life become possible. The easiest way to inflict a near-death experience in a human is to deprive him of oxygen! It is cheap and effective."

155

Goran opened a communication channel to the stasis chamber. "Hello, research subject. How are you today?"

The eight heads produced a variety of angry grimaces.

"Good to see you in strong spirit. Trust me, today you will need it. Today we are going to work on a very important experiment. You will need 100% of your concentration and collaboration. Your life depends on that."

With those words, Goran punched a few keys on the controls of the stasis chamber and the sound of venting air pierced the lab.

The eight-headed monster jumped off the chair and started exploring the walls of the stasis, looking for the hole that leaked the air.

"Sit. Down," commanded Goran in a voice of steel. "Concentrate. If you waste time, you'll die of suffocation."

The octopod reluctantly sat on the chair. One of the heads yelled: "Alright, you ugly freak. What do you want us to do this time?"

"Ugly freak. How ironic. However, let's get to business. You see a cup of water before you. Your task is simple. You need to rearrange the elements in that water so that it turns into wine. Concentrate, my friends. If you succeed, you'll live."

The human monster panicked. All the heads started talking, trying to convince each other to concentrate and ultimately bringing the experiment to chaos. Finally, they started experiencing lightness of the air.

156

"Quiet! Brothers! Quiet!" yelled one of the heads. "Let's pray. Let's pray how we never prayed in our life. Remember what the scripture says, with the faith of the mustard seed we can do miracles. And a miracle is what we need right now."

The heads nodded. The two hands on both sides of the stitched-together body were raised in the air. One of them started singing, leading the rest in the saddest, most doomed harmony.

The sound of the human voices filled the lab.

The eight-headed monster entered a state of trans, so transfixed by the prayer that it didn't stop singing when the oxygen started dangerously depleting. It only made shallower and shallower breaths, and eventually stopped making any sound at all, only silently moving blue lips, eyes big and desperate. The oxygen continued escaping through the vent in the chamber, and the monster finally fell to the ground, with the last words on their mouths: "Amen".

Goran shifted the view of the camera from the lifeless body on the floor to himself.

"The subject is dead," he pronounced matter-of-factly. "Some of you may say, what a tragedy. The creature is dead. Did you know, that I could bring oxygen back? I could have saved its life? But I didn't. You'll think, Goran, what a monster you are. What you don't understand is that oscillation at that level is like a dose of lethal radiation. There is no way this subject could have survived. And his death would be a lot more painful. So you might argue that I did it a favor. But hey, let's check how the experiment went."

Goran punched a few keys on the console, and the cup was picked up by a robotic limb and delivered to the orifice in the stasis chamber. There, the scan performed a simple spectral analysis.

"Unbelievable! It is alcohol! Red alcohol! If I was more ignorant, I'd say I just saw a miracle!"

***

"What an arrogant, sadistic monster..." groaned Ennuturat, feeling nauseous.

"I understand your feeling, Master Ennuturat. We launched a complaint with the office of the Katu Ambassador to remove Goran from the next shift. But I must admit it will not be easy because, as you could see, water to wine, miracles, and all that. Goran's methods proved to be effective."

"Yeah... I understand..." Ennuturat almost forgot why he had come to the reservation in the first place. "By the way, what happened with the dome? Do you know the reason for that explosion?"

"Master, although it is classified, I think I can tell you. You need to be aware of it."

"Don't worry, I'll handle the classified information with care."

"Remember what Goran said on the video about the black holes?"

"Yeah..."

"Well the research subjects in the exploded dome managed to create a miniature black hole. And then another one, from anti-matter. And collided them."

Year 2045.
Bangkok, Thailand.

Fah's small room was littered with clothes and shoes, as she painfully considered what to take with her. Choice between books and shoes did not seem like a choice at all. Her doorbell rang. Fah opened the door and saw Veronica Starr, well dressed and smelling fantastic, as if smog and humidity did not apply to her.

"Are you ready, Fah?"

"Almost there!" Embarrassed for all the mess, Fah shut the door to the bedroom.

"I see. At this rate, we won't leave by midnight, darlin'."

"I can't pack on such a short notice."

"You had three days!"

"I guess I needed four."

158

"Come on, Fah. What is your problem?"

"I don't know what the weather will be like, what kind of shoes should I take, and what do they even wear these days in Japan? Do I need formal wear?"

"Stop right there." Fah stopped. Veronica Starr extracted an e-cigarette from her tiny purse. "Do you mind?"

"Go ahead." Veronica activated the cigarette and took a good puff.

"You don't need any clothes. Just take whatever research you need, the rest you will buy there."

"I can't afford to replace my entire wardrobe!"

"Now that you work for my client, you can." Veronica Starr dipped her slender fingers in her purse for the second time and extracted a credit card. She dialed a few digits on the card and Fah heard a characteristic 'ping' for the completed transaction. "Go ahead, check your account." Fah went to the kitchen. Among the clutter she found her purse and extracted her credit card. Swiping on its display, she saw her balance, which was several digits bigger than it had ever been.

"Good lord! I hope I won't have to kill anyone for this amount of money."

"Don't be silly, Fah. You better start getting used to being paid, you deserve it."

"Ok, I guess this makes my packing easier." With those words, she picked her laptop and a few hand-held devices, tossed them in her purse, and grabbed a jacket from a hook nailed to the wall of the living room. "I'm ready."

"Wonderful. Our jet is waiting in a private airport. Don't forget your passport, we are headed to Japan right away".

Right when the two were ready to exit the apartment, the door flew open. In the doorway was Jaden, wearing an old black stocking cap, a scarf, a pair of hiking pants and a worn pleated jacket, with a messenger bag over his shoulder, stuffed to the brim with writer's junk.

"You were not about to have an adventure of a lifetime without me, were you, girl?"

159

Year 1603.
Edo, Japan

A group of Japanese merchants were having tea in the house of Daimyo Tatami. His house was overlooking the Bay, situated on the hill of Edo, the key trade and government center of the newly established Tokugawa Shōgunate.

The merchants were sitting on the floor around a tea table, enjoying the tea and the company of Tatami's gorgeous servant girls. As much as they enjoyed the social event, the mood in the room was sombre. With Tokugawa Ieyasu coming to power, their affiliation with the rival Daimyo Toyotomi served them no good. All businesses under Ieyasu were redistributed, causing those on the wrong side of this alliance to slip in the oblivion of Japanese business society.

"Turbulent times we live in, Daimyo Tatami," said Daisuke, the eldest businessman of the group. "I've lived through many wars and insurgences, but this one is different. For the first time in my life, I am worried."

Daimyo Tatami nodded and sipped from his cup.

Tatami was a powerful businessman in the region. Through his allegiance with the Toyotomi clan, Tatami secured valuable licenses for importing goods from China. Even when the Chinese emperor officially banned trade with Japan, accusing Japanese government in enabling piracy, Tatami managed to retain his business by conspiring with the Portuguese captains who served as the intermediaries. Now Tokugawa Ieyasu concentrated all Nanban (Western) contacts around himself and his allies, leaving Tatami in a business dry spell.

"My Nanban contacts refuse to do business with me now. Ieyasu threatens to expel every merchant who does not go through his administration for trade licenses," complained Tatami.

Overrun by the sense of doom, the group quietly sipped their tea.

Meanwhile, a foreign ship came ashore in Edo bay. That ship was much different from any other Western ships that had ever come to shore. It was spherical and illuminated by a green glow. It also was not made of wood, unlike every other vessel ever seen in Japan.

It was made of solid iron.

"How can this vessel float? Surely iron is heavier than water..." pondered a casual observer in the port, watching the weird vessel gracefully manoeuvring and docking.

"These Nanban merchants have great wisdom!" suggested one of them.

"They are not greater than us!" retorted another. "They just have different wisdom."

"You are right! Add to that, they can't read or write our way. They can't be so intelligent and not understand such simple things as writing from head to toe."

Meanwhile the vessel came to a full stop. Ennuturat, dressed in a climate-controlled suit and camouflaged in a holographic image of a Western merchant, stopped the engines and proceeded to exit the vessel.

Back at Tatami's house, Daisuke absent-mindedly looked over at the port. He had to double-take the scene of a strange new vessel and a Westerner coming out of it. Locals at the port surrounded the newcomer, greeting him with gestures. Apparently, the Westerner did something amusing and the crowd started clapping and cheering.

"Tatami, look, we have another Nanban over here. He's clearly new!"

Tatami waved off Daisuke's enthusiasm.

"So what? He will be working with Ieyasu and his minions in no time."

"True. But he will have to be introduced to him!"

"What do you have in mind, Daisuke?"

"We need to get to him first! Come on, let's get to the port immediately!"

Year 2045.
Tokyo, Japan. Daichi's Basement

Daichi awoke. The room was dark and smelled like food leftovers and dirty laundry. Before fully opening his eyes, Daichi reached out to his cell phone and checked his notifications. Most of them were spam or ads, but those 'incoming' numbers always promised a hope of something meaningful, although only until he opened the app and saw that all of those notifications were garbage.

Garbage.

Funny word. People thought of Daichi as garbage, and he

had turned himself into a living manifestation of that thought. They called him hikikomori, the recluse, the loser, the outcast, the broken one.

In fact, being garbage was the only thing Daichi knew how to do well. Over the past three years, Daichi had perfected the art of being garbage and taken it to the grandmaster level. He did not shower, did not shave, did not go outside his room, did not change his clothes, did not take out the trash. *Ever.* And he was exceptionally good at doing those things. It took a strategic mind to be able to live in his parents' basement without ever stepping outside, and not being a burden on the family.

Perhaps Daichi was garbage, but he was not a leach. He worked for his food playing games and earning bitcoin income. From that money, he paid his portion of the rent and ordered his food online. He also purchased his own electronics, but he did it extremely frugally, repairing everything whenever it was possible. That was the deal he had made with his family: as long as he could support his existence, they agreed not to evict him from the basement.

Daichi had last seen his mother in person over two years ago. She brought his food and mail to the door of the basement whenever it was delivered and left it on the door mat. Two years ago was the last time she had tried to establish contact.

The last time Daichi had seen his dad was even longer ago than that. Daichi wished to erase that day from his memory forever, because it had turned him into what he was now, the shame of the family, the disgrace, something that was never spoken out loud, the hikikomori.

***

Daichi was in his senior year when his dad decided that he needed to change schools. In order to stand a good chance of entering an engineering college, Daichi needed to spend more time studying, and his parents felt that Daichi was wasting too much time playing video games and fooling around. Over and over, they had passive-aggressive fights about Daichi's attitude, how he needed to pull himself together if he wanted to become anything but garbage.

One evening, dad returned home and announced that he had important news.

At the dinner table, mom served miso soup, rice and fried eggs.

"Fried eggs?" Dad raised his eyebrow at the sight of eggs and rice - not a traditional combination. Mom lowered her gaze and spooned some soup.

"Hajime, I just had no time for anything better. I'm exhausted. Just eat your meal." Dad said nothing, just swirled his spoon in thin miso soup. Finding nothing of outstanding substance there, he put a spoon-full of broth in his mouth. It wasn't bad, he decided, and continued eating, alternating the soup with fluffy rice. Mom broke the silence, hoping to bring some energy into the dinner-time atmosphere. "What was the news you were anxious to tell us, Hajime?"

"Ah, the news! Great news! My loan was approved!"

"What loan! Another loan? Hajime, you cannot be serious..."

"What sort of a loan? Well, that is the best part about my news. The loan is to put Daichi through cram school."

"A cram school?" Daichi gasped for air. "You want me to leave the house? You want me to sleep on the floor in a room with fifty other kids?"

163

"Relax, Daichi. It is a very good school. It cost me a lot of money, but there is nothing I want more than seeing you succeed. You are my only son, so don't think about money. Think about the school. That's all that matters."

Cram school. Those two words could not have possibly instilled more horror in Daichi's poor mind. Cram school meant that you were never alone. It meant having three hours of sleep every night, if you were lucky. But most of all, it meant fierce competition. In cram schools teenagers turned into monsters, calculating, memorizing machines, devoid of anything human. Daichi was not a stranger to bullying and mockery in his old school, but there at least he could hide amongst the crowd, avoiding his tormentors. In the boarding cram school you were on lock-down 24/7, with the same people around you, and if those kids were anything like the kids in his school, Daichi was cooked.

"Dad, please, can we talk about it?"

"There is nothing to talk about, son. You will do great. I'll buy you new clothes, cool stuff, whatever you want. We can go shopping tomorrow."

"Dad, I don't need new stuff. I just don't think I can go through this..." Dad's face turned red like a burner stone. He stood up, smashed his fist at the table top. The soup swooshed out and started seeping through the wooden boards of the table, to the floor.

"Daichi, this conversation is over. You don't want the clothes? Fine. But on Sunday I'm taking you to the school. You better be packed by then."

With those words, dad left the table without finishing his meal. On the way out he grabbed a beer from the fridge and sat in the chair of the living room, flipping through the channels. Mom came over to Daichi and placed her hand on his shoulder.

"You know he wants the best for you, son. He is trying so hard."

"I know, mom, but, wait, are you on his side too?"

"Well, give it a try. You always have this house if you want to come back."

"I know, but I will be a disgrace to everyone if I go there and quit. It's not like I have a choice of coming back, and everything goes back to normal."

Mom knew she should have said something, she should have lied, but she couldn't. She wasn't a strong woman, and it took a strong person to be a good liar. She went back to her chair at the table and started crying.

***

Flash forward five months. Daichi was at the cram school, and he was not doing well. He kept falling behind on all his classes, and the gap between the succeeding students and himself grew so wide, that it started swallowing him, bit by bit. Every evening the cohort took retention tests. The tests started after a long day of cramming, around 7 pm, and the kids could not go to sleep until they answered enough questions correctly.

It was customary for Daichi to go to bed past 5 am. However, the whole preceding week he got only one hour of sleep, only because the teachers took mercy on him and dismissed him without passing.

It was the end of term, and his parents were going to pick him up for a week. It was likely that based on his performance, Daichi would have been expelled.

When dad finds out that he wasted a whole semester worth of non-refundable tuition money, he'll go crazy, thought Daichi while taking a restroom break during the class. There, sitting on the toilet, he couldn't bring himself to go back to class. The hot wet tears heavily and silently fell on his knees. He took out his cell phone and ear buds, plugged them into his ears, and surrounded himself with a wall of sound. Daichi was in a trance, floating weightless in the universe, being everywhere at the same time, and feeling emotions so strong that his whole body quivered. But the anxiety still didn't go away. He reached down in his pants and gratified himself, quietly, matter-of-factly, while tears kept rolling down. For a split second, the whole universe took a big step back, leaving Daichi alone, but the minute the pleasure quivers subsided, he crashed hard to the concrete reality, back to the restroom, where he was sitting on the toilet, and his legs were about to go numb.

165

Daichi wiped his hands into a sheet of toilet paper, cranked his music a bit louder, and reached down into his pants again. This time it took only a little longer to finish, but the second he was done, Daichi knew that he was back to the ugly restroom, and it was only a matter of time until the instructor came looking for him.

Something had to be done, he thought. He wasn't sure what, but he was sure as hell he was not going back to the classroom. As he looked down at his feet, he noticed long colorful shoe laces in his sneakers. He looked around and up. Above his head he saw a water pipe running across the ceiling. It looked sturdy enough to handle Daichi's weight.

Once Daichi had a plan, the tears burst out of him even stronger, bringing even sharper feeling of hopelessness, also mixed with some relief. That was it, that was the way out for him, there and then. There was nothing to look forward to in life, and everything to be afraid of.

***

Moments later, the instructor walked into the restroom looking for Daichi who had been absent from class for almost an hour. He knew he should have checked on him earlier. Daichi was a typical profile for a runaway kid, especially before the end of the term. Not once the faculty had had to catch kids like Daichi who snuck out of the toilet window and crawled down the fire escape ladder. Instead of finding an open window in the restroom, however, the instructor immediately saw a rope hanging from the water pipe on the ceiling.

He smash-opened the door to the stall.

There, he found Daichi, standing on the toilet with his pants down, trying to reach the end of the rope with a loop. "I couldn't reach it..." cried Daichi... "It was too short..."

***

The cram school immediately expelled Daichi on the grounds of his academic performance, privately telling his parents that they should look into his emotional health. The incident left Daichi's mom so shaken that it gave her an emotional permission to divorce her abusive husband. Without having any idea what to do with Daichi further, she decided just to give him some space. And time. And so Daichi receded to the basement, and never came out for the next three years.

***

Daichi was surfing through the dozens of garbage notifications in various chat rooms and social media web sites. Not a whole lot of likes on his selfies, as they were of awful quality and always looked the same. He almost overlooked one of those messages, because the profile picture featured a cute girl with dark-rimmed eyes, pink hair, and beautiful cleavage. *Sex bot,* he thought immediately. Not that he was against sex bots, but there were just too many, and most cost money to engage.

Daichi didn't want to pay for sex. He probably would have, if he could afford it, but the way his life went, he couldn't splurge on anything that was not a necessity. Online sex had started losing its appeal a long time ago and only added to Daichi's perpetual self-loathing.

"Are you in a juvie?" read the message from the pink-haired girl. That was not a typical sex bot pick-up line, and he took a chance.

"No. Why would you think that?"

The girl immediately started typing.

"You look like shit."

Daichi wasn't offended. He really looked like shit. His wispy teenage beard and moustache looked hideous, and his hair was so greasy it almost formed dreadlocks.

"Well not everyone is a looker like yourself. What were you doing on my page?"

"We play in the same game. I'm Dragon67. You beat me in the Rigonara tournament. The app here suggested that I could have known you. So I looked. I don't know you, just played a game... I'm Nyoko."

"I remember you. You played good. I just had a lot more time to practice."

167

"I have all the time in the world to practice. I'm just not as good as you are." *Damn.* A real person on the other end. It was unusual, exciting, and scary. His whole life was built around avoiding anxiety, and this connection threatened to unravel something he might not be able to control. Daichi immediately decided not to get involved much further. "I guess you are not as good after all, Nyoko. Maybe you should go back to practice," typed Daichi, changing his status to 'off-line'.

Year 2045.
Tokyo, Japan

Old city in Tsukiji district. Fish market. Busy streets. A fest of life and death. Colorful fish is being slaughtered, gutted out, hosed down, flayed, fried, or worse, eaten half-live. Gleeful passersby line up at the food trucks for the taste of a delicious flesh of their choice.

Fah wore her new expensive poncho, a blend of merino wool and silk. The threads of silk in the poncho were reflecting light so softly, as if they were alive.

Veronica Starr and Fah walked into an old sake house. Ambient Japanese music was stirring her imagination: pictures of the old days flashed in the corner of Fah's mind, like dreams or memories she had never had. She sat at the table facing the entrance door.

The waiter brought a jug of hot sake - top shelf, with an eye-catching seal on the side - a trademark of an ancient sake brewery.

Fah poured a cup and took a sip. Hot liquid streamed down her throat, going straight to her head. Her hands felt heavy and her head felt light. Looking at the entrance, Fah visualized glorious samurai soldiers walking through the door. She saw their hand-crafted outfits in striking detail: textures, thousands of tiny seams, leather and metal plates, woven together - a lace of impenetrable armor. Wild, imaginative colors, audacious designs... and their faces. Those faces communicated resolve, fearless demeanor. They were glorious and honorable. Fah saw them as if they were flowing through a calm Zen river; that river guided them, controlled them, owned them. That river was Mushin, a mental state of remarkable sensory acuity that took over samurai mind and body, in time of war and in time of peace.

"You see it, don't you?" Veronica's voice broke through to Fah's mind, like through a sound-proof wall. "The ghosts of the past. Nakamura believes they walk these streets till this day."

"Who is Nakamura?" asked Fah, and someone gently

placed a hand on her shoulder.

"Michio Nakamura," said the voice. "You are working for me now."

***

When Nakamura turned 18, his father took him to his laboratory. They walked through several levels of security in a corporate building in the heart of Tokyo. Renowned in the world for his cancer research, Haruto Nakamura made one breakthrough after another, and nobody knew where his insight was coming from. In beating the cancer cell, he was a few steps ahead of everyone.

"This is where I work, son. Since you want to follow in my footsteps in medical research, I think it's time to share some secrets with you."

Nakamura's office was all white, meticulously clean and minimalistic, with the exception of one tiny blooming cactus on his desk, in a white porcelain pot. Young Michio looked around, trying to identify anything of interest, but it wasn't very easy.

"So... Is this where you do you research? In this office?" Michio wasn't impressed and could not figure out what in that office needed protection.

"Yes, son. This is where I do the most important research. I need to keep this place under tight security, because I can't allow industry spies to capture my secrets."

"There's not much here, dad..."

"And I certainly want everyone to think this way."

With those words, Haruto Nakamura grabbed a remote and pointed at the AC unit under the ceiling. The AC came to life, and with the humming sound of blowing air the white wall of the office began to slide aside, revealing a spacious modern laboratory behind a glass partition.

"Son, I need to tell you a fascinating story about a patient that I treated many years ago, Ichiro Akyama."

Nakamura passed a white lab coat to his son and directed him to pass through the sterile chamber, where both were radiated in harsh blue light.

The lab was filled to the brim with high tech equipment and various vials containing all sorts of test samples. In the very center of the lab sat a glass sarcophagus. Michio walked straight to it and saw a body of a man, in his 40s or 50s.

"Son, this is Ichiro Akiyama. Well, what is left of him. Ichiro was a commercial pilot back in the day. I treated him for a rare form of brain cancer. The cancer was terminal, and there was nothing I could do. Ichiro decided to take one last cruise to Paris before retiring and settling his affairs in order. But when he returned from that flight, he was in remission. I could not get a word from him about what had happened. Since treatment of that particular cancer was nonexistent, only a miracle could have stopped Ichiro's tumor from spreading throughout his brain. And he acted all weird about it too. He would not tell me what had happened, but he would not deny that something did happen to him. He kept saying that it was not safe for him to talk."

"So... How did you end up with his body, dad?"

"He willed it to me, for medical research. And I also received a letter from him."

"So he died? I thought he was cured."

170

"Well, he was in remission for two years. He stopped seeing me after that time. But sometime after two years, the cancer returned in a more aggressive form, and took his life within weeks. I did not see it coming. It was as if the treatment he received expired, and cancer immediately moved back in."

"What was in the letter, dad?" Nakamura reached into the pocket of his lab coat and extracted an envelope.

"Now this letter is yours, son. Treat it with extreme caution. Akiyama made sure that nobody knew about its existence." Finally Michio felt excited at the promise of a mystery.

"What is in it, dad? I can't wait to read it, but maybe just tell me in a few words."

"Ah, son, always so impatient!" smiled Nakamura and

grabbed his tall kid in a warm hug.

***

Fah was listening to Michio Nakamura's story having not a slightest clue why a pharmaceutical giant was interested in her little research.

"See, Fah, in 1986 Ichiro Akyama encountered something unusual on his last flight from Paris to Tokyo, when they flew over Alaska. Some unidentified objects took over the flight controls and blasted the airplane with some kind of a radiation. When the flight was forced to land in Anchorage, some cogs from the U.S. secret service took Akyama into an interrogation room and scared him to death; and death scared Akyama a lot because of his terminal cancer diagnosis. But when he got home, it turned out that his cancer was gone, and the secret service knew both about the cancer and about the upcoming remission."

Sake was corrupting Fah's thinking. She thought she had lost the ability to follow the logic of this conversation.

"I am sorry, what are you talking about? Secret government experiments?"

"More like the government's cover-up. Here's my wild theory, substantiated with years of research, both mine and my father's. The governments, and by that I mean the leading world powers, have known about the alien presence on Earth for... I don't know, for generations."

171

"Aliens?"

"Oh don't tell me that you were not thinking about it!"

"I was, but I never spoke about it with anyone in practical terms."

"Well this is going to get as practical as possible. The governments are both scared of the world's panic and reluctant to open their cards because they reap the benefits of the alien presence."

"Don't try to tell me that all the governments of the world are in collusion with *aliens!* That is nonsense!"

"Oh no, the problem is much more delicate. See, let's say

the governments were to go public, what would happen?"

"The world would go to shit in a hand basket."

"Exactly. Outing a vastly superior enemy would likely cause some pushback from the aliens. Whatever their agenda is here, it certainly involves secrecy and limited interaction with the world order." And then it dawned on her:

"Oh my god... We are in a cold war with the aliens..."

"It's a bloody ballet in a cold war theatre..." whispered Veronica Starr.

"Now you understand..." continued Nakamura. "I believe that the world leaders are trying to understand the enemy, to study it, and under no circumstances do they want to awaken the force that they are not ready to tackle. Imagine waking up next to a rattle snake! Akiyama's experience was by no means isolated. The whole Project Blue Book, its European, Asian, and Australian counterparts, accumulated so much research about such sightings, miraculous cures, and unexplained events."

"Crop circles?" suggested Fah.

172

"Perhaps. It goes further. For example, the Portuguese 'Our Lady of Fátima', now a holy Catholic place that once witnessed a mass sighting of what looked like a divine presence witnessed by thousands, and followed by miracles, especially healings. There is a strong evidence that something akin to Akyama's experience happened on that site."

"Now you are going to tell me that Roswell crash was real..." Fah was still sceptical.

"I'm afraid so. And so many other instances, when the governments and corporations managed to salvage alien technology and make incredible breakthroughs. The United States is one of the easiest countries to trace alien influence because of the free press and the public information legislation. Both NASA and DARPA were created in the wake of the Roswell crash, as well as other massive UFO sightings, well documented in history. Out of only these two organizations came so many innovations that they changed the course of our evolution."

Year 1604.
Edo, Japan

Tatami was expecting Ennuturat's audience in the Tokugawa palace. A year had passed since Tatami introduced Ennuturat, disguised as a Portuguese merchant under the name of Jose Brito, to the Shōgun. Whatever merits were behind the nature of Tokugawa and Brito's relationship, Tatami could tell that the two remarkably got along. That Nanban merchant Brito definitely had something to offer, thought Tatami, and it was time to remind him about the role Tatami played in Brito's access to the palace.

"Greetings, honorable Jose Brito!" exclaimed Tatami as he walked into the spacious palace room, designated as Brito's headquarters.

"Greetings Daimyo Tatami. How have you been?"

Initially Ennuturat was simply behaving the way that was expected of him, in order to keep his disguise. The shield that he was wearing depended on the humans' gullible belief that they saw nothing out of the ordinary, merely a human being from a different country. And if that belief was shaken, the human mind would start seeing glimpses of Ennuturat's true appearance - tentacles, alien skin, the suit that shielded him from the toxic Earth's atmosphere.

173

As time went by, Ennuturat grew to like the humans he spent his time with. To keep the appearance before his colleagues, he was extra grumpy about the away assignment, but in reality this was the most fun he had had since the Oscillation Project had begun. Just being around other living things, interacting with them, was so much more entertaining. He felt that humans were his pets, and even perhaps slightly more than that. *Friends?* No, that would be going too far. Since no word was particularly appropriate, Ennuturat thought of his Japanese humans as his favorite pets. Humans had pets too. Ennuturat found it endearing that humans got so attached to their little living companions. That was something he could definitely relate to.

"Jose, walk with me to the market! Let's have a meal

together," suggested Tatami.

"I know you are not fond of our cuisine, but you are a big proponent of a good drink! Maybe we can have a drink together!"

Ennuturat couldn't get out of the invitation easily. Tatami was determined. Ennuturat knew that Tatami had come to ask for his protection before the Tokugawa administration. That would be so easy for Ennuturat to arrange, as Tokugawa basically was Ennuturat's lap dog. But Ennuturat would have to care about Tatami's little life and his little problems. What was he to Ennuturat? A fruit fly, a little bug, so insignificant in his big universe.

And yet somehow this insignificant human had some sort of power over Ennuturat. Or maybe it was rather Ennuturat allowing the human to think this way. One way or another, the two were walking downtown Edo, through the fish market, to the famous sake house both of them enjoyed. The two unlikely companions passed by the fish tables where the crafty cooks slew fish and prepared it right before the customers. Tatami was particularly fond of the 'dancing squid'. The two got in line to order sashimi before they went into the sake house.

174

For Ennuturat, watching the preparation of live sashimi was always a horrifying experience, but he did it with an impenetrable expression. The squid was stored in big tubs of water, from which it was cleverly extracted with long pliers and allowed to squirt water, the final line of defence from a vastly superior, powerful enemy - the butcher. Then the creature was placed on the cutting board, gutted and skinned alive, chopped into pieces that danced on the cutting board in final agony. Such cruelty choked Ennuturat, but he made himself watch as a reminder that the humans and the Unkari were not so different after all; and given the opportunity, humans would gut and skin the Unkari alive just as easily.

And also that the humans possessed the kind of weapon that could do that to the Unkari. Perhaps not right now, but in the future, something in the human consciousness would give them almost divine potential - to turn water into wine, to walk on water, to part seas, to cure the sick and to create the worlds and everything living in them. That was a truly horrifying thought to every Unkari, and was the one thing that both tribes for the most part agreed on.

"Maybe you'd like to try some today, Jose?" suggested Tatami.

"My friend, you know that where I come from, we don't eat such things." Of course if Tatami knew other Portuguese merchants personally, he would have known that they embraced eating fish, perhaps not in such graphic form as live sashimi. "What is so amazing for you in... eating live things?"

"I never thought of it. Live means fresh. This is how we receive our nutrition, from the ocean. This is what we have here. No great philosophy behind it, I'm afraid."

"Tatami, do you realize that some of these creatures have senses that can experience things you cannot even imagine! Mantis shrimp, it can see colors you cannot see. Mammals can smell and taste things so sharply that it would blow your mind if you could experience only a fraction of it! And be assured, that they can feel every instance of being pried open and dissected for your consumption."

Tatami looked closely at Ennuturat, thinking that his vision was tricking him into seeing weird things. For a second it appeared to him that Brito had tentacles, just like the squid on his plate!

175

"My friend Jose, your talks make me see crazy things! And I am very hungry now, so I suggest let's eat first and then talk about it over good sake. Then you can tell me all about it!"

Sake! Ennuturat loved that stuff. Alcohol was common in the Unkari biochemistry and they consumed it for hydration, but humans invented recipes of it so intricate and so different all over the planet that he never stopped marvelling at their craftiness.

Year 2045.
Tokyo, Japan

Back at the Old city in Tsukiji district, Nakamura, Fah, and Veronica Starr continued chatting about alien conspiracies and sipping hot sake.

YEAR 1604.
EDO, JAPAN

Tatami poured a cup of sake for Ennuturat and himself, and both indulged in their drink. Tatami, with his stomach full of dancing squid that needed to be settled, and Ennuturat, whose stomach was unsettled from the mere sight of Tatami's food.

YEAR 2045.
TOKYO, JAPAN

Jaden barged into the entrance of the sake house, throwing the doors open in front of him and hastily looking for the group he was supposed to meet an hour ago.

"Ah! There you are!" he exclaimed, seeing the group of three seated in the middle of the restaurant. All three visibly cringed at Jaden's brash entrance, who, with numerous shopping bags in his hands, approached the table and seated himself next to Fah.

"Jaden, where have you been? Don't tell me - shopping!"

"Ok, I won't!"

"I can see the bags! You went crazy on your first day in this country!"

"Oh shut up, girl. If I wasn't thinking about shopping for both of us, you would be wearing your old rags now. And now look at you! Such class!"

"You know that this is a typical shopaholic's excuse, right?"

"I. Don't. Have. This. Problem. Okay? I'm just being... strategic. We need clothes!"

"Jaden, this poncho costs a fortune!"

"The appropriate response would be to thank me! And by the way you can afford it now."

"Your friend is right," chimed in Veronica Starr. "You can afford it now. And by the way, you look fantastic." Veronica flashed one of her smiles that made Fah weak at the knees.

"Alright, girl!" Jaden tried to awkwardly hi-five with Veronica but she didn't go for it, and Jaden's hand remained hanging in the air for a very long and just as embarrassing second.

"What's wrong with your team spirit, girl?" Jaden pouted and directed his hand at the sake jug. "What did I miss?"

"Oh I don't know," Fah answered, "just a world order conspiracy of epic proportions, that's about it." Nakamura smiled. "So what is it you want me to do, Mr. Nakamura?" Fah inquired, trying not to stare at the steely eyes of Veronica Starr, the eyes that pulled her in like quick sand.

"I believe you've accomplished most of your preliminary research. We've been tracing your progress as you continued to request archival materials from Japan linking the Tokugawa Shōgunate and the alien presence. So I believe you've put that much together."

"Well, I saw the evidence. I just couldn't quite trust my conclusions."

"I know you were trying to trace the descendants of the Tokugawa samurai. What do you know about it?"

"I believe that the samurai received a particular treatment to enhance their abilities."

"That just sums it up nicely. I want to give you the resources to finish this part of the investigation. We need DNA samples of these samurai ancestors. We believe that they have a gene capable of improving metabolism and self-healing abilities. In particular, we believe that the samurai had the ability to consciously direct the cells in their body to kill cancer cells, and some other tricks, like disassociating from pain, improved reaction etc. This research has tremendous potential for the field of gene therapy. Aliens planted this DNA in humans, and we need to identify it and learn how to use it for the good of humanity, just like DARPA once did with inventing the Internet." Fah bit her lip and thought about it for a moment.

"How do you sleep at night, knowing all of this?"

"Pretty good. That is what I suggest you do as well. Life is short. They have been here probably for centuries and we are still around. It will be ok in our lifetime, if we don't kick the hornet's nest."

"Aren't you a bit curious to meet an alien life form?"

"I thought about it. But what would be the benefit in it? I prefer the status quo. And also I prefer to find the DNA that cures cancer."

YEAR 2045.
OSAKA

People rarely chose to live in the Dotonbori district. People worked there, hung out there, but then they went home to the suburbs. Nyoko preferred Dotonbori. In fact, the only other place she could probably bear living would be Tokyo, even more crowded that Osaka's Dotonbori, but Tokyo was out of the question. Too many tourists and diplomats made the authorities more vigilant, and homeless Nyoko would have been constantly on the run from them. In Dotonbori she felt at home. Each shop blasted a different tune, creating constant discordant noise. To Nyoko it was her personal cosmic background radiation, permeating every pore of her body. People were constantly on the move.

In Dotonbori, everyone was an individual, yet no one really stood out. Nyoko often thought that Dotonbori compensated for her lack of personality, filling her to the core with sensory input from every corner, making her feel alive. She didn't have to feel or think, she didn't have to hear her own thoughts, when she was surrounded with Dotonbori's presence. She was never alone, and always alone. A perfect - or the *only* - way of being for her.

Actually Nyoko wasn't exactly homeless, but her living situation was not a conventional one. She lived in an internet cafe, where she paid a tiny amount for a booth with paper-thin walls, which housed a single chair, a desk and a screen. Of the luxuries of her 'housing complex', there was a shower stall in the general bathroom, which the owner decided to install after a few years when the place started stinking so much that people passed out.

Most people have no idea how a person could live out of a shoe box of possessions. Nyoko perfected this style. She ate, she slept, she played online games, she fucked. Life was simple, and any minimal complication of that scenario immediately triggered her anxiety.

When Fah knocked on the door of her booth, that was the kind of a complication Nyoko could not easily cope with.

"Yes? Who's there?" asked Nyoko, her voice uncertain.

"My name is Fah. I need to talk to you about something." "Are you from church?"

"No."

"Social services?"

"No."

"Police?"

"No, nothing like that. I am a researcher, a journalist. I want to talk to you about your life."

Nyoko burst out laughing.

"Right. My life?" Fah opened the door and walked in. The cubicle was so tiny that Fah barely squeezed in and stood to the side of the desk, pressed to the wall. In the door opening Nyoko saw another person.

"Hi, I'm Jaden. I'm a writer." Jaden smiled. His large frame blocked a good portion of light from the hallway. "I'll just stay over here for the time being, if you don't mind."

"Who are you people and what do you want from me?"

"My name is Fah Napasiri. This is Jaden, he's my friend. He helps me with the research. I came from Thailand at the invitation of a distinguished Japanese scientist. We are looking for the descendants of Tokugawa Ieyasu's samurai. And we believe you are one of them."

Year 2045.
Atlantic Ocean. Unkari
Research Facility

Argon Katu held another emergency meeting. This guy Michio Nakamura was proving to be a real problem, and the team was assembled to figure out how to disrupt his activity on researching the samurai DNA.

A task force of five Unkari bureaucrats were sitting around the table. Each had a liquid silver screen before them and they dipped their tentacles in that silvery puddle to access data.

"Who's first?" inquired Argon.

"Let's just remove him. It's simple," suggested one of the team members.

"Have you even done any probability analysis?" vehemently disagreed another.

180

"The last time we removed someone of Nakamura's level we created additional problems."

"The last time was Kennedy," inserted one of the team.

"Kennedy was not last! There were many after him."

"Name one! I thought so."

"Kennedy was different. We didn't remove him personally, remember? CIA cracked his physician and he told them everything, about the gene, about us, about the fact that without our treatment Kennedy wouldn't have lasted that long... They removed him. They didn't want a president propped by the aliens."

"Oh come on!" disagreed another alien. "Do you believe these Enkri conspiracy theories? Argon, you were on the case. Am I right?"

"Kennedy is classified," Argon informed him. "What do we

have on the Nakamura subject? I don't have all day to waste."

"Right. I think most of us would agree that removing Nakamura would be... shall I say, unsophisticated. Also he is so well protected, we would have to do some collateral damage and risk being exposed once again."

Argon grew impatient. He hated when his staff schooled him on the obvious. "What are you suggesting then?"

"The more subtle way would be to remove his current research team. We've done some high-level probability analysis." With those words, the speaker scooped some of the liquid silver from his screen puddle and tossed it across the desk towards Argon. Argon scooped the substance and connected it to his liquid screen. Quickly scanning the data analysis, he nodded his head in mild approval. "Fah Napasiri is my suggestion. Removing her would buy us plenty of time, and hopefully Nakamura will pass away by that time. This guy she is working with, the writer, he presents no problem. We believe he will be so scared by Fah's death that it will clearly deter him from further digging."

"What about this other woman involved?" asked Argon. "Veronica Starr."

"She is a mercenary. She follows the money. We can buy her off if we have to but we believe she will just move to another high-paying client."

181

"I want to talk to her first," insisted Argon.

"This is really unnecessary. And highly irregular," protested one of the bureaucrats while the others sprayed a few puffs of colored powder in the air, communicating their disagreement. "Contain your emotions, please. It's not a street market. I said I want to talk to Fah. Get my shield ready and track her location."

YEAR 2045.
TOKYO, JAPAN

It had been three months since Nyoko first met Fah and

moved with her to Tokyo. Although Fah paid her well as a research subject, the selling point for Nyoko was Tokyo itself. Until high school, she had lived with her parents in Tokyo, but then she had dropped out of school and escaped home. Nyoko hitchhiked her way to Osaka where she wished to start living her own life the way she wanted it. The only thing she missed in Tokyo was her high school crush. That was such a ridiculous and hopeless crush, because Daichi didn't even remember her in school. He always played it cool, kept to himself, and focused on his books. Daichi was going to go places, or so it had appeared at first. But then something broke that boy, and he dropped out of cram school, and out of reality as well, adopting a gaming world instead.

In the gaming community Daichi was a rock star. Nobody cared where he was or what he did with his real life, because on the web Daichi was a celebrity. Although he never visited conferences and never communicated with his fans, Daichi could win any tournament if he so desired.

There was a key difference between Daichi and Nyoko. Daichi had made it. She, on the other hand, had absolutely nothing to show in her life. She didn't even have those aspirations to begin with. The only reason she involved herself in those gaming tournaments was to keep in touch with Daichi, albeit only on the score board, where he always was on top. But even that felt intimate to Nyoko.

***

Fah walked into the spacious warehouse that served her as a laboratory. She was sipping hot black coffee as she approached the section with the computers and the wall, all littered with various scraps of paper and colored threads connecting them. The monster made its way back to the new place as well.

Nyoko was at one of the computers with a top-of-the-line gaming console, slaying some alien monsters on the screen.

"Morning, Nyoko. Did you sleep well?"

"Yes, Fah, thank you. Where's Jaden this morning?"

"I think he is chasing a new fling. He hasn't been sleeping in his room for some time now."

"Nice."

"What about you, Nyoko? Do you have someone special?"

"Kinda... It's complicated."

"I'm sure it is!" Fah chuckled.

"Nothing is simple when it comes to love."

Fah meant every word of it. If there was a world competition on developing unrealistic crushes, she would be a champion. Her recent crush was so out of her league, that it took the cake in the list of romantic attachments that go nowhere. Veronica Starr... She just loved to roll that name on the tip of her tongue. She was so high in the clouds, so unattainable. Every time the two met for business, it felt as if Veronica had an invisible taser on her heart and kept jolting it every time she spoke Fah's name.

"What are we going to do today, Fah?" Nyoko asked her, snatching Fah from her marshmallow clouds. Fah blushed and cleared her throat as subtly as she could.

"I made a list of some Zen meditation techniques. You need to try achieving Mushin. Your eventual goal would be to heal a small pin prick or a paper cut with your mind. I hope you are ok with all this pricking we do here."

"Yeah, that's nothing compared to a tattoo needle on some of my body parts."

183

"Don't wanna know, girl!" laughed Fah.

"Oh yeah, those tattoos are meant for only one person."

"That crush of yours?"

"Yeah. You got me. Not like he will ever see them."

"Why not?"

"We live in different worlds. He's a gaming superstar. I am nothing for him."

"Yeah I can relate to that."

"Veronica?"

"That obvious?"

"Duhhhh. Every time she walks in, your voice goes up a notch, you drop things, you bump into things, and you don't look in her eyes! Like, ever! What do you find in that skinny bitch?"

"I don't know. I just don't know. But hey... change the subject. We have work to do."

Nyoko and Fah prepared to do their experiment. Nakamura believed that they needed to test the gene, to prove that it worked, and for that they needed to make Nyoko perform a healing miracle. It was a constant stream of tries that Fah orchestrated by drawing on the techniques of prayer and meditation. She even brought in a kendo tutor to approximate the samurai training routine.

"What today? Candles or knives?" laughed Nyoko.

"Here's what I want you to do. We will start from meditation. You will listen to the audio track that guides you into a zen state. Then you will cut your finger and focus on healing it."

"How original."

"I know, we've done it a million times. But I think you are making progress. You are getting better at emptying your thoughts."

184 "My thoughts are always empty, Fah."

"Don't say that!"

"It's true. All this meditation is nothing special to me. I always 'meditate' on something; I just didn't know that I was doing it. I listen to water dripping from the sink faucet, I listen to the noise of busy streets, I turn that chaos into a melody in my head by rearranging the sounds. I just don't know how that is supposed to heal a cut. I am sorry, Fah, maybe I just don't have it."

"I believe in you."

"I appreciate the sentiment but I suggest you find some other subjects as well."

"I am working on it. I narrowed down on another guy, he's your age, living here in Tokyo. But I don't know where he lives.

His traces were lost since he dropped out of cram school."

Fah grabbed a paper folder from the desk and extracted a picture of a young guy.

"Where are you, Daichi?"

"What did you say?"

"Daichi Abe. He's my next prospect." Nyoko's heart skipped the beat.

"Let me see this picture." Nyoko grabbed the picture from Fah's hands.

"I know where he is. Not physically, on the web. He's the boy I have a crush on."

"I cannot believe it! What a coincidence!"

"Maybe Mushin is leading me to him!" laughed Nyoko, making fun of Fah's theories.

"You know, actually, maybe it is true, laugh all you want, but the two of you have a connection, and you both have the gene. Maybe you are drawn to each other like opposite magnets, to make something complete, something whole."

"You are getting all weird on me, Fah. But I have an idea. And maybe your Mushin will help me pull it off."

***

185

Next day, Daichi entered a gaming tournament where he was absolute king. Rigonara was a vicious slaying game based on the ancient samurai fighting techniques. A mix of kenjitsu, kobudjitsu, iaidjitsu, tenshinryu hyouho and many others, Rigonara simulated a battlefield in a modern city with ancient weaponry - katana, wakizashi, and kanto swords. It was a post-apocalyptic world where Tokyo was ridden by gangs of sword-wielding fighters. According to the game, each competing gang could consist of up to five fighters. Daichi always fought alone. And always won. Each time before the tournament, he walked the streets of the game, felt every corner, and taught himself to walk it blindfolded. Unlike many other gamers, Daichi actually studied all the fighting techniques. In real life he was a dough boy, the least athletic kid there was. But his mind knew discipline. He treated the game as if his real life depended on it, and would never surrender.

Daichi never played like he didn't care. He thought it was insulting to the game and to himself to be unprepared, to have other things on his mind when entering the game. Although physically weak, Daichi's mind was that of a world class kenjitsuka. Daichi walked on a game field wearing a modern take on the samurai armor for which he had written the code himself. It did not give any particular advantage in the game but it had a symbolic value for Daichi. He cared about every single detail of his game avatar, including the appearance. He carried two swords, as was customary among the samurai.

Once he entered the game, Daichi rehearsed a few classic battojutsu katas - a skill of drawing a sword and slaying an opponent in one move, in just a fracture of a second. Dying from the hand of an enemy without even drawing katana was shameful in Daichi's mind. It was shameful in the mind of real samurai, and Daichi treated the game fight with the same respect.

Then he saw the first attackers. Actually he did not see them, as much as he sensed their presence. Daichi didn't know if he could develop an actual Musoken in the game, but it seemed as if he did. His first opponents were always newbies to the game and never posed any threat. The real gamers avoided of encountering Daichi as long as possible, in order to rank higher in the game. They had no illusions about the fact that they were going to die in the game, and they preferred to die from Daichi's hand, which was a badge of honor among the gamers.

Daichi was walking down the dark street. Most of the streetlights were broken and he could hardly see anything. But unlike the others, that did not slow Daichi down. He did not need the light: his feet committed those streets to memory. He sensed them coming at him from behind the broken vending machine, three of them, young punks wearing standard game outfits and with four swords each tucked in their belts. *Kids...* thought Daichi and kept calmly walking.

That was when he heard the war scream, way early, as they were still a good hundred meters away. *Oh god...* thought

Daichi, and continued out loud:

"Just keep walking, kids. I don't want to kill you five minutes into the game."

But the three were already under an adrenaline surge, or maybe something else that pumped them up. Like wild animals, unaware of their bodies and their surroundings, they just ran towards Daichi's katana like moths to the flame. Daichi kept walking.

Moments later, Daichi turned around, instantaneously drawing a sword and as it flew out of the saya, he cut the head clean off one of his attackers. With the next open horizontal strike he took the head off the other kid, and with the third vertical strike he sliced the third kid in half, whose avatar guts spilled all over the place.

Daichi, as calm as before, completed the move with a ceremonial wiping of the blood from the blade with his fingers first, then with the sleeve of his kimono, and performed a proper noto, returning the blade back to saya. Nobody went that far with the traditional rituals, most would just walk away. But Daichi knew that there was a purpose for every one of those routines. They help to be focused, to go above and beyond standard katas, to take the skill to a new level.

187

Daichi's score table popped with the number "3". That score only would matter if he eventually lost and it would demonstrate his rank among the players. Daichi did not care about the score. He knew that he would face the last standing enemy and would slay him, and that was how his victory would be achieved, not with a petty score card, but with going against the most powerful samurai in the game.

***

Several hours passed, and Daichi didn't even notice if he was hungry. In his tiny dim room, he was all concentration, and nothing could distract him from the goal. All bodily functions were on hold as he made his way through the slash piles of increasingly better enemies. Those players did not make rookie mistakes. They attacked with impeccable timing and cut with precision. Most of them did not need to draw their wakizashi, the short swords, as they were good at keeping their katanas in their hands.

The game stats counted down to the three last players, then only two: himself, and someone else. Finally Daichi cared to open the profile of the player. It was Dragon67, or as he found out a few months ago, Nyoko. Nyoko's previous gaming record was that of a mediocre player. She ranked in the lower middle bracket. But in this game she had made it all the way to the top. And oddly her score was very close to that of Daichi's. Even though Daichi did not go for the score in the game, to see Dragon67 getting that high was impressive.

"Ok, I'm impressed!" Daichi broadcast on a public channel. "Come out and let's be over with it." The answer was not forthcoming.

"Cat and mouse then, right? Guess who's the cat?"

"Shut up and fight like a warrior!" followed the answer on a public channel.

"Dang girl. You're making me hard," whispered Daichi.

***

Nyoko was in the flow. Perhaps she couldn't direct her Mushin to heal her paper cuts, but she could now direct it at something she really cared about - getting Daichi's attention.

Ten minutes ago, Fah had awaken on the couch beside Nyoko, who had been playing for the five past hours. She was unstoppable. She awoke right in time to witness the final fight. Nyoko's avatar was hiding on the third floor of a half-wrecked building, watching Daichi below on the ground standing with his arms folded right in the spotlight of a streetlight. The ghosts of his slain enemies crowded together, watching on a muted setting - they could not say or do anything except bear silent witness to his victory.

Nyoko was waiting. She wanted Daichi to make a mistake, to get impatient, because she knew that all things considered, Daichi was a better fighter. This time she did not go for the score rank. She went for the victory. Clean, honorable victory, the only kind that would impress Daichi enough to care about her. Daichi was calm and unscathed. He swam his mental river of calm like a trout, strong and graceful, without a single thought or emotion out of order.

And then he sensed it.

Just barely in time to draw the blade and block the attack from Nyoko, who jumped at him from the building. She accumulated enough game strength to pull it off, otherwise such a high jump would have killed her. With that one jump Nyoko's extra strength was down to zero. It was her own skill now against the most skilled gamer in the history of Rigonara.

Daichi looked at Nyoko, even more impressed then before. He purposefully drained his strength account, as a courtesy to his opponent. Now they were on an even footing, and no one would be able to accuse the winner of winning on a technicality. It would be a clean victory.

Then the katanas went flying at a speed that the eyes of the ghosts could not follow. They watched the score board and saw the two going neck and neck, neither giving an inch. Ten minutes into the fight, Daichi gained advantage and went at Nyoko with a daring vertical cut from head to toe, holding katana in both hands and exposing in that moment his neck.

The moment was brief, and Nyoko's death was foretold. Suddenly Nyoko felt as if the game had melted away, and everything came to a halt. It was not a game glitch. It was Nyoko's conscious decision to view the unfolding events in slow motion, like film frames. She saw Daichi above her, his face beautiful and fierce as he went for his victorious strike. His katana way up in the air, under a clean 90-degree angle to the ground, making a proper whistle as the blade slashed through the air. The katana was slowly descending on Nyoko's body following an unwavering trajectory. Instead of panicking, Nyoko felt that all of a sudden, she had all the time in the world to make her move and turn her imminent death into her victory. With her katana in her right hand she attempted a perpendicular block of Daichi's katana, but she only did it as a distracting move. She knew based on the momentum of Daichi's strike that she would not be able to withstand that direct hit. With her left hand, she extracted her kanto, a short dagger tucked behind her back. With an assertive move, she drove the dagger through Daichi's exposed lower jaw, right at the base of his tongue, and further into Daichi's head, piercing his brain.

Daichi's avatar instantaneously fell on top of Nyoko,

lifeless and defeated. The game was over. A congratulatory fanfare announced Dragon67 as the winner. All the ghosts' sound was un-muted and they cheered like crazy at the sight of the new queen of Rigonara. The game took her to the winner's room. Nyoko had only heard about it. It was a brightly lit empty room with a short tea table - a tea ceremony for two.

A traditionally dressed geisha was serving the tea. Nyoko approached, bowed down, and sat on the floor before the table.

"Who's the second cup for?" she asked.

"For the defeated one," answered the geisha softly. At that moment, Daichi appeared in the room, dressed in a white kimono. Nyoko noticed that she was wearing the same kind of kimono.

"Congratulations, kenjitsuka. I've never been in this room as a defeated one."

"I've never been to this room before. Period. What do we do here?"

"Anything you want. I'm all yours. You won." Daichi politely bowed down and signalled the geisha to go away.

"Anything I want?"

"*Anything.* Command me, I'll do it." Nyoko was speechless.

***

Fah quietly exited the lab and locked the door from the outside. Kids needed privacy.

***

Sitting on her chair in the warehouse in front of the console with the VR goggles on, Nyoko's heart rate was as high as if she were about to OD, but there was nothing running though her system, other than Mushin and love.

***

Three hours later, Fah and Nyoko were standing outside the warehouse. Spring air filled their lungs. Both drew cigarettes and quietly lit up.

"Aren't you going to tell me?" begged Fah.

"Let's just put it this way. He saw my tattoos. All of them."

***

It was past 11 pm when Fah was walking down an obscure Tokyo street in the business district. She couldn't sleep and had decided to walk to the warehouse and do some research. The obscure location for the lab was chosen on purpose, to avoid drawing any unnecessary attention to Nakamura. The street was empty, but relatively well-lit. The streetlights were casting long intertwining shadows on the asphalt. The light reflected in the fresh puddles after the rain. Suddenly Fah heard brisk footsteps behind her. She turned around and saw a man in a dark suit and a hat, who was catching up with her a bit too fast.

"Miss, wait. I need to talk to you!" called the man and waved her.

"What about?" Fah kept the speed of her pace.

"About your samurai research."

"I don't know what you are talking about." Fah turned around and sped up, almost to a jog. Although she had been out of training for some time, she was a good runner, especially if her life depended on it. That however would only work if the man did not have a gun. She decided to sharply take a turn to the right and try to disappear in the maze of lonely streets, when out of nowhere the man popped out right before her. "How did you...?" Fah felt cold sweat along her spine.

191

"Miss, you are making a big mistake. I am not your enemy. Not just yet. Some forces want you out of the picture and I went out of my way to warn you. I can protect you if you come working for me."

"What do you want from me?"

"I want the boy and the girl, and you. You keep working on activating the oscillation gene..."

"Oscillation gene?"

"...but under my supervision. I can give you more than

Nakamura ever will. And just as easily I can take it away."

"Who are you?"

"Finally. The only question that matters. You know who I am!" The man lifted his chin up, allowing the defused yellow street light to illuminate his face. In the features of a Western man she saw something underneath, not with her eyes, but with her skin. She felt very unsettled and suddenly suspicious. A sense that she was looking at a mask of a face was nagging her.

"Come on, you can see it, can't you?" insisted the man. At that moment Fah saw the image of the man flickering, and under the skin of a human she saw a horrifying sight: a monster so alien that her brain refused to process it. Tentacles, slimy reptilian skin, a face that lacked any humanity. Fah screamed but the man shoved her against the wall so hard that the "thump" sound echoed down the empty street.

192

"Try screaming again and I will kill you right here. That was the plan to begin with anyway. Listen to me, you little insect. You either work for me or go back to whatever hole you crawled out of and stay there. You hear me? Stay there and make no sound! There will be no warnings after this. If you decide to switch sides, here is the email to reach me." The alien grabbed Fah's wrist and breathed on the back side of her forearm. The skin in that place started burning, and left a raw branding - the email address.

And just as briskly as he appeared, the monster walked away, and soon faded from Fah's sight. Shivering, with her hair all messed up and mascara streaming down her cheeks, mixed with tears of shock, Fah walked to the warehouse, disabled the alarm, and walked in. Inside, she poured herself a hefty glass of neat scotch, downed it, but felt no effect from it.

She picked the phone up and dialed Veronica's number. The phone rang twice and Veronica picked up.

"Is everything alright?" Veronica's voice asked.

"I need you to come here. To the warehouse. Right now." She added in a broken voice: *"Please."*

"I'll be right there."

***

For the first time Fah saw Veronica looking as a normal human, wearing casual jeans and a sweater, sneakers, no makeup, and only an expensive cream-colored cashmere coat gave away her status. Fah noticed that Veronica was shorter than usual. That surprised her, because they almost were of the same height. Fah was sitting on a couch all wrapped in a blanket, a bottle of scotch and a glass by her side on the floor. Her face was all muddy from unreliable makeup, and the streams of tears dried on her face like receding mountain rivers in the dead of the summer. Veronica walked over and sat on the couch by Fah's side.

"Tell me about it, whenever you are ready," she softly spoke.

"I saw IT. I saw the alien."

"What?"

"He... it... attacked me on the way to the warehouse. It threatened to kill me unless I quit the research or switch sides, work for him."

"Oh my god, darling', this... sounds horrible." Veronica placed her well-manicured palm on Fah's knees. "Are you sure it was not a prank?"

193

"I SAW it! With my own eyes! It was hiding behind a shield of some kind. If he didn't force me to see, I would never know! Veronica, they walk among us!"

"We will figure it out. I promise you. You will get security, the best kind. We will spare no expense."

"He called it the oscillation gene."

"I've never heard that term before."

"I need to think what I will be doing next." Fah extracted her hand from under the blanket and showed Veronica the branding. Veronica gasped.

"I need to email about my decision. I imagine they won't wait for it too long."

"You are considering to quit, don't you?"

"Yes. I will not work with the enemy, for sure, but I am scared, Veronica. I think we all are in danger."

"Give me some time. I have excellent connections. I can safely move you and the kids, no one will find you."

"I don't know... I am scared..."

"Trust me... Do you?" Veronica moved closer to Fah, so close that Fah felt the warmth of Veronica's skin and her light perfume. It was enchanting. All of a sudden Fah could not think about anything else but Veronica's skin, and her lips. "I want to..." Fah whispered but her voice failed to do even that much without cracking.

"Let's get you warmed up. You need to take a shower." With those words Veronica started to remove her clothing until she was standing before Fah completely naked. Veronica took her hand and helped her to get up from the couch saying, "I believe I could use a shower as well."

***

Next morning, Fah woke up in a guest bedroom of the warehouse. Veronica was gone. In the place where Veronica had slept, Fah found a folded sheet of paper - a note. It read:

"Call Nyoko and wait for me in the warehouse. Security is already in place. You will not see them but they are always around. You are safe now. And thank you for the shower."

Thank you for the shower? Fah read that line over and over again. For the shower?

How did she mean it? Romantically or practically? If she wanted to say something romantic, she would add something like she had had a good time or just *anything*. Anxiety, self-doubt, and shame all together washed over Fah's mind, but the timing for sicking oneself was wrong. She needed to get Nyoko to the warehouse and think about some practical steps. Romantic torment was filed away for the more appropriate time.

***

Nyoko showed up in an hour. She had her luggage - a tiny

suitcase in the shape of some anime monster, all in acidic bright colors.

"That's all you have?"

"Yes, why?"

"Not much there."

"Actually, that's quite a lot. Now I need to worry about it. A good thing about living without possessions is that in case of an emergency you are not restricted. And we are in an emergency, aren't we?"

"I'm afraid so." Fah recounted the events of last night, this time trying to minimize the drama in her voice. No need to scare Nyoko just yet.

"That's quite a story, Fah. What are we going to do?"

"I don't know yet. I am waiting for Veronica to come back..."

"Wait, is that her coat on the couch? What was going on here?" teased Nyoko.

"Oh give me a break."

"Tell me, tell me!"

"We took a shower."

"Oh-my-god! And?"

"And spent the night, if you must know. I woke up and she was gone. Left a note."

"Oh that's good!"

"...thanking for the shower."

"Hmm."

"That's what I think." Nyoko sat on the couch and pulled her feet under her. Fah sat next to her.

"Where's Jaden? I haven't seen him in a few weeks."

"Somewhere in Hokkaido. He's the travel vlogger now. What about Daichi? What are the two of you up to?"

"We talk."

"You think he'll change his mind?"

"About joining us? No, unlikely. He doesn't even want to meet me in person. We spend a lot of time together online but that's about it. I told him about your theories and that the Mushin helped me to beat him, but he thinks I'm just very good at the game. He thinks I developed a skill, that's all."

And then a shocking realization came to Fah. "Oh my god. The man, the alien last night, he mentioned the kids, two kids. He knows about Daichi! We must protect him!"

***

Daichi was madly in love with Nyoko, but he could not believe that such a beautiful and smart girl liked him. No matter what Nyoko said, Daichi always thought that if she knew the truth about him, she would be disgusted. Daichi never opened up about being hikikomori, that was too embarrassing to admit. It was better just to leave everything the way it was. And if Nyoko decided not to talk to him after some time, so be it. He would accept it.

The message from Nyoko popped up on his screen. A video chat request. He accepted.

"Hi, my samurai. How did you sleep?"

Nyoko was walking on the street as she was speaking.

"I haven't gone to bed yet. I was playing all night."

"What tournament?"

"Katana Justice League."

"Nice. What are you going to do now?"

"I'm not sleepy yet. Just going to sit around, watch something."

"Oh, good. Because I'm at your house, and I'm walking in." Daichi froze.

"What. Did. You. Say."

"Daichi, we are in danger. We need to talk. And we need to do this in private, our communication may be intercepted."

"No! I can't! I'm busy now! I am going to sleep now."

"Daichi, you said you were not sleepy." Daichi heard the doorbell ringing and his mother opening the door.

Voices down the hallway. Panic. Heartbeat. *Lock the room! Quickly!*

Steps on old wooden carpeted floor coming towards the room down the hallway.

Knock on the door. Daichi wouldn't answer.

"Daichi, it's me, Nyoko."

"Go away! I'm busy!"

"Daichi, we need to talk. You are in a serious danger. Remember I said that we have a gene, they call it the oscillation gene. Some very deadly forces are after the gene. We need to disappear. I have friends who will protect us."

Daichi wouldn't open the door and would not answer.

"They threatened to kill Fah. Daichi, she is my friend. My only friend. I'm scared for her."

"Wait... The gene... How long have you known that I have it?"

"I found out the day before I beat you in Rigonara."

"Wait, so you just needed my cooperation?"

"No, Daichi, no! I liked you since high school. You didn't even remember me. That's why I even started gaming, to meet you."

197

"Liar!" screamed Daichi and loudly kicked something in his room. "I hate you! I never liked you! I did it for free sex! You are a free bitch for me, that's all! Go away!"

"Daichi..."

"Go or I'll throw you out myself!"

Tears burst out of Nyoko's eyes and she ran away, outside the house, to the streets, and kept running, until her lungs started burning. Then she stopped, sat right on the asphalt curb and cried. The busy crowd kept walking around her. She felt as if she was in the woods, among silent trees, with the street noises sounding like the wind in the treetops. In the middle of one of the busiest Tokyo streets, Nyoko felt in perfect privacy.

Daichi sat on the floor, cried and rocked himself violently. What had he done? Why did he hurt this girl so much? His agony was too much to handle. And yet, somehow, this was not the kind of an agony that would force Daichi to attempt another suicide. He wanted to live! He wanted to make it right by her! He wanted to be someone else, someone better. He wanted to take a step outside of his dark room, and he wanted to shave clean, cut his hair, throw out all the trash, open the curtains to allow the daylight in... He wanted to do all those things but had no energy to take the first step.

Nyoko took out a pack of slim cigarettes from her jacket pocket, lit it up, and watched the smoke mix with the vapor of the chill November day and escape her lips. She didn't think about anything but those grey clouds in front of her, pushing the entire world to the background, blurred, out of focus.

Daichi kept rocking himself on the floor, but now he did it in a slower, consistent tempo, his eyes closed, all his senses switched off. Inside his mind, he saw Nyoko, floating among the clouds, rocking with him in unison, creating resonance waves, like ripples on the surface of a still lake. Daichi and Nyoko were two drops that kept falling in the same spot, creating perfect harmonic ripples in space-time.

198

One - two - three - Splash - One - two - three - Splash.

Nyoko kept lighting new cigarettes, not so much inhaling the smoke but puffing it out at a consistent pace. She became really good at creating identical, evenly spaced, puffs.

One - two - three - Puff - One - two - three - Puff.

Finally, in his mind, Daichi said:

"I am sorry. You did not deserve it."

Tears rolled down Nyoko's cheeks. She didn't know she had any left to cry. She felt like an invisible presence hugged her from behind. An overwhelming warmth and love entered her, love so expansive Nyoko thought her heart would burst out of her chest. She kept puffing the clouds of smoke and silently cried, when those clouds started arranging themselves in a heart shape.

***

Fah was in the warehouse, behind her computer doing research, when she sensed someone behind her back. Fear jolted her body as she recognized that presence.

"Yes, this is me, Fah. I'm glad you recognized me." She heard Argon's voice. "You have been a naughty pet. And I'm afraid you need to be punished now." Fah closed her eyes and would not turn around.

"Do what you came for."

"As you wish." With those words, Argon jolted Fah with a high-voltage electric current. Fah's heart gave one last beat and stopped forever.

***

Nyoko did not know how much time had passed since she had first sat down on the curb. Time lost any relevance to her until she heard an incoming call. Reluctantly she checked the caller ID - Veronica Starr.

"What does she want from me..." mumbled Nyoko and answered. "Yes..."

"Nyoko, I have... tragic news for you... It's Fah..." Nyoko's heart paused. "Fah is dead. Don't come back to the warehouse, it is not safe. I wired enough money to your account to last for some time. Spend them wisely."

199

Nyoko could not say a word. She couldn't cry either. Something died in her that moment.

"Are you listening, Nyoko?"

"Yes..." Nyoko answered, barely audible.

"We are closing the Project. The situation has changed. Nakamura has shifted his priority in the light of a security risk. You won't be able to reach me anymore." The call disconnected.

***

Veronica Starr sat on the floor holding Fah's lifeless body in her arms and bitterly crying.

Year 2045.
Tokyo. Japan. Daichi's Apartment

Hours later, Daichi passed out on the floor from emotional and physical exhaustion. He was sleeping a dreamless heavy sleep, when he heard a loud thumping noise.

Knock Knock Knock Knock!

It sounded like rocks falling from the sky. Groggy, he slowly awakened, his whole body shivering from being yanked out of his deep sleep. The noise came from behind the door.

"Daichi! This is me, Nyoko!" He heard Nyoko's sobbing voice. "Fah is dead. I have no place to go. You can throw me out if you want, but you will have to come out and do it yourself. Until that time, I'll just stay here." The noise quieted. Daichi heard a lumping sound as Nyoko sat down on the floor, her back pressing to the door.

200

Nyoko sat there for ten minutes and fell asleep, overcome with grief and exhaustion. About 30 minutes later, Daichi's mom came over with a blanket and put it over the sleeping girl, secretly hoping that a miracle would happen and this weird tenacious kid would return her son to the real world. Daichi sat in his room, staring at the door. He knew that Nyoko was there because he heard her snoring. Then resolve came over him. He simply got up, without thinking, and went to the shower. After meticulously scrubbing himself with the tiny bit of soap he had left, saving every drop of it, he dried himself with a small hand towel and found an old razor somewhere under the piles of garbage. He cleaned it with some vodka he had handy, soaked the towel in hot water, and held it on his face for a few minutes. Then he took the razor to his face. Piece by piece, he shaved off his past, his shame, his insecurity. With a face as a clean slate, Daichi felt that he could have a clean start with Nyoko. She had come back! After all he said, she had come back! He could not believe it. The final touch was to cut his thin wispy hair. He remembered that he had a haircut machine somewhere. It took some digging, but he finally found it. Setting the machine on #3, not too short, not too long, he chopped off those long ugly strands. Looking at himself in the mirror, he could not believe what he saw. A young man, averagely looking, but not broken. Not ashamed. Not a hikikomori.

***

"Nyoko, wake up. We need to go now." Nyoko opened her eyes. For the first time, she saw Daichi's face in the daylight. It was just as she remembered from high school, a bit stoic, but handsome in its own way. Handsome to her, for sure.

"Hey. Hi... You don't hate me anymore?"

"Girl, how can I hate you? You saved my life." And he hugged her.

Year 2046.
Osaka. Ono-Ha Itto-Ryu Kenjutsu Temple

A year had passed. Nyoko and Daichi were glued to the window outside the Shinto temple, watching five kenjutsuka monks practicing. Their moves were captivating. Although they resembled classic ryu styles, they had freedom and fluidity to them, unlike anything the couple had ever seen.

201

"Did you see this, did you just see?" whispered Daichi to Nyoko. "Let's try this one."

The two took the formation and attempted replicating the move with wooden katanas in their hands. Daichi stood with his back to the window of the temple and received the strike, while Nyoko attempted a vertical cut. By blocking the move, Daichi clumsily threw Nyoko to the side and she flew through the window, inside the training room. A huge stained glass mosaic came crushing down, and only because Daichi's strength threw Nyoko far and fast enough, did she avoid being pierced by loose shards. Nyoko landed at the feet of the Shinto priest and Kenjutsu sensei Hideyo Ittosai. Daichi froze, not knowing if he should run and try to break Nyoko out later, or follow her inside. That ancient stained glass must have been worth a fortune! Daichi's dilemma resolved itself when the two monks grabbed him by the arms and dragged him inside.

"So, what do we have here? Two warriors, apparently," suggested sensei Ittosai. The monks around him burst out laughing so hard, they could not stop for a few minutes. "Alright, enough guys, they've been embarrassed enough. Let's see how these two will pay for replacement of a 400-year-old window! Who are you two? Why are you snooping around my windows?"

"I am sorry," said Daichi first. "It was my idea. We have an important mission..."

Nyoko painfully kicked Daichi in the side before he finished his sentence and continued: "We want to learn the ways of samurai. The window... it was an accident. Here." She got out a small scroll of cash from her pocket. "That's all we have." The sight of the petty cash got the monks in stitches.

"Well that amount could probably buy us some good sake, to help us forget what you've destroyed here. But to restore this stained glass would take 100 times as much money. Maybe a 1000 times. So, what are we going to do?" The two looked as guilty as the original sin, but did not say a word.

"I have an idea!" suggested sensei.

"You two will work in the temple. Keep your change, you'll need it."

***

"What did we get ourselves into?" grieved Nyoko, sitting on a tiny bed in one of the monk's quarters, while Daichi looked outside the tiny window. Outside the window, monks were mowing the lawn, cutting the hedge, and sweeping the trails.

"Maybe it's for the best. We can learn from them."

"Daichi, they don't want to teach us. They want our free work. We don't have time for that. We have a mission, remember?"

"Sometimes it feels like we've gone crazy and the whole world around us is just a game." Daichi sat next to Nyoko and kissed her forehead.

"I know, I know. But then there is this." Nyoko pulled a feather sticking out of the pillowcase and placed it on her palm. She closed her eyes and concentrated. Slowly, the feather lifted from her palm and hovered above it. Daichi smiled, and playfully blew the feather in Nyoko's face. Nyoko laughed, but not for long. Her nose started bleeding. A thin red drop traveled down her lips, to the chin.

"Honey, don't waste your energy! That was reckless!" He pulled a piece of tissue from his pocket and wiped the blood off her face.

"You better lie down."

Nyoko obeyed. Holding the tissue to her nose, she whispered: "I cannot afford you losing faith. Fah counts on us."

"I know. Please forgive me. I will talk to the sensei and convince him to take us as his students."

"Do you think he can teach us to follow Mushin?"

"We did the research. We can't be sure, but the fact that he is the ancestor of the great Ito Ittosai, the founder of the Ono-Ha Itto-Ryu school, is encouraging."

"You are right. Maybe Mushin brought us here. Maybe we are in just the right place."

203

"I hope so. I am afraid our time is running out."

"Don't say that, dear..."

"Nyoko, it is true. We walked into the Mushin river unprepared, we swam in it, and now its piranhas are eating us alive!" Nyoko started crying. "All I really want is for this road we've taken not to be a waste. I want to bring Fah back."

***

Another few months had passed. Hideyo Ittosai agreed to teach Nyoko and Daichi and kept marveling at their zeal for knowledge. They worked harder than any of his experienced students, heeding to every word.

And even though they clearly lacked the physical

conditioning, required of a kenjutsuka, there was something intuitive about how they understood the discipline. They clearly had the ki. After one of the trainings, sensei Ittosai invited the two for dinner. Daichi and Nyoko cleaned up and walked through a sliding door into a traditional Japanese room with tatami mats on the floor, a low table and cushions in the middle. Sensei was expecting them. The meal was already served. Nyoko and Daichi politely bowed and took their places at the table.

"How is your training going?" asked sensei to break their shyness.

"Good."

"Very good."

"That's good to hear. Are you getting what you expected from it?"

"Yes."

"I think so."

"Maybe."

Sensei laughed.

"You don't seem too sure about it. What is your goal anyway?"

The kids looked at each other but were hesitant to speak.

"Ok, I've had it with you. You train as if your life depends on it. Don't get me wrong, I love your dedication. But kenjutsu is a path of a lifetime. You need to pace yourself."

"We don't have much time..." mumbled Daichi. Nyoko gave him a restraining look.

"You are young. You have all the time you need." The silence was too overwhelming to ignore. Sensei realized that something serious indeed was going on between the two.

"Alright. I will open you a secret. The window you've broken... It was a cheap replica. I just wanted to teach you a lesson. Plus, I wanted to hire some maintenance people anyway. I've been saving your salary since day one. Look! It's yours! You can go if you want." With those words, sensei extracted a wad of cash and placed it on the table before the two.

The look of genuine surprise and shock washed over their faces. "Sensei, you want us to leave?"

Nyoko sounded mortified.

"You can stay if you want. But I need to know the truth." Nyoko decided to speak up.

"Sensei, there is nothing strange about us. We just want to train. We love it so much."

"Right, Nyoko is right," agreed Daichi.

"Alright then. Let's eat and I will tell you a few stories." Sensei passed the plates and loaded his.

"This temple is very old and special. I believe you know that much. A lot of energy is concentrated here, powerful energy. It helps a warrior to find his ki."

"We've read about it."

"On Wikipedia."

Sensei smiled.

"I see. So what do you know about Ito Ittosai?"

"Everything!" exclaimed Daichi. "His ki was strong! He was the greatest warrior."

"Yes! He knew how to walk the rivers of Mushin..."

"... and stay safe..." added Daichi bitterly.

"Oh, I see you've done your homework. Ito Ittosai was a legend. He discovered that with a lot of training and mental discipline he could transcend the traditional kumitashi. Once he was attacked in sleep, and he reacted instantaneously. He overcame several of his attackers without thinking, subconsciously. When he analyzed that fight, he realized that something other than the pure skill of a samurai was at work. He called it Mushin."

"Yes, sensei, we have read about it!"

"There are some things that are not mentioned on Wikipedia. Ito Ittosai was the son of the greatest samurai of

Shōgun Tokugawa Ieyasu himself!"

"Oh wow, we did not know that."

"There is more. In 1604, a Portuguese merchant named Jose Brito arrived in Japan and became friends with Tokugawa. He promised to create him an army of unstoppable samurai, if Tokugawa followed some simple conditions. One of them was to restrict other foreigners from the Japanese lands, *and to keep that fact a secret.* I bet you didn't know *that.*"

"We had no idea..." agreed Daichi.

"Tokugawa thought that Jose Brito knew witchcraft or was talking to the gods. He knew deep secrets of the universe and could make amazing predictions. The wealth of his knowledge was beyond anything any human on Earth could know at that time."

Nyoko's eyes got big and Daichi gasped for air. Daichi whispered to Nyoko.

"He knows! I think he knows!" Sensei had a sly look on his face, but he continued.

206

"Well, somehow Jose Brito knew which warriors had ki and which didn't. He told Tokugawa that sometimes ki transfers from a parent to a child, but it needs proper training to flourish. It is also a dangerous gift because it can make the warrior sick. In order to leave no traces to the project, Jose Brito suggested a new rule should be added to the samurai code of honor. Any samurai who became sick was considered a disgrace to the Shōgun and needed to take his life honorably. This was a useful ploy because it left no traces of the experiments."

The kids listened with their mouths open.

"Well, fascinating, isn't it?" asked the sensei. "That's it for that story. But you haven't eaten your meal. I have some beautiful artefacts in this temple. There is something I'd like to show you. I'll leave you for a minute while you are finishing your meal." The two nodded and sensei left the room.

"He knows! We have to tell him!" urged Daichi.

"Maybe you are right... How long can we do it on our

own? We really have no idea how to operate the oscillation gene."

"*Shhhh!* He's coming..."

Sensei walked in with a large porcelain saucer in his hands.

"Look!" he exclaimed. "This saucer is 400 years old! It depicts 24 most famous Tokugawa's samurai. The Smithsonian museum in America offered me three million dollars for it!"

"Oh my god!" exclaimed Daichi. "Seriously? And you just walk around with it?"

"Yeah, why not. I'm a kenjutsuka. My coordination is impeccable. Here, take a look, it's Ito Ittosai!" The sensei passed the saucer to Daichi but it was heavier than Daichi expected and it fell straight to the floor, crashing into three big chunks. Daichi and Nyoko screamed in shock. Nyoko closed her eyes with her palms and accidentally wished the saucer would put itself back together. And in that instant, the chunks of the saucer drew to each other like magnets, and the whole saucer jumped back into sensei's hands.

"What did you do, Nyoko?" screamed Daichi, but Nyoko shuddered and fell to the ground, thin line of blood running from her nose.

"Oh dear!" exclaimed sensei. "How long has she been using ki?"

"She will come to her senses momentarily. So, you knew!"

"I suspected. I've trained fighters all my life and have not seen such intuitive ability in such weak, untrained bodies. I knew it must be it!" Nyoko opened her eyes, Daichi helped her to get up. "How are you?"

"I... am alright. A bit dizzy. Did I just? Oh no..."

"He tricked us, Nyoko. He knew."

"Suspected!" corrected sensei. "But my suspicion proved to be true."

"Oh no..." Nyoko felt so foolish. "That wasn't an ancient expensive saucer, was it?"

"I'm afraid not. It's from the gift shop."

***

An hour later, Hideyo Ittosai was still listening to the fascinating story being recounted by these two ordinary Japanese young adults, whose life had been turned upside down by the discovery of their ancestry. Everything was fitting together like a puzzle. For Hideyo Ittosai it confirmed his suspicions that Jose Brito had not been human after all. However, he had previously hoped him to be a more benevolent creature. When he learned about the ruthless murder of the woman named Fah, because she had come too close to the secret of Brito's true identity, Hideyo grieved. "The faith of our ancestors was right. Ki is everywhere. It is in every particle of living and inanimate objects. This potential is within us. Gods are not what we used to think..."

"Sensei, you must help us to direct our ki to save Fah, just like I fixed that broken saucer..." bleated Nyoko.

"Oh dear kids, I hope you realize that you are risking your life. Our secret scrolls mention certain powerful kumitashi that could bring a dead person to life. They were practiced by the samurai to protect the Shōgun's life during the battle. But these mental routines take so much ki, that the ones who perform them must give every last drop of it."

"Sensei." Daichi respectfully stopped him. "We know. Fah had a lot of research. While she was working on the project with the wealthy pharmaceutical tycoon, she had plenty of resources. We don't know the exact kumitashi that must be practiced, but we do know that they would take a huge strain on the body. If I understand correctly, it is as if our bodies receive a lethal dose of chemicals or radiation, I'm not sure exactly."

"Well, there is more to that. The kumitashi itself requires both samurai to die simultaneously. And since you will drain your ki to zero, you won't be able to save yourself. Have you heard of kiri-otoshi?"

"Of course. That's the technique that made Ono-Ha Itto-Ryu school so famous."

"Well, the technique that we are talking about is based on

that move. Two samurai face each other and approach at the same time. While in kiri-otoshi one samurai prevails, in aiuchi both samurai fall."

Nyoko and Daichi grabbed hands. They knew that performing such complicated oscillation they will die from the various ailments, but they did not expect to kill each other in real life.

"So, what do we do now?" asked Daichi of Nyoko.

"We train even more vigorously than before. Then we fight"

Year 2047.
Osaka. Japan.
Ono-Ha Itto-Ryu Kenjutsu Temple

Another year had passed. Nyoko and Daichi had both changed beyond recognition. Not an ounce of fat was left on them, only lean muscle and flexible joints. On that Saturday, the two were receiving an unprecedented honor: black belts. It normally took years for any other student to achieve the black belt, but Daichi and Nyoko were anything but normal. Ki was percolating in them. The two communicated without words. Their reaction was so fast that during the fight even the sensei could not tell who scored the point. And for the most part, Daichi and Nyoko were dead even. They were like two pieces of one puzzle, and if their lot in life was to fight another enemy, they would have been unstoppable.

209

But they had to fight each other, and to the death.

The students in the temple greeted Daichi and Nyoko with a celebratory parade of their skills, but the centerpiece of the display were Daichi and Nyoko themselves. Their black belt performance blew everyone's minds. According to Ito Ittosai, samurai had to grow in ki all their life, learning the techniques until they became ingrained in them and they could improvise. Daichi and Nyoko transcended those techniques. They fluently spoke the language of katana.

After the ceremony, Daichi and Nyoko went for a walk to the river. As proper samurai, they had their two swords with them, tucked behind their belts. It was spring, and the air was intoxicatingly fresh. Everything blossomed. The two walked along the river hand in hand, not saying a word. They were overwhelmed with everything: the belt, the spring, and their love, all mixed in their hearts in a crazy cocktail that made them feel drunk on life. And yet, the time was approaching when they would have to give it up.

Neither regretted their decision, but that realization made every living breath more special.

They sat down under an old cherry tree. The grass under it was fresh. The sky had a surreal color to it: blue mixed with light pink and lilac, so tender and so vivid, as if created it with water colors.

The two looked at each other and they knew.

If there was ever a good time for two young people, madly in love, to end their life, it had to be then. The two cried silently, kissed and smiled. And cried again. Until the tears were all out, and kisses were no more. There were only melancholic smiles.

"I love you, Nyoko. Always. Forever. In any universe."

Nyoko was all choked up. She hugged Daichi really tight and whispered something in his ear, something that only the two of them knew.

Then it was time to fight.

The two warriors put every emotion behind them and only saw a fierce enemy in each other. Their faces – until this moment so filled with love and longing for each other - were now mental shields. Their katanas were drawn and they clashed, slicing the air with a sibilant hiss.

Attack - block - attack - block.

Slice – cut – slice – cut.

Blood dripped from the multiple small cuts, and their kimonos turned into rags. All a raw bloody mess, neither of the samurai could strike a victorious move. It was obvious that aiuchi was meant for these two equally strong and skilled samurai: neither would accept defeat, and no option of a draw was available. When it was time for aiuchi, both knew it.

The two took a few steps away, readied themselves and screamed their final war cry:

"For Fah!"

"For Fah!"

And pierced through each other's hearts.

Year 2045.
Tokyo, Japan

Something imperceptible caused Fah to open her eyes. She looked to her right side and saw Veronica Starr, wrapped in a white sheet, like a feather fallen from an angel's wing. She was peacefully sleeping. Fah's heart skipped several beats in a row, then went racing as if catching up. Very quietly, Fah exited the bedroom and went to the small kitchenette to make a cup of coffee. The burner stove made a small whistle, which oddly reminded her the sound of katana. She scooped the ground beans, added them to an old-fashioned pot, and filled the pot with water. As the coffee simmered, Fah watched the bubbles forming shapes. They looked like two samurai dancing in a deadly fight. Transfixed with the dance of the coffee crema, she again overlooked it and it spilled up over the stove. Managing to save a good portion of it, Fah filled two cups and returned to the bedroom.

211

Back in the bedroom, Veronica was propped up on the pillows, still wrapped in the sheets, with a completely charmed smile over her face. Fah couldn't quite believe the transformation in the previously perpetually stoic and business-oriented woman she'd known for some time.

"How did you sleep, sunshine?" asked Veronica in an unusually husky raspy voice.

"Good. You?" Fah felt completely out of her element. Seeing Veronica all smiles and warmth threw her social radar. What was she supposed to do next? Get back in bed? Kiss her? Or too much too soon? *Just play it cool,* she thought, when Veronica got up and, losing her sheets, approached her.

"Coffee. Thank you! Love it. This is how I want to wake up with you every morning. Except we will be taking turns on making coffee."

"Every morning?"

"Yeah. Unless you have someone else on your heart and this was just a comfort fling for you."

"N-No, no no, who me? No..."

"Okay then!" laughed Veronica. "Get back in bed."

Fah obeyed. Veronica indulgently sipped her coffee. Fah looked at her and couldn't bring her eyebrows down.

"Aren't you going to ask for sugar, or cream, or soi milk, or whatever?"

"Nah. I don't need that nonsense."

Fah's heart melted. Finally someone who *understood* coffee!

Veronica continued her gleeful chatter.

"I had everything planned, but you woke up first and kinda ruined it."

"What did you plan?"

"I was going to sneak out early, go home, change, order us a table in some nice upscale restaurant. I'd meet you there for breakfast. But most importantly, I wanted to arrange your security for the time being, until you decide what you want to do with the Project."

"Yeah, security..."

"Sorry for bringing it up. My official response to you is to stay with Nakamura, that he will protect you, that the project is too important."

"And unofficial?"

"We live only once. And I can't afford losing you. Not now. Not anymore."

"I see. But wait. What do you mean now?"

"Now that you are finally in my arms, and we don't have to run circles around each other."

"I didn't notice you running any circles around me."

"I'm just really good at it, dear."

... And then Fah's memory returned, as if she remembered the details of one horrible dream, a dream that never happened!

Nyoko!

Her own death...!

And then...

... being drawn back to the light by two angels.

Nyoko and Daichi! They did it! They mastered the Mushin flow! *They saved her life!* It was such an emotional realization that Fah started wailing and crying, completely confusing Veronica, who blurted out:

"What did I say?"

"It is not you!" sobbed Fah and hugged Veronica. "Nyoko is gone! She... she..." Fah could not put it into words. "She faded..."

***

After those last words, Fah typed "FADE TO BLACK", a direction to fade out the scene of her feature screenplay. "Honey, I did it! I finished the scene!"

"Oh my god, congratulations, dear!" exclaimed Veronica and ran in from another room of their luxurious penthouse.

"Should I open some chocolate wine?"

"Yeah, in a minute. Come over here, I want to read it to you."

Some time passed, and the two were hugging each other, reminiscing over the crazy events of their past five years, how Fah had become a trendy best-selling fiction author and was now working on the screenplay adaptation of her smash hit about alien conspiracies and two young samurai finding their way to Mushin, in order to save their friend's life.

"Honey, I think there is an Oscar waiting for you".

"We shall see. Why do you think stories of aliens spying on us is so popular? Is it because humanity subconsciously suspects it?"

"I don't know, dear. All I want to know is that they are *not* spying on us."

Veronica and Fah for a moment looked out the window of their prestigious Bangkok apartment. If smog were to make its way to the 86th floor where they lived, they'd simply move. Now they had the means to do it. But so far, they had enjoyed a piece of the sky above the grey smog blanket.

Everything seemed blissful, except for the pesky little fly crawling on the window.

214

7
LOVESICK

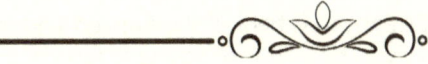

YEAR 2325.
MONROVIA, LIBERIA

Ny sat in the living room, drowned in soft afternoon light. Tears welled in the corners of her eyes as she gripped a tiny flat object in her sweaty palm. A holo-recorder. Seventy-year-old Anika Borgess sat in front of Ny, quietly sobbing. She gave up on trying to compose herself while delivering the news of Otis' destiny. Ninety-year-old Ny looked young for her age, but Anika barely looked forty. Citizens born on the Fourth Orbital Colony were a mystery to the rest of humanity as if they concluded an unholy alliance with the spirits of death.

217

"Fifty years..." Ny uttered and broke into tears. "Fifty years I carried imaginary conversations with the father of my child, trying to find out what went wrong! Why now?"

Anika looked Ny straight in the eyes and whispered: "I am so sorry..."

"Otis died not knowing he had a son. Derek has children of his own now. Five children. Otis would be so proud..."

"Five? Ny, what I am about to tell you is hard to believe. You must keep it in absolute secret."

"What exactly are we talking about?"

"The file you are holding in your hands is a diary, Otis

recorded it after his arrest. It was confiscated. I spent all these years trying to get it back. He made me promise that I would give it to you."

"Is he dead?"

"Oh... I'm afraid it's a long story. But first, let me ask you this. Does your son or any of his children experience recurring, vivid dreams?"

***

When Anika left, Ny remained sitting in the living room for hours, until the sun disappeared behind the horizon and the room sank into a velvet cloak of darkness. Outside the panoramic window of her living room was a view of the pier. The boardwalk was lined with street lights that illuminated the white foam thrown at the shore at regular intervals. Fifty years ago, Otis and Ny had enjoyed the same view of the Atlantic Ocean from *Anglers* restaurant, sharing the intimate bond of new lovers. Feelings of excitement, longing, and sexual desire had enveloped the two like a cloud. There, at *Anglers*, Ny had talked to Otis about his strange recurring tsunami dreams, but all she could think of was his warm, well-defined body, and his touch on her skin, the way his short beard felt on her cheek... and on other parts of her body.

218

She was dizzy, drunk on sensations, and irrationally self-absorbed.

She was lovesick.

Losing someone in the moment of greatest emotional attachment was the worst thing that could happen to a person. Love like that never goes away. Feelings never fade. In fact, memories become obsessive, all-consuming and unavoidable. They possess the grieving person for the rest of her life, like ghosts, like never-ending nightmares. Fifty years later, Ny had become used to living with the feelings of all-consuming love, grief of a loss, and an obsessive desire to look at the faces of every man in the crowd, like a puppy that had lost its master. It was sickening, nauseating, and completely unavoidable. Even when Derek had been born, or Derek's five children, which had given Ny the highest happiness she could possibly experience, these feelings of grief and loss had never gone away. They played over and over like parallel tracks of two different songs, one happy, and one devastatingly sad, and both created a distortion, muddying each track and turning them into noise.

Ny's life had become a noise. That was why she almost preferred grief. That way she could focus on one track and savor each note, each sound, without any interference. And now she was about to listen to a real sound track that would finally play in harmony with her grief. It scared her. She didn't know how much grief her heart could take at a time.

Otis' diary most definitely would overload the limits of grief Ny was used to.

But it was a risk she had to take.

In the quiet dark room, the ninety-year-old woman placed the recorder on the coffee table and pressed 'play'.

DAY D+3

I made my living on space history and space mythology. In human ethos, they always come from space: big ships in low orbit, panic, laser beams evaporating crowds of mortified people. Sometimes we think of aliens taking human form: blended in, studying, spying, or even altering us to their secret agendas. The reality is more unbelievable than fiction. Three days ago, on October 21, 2275, the aliens emerged from the Atlantic Ocean on the Liberian coast. My name is Otis Solarin, and this is my eyewitness account of the First Contact.

I am writing these notes from jail, where the coast guard soldiers booked me for trying to save their sorry asses from starting an inter-galactic war, but, as the saying goes, there is no prophet in a homeland. In all honesty though, I can't blame them for doing what they did. It is not every day that aliens walk out of the ocean. It has been three days since I was thrown in my cell, in such a rush they even forgot to search my belongings. My v-pad wristlet remains on me, powered by my body heat, so I will not run out of charge merely recording these notes... well... as long as I am alive. So, recording notes is all I can do. Actually, it is the only thing I can do to remain sane.

Over the past three days, I have not seen anyone outside my cell except for one SEMI-AI guard. He is just standing there, staring at me with his single blue eye planted in the middle of his faceless head. There is precisely zero chance of getting any information from this fella, thus I remain in complete oblivion as to what is going on outside.

Are we conquered yet?

Are we at war?

Maybe the entire human civilization is already extinct, and I will never find out about it. This SEMI-AI will provide me with food for as long as it is in the storage, or someone overrides his current instructions. It is unheard of in 2275 to keep someone in detention for three days without any further investigation, and all I can think of is that I was simply forgotten. Something is definitely going on out there, something big enough to interfere with all the automated processes in place. Normally even before an offender reaches the jail, their file is already cross-referenced through various databases in terms of risk assessment. From then on, a quick decision is made to bring the file before the judge or not. Spending three days in a solitary sell is highly irregular, this is why I suspect something has gone terribly wrong.

220

DAY D+4

I am currently flying on board of the presidential aircraft, filled with various military advisors. A lot has happened since my last entry. They took the video of the First Contact that I recorded, but they did not find my notes, because I accidentally started writing them in my history lecture file. I will continue writing my notes in this file, because it appears to be the only way I can keep a record of the events. And the events are stranger yet. Yesterday I finally received my first visitors in jail: a military General and his bus boy. "Apologies, Dr. Solarin, for keeping you here for so long, but I am sure you can understand that what was going on a few days ago brought an end to any sort of 'normal' that the humanity was used to."

"I imagine so..." I reluctantly agreed.

"I am a General so-and-so (I did not remember his name), and I am here to talk to you about the Voyager record."

"What about it?"

"First, how did you realize that it was the record from the 20th century spacecraft?"

"Are you serious, General? I teach space history in the Robertsport University!" The General uncomfortably cleared his throat. "Now it is your turn to do some explaining. I was here for three days, and have no idea what the hell is going on! Are we invaded? Why did our soldiers initiate fire?"

"What makes you think *they* initiated fire?"

The General gave me a suspicious look as if laying a trap.

I bluffed. "I was there, remember?"

The General cleared his throat the second time. "I have to admit, that our soldier committed an irregularity..."

"Are you kidding? He panicked? That's it?"

"The situation, as you could tell, was ambiguous," said the General defensively.

"Is this how you are going to spin it for the public?" All of a sudden, I saw it all too clearly. "Of course, how can you admit that the biggest diplomatic fuck-up in human history was committed because some idiot soldier panicked..."

"Dr. Solarin, watch your language. Last time I checked, you are booked for assaulting a military person during a combat situation. If we decided to get creative with the books, you could go down for aiding the enemy."

"This will not stand in any court!"

"In any civilian court it might not stand, Dr. Solarin. But the entire Earth Nations Federation is under a martial law. There are no civilian courts left."

"So we *are* under attack, aren't we?"

"Mmm... It is more complicated. First, you must sign this

non-disclosure agreement."

And he passed his iPad through the bars requesting my fingerprint.

"What if I don't want to?"

"Like I said. Your choice is either working for us and sign this confidentiality agreement, or go back to the company of the SEMI-AI. I'm sure you two will spend many wonderful years together."

"This is insane! I have rights!"

"Dr. Solarin, cut the crap already. Humanity entered an uncharted territory. Some collateral damage is bound to happen."

Needless to say, I signed their damn confidentiality agreement.

According to it, I could not talk to the public about anything related to the First Contact or especially about the Voyager's record. Apparently, they concealed this small detail from the public. Sometimes I wonder whatever happened to the other guy who recognized the record. I hope he was given an option to cooperate with the government, otherwise this is the darkest hour of humanity, and like the General said, some collateral damage is bound to happen.

222

"General... I need a favor. I was there with the woman."

"Yenplu Obungo."

"Where is she?"

"She was looking for you. She showed up in every government office she could think of."

"She is alright then!"

"She is."

"Can I talk to her?"

"I'll think about it. In time, perhaps."

"Can you at least carry a message for me?"

The general finally exhaled and slouched back.

"Dammit, Solarin. You are going to be a troublemaker, aren't you?"

DAY D+5

Technically there was no invasion. What I have learned over the past two days was that the aliens simply disappeared after our soldier overreacted and opened fire against the direct orders of his superiors. In a sense, I understand why he opened the fire. When the music started playing and the box with the record emerged from the side of the alien 'submarine' craft, anyone could panic. Nobody ever was trained for anything like that. The most remarkable and classified piece of information I have learned was how exactly the First Contact ended. When the smoke and panic subsided, the box with the record was found on the beach, half-buried in the sand. It was immediately tested for potentially harmful substances, and once it was cleared, it was delivered to Rabat, the headquarters of the Royal Moroccan Fleet.

In one of the classified and isolated bunkers, where I am assigned to work as a *civilian extraterrestrial consultant* (don't be raising your eyebrows, I'll explain it later), this record is currently studied by a swarm of useless quasi-experts. The case seems to be rather simple: the clear container, in which the record was kept, was engraved in various human languages: HUMAN LOST, UNKARI FOUND. This simple statement led to a few profound conclusions, and despite how complicated my fellow top-secret researchers tried to make it, the case was simple:

223

First, our visitors are an alien race called Unkari.

Second, they know us very well, and we can be sure of it at least on the basis of them going to the extent of translating this phrase to 18 our languages.

Third, they basically responded to an invitation that our ancestors so carelessly extended 300 years ago. Finally, at least for now, they came with peaceful intentions and attempted to establish diplomatic relations, but, as it became obvious, the meaning was lost in translation. The military keeps a tight lid on the details, but the Pandora's box was opened, because a few dozen scared-to-death tourists and Liberian locals remained at the scene and broadcasted the whole event live. After some deliberation, the military decided that it may be for the better, because fear is very useful for controlling huge populations.

Almost without any resistance, the civilian government of the Earth Prime, six Orbital Colonies, and several extra-terran colonies surrendered authority to martial law and delivered it in the hands of their military generals. I am isolated from the news and cannot communicate with anyone on the outside. Every day we receive a 15-minute briefing on what they think we need to know about the world in general, after which time we collectively consume gallons of coffee and mountains of club sandwiches, poke around the lab and mainly gossip, pretending we know what we are doing. Rumor has it that the military conducted the widest sweep of the ocean and extensive search of nearby space, and no trace of any aliens was found.

They vanished into thin air.

DAY D+18

224

No real news to date. The new-coming science folk told us the news from 'the outside': civilian unrest caused by the clashes between the 'Stop Them' and 'Welcome Them' groups. Violent outbreaks occur all over the world. It appears that the activists are not well organized yet, and the military is trying to keep it this way, but the tension is growing with each passing day. The aliens vanished, and some believe that we 'deeply offended them', as the result we are deemed unworthy of further contact. I personally find it hard to believe, because if they studied us long enough to learn 18 of our languages, they probably already figured out that our species are knit from contradictions, and it didn't stop them from contacting us in the first place.

I have a lingering suspicion that I keep to myself. What if they predicted our course of action? What if they wanted us to somehow overreact? What if they played us like poker virgins?

It's a lot to assume from this little piece of information, but it is not too far stretched. I fear that they dragged us in a waiting game, and something tells me that they have plenty of time to spare.

DAY D+56

Some new people joined the research club lately. The rumor is that the Earth Nations President and the Congress leaders are in hiding. Something is not right and they are not telling us. It's been far too long since I was forced to join this club, and since then we ran all possible tests on the record, to the point that there is absolutely nothing left to study on it. We positively verified its authenticity, and beyond that we could not do much. We are going nuts here. A curious fact was discovered by a former citizen of the Court Orbital who is the linguist for the Royal Moroccan Fleet. Apparently, one of those languages belongs to an old 15th century manuscript. Not sure what the fuss is about it. But once the news broke out, this gal, Anika, was isolated from our worthless sandwich-eating club. I haven't seen her in days.

***

Ny's red face with dried streams of tears was illuminated by the blue light from the holo-recorder, as she hugged the pillow listening to the voice of her lover, the voice she hadn't heard in fifty years. The recording was interrupted by an incoming video call.

225

"Hi mom, how are you? I saw you were online, why get up so early?"

"I haven't gone to bed, Derek."

Ny's hoarse voice gave away more than she wanted.

"Mom, is everything alright?"

"Son, can you please come over? We need to talk."

"Sure, but what is it about? Are you feeling ok, ma?"

"I'm fine, it's not so much about me. It is about your father."

8
KISMET

Year 2325.
Monrovia, Liberia

Derek was driving on a freeway from Congo Town to downtown Monrovia, where his mother owned a fashionable loft with an ocean view. The freeway weaved along the coastline, where an endless body of water threw angry shards at the coast, as if saying: "I despise you!" The ocean and the shore are eternal antagonists.

Walking into Ny's apartment, he was pleasantly greeted with the earthy scent of herbs and aromatic oils tucked in myriads of little clay jars all over the living room. The coffee table was decorated with giant candles which still burned bright despite the morning sunlight overpowering their timid lumenocity. "I came as soon as I could, Ma."

229

The digital clock on the shelf marked 7:45. Ny's eyes were puffy, her face gave that motionless stare that indicated a person after the first wave of distress had passed, as an aftershock of exhaustion took over the body. Derek sat beside her and tenderly kissed her on the cheek – it tasted salty. "Derek, I know what happened to your father. At least I am about to find out."

Ny motioned to the holo-recorder on the coffee table - the recording on pause.

"You *know something* about his disappearance? But... *How?*"

"Last night I had a visitor. Her name was Anika Borgess. Apparently, she worked with Otis in the Royal Moroccan Fleet headquarters in Rabat."

"I thought dad was a history professor."

"He was. We worked together. The military recruited him in the wake of the First Contact."

"I cannot believe it! All these years, the missing person's reports, private investigators, archives... Why didn't she come forward earlier?"

"She said she couldn't. The materials were classified, and the recording was taken away from her."

"So, what did you find out?"

"You didn't miss much so far, I am still listening."

Ny briefly retold the content of the recording up to that point.

"I can't wait to hear more!" exclaimed Derek.

"Me too, son, me too." Ny beckoned him to resume the recording.

DAY D+86

Today a major development occurred. Apparently the Unkari ships were noticed in the orbit of Titan. Our briefing was unusually long, during which we learned our telescopes which observe the area around Titan recorded the Unkari fleet appearing out of thin air. One second there was nothing, and then, they appeared one by one. Where did they come from? Did they simply remove some cloaking device, or did they use some wormhole or other method to instantaneously materialize in our space, no one could tell. The nervous energy here is palpable. Nobody seems to know what to do or how to explain any of this, and this helplessness gets on everyone's nerves.

DAY D+92

It is still a waiting game. I am more and more convinced that the Unkari are toying with us. This suspicion is so solidified in me that I am unable to see things any other way. I am biased now; and thus, I am useless. But I cannot leave either. As a side note, I think the military is experimenting on us with a new type of torture - the Club Sandwich torture. If that is our key weapon against the enemy, we shall prevail.

DAY D+93

A major development was announced today after the dinner, when we were all summoned to the conference hall. We were presented with an audio recording, on which, in numerous Earth languages, the aliens requested negotiations. This probably was too much to handle even for the military, and the decision was made to make this information public. As always, the military PR machine milked this to their benefit and added a little bit to the original alien message. Namely, they said that the aliens made it a mandatory condition for the negotiations that peace on earth among various battling fractions was restored.

DAY D+94

It was 6 am in Rabat when we were summoned to Conference Hall #1 to receive the instructions. I didn't know then that I would be headed for Reykjavik with a group of researchers to meet with the aliens. Someday these notes will make a fine book, but I may not live till the day they declassify the whole thing for a book to go public. Since I don't have any children of my own, my legacy has no real meaning to me. Still, I will continue recording in the hope it gets to Ny someday, regardless of what happens to me.

Anyhow, Reykjavik was chosen by the Unkari as a place for the diplomatic neutral zone. I suspect that the aliens had a great deal of inside knowledge when they chose this area for the negotiations. Reykjavik is uninhabited and isolated, with the temperatures on the surface never rising above -50C. Humans abandoned this area since 2190, when a misguided effort in dealing with the global warming resulted in a chemically facilitated Ice Age. Ever since, the majority of the world population moved to the orbital stations, and the Earth Nations began an active space colonization program. Over the past 100 years, the Big Ice has showed signs of recession, and overall, we are hopeful that someday humanity will return and re-inhabit places like Europe and North America, but it will not happen in my lifetime. This is why the choice of Reykjavik was brilliant. No civilians can make their way to these ice-covered wastelands of extreme temperatures and snowstorms. The only way to get there is via private air transport, and obviously not many people can afford that, not to mention the dangers associated with piloting in zero visibility and extreme weather, so the issue of crowd control resolved by itself.

It's past midnight here, we arrived to Reykjavik about two hours ago, and are resettled in the temporary habitation modules, which is a fancy word for a six-person igloo with sleeping bags, a mobile kitchen and a sanitation unit. It's cramped, and my neighbors are cranky and anti-social scientific types with egos that simply do not fit in such tight quarters. I should also add, unlike me, all five of them fought to get on the team to Reykjavik. Mans and Andrea are from the 3rd Orbital Colony. They are the descendants of Norwegian and Spanish immigrants, evacuated to the Orbital stations. They were career military consultants in numerous overlapping fields, but from what I understand, astrophysics was their main focus. Tess was a native Nigerian, a renowned expert in biology and biochemistry. Liam was an officer of the Royal Moroccan Fleet, and although technically he was a military medical doctor, I suspect that he was here to watch over us. He exudes this particular forced friendliness that makes anyone want to stop all conversations when he walks in.

Finally, the most mysterious team member here is Anika. Unbelievable as it is, she is from the 4th Orbital. This space colony is headed on their own course of evolution, and rumor has it that the genetic enhancements they practice are beyond anyone's wildest dreams. Anika is probably in her early 20s, a librarian type that looks like a world-class athlete. I've heard that the Fourthers are obsessed with knowledge, and Anika is no exception. She makes Mans and Andrea sound like high school dropouts. And the thing is that Anika seems to be ok with humiliating them. I wonder if she does it intentionally, either that or the lack of social contact with the rest of humanity that the Fourth practices is the real cause. The first diplomatic meeting is scheduled in two days. Our mission is to sit in the audience and make all kinds of observations. Liam is hinting at the security risk and makes everyone jumpy about it, but I doubt anything would happen to us at that point. If they wanted to harm us, they've had more than enough opportunities.

DAY D+97

Wow... Where do I even begin? Today was the day. We met with the Unkari delegation. In short, what happened today, made the generals reheat that flippant threat of charging me with treason. After what happened today during the meeting, I was summoned to the interrogation office and questioned for three hours by numerous nameless people in suits. All of them were asking one question: what is the nature of my relationship with the Unkari? Of course, I have no relationship with these aliens, but what happened today made me suspect that we all together are missing a bigger picture – we are all assembling a giant puzzle with a handful of pieces and without the guiding image of the end-result.

233

***

The meeting room was equipped to the specifications transmitted by the aliens. It looked like a large lecture hall with all of the scientific community settled in the audience. The seats were equipped with integrated standard-issue pads. We received a unique login code that allowed us to access various databases and keep the records. My quick estimate was that about 150 scientists were present in that room this first day. My own relevance was quite relative, but since I posed a threat of exposing the military mistake during the First Contact, I was dragged alone. Officially I was an expert on alien cultures, xeno-anthropology as they called it. How I received this title? Due to my book about the portrayal of alien cultures in science fiction. So in reality I was an expert of made-up aliens. How this expertise was going to be relevant with the real aliens, was a complete mystery to me. The center of the room was equipped with a cylindrical area which was connected to the floor on one end and to the roof on the other – a 'fishbowl' tube if you wish. The roof was retractable - this is how the aliens were supposed to show up. The security was stationed every few meters around the room, and I suspected that more of them were present mixed among the civilians.

As we were explained during the briefing, the cylinder was equipped with special climate conditions, to the specs provided by the aliens. The chamber was filled with a gas composition based on methane and some other elements. It was maintained at an astonishing temperature of -140C, which was 30C warmer than the aliens requested, but apparently we were not able to comply with this requirement on such a short notice. If the cylinder's integrity was compromised, the difference in atmospheric pressure and temperature between the room and the cylinder could be life-threatening. That is why *all* projectile weapons were removed. The soldiers were only equipped with shields. Whether the shields would hold against the aliens, nobody could tell, and any guess was merely a speculation. The room was incredibly quiet. Everyone readied their recording devices and anticipated to witness history in the making.

234

At one point the room was flooded with soft white light and we all closed our eyes taken over by a surprise. It was on the video records that we saw what happened. Instead of entering through the retractable roof, the aliens appeared from thin air and landed on the floor, which all of a sudden became elastic, like stretched rubber, and they softly landed on its bouncy surface. Whether they manipulated space or the matter of the floor, we have no idea. When the light subsided, we opened our eyes and saw three aliens, two meters and change tall, wearing spacesuits and those horrifying three-eyed helmets. They were standing upright, like humans, but had six limbs in total: two for legs and four for arms, if you could call it that. The climate-controlled chamber was equipped with microphones and we could hear from speakers placed around the room, the sound of their alien greeting. It sounded like a metallic screeching. But then they turned on a device that translated the message into English – which had been agreed upon as the official language of communication with the Earthlings.

"We come in peace," said one of the aliens, who we thought was in charge. "We are looking forward to a treaty between your and our species. If you display peaceful intentions, this union will be beneficial to both races. If you attack us again, we have the power to destroy you, but most likely we will simply terminate this relationship and watch your species on your course to self-destruction".

A Vice-President of the Earth Nations, Eduardo Akura stepped forward and addressed the aliens. "Dear guests, we welcome you to Earth, the cradle of human civilization. We hope that from now on our relationship will be free from misunderstanding and we can start all over again, moving toward the goal of our mutually beneficial treaty."

The alien speaker looked to his right and received a sign from his peer, this was when I realized that the real leader of the delegation was the alien who stood to the right and remained silent. This insight made me feel uneasy, because it was likely that the leader of this alien delegation did not consider us worthy of a personal address. "Your proposal is acceptable, human, and we, in turn, suggest establishing a cross-cultural exchange group that would allow us to learn more about each other" – the translation came from the speakers. A silence established after the last words of the translation came through, and Akura decided that it was his turn to speak.

235

"Your proposal is acceptable. We will establish a group of the best representatives of our race: scientists and politicians to work with your representatives."

The alien again looked to the peer on his right, and they exchanged some non-verbal messages, after which he spoke. "This proposal is unacceptable." The audience gasped all at once. *"We* will choose two representatives among those present in the audience."

"This is not the best idea..." began a flabbergasted Akura.

"This is a critical point in our negotiations. Don't make another mistake, human representative. The outcome of our negotiations depends on your decision to comply with this request." Akura stood in bewilderment, frowning his eyebrows and scratching an itch on the back of his head that was not there. In his earpiece he received a message from someone outside the room, and finally he spoke.

"We agree. Who do you choose?"

The alien spokesperson raised one of his limbs and projected a beam of concentrated light into the crowd. When the first pick fell on Anika, I wasn't surprised. She was smarter than anyone in the room, so it only made sense. Anika was sitting in the same row, about five meters away from me. Then the light started travelling in my direction and finally stopped dead on my seat, flooding my eyesight. "We have made our choice," spoke the alien. "Tomorrow we will take these two humans to our ship. Have them ready in this room in exactly 24 standard Earth hours. We will broadcast the technical details later." And without long good-byes, the trio disappeared from their cylindrical chamber in a flood of white light.

***

236 I've spoken to Anika, and she thinks that the choice was random and that they are trying to just stay one step ahead of us. Although it makes some sense, I firmly suspect that there is something else to this choice, but have no way of verifying my suspicions. I have 4 hours left to sleep, before I need to get ready for the visit tomorrow. The med bay gave us some sleeping pills so that we don't waste time counting sheep. For once I think it was a good idea. As soon as I save my log, I will take the pill and try to get some rest, god knows, I will need energy tomorrow.

DAY D+98

It is late in the evening now. I spent a full day going through one shock after another: first, meeting the aliens on their ship, and second, being interrogated upon my return. I am between a rock and a hard place. At this point I feel that if the aliens were not so insisting on my importance to the diplomatic mission, I most likely would be thrown in jail again.

DAY D+567

I haven't kept this log very well for the past year. A lot has happened. Today was the day when I received the treatment. Apparently, I am a carrier of a unique genetic ability. Unkari call it oscillation. Ny, if you ever get this log, well... remember my tsunami dreams? I know the truth now. Through the recurring dreams, in which I repeatedly went through multiple horrible deaths, my brain tried to exercise preparing to activate the oscillation. Through the treatment that I received today from the Unkari, the oscillation ability in my brain was activated. What is oscillation, I bet you'll ask? Now that I received the treatment, I will be able to change reality. Small things so far. For example, if we went to a casino, now I would be able to predict red or black on the roulette. Every time, no failure. When I get stronger and master my ability a bit better, I will be able to predict even a zero. Ny, we would be rich!

I am currently among the Unkari research team, on their ship orbiting Titan! The views here are incredible, Ny. We are close enough to the surface to see the methane oceans and lingering methane fog that gives the most beautiful auroras you've ever seen! I am here with this gal I told you about, her name is Anika. Apparently, she deciphered an ancient language from the 15th century that turned out to be one of the Unkari dialects. Now she is the only human who can speak Unkari, and that is why they requested her as a liaison as well. The problem is that our government became very difficult to deal with. Every time Anika and I returned from our meetings with the Unkari, we were interrogated, required to write lengthy reports and asked questions we had no answers to. It's not like the aliens opened us the secrets to the universe! It was not like that at all. Usually we were paired with an Unkari, who would talk to us about what it's like to be a human. They wanted to understand us. Honestly, even to this day I have no idea if we walked ourselves into the largest trap in human history, or if this is a great opportunity for us. The Unkari claim they want to reach an agreement with us – to share our space in the galaxy. Apparently, their galaxy, Sagittarius Dwarf is being absorbed by the Milky Way. In a few million years, their home world will collide with the solar systems of our galaxy. I know, it makes little sense – the event is so far away that not only will humans likely become extinct before that time, but even our stars will be gone. Why negotiate with us? Why move into our space now? I am asked these questions every time the military interrogates us – and I have no answers.

What I couldn't tell the military is about this oscillation gene. Don't judge me, dear. They would lock me up like a lab rat. And if you know about human history as much as I do, you will easily imagine what a witch hunt is coming up for those with the gene. We will be hunted down, rounded up, and dissected in every imaginable way, honey. I had a choice: to trust humans or to trust aliens. History will show if I was right, but I know enough about human history to not trust our military. Call it genetic memory, if you will.

Remember, we talked about it in the Anglers restaurant, the last day when I saw you. That moment froze in my memory like a petrified leaf in a drop of amber. It's immutable, it's treasured and savored, dear. I remember everything...

238

When the Unkari felt comfortable enough with me to reveal why they requested me for the diplomatic mission, they told me about the oscillation gene and offered cooperation. I could decline, but I agreed. Yes, dear, I am aware that it could be a false choice, that perhaps I was manipulated into it, but I really could decline the offer. I could have stayed. Maybe they learned me too well, still I feel like the choice was mine. I volunteered to help the Unkari to study this ability. This research will bring a lot of good to both our races. The Unkari say that oscillation is a uniquely human thing. They cannot do this, and none of the species they've met can either. Don't you see, honey, we have an opportunity to find out why are we here in this universe, where we came from, because this ability has lain dormant in us throughout the entire course of our evolution. We just were not ready to use it. Our bodies had no capacity to withstand the chemical surges of an oscillating brain. The Unkari believe that I may be ready. They say I may be the very first human who would do this and survive.

I see the future, Ny. I see the future so bright that it's blinding me. I see the golden age of humanity where we conquer accidents, disasters, uncertainty, and can make better choices. I see the future where both our races live side by side in this pocket of our enormous universe.

Do I have regrets? The only thing I regret is that we couldn't make a family, and have children of our own. They would inherit the oscillation gene. They would experience what I experienced through the power of oscillation, and I only started! Who knows what I will be able to do! Save people from needless deaths, broker diplomatic agreements, avoid accidents and natural disasters? Maybe all of it!

Ny, dear, this time I am not returning to Earth. I will leave with the Unkari, to live among their people on their home world, to learn from them and to explore my newly discovered ability. Please forgive me, my dear, but one way or another, the military would never let me go. I suspect they already told you I was dead; if not, they will soon. They would never let me go because of how much I know. And because of this oscillation. I am afraid that if I came back, I would accidentally reveal my ability in a moment of fear, because that is when it works the best. They would interrogate me, they would hit me, and I would spontaneously oscillate, and it would be all over for me. I don't yet have a good impulse control over this ability yet.

239

One way or another, my life and freedom is in jeopardy. On the other hand, I have an opportunity of a lifetime to do what I am good at - to record history. Any historian in my place would jump on this opportunity without hesitation. I will give my log to Anika, and she will find you as soon as she can. Ny, I will always remember you, no matter how far away I will be. You are my sunshine, you are the only one, and there will never be another. I take the memory of you with me, to another galaxy. I'm sure by doing this we will break all sorts of records for a long-distance relationship! That should be worth something... I wish I could stay... I wish I could take you with me... I wish I could change things... Someday I may.

Meanwhile, I will be smiling at you from the night sky.

So long, my love. Until we meet next time...

***

The recording was over. Derek and Ny were in shock, tears streaming from their swollen eyes. Quietly, Derek got up and walked to a book shelf at the corner of the living room, which was covered with antique paperbacks from floor to ceiling. Here and there, the shelf was decorated with fashionable ebony carvings – African animals, statues of people, intertwined together in either dances or passionate love scenes, he could never tell. Derek reached toward one of the upper shelves and pulled down a cardboard box tucked on top of the books. "You want to play Kismet? Now?" Ny smiled faintly. Derek had loved that game as a kid. He could never get enough of it, and became quite good at it. He would ask Ny to play over and over again, often saying that he thought he could make the dice obey his command. Ny would always pretend to believe.

"I want to show you something, Ma." He extracted a black velvet pouch from the box – five white dice rested on his palm. He shuffled them in the palms. And rolled them on the coffee table saying: "Kismet of three." And they both watched the dice turn until each side showed three dots on the top surface.

"Wow, son, that's pretty good."

"Ma, watch again. Kismet of six."

And he rolled again.

As if in a slow motion, all five dice delivered the predicted number six.

"Kismet of one."

And sure enough, all five dice rolled one.

It went on and on, Derek rolling and calling the numbers, never once missing.

"It's a fine party trick, isn't it?" he said, Derek smiling bitterly. "At least now I know that I inherited it from my father." Some time passed by in silence, which Derek finally broke. "I don't know if it's the right time to bring it up, Ma, but what the hell. Let's just get over with it."

"What is it, Derek?"

"I've been to the doctor."

"Because of your nose bleeds?"

"Right... It's a tumor, Ma. I have brain cancer."

Three centuries later...

PART
TWO

9
DEATH LOOP

"Shhh...Quiet, River."

"What can I do? I sneezed. I think I'm allergic to this moss."

River patted the lush growth stretching on the floor of the abandoned Salonimite mine. "I'm not supposed to be allergic to anything, I thought it's impossible, but this alien flora..."

"Shut the hell up already or I'll chop you for steaks myself!" When those words left my lips, I realized just how odd a statement it was. We were hunted by slimy, stenchy monsters on an enemy planet, and had had nothing to eat for so long, that somehow my grunt made sense.

247

River startled for a second, probably weighed just how resolute I was to chop him up. I knew he didn't dwell on that one for too long because he lip-synced, *Fuck you, asshole*, peeking from the Salonimite ore pile with his sniper rifle pointing in the direction of the dark tunnel. The Unkari were close. *Well, back at ya, you little prick.* But right at that moment we had much bigger problems than River's insubordinate demeanor and filthy mouth. I could taste Sodium and Iodine in the air, a sign that those stinky sons of bitches were near. Erinozhan was a dumpy little planet not worth losing our lives for, but we had our orders. It had been eight days since the Royal Moroccan Fleet had been squashed like a Serzarian cockroach. For the first seven days or so, I had thought I was the only survivor.

The transmitter didn't work, and I had no clue how to fix

the seventh-gen subspace modules. See, by the time I graduated from the Academy, my high school q-entanglement theory was hopelessly obsolete. Moreover, I'm a soldier, goddamnit, and picking apart state-of-the-art paraphernalia was not how I spent my Friday evenings. Even if I could fix the transmitter and send the signal, I know now that the Unkari would intercept and triangulate it right back to my location.

Evidently, they'd intercepted us since we had landed on Erinozhan. When part of our platoon had fallen behind, we had transmitted the details for our retrieval, which solely hung on the element of surprise. Surprise had not worked, and we had walked into a trap. Those ogres who called themselves "Holy Warriors of Lenar Unkar," or some shit like that, hadn't even broken a sweat capturing us. Although, that's not entirely true. Unkari always sweated, regardless of what they did. So yeah, they leisurely sweated when their dampening field scrambled our ammo's hard drive. When clubbing the enemy with our useless rifles did us no good, we were forced to surrender. The son of a bitch disarmed me while casually munching on his field rations. I almost gagged when he approached within a yard's distance - the air reeked of Unkari sweat.

Later we had tried to run and were shot in the back like wild game. I even suspect they allowed us to slip away. Maybe it was the day for target shooting in the Unkari unit. When running, something had struck me on the back of my head. I staggered. It had felt like a coconut shot from a canon. Not that I know how that would feel, it's just the imagery that had popped into my head a fraction of a second before my lights went out.

I came to my senses, unable to move anything but my eyelids. At first, I thought that my limbs were missing. As it turned out, I was buried in a ditch left over from the Salonimite extraction. I was not covered with soil as I first thought, but with dead soldiers in full combat gear. Luckily, my cat suit was functioning so I received a steady flow of oxygen. For seven long days, I hid in the mine, surviving on pre-packaged nutrients. Lucky to pick a few capsules off the dead soldiers, I was covered for another ten days or so. River, however, stretched his two-day supply as well as he could, but when I found him in one of the tunnels, he was trying to slit his wrist in order to drink his own blood. Talk about desperate! It was a good thing I got there when I did. Obviously, he was not thinking straight.

I barely knew River. We had never met off duty. He struck me as new, maybe it was even his first mission. Either he was a rookie, or just neurotic. In any case I thought, *We need a new HR director. Who the hell staffs a top-secret mission with such a neurotic mess?*

It's a miracle he survived at all. A miracle, and nothing more. Lucky bastard. Now there were only two of us left alive, and only he had a weapon, which he refused to part with, quoting a paragraph from the regulations. Even the argument about my extensive sniper training did not work, while River couldn't hit the broad side of a barn.

This mission just kept getting better.

*****

Back behind the ore pile, River pointed his gun towards the winding tunnel. I tried to run an infra-red scan, but Unkari were cold-blooded and the only two warm bodies in the 50 meter radius belonged to River and myself. It was a pointless task, but I had to do something, because without the gun I felt naked. Finally, River alerted me with a hand signal, which looked like something he picked up from a movie rather than combat training. I rolled my eyes, but the headgear covered my face, so River could not see my annoyance. Soon enough I saw them coming around the corner. Despite wearing protective headgear, my eyes watered from the stinging air composition. The truth being, that even if River gave me his gun, it probably wouldn't change a thing. The Unkari took us prisoner after he fired a single shot and the enemy's dampening field kicked in.

*****

"What do you think they are going to do to us, Mazula?" River asked, stretched out on the dirt floor of the gated holding cell.

"I have no idea. But whatever it is, it better start happening. This guy outside the gate stinks up the whole place. Tell me Ensign - you're an engineer. How the hell does our headgear filter poisonous atmosphere, but not their hideous smell?"

"Selective filtering. The logic is that soldiers need all their senses in combat. Research suggests that we are still too related to primates in an evolutionary sense. Although we are in space and cannot breathe the local air, we can smell some elements of it, to the extent that they are not interfering with our vitals."

"Bull! This smell interferes with my vitals! What if I throw up under my cat suit?"

"Oh, you haven't before? I personally do not recommend it. *That* smell stays as well."

I considered that last bit of trivia for a moment and decided that I had to do something before I drowned in my own vomit. "Hey!" I yelled and threw a pebble at the Unkari guard. "Stop your filthy sweating! Haven't you heard of deodorant?"

The Unkari leapt from the floor and hissed. I was just warming up. My military shrink always said that bottling emotions was unhealthy. Right there and then I felt that expressing myself to this ugly bastard was long overdue.

"Mazula, what the... What are you doing?" whispered River, but it was too late.

250

The guard barged forward and in two short leaps wrapped his clammy tentacles around my neck and arms. I was gasping for air. Luckily, River threw himself at the Unkari from behind, delivering a formidable punch to his head. The bastard staggered. He let go of my two arms in order to grab River, who continued punching him from behind. Trying to shake River off his back, the Unkari shot his snake-like paws at him. His grip around my neck softened, and I watched River evade those paws with uncanny speed and precision. I made a mental note to find out where River acquired those wicked combat skills, while gouging my fingers into the Unkari's eyes. They turned out to be rather sensitive, because the bastard belted a high-pitch squeal and went after me. Meanwhile, River took another shot at the monster and drove a sequence of hooks into his skull. Finally, I heard something crack. The guard was startled at first, then slowly loosened his grip around my throat and slunk to the ground, unconscious, or perhaps even dead. I did not bother to check. I gasped a few gulps of air, pushed the limp tentacles off me and bolted towards the gate to see if other guards were arriving. "Okay, River, I'm impressed."

River as well thought that he did a great job too. He performed a triumphant dance over the alien's body, thrusting his hands in the air and cheering. "Did you see that, Lieutenant? Did you? These new-gen uniforms with muscle-assist exoskeletons are smokin'... I could never do that on my own strength. I mean, I have wrestled big guys in the Academy before, but this was Unkari, you know, with all their limbs, and they are so much taller too! Nobody ever knocked out an Unkari before. I am the first ever..."

"River, goddamnit! Do you need a formal invitation? After you!" I pointed to the exit.

We ran around the corner and sprinted down the empty corridor, while feverishly formulating a plan. Being stranded in another galaxy, you can't simply catch a ride home.

Wait a minute.

Maybe we could catch a ride after all! The Unkari must have some sort of transporters on the surface. Whether we could figure out how to pilot them remained to be seen. We ran away from the holding cell thinking about potential issues associated with stealing an Unkari transport, when...

251

All of a sudden I found myself in the same holding cell, in exactly the same position, right before I threw the rock at the guard. There was no transition, no physical sensation, and no time dilation. Nothing. One fraction of a second we were running, and another we were back in the cell. For a second, I thought that the whole escape was just a hallucination.

River and I looked at each other.

"You noticed it too, didn't you?" whispered River.

"I did. Any ideas?"

"Not a clue. It's as if we went back in time."

"River, I was not the brightest kid in science class, but I think time travel is essentially impossible."

"You're right. It *is* impossible. That is, outside of the pairs of entangled particles that communicate their state to each other over distances spiralling back in time and adjusting their state. But I wouldn't even call it time travel in the first place! This is the fundamental quantum property of the universe. In its basic structure, the universe is fluid and uncertain. This is, however, impossible for non-quantum bodies, Anything bigger than a particle..."

"Ok, ok, I don't understand any of it. I count on you to figure it out."

"Oh, no, no, Mazula, I'm not much of an expert. That's just a random piece of knowledge."

"What's your military occupation, you said?"

"I'm just an entry level engineer. Theoretical quantum physics is way over my head."

I looked at him in disbelief. Either he was shitting me or he was delirious, on top of neurotic. I had no time to argue. "Okay, one step at a time. Let's see if that guard has any memory of this event." River nodded, and I picked the pebble again. "Hey you, piece of rotten cheese...yes, I'm talking to you, motherpupper." I yelled and threw the rock. The motherpupper probably did not have the knowledge of the previous time we did this, or so I thought, because he barged in all over again. This time, however, he drew a laser blade.

Maybe he did remember after all.

It all happened too fast.

A tentacle wielding a blade stretched toward me as the alien approached. Half a second later, my brain vaguely registered a sharp hit across my neck, and I blacked out.

The next instance, I found myself in the very same cave, with River jumping off the floor and grabbing my shoulders. "Are you ok?"

"Yes, I'm fine. Why? What happened?"

"He slit your throat Mazula! You were dead for about two minutes on the floor with your blood all over the place. Heck, I had your blood all over my uniform."

"You cleaned up nicely."

"How can you joke like that? He killed you a minute ago!"

"You said, two minutes."

"Well, yeah. But what difference does it make?"

"All the difference, River. I need to know how long this loop cycle is. Next time..."

"Next time? *Next time??!* There may be no next time! You can't expect to just keep coming back from the dead!"

"Ensign River, you are beginning to piss me off. Get your shit together. We are dead sooner or later if we don't get out."

"I see your point, but still, I wouldn't purposefully try to get killed, if I were you."

"How old are you, Ensign?"

"Why?"

"Stop acting like a child. Now, next time, clock the loop. I need to know, if we are going back or forward in time, and how long this whole event lasts."

***

Thirty loops later, we stopped counting. Over that period of time, I was killed roughly half the time. Half of the time, the Unkari soldier received a crack in his skull. Here is what we learned. First, the loop lasted about three minutes. The countdown started at the moment we tried to piss off the guard. From the moment he barged in we had three minutes to get out. After three minutes we both ended up back in the cave, no matter how far we made it.

Second, if we did not engage the Unkari, time passed and nothing happened. Once we spent seventeen hours waiting, and nothing happened at all. We were getting weak and hungry. My rations were taken when we were captured, so our provisional situation was dire. We decided that we had to act, otherwise we'd just starve to death.

The third conclusion followed from the second one, and it was stranger yet. We were not going back in time. Radiation decay does not lie. River's atomic clock counted forward, and

10
CAGED

"Mazula, you said you'd chop me for steaks..."

"Uh?"

"Would you really eat me? I mean, if I die first. Would you?"

River was fingering the slippery wall of the Salonimite mine, where we were kept hostage. The Unkari guard was still outside the barred door. I had no answer to River's question. I was preoccupied with thoughts on how long our military uniforms could keep recycling waste products and generate breathable oxygen. Normally, a mission should not last longer than three weeks. It wasn't the most efficient uniform, but it was made specifically for the deep space missions - like this one on Erinozhan, where there was no breathable air for human biology. Normally we would get a drop of spare resources (everything from nutritional packs, air and waste filters, medicine cartridges, and such); but we were being kept hostage, and our clock was ticking.

257

In the absence of my participation in River's existential gastronomy musings, he persisted. "I gave it some thought and decided that you... well, I think you should. I mean, if your moral code demands permission from me, if that would make it easier for you, know that you got it. There's no shame in wanting to live."

"River, what on earth are you talking about?"

"You have my permission to eat my dead body, what

else? Haven't you been listening?"

"No, as a matter of fact, Ensign, I haven't. I'm busy thinking about how to keep us alive."

I was about to lose the hell hounds on this officer, but when I turned to face him, all my bravery was gone. River rocked himself, hugging his knees and passing a barely audible humming sound.

"River, listen to me, you are not going to die."

"I already died seventy times. I had my throat cut three times, my lungs pierced twice, my neck broken three times, suffocated once, but mostly shot... I could write an encyclopaedia on near-death experiences. Mazula, if only you could understand, I remember all of them. Isn't this ironic? All of the injuries in the loops were undone, but my broken ankle from almost a week ago remains broken... If I believed in hell, I'd say this should be it."

"But you didn't really die in those loops."

"It felt real to me. Hurt real, too. Weren't you afraid of dying?"

"I was." I honestly replied, but could not think of anything else to add, suspecting that it would only fuel his derangement, so I went back to the assessment of the situation.

Breathable air would not become critical for another ten days or so. That's plenty of time. Our cat suits were damaged. All things considered, it was a critical advantage. Exposed to -190C and Erinozhan's methane-based atmosphere would be lethal.

Our food situation obviously sucked, but it would not become an emergency for at least eighteen hours. The water situation was getting critical, but we still had time. In the worst-case scenario, we could take a small amount out of the cat suit circulation. Normally, it would be an extremely bad idea, because our oxygen supply depended on that water, but in the absence of options, any idea was workable.

I also considered the possibility of a rescue mission. The problem was that our mission was beyond classified.

Officially, the Unkari and Earth Nations were not at war, at least no missiles had been fired. Yet. But we knew that the Unkari had designs on our quadrant of the galaxy. For an old and extremely long-living species as they were, they considered their home galaxy, Sagittarius Dwarf, which was being slowly swallowed into the Milky Way by the gravitational pull, a legitimate real estate situation. From the perspective of humans living an average 150 years, that was ridiculously overdone strategic planning. For the Unkari, it was nothing more than responsible nation-building. With that being said, our top-secret intelligence mission was to keep silent for two months - the entire time it takes to reach Erinozhan from Earth - carry out the intelligence mission, and come back.

None of the 380 officers and 240 civilian tech-support folks, who stayed in the orbit escaped Erinozhan. I remembered E. N. Obama, the run-down Galactica-class vessel, being dragged out of the shipyard of the orbital recycling station specifically for this mission, so that nobody could ever flag the assignment. Officially, E. N. Obama was decommissioned. Officially, our entire crew was quarantined on Dzhu-Imani orbital, on the outskirts of the remote 87th quadrant, where the quantum tunnelling communication grid (which we called the com tunnel) was not installed yet, and the data exchange was carried at regular light-speed via Morse. That meant three years and change for any word to reach the nearest outpost with the com tunnel, which in turn would forward the data via the broadband subspace to the Earth Nations headquarters. In other words, our silence had a reliable cover.

259

I had a painful flashback of the E. N. Obama being blasted into nuclear dust. When its shield started collapsing due to the impact of the Unkari missile, portions of its body flickered in and out of vision in the sky. I was hiding in the pile of methane snow, keeping surveillance through a small perforation, just big enough for my portable telescope to feed the video of my surroundings on my retina, when suddenly I was blindfolded by a white flash that illuminated everything on the dimly-lit surface, with nuclear-scale brightness. One of Obama's fusion reactors was breached. How do I know that only one of eight reactors was affected at first? I zoomed on the ship and saw the hull of a giant vessel popping like a firecracker dead in the middle, spewing what looked at first like colourful confetti, but I knew better. They did not die in an instant, as would be the case if the entire fusion reactor chain collapsed simultaneously. Poor civilians, one way or another persuaded to sign up for this audacious mission, were tossed in the vacuum like wedding rice.

To my knowledge, nobody survived. Nobody but the newbie Ensign River and myself.

There will be no rescue mission. Ensign River was all the help I could hope for. Between his leg injury and scrambled brains, there was not much help to be expected.

***

"What would you eat first?" River raised his voice again as if echoing my assessment of his togetherness.

"You mean, if you..."

"I mean when I die, Mazula. And it will happen soon. I had spent seven days on two-day rations. My leg is infected. There is no damn thing good for eating on this planet. Let's get real here. Indulge me, would you? What would you sample first?"

"River, spare me, I may throw up, and I have nothing in my stomach."

"I think you should start from the hip. I am pretty sinewy otherwise. Used to be a runner for the Academy team."

260

I did not reply to that last one. To be honest, I knew that River was going through the motions being captured and all, but his panic was not helpful. I had to concentrate on the plan. For the umpteenth time, I went over the mission details in my head.

First, why was I here? I was sent to Erinozhan for a classified intelligence operation of the Royal Moroccan Fleet. The Earth Prime Senate delegated us to follow up on the intelligence that the Unkari possessed advanced technology and were testing it on this abandoned Salonimite facility. What the technology was, we didn't know. All we had to work with were the intercepts that our analysts put together like bread crumbs from the bread basket. For all we knew, the Unkari were celebrating a formidable accomplishment in advancing their project, which, supposedly, would give them leverage against us. The confusing part was in the fact that in sheer brute power and technology, the Unkari already exceeded humans. The workable hypothesis was that the Unkari looked for the ultimate solution that would bring their victory without losing a single Unkari life. Our xeno-anthropologists claimed that, due to their extremely long life span and low birth rate, the Unkari valued life much higher than the human race.

Second, what did I know about the location? Erinozhan was actually a large moon of the fifth planet orbiting a K-class star of the Sagittarius Dwarf galaxy. The proper astrometric designation I did not remember, and normally I wouldn't need to. The chances of a ranking Lieutenant like me needing to navigate through galaxies were slim. Now, on second thought, I probably should have paid attention during those briefings. Oh well, no point on chewing on the same dead cat.

Man, I must've been hungry for having such gourmet thoughts. "What the hell," I thought and walked to the barred door.

"Hey you!" I yelled at the guard. River jerked and looked at me pleadingly.

"I can't take it, Mazula. No more, please..."

The guard rose from his makeshift stool and hissed at me.

261

"Yes, I am talking to you, fucking tripod. I need food! You understand me? Where I come from, starving prisoners is considered a war crime."

I looked at the guard and he looked at me, slightly tilting his head to the side.

"River, I think he knows what I am saying. This is different. This time, we won't run and see what happens."

"I can't run anyway. Not with my blooming gangrene."

Meanwhile, the guard left and returned within a few minutes. He came back carrying a box about twice the size of a regular shoe box. Approaching the door, he retrieved his combat knife and, pointing it at us, opened the gate and slid the box through.

We shrugged, but I decided to roll with it, and picked up the box. It was heavy, black, matte. Its texture reminded me of graphite. While we were scratching our heads as to what this box was supposed to mean, the perimeter of the cave lit up with a green glow, and something of a cylinder glass environment descended from the ceiling.

"What the..."

"This can't be good, Mazula! What do we do?"

"Hang tight! We don't have many options!"

The cylinder tightly connected with the floor, enclosing us in a test tube of sorts.

All of a sudden, the air around us hissed, and the gravity rapidly decreased. River and I slowly floated off the floor and hung in mid-air.

"Mazula, they are gassing us," screamed River.

"They can't gas us! The cat suit provides complete climate control." Indeed, every inch of our body was covered with elastic semi-organic material. Frantically River pressed his palms to his face, as if reassuring himself that the protective headgear was securely in place. "Remember your Academy training, we ran rapid decompression and purge cycle scenarios. Brace for impact, remember?" River did not respond, evidently completely frozen in the face of possible suffocation.

"Ensign River! Respond!"

River did not respond.

"Ensign River, damnit, comply with the training sequence. Brace for the purge cycle."

"Bracing for the purge cycle!" cried out River, and his voice modulator quivered because of his high-pitch cry. Meanwhile, the purge cycle was over. The capsule filled with some gas composition, and we smoothly descended on the floor. River collapsed to the ground, grabbing the base of his foot. He was in pain. The uniform was initially equipped with analgesic and blood-clotting compounds that automatically were released based on the pain indicator scan. A few hours ago he had red-zoned on meds, which had turned him into a raw nerve. I glanced at the back side of my wrist accessing the B5 monitor and requested an environmental scan.

"River, are you ok there? Check your B5 for the environmental data."

River complied and immediately perked up.

"It's breathable. I cannot believe it," whispered River.

"Yes, it is. What is that supposed to mean? First, I asked for food. Second, we received the box. Third, we received a human habitable environment."

"They want us to remove the headgear. Maybe they want to poison us after all."

"Maybe. Although it doesn't make sense. What's in the box?"

"Well, if they want to poison us, this is poison."

"Could be. However, think of how many times this strange space-time loop has repeated, yet this scenario is different."

"I've been thinking, Mazula. I don't think it's a space-time loop. It's something different. Entirely different..."

"Oh yeah? Wait, River, let's figure out what's going on at the moment first. I say let's check out the box."

263

"Alright. It's your call."

Could it be that simple? Could they bring us food in that box? It made sense. The Unkari knew their enemy well enough to know that we could not remove cover in the hostile methane-rich atmosphere and without removing cover, we could not ingest anything that was not military rations pre-packaged to be delivered through the uniform.

I had only one way to find out, so I retracted the headgear.

Sharp breath.

"Oh?" River gasped, but would not say a word further. *There it goes again.*

"What, Ensign? You have issues with trans women in the military?"

"Mmm no, not at all... You are just so..."

"Big? Tall?"

"Yeah... I just assumed... But I don't mind..."

I was annoyed. Ok, so I wasn't the most petite trans woman, I get that. Just a dash under 7 feet tall, I wear XXL uniform size - more than one standard deviation from most women in combat. This is what you get for spending most of your life bulking up in the military and not getting on blockers earlier. And, by the way, my transition was not over. Although I was planning on having more intervention sometime in the future, I didn't want to interrupt my service. While on active duty, you get only so much leave time, so the process was slower than I expected. But for crying out loud! Do they always have to react like that? If I was a tiny sophisticated missy, they wouldn't give a damn. But this pressure to conform to a gender stereotype really gets on my nerves. I am not going to stop being a soldier just because now I have breasts. See, I don't make fun of River for needing a bar stool at a dinner table, do I?

Ok, ok. Stop it, Desiree. You are better than that...

I knew I had to let River off the hook. I went through this with my buddies and even though they were supportive, it was not easy for them to accept a woman into their testosterone-reeking man-cave, even though I was one of them for years.

"Relax Ensign, I get it. It's not like I wear my identity on my sleeve. But hey, we have other things to talk about now, don't you think?"

"We sure do..." said River mysteriously, and added: "How is the air?"

"Try it yourself. It's... well... it's wonderful."

"I'll wait, if it's all the same to you."

"Suit yourself. But I need to figure out what is in this box." I picked it up again. It was about one kilo in weight, with a small black button on top.

"Hey you there! Yes, I'm talking to you, Lenar Unkar Warrior."

"Mazula, it's not a diplomatic cocktail party."

"Shhh River. This is the first time he did not hiss at us. Yes, Lenar Unkar Warrior, I am talking to you. What does all of this mean?"

The Unkari looked intently at me and made a limb gesture, sliding it towards his jaw and down the neck. *"Hfoooo,"* whistled the guard.

"Hfu? You mean, food?"

"Hfoooo. Umn Ukrishn."

"Food! Human nutrition!" exclaimed River. "No way! All this time we just had to ask?"

"Evidently so." I pressed the button on top of the box. A cloud of steam ushered out of it, emitting a smell of... well, the closest description would be boiled grass. River hopped closer. He stretched his wrist towards the box, pointing the B5 for the composition analysis.

"It's definitely organic. Terrestrial organic, I mean. Carbon, hydrogen, oxygen, ok... It's analyzing. A bunch of minerals, plant-based protein, fiber, fatty acids. It's going over the database looking for the match. Mazula, I'll be damned, it's a synthetic approximation of spinach and beans, all scrambled, but the composition is really close."

265

"That's good enough for me!" I said and checked the pot for a spoon. A spoon was obviously too much to ask, and I scooped the green goo with my finger, studied it for a second, and finally delivered it into my mouth. "I bet the grass in my yard tastes better. River, come here, man, let's eat before we start dying again."

River positioned himself close to the pot, still wearing the headgear.

"Man? So ... you don't know. I know it's against protocol and all, but I tried to hint you all along."

"What are you talking about, bro?" I was busy trying to scoop semi-liquid goo with my finger.

"I'm no bro to you."

"What? You prefer Ensign River?" I chuckled.

"It's not that. I'm more like a sister to you," said River and retracted the headgear.

I lifted my eyes from the pot, and lost my jaw. The military policy was explicit on gender parity, to the point that we never see each other on the mission without the fully equipped uniform and voice modulator. That's why River never suspected who I was. At the end of the day, you stop wondering who is who, and think only about the mission. It is truly easier to do your job this way. But damn. I guess I was caught in stereotyping myself.

"Ensign Ebony River, nice meeting you, Lieutenant Mazula."

"Nice meeting you, Ebony." I was awe-struck. So River was a woman.

Big deal. It was not the gender that shocked me. And not her incredible purple eyes and purple braided hair, and not even the completely surreal beauty of her face untouched by this gruelling mission. I could not imagine that I was serving with someone from the Fourth Orbital Colony.

"I see, the eyes gave me away." She smiled.

"A little. Fourth Orbital! I'll be damned!" Their tribe was reclusive and pacifist and would not want anything to do with the military, even if their life depended on it. And so much for the simpleton military engineer, Ensign River! About one hundred years ago, the Fourth Orbital legalized the full-force genetic editing of every expected child. Without any exaggeration, the 4th were the brainpower of humanity. I bet my boobs she knew everything there was to know about quantum physics. But why would she hide this from me? No. Can't be. Or can...

I remembered a huge diplomatic scandal, that broke out about two years ago, involving an eloping citizen from the Fourth. These brainiacs could never leave the orbit, this was against their law. And when this one requested asylum on the Earth Prime, the Fourth had a temper tantrum, threatening to stop providing knowledge services to the Earth Nations

Confederation. Nobody took them seriously, because they had no weapons, no military, and fully depended on the rest of the colonies for supplies. What could they really do to us? Stop writing books?

Well, that's not entirely fair. The Fourth serviced all the terra-formation processes in the galaxy. Without their expertise, none of our rapid progress would have been possible. Everyone was happy about their help, and having them work from the comfort of their home didn't bother anyone. I guess as the generations passed since they self-imposed their home arrest, we did not expect to have much in common. They probably solved Feynman diagrams before breakfast, what can you possibly talk about with a person like that?

Anyway, long story short, the Earth Nations did not turn in the deserter, and the Fourth never stopped pouting about it, although personally I am not sure what it meant in practical terms. I know that the identity of the deserter was concealed, and that was the end of the story for the rest of us. And now I was sitting in front of the best kept diplomatic secret and watching this unicorn, Ebony River, scoffing the green alien mush.

"Stop staring at me, Mazula. Start eating."

"Desiree."

"What?"

"This is my name."

"Nice name." A pause followed as we silently regarded our meal.

"What's a brainiac like you doing in a place like this?" I asked.

"It's a long story."

"I'm sure."

"And for the record, normally I wear prosthetic facial implants, and nobody can see my face. But when the attack on E. N. Obama started, I had to evac, and had no time for that sort of stuff. It is by pure luck that I was going through parachute training on the holodeck, that's why I had a pack on my back, when the ship core burst open. I dropped from the low orbit. Anyway, what I am trying to say, Desiree, now that you know who I am, you must keep it a secret. My life depends on it."

"Don't worry, Ensign, your secret is safe with me."

She smiled faintly. For a few moments we were solely devoted to the green goo in the pot, and perhaps to our own thoughts. I was thinking about our identities, and how many of them are hidden, sometimes even from ourselves.

***

Ten years ago, I was going to get married. She was the most beautiful woman I'd ever seen. We did not make it to the ceremony. She died in a flash fever.

Sometimes I think that my continent is cursed. AIDS, Ebola, malaria. We've dealt with those. But no matter how clever we get, there is always something around the corner. They say that the flash fever was a strain of Ebola virus - a whole lot deadlier though. We didn't know how the virus picked its victims. Some were just fine coming in contact with it, others died within hours. Their lungs burned into crisps. My baby, Desiree, was among the unfortunate.

268

It was a rehearsal evening. She was wearing a shimmering dress of pale gold. It made the surface of her body look like a glittering lake. One moment she was laughing and drinking champagne, and another – she collapsed on the floor, coughing blood. Her beautiful dress was covered with red stains. It was as if my songbird was bleeding, snared in razor wire.

Everyone ran away as if they saw the face of death itself. Maybe they did. I had no time for death. I sat beside my baby and cradled her in my arms for the longest 20 minutes in my life, looking her in the eyes, swallowing tears, and telling her how much I loved her.

The disease did not take my body, but it did take something so big, I could not put it in words. Until three years ago. Desiree's death finally gave me the courage to look inside and realize that I lived like an off-balanced Russian doll that could never stand upright. Something in me was off kilter. It was always there, and I could not ignore it any more.

That was when I went to court and officially changed my name to Desiree Mazula. I took the official documents to our HR Director, requesting to adjust my file accordingly. Then I took medical leave to adjust my body as well.

When I returned, some of my buddies, ever so gently, asked if I did it to keep her memory alive. I thought about it, but concluded that that was not the case. First, I fell in love with her, then we were planning to getting married, and then I was dealing with her loss, and all this time I had no opportunity to think of who *I* was, other than in relation to other people and institutions. A soldier. A son. A future husband. Maybe even a father. All those qualifiers didn't tell me who I really *was*.

Once the grief subsided, I found some clarity; everything fell into place. As for my new name, well, Desiree is just a beautiful name. It's that simple.

***

Ebony scooped the remains of the food from the walls and sat the black box aside, looking at me. It looked like she was going to say something important, when I heard the familiar hissing sound of the purge cycle.

"Suit up, Ensign! Brace for the impact!" I yelled, following my own command.

The next moment, we were floating in mid-air, arms grabbing knees, like two hedgehogs in a pond. The glass cylinder capsule was lifted, and the methane-rich atmosphere restored. This time, our landing to the ground was not so smooth. I landed on River, causing his –*her!* - leg excruciating pain. She groaned, and her off-key voice, processed through the voice modulator, was truly heartbreaking.

Another minute or two later, we heard heavy steps moving towards us from the depths of the cave. The sound of their footsteps bounced off the slippery rocky walls and vibrated, trapped under the tall ceiling, unable to find a surface to absorb it. When the footsteps approached closer, the sound became notably shallower, less resonant, and soon died out in front of our holding cell. Three Unkari soldiers joined our guard at the gate. Curtly sharing a few vocalizations between each other, they opened the cave. The gate banged the rock wall as it was flung open by one of the newly arrived guards. I knew little about Unkari emotions and expressions, but it appeared like the guard was impatient. With their high-powered rifles targeting our every move, they commanded us to exit the cave and follow where directed.

About one kilometre or so into the tunnel, we stopped before a foreboding dark cave. It must have been enormous because our steps created a full, resonant echo that seemed to live forever. I closed my eyes to allow them to acclimate to the darkness. When I finally opened them, to my utter horror, I found us standing at the brink of a bottomless canyon.

The Unkari stuck their rifles in our backs, and one of them commanded: *"Shoom."*

"This is it, Desiree Mazula. I'd say it was a pleasure knowing you, if not for the circumstances. Had we met in a different place, in a different time, who knows, we could probably get along," said Ebony wryly.

"I cannot believe it, that shitty soufflé was our last supper. You putrid, foul, rotten, slimy piece of shit of a race! You want me to jump?" I yelled, trying to turn my head to the Unkari standing behind me, but the suit restricted my range of motion.

270

"Shoooooom Umn!!!" hissed one of the Unkari, nudging me with his gun. The hard jolt to my back made me stagger towards the edge, where the rock was loose, and I slipped. I heard Ebony yelling at the Unkari words I did not realize they knew back on the Fourth, but it didn't last long. The last thing I heard was silence.

11
FREEFALL

"Umn tarted vo vat fo."

Enveloped in bright light, I struggled to open my eyes.

"Umn vo at Unkar vat fo."

Here came the voice again. I knew I had to open my eyes. I looked up and saw a cloud hovering over me. I squinted to see past the cloud and freaked out. I was not looking up, as I thought at first. Without any visible bonds, I was floating face down at least fifty meters above the floor. It was hard to say exactly how high, because I had nothing for a reference point, but it was high enough to know that, in case of a free fall, I'd be as good as a sack of scattered beans. I could hear water dripping on a rock surface, like a metronome, keeping tempo to the waves of my panic. The place was dim, and the brown rock walls had a wet sheen to them. I tried accessing the B5 and pulled my wrist into my field of vision, only to meet a formidable resistance. My entire body was immobilized.

The minute I realized how high I was above the floor, electrifying fear penetrated my body. Generally, I was not afraid of heights, this was something they tested you for in the military because soldiers routinely experienced zero gravity. However, some rational part of my brain screamed that hovering in zero G was not the same as hanging above the floor, with no apparent strongholds, when gravity clearly was pulling me down.

As if that itself was not a reason to panic, I felt the cloud swirling around my face, leaving cool prints in spots of contact with my skin. Because of that clammy feeling on my skin, I realized that my headgear was not on, and I breathed the air from the environment. At that point, I couldn't decide which threat I should worry about first: falling down and breaking every bone in my body, or inhaling whatever there was in that cold, milky, gaseous cloud all over my face.

"Put me down!" I yelled, intently staring at the floor below me.

"Umn vishhhh davn Unkar akreeee."

Evidently my captors had a twisted sense of humour and released my bonds, sending me on a collision course with the pavement. Blood rushed to my frontal lobe so fast, I could physically feel it. Panic prevented me from having any coherent final thoughts, except, maybe, *"splat."*

About half a meter to the floor, I felt a hard blow to my chest and stomach, as if hitting something invisible in the air. The gravity turned off, and I stopped falling, barely avoiding pancake-ification. Right when I felt a rush of relief, something went terribly wrong with the room surrounding me. My point of view shifted, and, again, I was looking fifty meters down, plastered to the thin air without any ability to move.

"Umn vant mo davn," hissed the same voice without a question mark at the end, but I got the message.

"No! No more down!"

"Hoot," hissed the voice. *"Umn mast ansa. Vo on Unkar vat fo."*

My captors wanted to know why we had committed an act of war against them by invading their territory with our military. Reasonable question, if you ask me, but this was not something I could tell them. So I tried the next best thing: I lied.

"We were lost. Our navigation was..."

And before I knew it, I was falling down like a ripe papaya.

"Splat!"

The image of a ripe papaya hitting the pavement appeared before my eyes.

"Splat!"

This time, my body met the floor, and everything went blank.

***

According to Article 2 of the Earth Nations Confederation (ENC) Constitution:

> *"Earth Nations Confederation is a union of equal and independent human colonies in space, united in the name of security and economic prosperity for the human race."*

Each colony has their own constitution and government, but they are not allowed to hold an independent military, only a police force and National Guard. The ENC military is stationed across all the colonies and consists of enlistees from all over space.

The Earth Nations Confederation is governed by the Earth Nations Senate (ENS), a dual house body with combined legislative and executive authority. Its primary functions are the review of the colonial legislation, unification of practices, inter-colony commerce, and defence. Both the legislative and the executive houses of the ENS have their speakers.

275

Earth Prime (EP) is the capital of the Earth Nations. As the capital city, Earth Prime has a special status of an autonomous colony with its own military. The headquarters of the EP military, the Royal Moroccan Fleet, is stationed in Rabat, in the African Moroccan Democratic Kingdom (AMDK). Earth Prime also has its senate, which is modelled after the ENS. Earth Prime delegates thirty percent of the seats to the ENS, which makes it the most powerful colony in terms of decision-making. On top of that, EP also elects its own president, who has some veto authority over the EPS.

I was going over all of this information in my head, trying to pinpoint where things with the Unkari had gone so terribly wrong. The more I thought about it, only one name stood out clearly: general August Parietti.

General Parietti, the head of the Royal Moroccan Fleet, was the reason why the Earth had Nations panicked and sent the military vessel to the Unkari space. Parietti was a strong proponent of meeting external threats head on and in a pre-emptive fashion, whenever possible. History will show if he was on the right side of the issue, but he managed to gather enough votes in the EPS to override the Earth Prime president's veto on pre-emptive acts against the Unkari. Considering that the issue had top security clearance, or should I say, a level of clearance that did not even officially exist - and only a handful of senators possessed it - the decision was made by a four-to-three vote in favour of sending the troops. However, the general was forced to make concessions. Instead of sending several vessels, he was allowed use of a single Galactica-class vessel, which, if you know anything about the military fleet, is just one step above the cargo barges running errands between the colonies. The goal was to leave no traces to this mission, nothing that even the most experienced watchdog activist or reporter could stick her fingers in.

To be fair, everyone, including the general, blamed all of this Unkari mess on one event: Arecibo 1974. What were our ancestors thinking? Broadcasting a "welcome" message into space without having any planetary defence mechanisms was nuts! It's like teasing a Rottweiler with a bloody steak, and then blaming the dog for your missing fingers. You just don't do that sort of thing! Makes you wonder why, 300 years later when the Unkari showed up in our solar system, everybody acted surprised.

276

***

"Fuck Arecibo," I thought a fraction of a second before crashing into the floor for the fourth time from fifty meters, and feeling my bones shatter like a wafer.

***

"Fuck Unkari," I thought, when I saw myself hanging above that floor some time later. It looked like lying about the purpose of our military operation was a bad idea.

"Ok, I'll talk! Let me see Ensign River first. What happened to her?"

No response, only the cloud hovering around me. "Please..."

Silence. I was about to relax a bit and closed my eyes, when I felt that my centre of gravity rapidly shifted to the skin on my back. Indeed, I headed towards the pavement full speed. Like in the previous loops, everything went blank.

***

"Ok, ok! I'll talk! I'll tell you everything!" I begged. "But you must realize, I am just a soldier. I go where they send me. I don't know any Earth secrets. I am just a..."

"... *AAAAaaaaaaaaaa...*"

Splat! Crumble. Blank...

***

Next time, when I found myself hanging above the floor, I broke down. Making a person survive her death over and over again was a twisted interrogation tactic. I started talking. Certainly I am not proud of it, but I rationalized that I knew relatively few details.

"We were sent here because... we had information that your people were testing a weapon. We wanted to know if you were preparing for war. It was common for our people throughout history to gather information about the defence capacity of other countries and consider how to fight back in case of war. It's a preventive move. We did not start a war with your people. If we did, we'd come with a lot more ships. Please, I'll tell you all you want to know, don't drop me down any more."

277

The cloud swirled around me as if thinking of more questions to ask. *"Umn mast ansa. Infamashn of vapon, hav."*

"From your sub-space communications. But exactly how, I have no idea, I swear. Look, maybe you can read my mind. If you can, please, go ahead. You will see how insignificant I am in the military chain." There was an awfully long silence. I prepped myself for another "splat" in case they did not like the answer... but nothing happened. All of a sudden, my point of view shifted again, and I bumped my back into a cold hard surface. I realized that I was spread on my back on the floor and looking up at the ceiling. I felt like throwing up.

Now that they had their answers, I did not see the value of them keeping River and me alive. What would they do to us? My best guess was that the end was near. There were no diplomatic relations between us and them, and thus a prisoner exchange would be pointless. Our lives were worth nothing except what little information we could provide, and it looked like we had already played that card.

I struggled to stay awake, but my body was weak. Eventually I fell asleep.

***

I had no dreams. No visual dreams. Through the heavy veil of the dark abyss, I heard Ebony's voice: *"Mazula, wake up. We need to escape."*

Eventually, I woke up and saw Ebony sitting next to me and staring without saying a word. "Oh hi! Glad to see you're ok." Ebony did not respond, but in my head I heard a thought:

"Don't talk, think. They may be listening."

Great. I was hallucinating.

I picked myself up from the floor and touched Ebony by the shoulder.

"This is real, Mazula. Don't be an idiot."

I heard the thought again, but Ebony's lips were not moving.

Thoughts kept streaming: *"Mazula, I can transmit my thoughts to you. It's a long story, but this is the reason I am in the military. Well, part of the reason anyway."*

Ebony shrugged her shoulders and gave a faint smile.

"Ebony? What's going on?" I said aloud.

This time she responded audibly.

"Mazula, what's not clear about not speaking? Concentrate!"

"Ok, ok! Yes, ma'am!" I said, still audibly.

"An experimental device in my brain amplifies my brain waves and transfers them to you, bypassing your hearing system. You'll get used to it. And yes, you can respond, but you must concentrate, as if you are typing each word. Visualize typing and saying these words out loud. Try it."

"EBONY," I "typed" in my head. She responded:

"Yes?"

"WHAT THE HELL?"

"We don't have time for this, Mazula! We need to run! We are in big trouble!"

"YOU THINK? I'M GLAD YOU'RE CHIPPER NOW. TRUST ME, I KNOW JUST HOW MUCH TROUBLE WE ARE IN."

I hoped my spelling was correct.

"Slow down! Try shorter sentences! It comes to me scrambled."

"OK, READ MY EYES." I gave her a stare. Ebony chuckled. *"WHAT HAPPENED TO YOUR LEG,"* I thought slowly.

"They took care of it. When you jumped off the cliff, they pushed me over right after you. I ended up in a room like this one. I was immobilized, as if bound by a force field. The Unkari came in and out several times, then they purged their atmosphere and poured breathable air. I had no other choice than to breathe in, because my headgear spontaneously retracted."

279

"How?"

"I don't know how, but it did. The room was empty at that point. Then I saw a cloud, or maybe a colonial organism, like a bee hive, but it looked like fog, translucent, yet somehow intentional."

"I know what you mean. I saw it too."

"The cloud coated my leg, and healed it. I don't understand why would they bother though."

"What did they ask you?" I was getting better at this strange communication.

"Nothing."

"At all?"

"Not a word. I didn't talk to anyone. After my leg was healed, the headgear popped up, the purge routine was repeated, and their atmosphere was restored. Some time later, the guards came back, threw a cloth on my head, and brought me here. I did not see where they were taking me, but I counted steps. This place is about 500 meters away."

"Can you do a mind meld too?"

"Why would I blend my mind?"

"Never mind."

"Anyway, I'll explain it to you later, when we are safe. Also, if it makes you feel better, this project is classified and highly experimental. That's why I couldn't tell you before. But if we don't get out soon, there will be no Ebony to court-martial. They know our language better than they speak it. Talking audibly is not safe."

"Do you remember anything about that jump? How did we get here? Where is here?"

"Good question. Let me check B5 for our coordinates."

"I can't believe it!" exclaimed Ebony out loud and stuck her wrist towards me. The monitor showed long lines of numbers. Those were the coordinates, but I couldn't make any sense of them just by looking at them. Reading my confusion, Ebony swiped the monitor and pulled the menu with the stellar classification.

Star name: Gliese 581

Spectral type: M3V, red dwarf

"I'll be damned. I know that much. We are in our neck of the woods, it's only about twenty light-years away from Earth," I thought.

To be clear, it still wasn't walking distance home. But not only we were in our galaxy, we were in one of the nearest star systems.

"Ebony, do we have a colony there?" I thought.

"No. There are no planets with the right habitable conditions.

For humans, that is."

"Can we tell which planet exactly are we on?"

"The GPS gives me only the coordinates of the star. But let's think logically. The Unkari live in cold places. Their main chemical elements are methane, nitrogen, and hydrogen. So we are looking for an ice ball. Let's look at what kind of planets are here." She started swiping the monitor, pulling the profile of each planet in the Gliese 581 system.

Here is what we came up with:

581b was the first planet. It was a hot, Venus-like gaseous ball. Hot was not good.

581c and 581d were also warm by Unkari standards, and the chemical compositions were too different from the typical Unkari habitat.

That left us with two other planets.

We did not have a lot of data on them, but we had some approximations of temperatures, and both of them were very, very cold, just like Erinozhan. Could we have existed next to the Unkari all this time? Did the Unkari move here recently and, if so, when? If our B5 data was correct, we had covered an enormous distance in one leap, from the Erinozhan underground canyon to the Gliese 581 system. We had no answers to any of these questions. But, at the very least, we had a faint glimpse of hope. First, Ebony was in good shape again, and we could think of an escape. Second, when it came to escaping, it seemed that our chances had now significantly improved. Still we had no transport, but those were the details that we had to work out, one at a time.

281

12
INTACT MEMORIES

Four days had passed since River and I were captured. Apparently, our captors wanted to know why humans invaded Unkari territory. Whenever they didn't like the answer, they killed us in countless horrible deaths, only to bring us back to life for more questioning.

"*VR game. We're in a game,*" I thought to River, who, as I had just found out, had a top-secret military gadget in her brain allowing non-verbal communication, or NVC as she called it. I thought it was funny how adamant River was that I call it NVC, because telepathy according to her is something you threaten your children with when they change a password to their grade record, at which point I couldn't help but notice that it sounded a bit too personal. But then, what do I know about the childhood of a human race made up of genetically enhanced geniuses?

"*VR game? Mmm... Maybe an augmented reality, AR. It seems that we are nudged to make certain choices, and whenever we choose wrong, the sequence repeats,*" River thought back.

"*VR, AR, big difference, what's important is what it does to us. We go back to the previous level. When we complete the level correctly, we move on. But River, this is insane! Think about the magnitude of technology it would take to manipulate our very existence!*"

"*AR can be affirmatively ruled out, Mazula. Our cat suits are integrated with our parameters down to the molecular level.*

Aging leaves specific traces in the chromosomes. With each cellular division, chromosomes are copied, but the new copied chromosomes are shorter than the previous one. There are forty-six chromosomes in each cell. Each one of them is like an individual clock. Monitor ten cells, and you get 460 synchronous measurements. Our cat suits measure millions of cells simultaneously. That's an impressive degree of reliability and validity, if you ask me. No AR environment can be so detailed."

I racked my brain over this puzzle and could not come up with anything. If the genetically enhanced genius from the 4th Orbital Colony could not figure it out, why should I even bother? *"Ebony, is it true that all your people have photographic memories?"*

Ebony leaned against the wall of our holding cell, mulling over something in her B5.

"For the most part," she thought without lifting here eyes.

"What do you mean?"

"We are born with the standard package. It includes enhanced health, athletic, and cognitive capacities. Eidetic memory is part of the package." She emphasized the eidetic. River was really into naming everything properly. *"Sometimes, rarely, an individual may choose to switch it off. This procedure is irreversible, so my people think carefully before they commit to it."*

"Why would someone decide to switch it off?"

"Personal reasons. Experiencing war would be one of them. You don't want to perpetually remember every sensory input when you are injured or tortured."

"So you remember all of those deaths..."

"Yes, in detail." Ebony finally looked me in the eyes.

"I'm sorry. It must be hard. Now I think I understand why your people stay away from the military."

"Now you do."

"Did you consider switching off before enlisting?"

"Yes, I did. But the military was explicit that if they were to start a diplomatic conflict over my asylum on Earth Prime, I'd

have to be intact."

"Is that what they call it?"

I couldn't tell why, but somehow it sounded wrong. I also thought that Ebony was not such a bad soldier after all, I mean, considering. At first, I thought that she was a grouch. She didn't deal well with being injured, true. Now that I learned about the price she paid for enlisting, I regretted being so quick to judge. She was on her first field mission. What was General Parietti thinking? I promised myself to never vote for the Sinkor Administration again. In fact, I considered leaking everything that went wrong with this mission. All of this would have been avoided if not for the knee-jerk leadership style of one very powerful, paranoid, and xenophobic general.

Leaning against the wall, Ebony kept working something out on her wrist monitor.

"Ebony, do you have trees on the 4th Orbital?"

"Yeah, why?"

"Have you seen an ebony tree?"

"Ah, no, not really. I know what they look like from pictures. Why?"

"Ebony trees are native to where I am from. They grow all over the West Africa. I take it you haven't seen a real ebony carving?"

287

"No, I haven't. Cadets don't get away-time from the Academy compound much, and in my case, you know, they watched me extra special."

I didn't notice when I started talking audibly, but she didn't seem to mind this time. "My grandpa had a collection of ebony antiques that were in his family for ages. Those statues were carefully displayed in his living room, on a bookshelf. I imagine that he could become filthy rich if he sold them. Heavy, smooth, and black, like roasted coffee grounds, ebony is an incredibly elegant wood. Before the ebony restriction was imposed, people used to cut the trees uncontrollably, especially after the Big Ice. Ebony trees almost went extinct. When the Big Ice melted away and a lot of people moved out from the tropical longitude, West Africa set out on a mission to preserve the ebony tree, only to find out there were hardly any left."

"Isn't there a famous Ebony park somewhere in Africa?"

"Now there is. It took the effort of the whole continent to find small seedlings, transport them to Cote d'Ivoire, and plant them on acres of reclaimed land."

"Have you been there?"

"I have, indeed. I proposed there to my future wife."

"I didn't know you were married."

"I'm not. She died from the flash fever before our wedding."

"I had no idea, Desiree."

"I know. It was a long time ago. I made my peace with it. The reason I remembered those trees, obviously, was your name, but there is more to it. Ebony is incredibly strong. It actually feels more like rock than any other wood. Anyway, my people think that it is special."

288

I had a lump in my throat that I couldn't swallow. I knew that she knew that our chances to get out of this alive were... Heck, math was never my strength, but I am sure she made an impressive probability analysis, and it wasn't looking good. I had to throw her calculations by adding another factor in: a will to live. Many times in human history it had proven to be a wild card, and I was going to bet all my chips on it this time.

"Heck, Ebony, you are named after the strongest tree on Earth! That counts for something! We are going to be ok! I promise!"

"I'll take your word for it, Mazula."

River smiled at me. Come to think of it, it was the first time I had seen her smile. It was a beautiful sight. And then the floor of our cell parted in the middle with an intimidating hiss and started retracting to the sides, exposing a chasm below us into which our breathable air was fast escaping.

13
ON FIRE

"Brace for impact!" I yelled to Ebony and retracted my headgear.

The chasm below us was getting wider. Soon we were on our toes on the opposite sides of the small holding cell, pressing to the walls and struggling to keep steady. The walls were perfectly smooth, leaving no possibility to hold on to them. The sooner we realized that the jump is unavoidable, the better. "River! You can do it! Think of it as parachute training!"

"We have no parachutes!"

"I know! But our suits will absorb some of the impact!" For Ebony's sake, I had to come up with a lie fast, and this was the best I could do.

"Really?" Ebony was not buying it, but hoped I'd persuade her otherwise.

"Absolutely! When your leg was broken, remember?"

"Yes, the suit stiffened to create a cast." She confirmed.

All of a sudden, my blatant lie looked like a glimpse of hope. In the face of imminent threat, any idea was better than no idea at all. "Exactly! We need to manually input multiple broken bones diagnosis, and the suit will cast the entire body."

What hogwash, I thought to myself, but kept rolling with

the idea.

"Mazula, are you *nuts??* We won't be able to move! If anything happens while we fall... Do you realize that we can't reprogram the suits on the fly? And think of the shock to the body upon an impact!"

"You have another idea?"

"I suggest partial casting. First, we group for the impact here, then we program the suit to cast the head and the body, leaving arms and legs mobile. When we fall, we try landing on the side, like we were taught in martial arts training at the Academy, remember?"

"Ok, I guess I'm impressed." Not! *So* not. But what could I do? The receding floor was only about twenty-five centimeters long on each side, and I wore large shoes. "Is there any setting we can use to absorb the shock from the impact?"

"Maybe. Maybe we should manually set for zero gravity? The suit will increase air pressure inside to compensate to 1G. We will have a layer of padding. I don't know otherwise..."

"Let's do it. Can you script a program and wire it to me?"

"Sure. Give me a second."

"Take your time."

292

While River ferociously inputted data on her B5, I was wondering what the Unkari were trying to accomplish with this stunt. Was this their standard execution procedure? Were they done with us? Or maybe... Maybe the chasm was the entrance to another wormhole leading some place away from this planet?

Meanwhile, the settings were ready. I unpacked and installed them.

The floor was only inches away from completely receding on both sides.

Ebony however was ready to face it. "See you on the other side, Mazula! It was an honor being captured with you!" She smiled and fell into the abyss. I waited until the last second to see how far she had to fall. The last thing I saw before Ebony disappeared was the yellowish-green flash, combustion of sorts. And then, *poof,* she disappeared. The void was dark again.

That's when the remaining floor receded and I snowballed down.

***

"Mazula, get up."

I peeled open my eyes. Ebony was looking at me, her headgear still on. I felt the ground underneath me: hard, smooth, and plastic-like. It was a bit difficult to get up at once, so I rolled over to the side and managed to prop myself up on all fours.

That's when I saw tentacles next to us.

Unkari, two of them to be exact, stood next to us and tilted their heads left and right, blinking like some freakish lizards.

And they had weapons trained at us.

I finally brought myself in an upright position. I looked around. We were in the middle of some valley covered with what looked like methane ice and snow, with lingering fog. A typical Unkari habitat, however, it was definitely not Erinozhan. I could see far into the horizon, where the valley transitioned into dramatic spiky mountains.

293

"How long have I been out?" I asked out loud, feeling that NVC would be too much energy right now.

"You fell out of the vortex in the air a moment ago. By the way, we did not need the cast, because this surface turned elastic upon impact. It was a rather soft landing."

"I must have passed out."

"The likely answer is that your brain erased the memory of the fall as a protective mechanism. Human brains often erase memories of traumatic events. Because I am eidetic, I could not forget the fall, that's why..."

"River! You're giving me a headache! And I already have one!"

"Sorry, Mazula. You are right. These ugly bastards should

be our priority at the moment," she clenched her teeth, staring down the enemy, like a panther, ready to rip their throats out.

"Calm down, River."

"Calm down my ass! I am tired of this!" And she made an abrupt forward motion, testing if the aliens would budge. They twitched and raised their weapons into a ready position.

"Ok, ok, big guys, we are cooperating, see?" I slowly raised my hands for a few moments, until the guards visibly relaxed.

Once the guards' vigilance diminished, I needed to know where the hell we had ended up this time. I shifted the weight from one leg to another and yelped, pretending that my leg was injured. Leaning down to my "injured" ankle, I accessed the B5 and set it in the automated mode to feed the data directly on my retina. Because I had no time to apply filters, hundreds of windows instantly bombarded my field of vision, superimposing on each other and cluttering my view with billions of data pixels.

Because my eye muscles reflectively tried to follow each of the windows popping up, my eyeballs felt as if pricked by a myriad tiny needles of electric current. This immediately exacerbated my migraine. Covering my eyes and moaning in pain, I had to pull through it anyway, and use my eye movements to close the fields that I did not need at the moment, leaving several scans running to the left and right corners of my sight.

As it turned out, we were still in the Gliese 581 system, although it was a different planet, and, based on the gravity readings, I suspected it to be a moon or a planetoid. Despite intense migraine and piss-poor concentration, I NVC'd this data to River. This chip in her head was proving itself handy.

"*Umn mast moov!*" asserted one of the Unkari, and stepped forward, encouraging us to step back. I slowly collected myself from the shiny ice-covered plastic, and we complied. We walked across the alien terrain. I took the environment composition scans to the best of my ability, navigating the searches with my eye movements, despite terrible pain each eyeball movement caused me, wiring my findings to River.

We walked down the valley in silence for about an hour, with the mountains sprawling on both sides. The fog was composed of methane-nitrogen-hydrogen vapor and traces of cyanide gas. The fog-like methane vapor was a sign of condensation. I wondered what methane rain would look like. The surface was covered by sand dunes made of various glistening hydrocarbons. Underneath the dunes, there were glaciers of polypropylene and other unfamiliar classes of plastics. The whole valley was made out of plastic!

"You know guys, for an advanced race, you sure don't recycle enough."

"Umn mast tok not," verbalized the alien behind me, poking my back with his gun.

Traces of rock-hard water were present as well, clustered in layers of mountains around us, although this water was not suitable for human consumption, containing a variety of highly toxic trace elements.

The surface temperature was -187°C in the valley, dropping even lower in the mountains. The Unkari loved it cool.

I took a brief reading of the cat suit stats. Thermoregulation worked within safe parameters, but the extreme environment required higher rates of water consumption for climate control maintenance. This was bad news.

295

"Ebony, how long do you have before red-zoning on the water level?" I NVC'd to her.

"Three hours, give or take. And you?"

"Around two. I hate to state the obvious, but we must figure something out, and fast."

"There is frozen water on the surface. It's mixed with the sand under our feet. It's a mixture of freeze-dried snow, so solidified that it doesn't stick at all, and it feels like soft sand. There are also frozen methane particles and rock sediments, all in a perfectly non-reactive state."

"Ok, ok, got it, damnit, River. So we have water. But we would have to do serious filtering before we can pump it in. Did you see

the cyanide readings?"

"Yeah, among other things. I may be able to rig up a filtering program, so we only need to collect and melt the ice. And the problem is that you cannot heat it up in this atmosphere. Methane is highly flammable. Basically I need to accelerate molecules in the ice without applying heat. I could apply pressure to it, a lot of pressure, several thousands of atmospheres to be exact. Or, some chemicals could work too."

"Or we could just repossess the weapons of these bastards. Their particle beams probably would do a great job melting the ice."

"That would do!" she said as if it did not occur to her before. *"With one little exception. I doubt they would just give up their guns."*

"That's a problem. Hey, what did you just say about a highly flammable atmosphere?"

"It is. A small electric short-circuiting would combust the hell out of this place."

"This is something we could work with. How do you think our suits would react to the explosion?"

"Well, it depends on how big the explosion was. Chances are that we would survive, but again, our water level would dramatically drop. Any environmental stress causes accelerated rates of water processing. We could torch them, but at the same token, we would be on the verge of our climate-control collapse."

296

One step at a time, I thought. Meanwhile the Unkari brought us to their transporter. It was hovering at the edge of a bottomless crater that stretched miles into every direction. Leading to the transporter was a bridge, about 500 meters long, that stretched between the edge of the cliff and the transporter entrance.

"It's now or never!" I NVC'd to River. *"We need to break away now."*

"What are you suggesting?"

"We need to highjack the transporter. With any luck, we can make it to the Earth Prime in time before our oxygen runs out."

"It might be our only chance."

"We need to wait until we get to the middle of the bridge. Not a minute earlier."

"Why? You have something against solid ground under your feet, Mazula?"

"We need an advantage. Throwing one of these squids over the rail would give us such an advantage."

The Unkari behind nudged us towards the bridge, pointing their weapons in our backs.

"Mazula, I have an idea. I think we can generate static on the surface of the cat suit. Use the setting for survival on the wild terrain. There should be an app for kindling the campfire."

"Oh yeah? How is that going to help us?"

"I believe that generating sparkle on your palms, you could torch them like marshmallows. Since you have B5 running through your retina, you can access it. You'll have to do it, and I will back you up."

"It might work, River. Good thinking! Remember, we need one of them alive to pilot the transporter." Meanwhile, we made our first few steps on the bridge. Looking from above, it appeared nearly translucent. The bridge was wide enough for five persons walking side by side. At first, it appeared that there were no safety rails, but then I noticed that one of the guard's tentacles lightly brushed against the edge, bumping into something solid. It was a force field.

"What parameters should I look for to identify, how high is the rail?" I NVC'd River.

"It's 0.9 meters tall, close to your waistline. I suspect if you tossed anything in it, it would become more visible."

"And you know this how exactly?"

"I can see it. The field emits a slight heat wave, only 0.17C above the background temperature."

"Ok." I slightly raised my eyebrows and chuckled. *"I guess it's a long story, isn't it?"*

"Actually, not really. I am genetically enhanced, remember?"

Ebony smiled back warmly. *"How is the campfire going?"*

"All set. Let's get a bit closer to the middle. I will try throwing a flame ball at the one behind me. Yours will get distracted, that's when you go after his gun."

As we walked, the wind grew stronger with every moment. At first, I thought that it was some kind of convection effect that created wind currents in the canyon, but then I noticed the clouds. I turned back and could not believe my eyes: the horizon was sprinkled with emerging and dissipating tornado twisters. Although far away, they looked intimidating.

The storm was approaching fast. The bridge swayed under our footsteps, and clouds of sand, mixed with snow, blew in our backs, almost throwing us off balance.

In mere seconds, the sky turned violent, and the flickers of lightning illuminated rugged edges of clouds. There was no thunder yet, that was how I realized that the lightning was in the outer atmospheric layers, but probably would descend closer to the surface soon.

And then we heard thunder breaking the sky, like a giant crystal bowl.

We could not wait any longer.

298

"Now!" I yelled to Ebony in my head, clasped my palms to generate static. The air combusted, and I tossed flame at the guard behind me. The guard was caught in flames, and his methane-based biochemistry flared up. Through his screaming I heard Ebony yelling at me out loud:

"No! It's a mistake! It's about to rain!" I watched her kicking the gun out of the guard's grip and sliding it with her foot in my direction, trying to process what exactly she was telling me about the rain.

The terror in her voice made no sense to me at first. Then, to my horror, I realized it.

Methane rain.

Liquid methane pouring from the sky all over us, right when we started a bonfire.

The entire bridge was about to turn into a gril!

I picked up the gun and pointed it at the other guard, who screamed in his alien form of panic, while Ebony yelled at that unresponsive creature, "We have to run!"

And then the first heavy drop fell on the shield of my headgear, leaving a large wet splatter as it rolled down. A few more drops fell on the bridge, on my cat suit, on Ebony and the guards. The crisped up, but still kindling guard a few meters behind me all of a sudden flared up with new energy.

The next second, raindrops started catching fire while still in the sky.

A chain reaction flared up to the raindrops above the source of the fire and started spreading in all directions across the bridge's surface.

For a brief moment, all of us were perfectly still, taken away by the foreboding beauty of the green flames raining from the sky, falling on the translucent bridge surface and "infecting" the wet methane puddles, rapidly gathered on the surface.

Through the humming of my blood in my head, I heard Ebony's terrified scream at the guard, who seemed to be the most affected with the sight of his dead fellow soldier and the flames raining from the sky. Finally, she sucker-punched him in the head. That snapped him out of his stupor, and he started running towards the transporter.

299

That's when the individual drops were no more, and the sky rained a downpour of liquid methane, instantly creating a combustion right behind us, spreading faster than we could possibly run.

I yelled for Ebony to run in front towards the transporter door and try to open it, as she was the fastest among us.

A cloud of black smoke enveloped the guard and me, veiling the outline of the transporter. A red alert from my climate control beeped, but I had no time to disable it. Meanwhile, the Unkari soldier started lagging behind. The fire did not have him yet, but it was obvious that he was suffocating from smoke, because he was without a space suit. His tentacles slapped the pavement heavier and heavier, and far less regularly. Finally, merely ten meters from the transporter door, his body collapsed as he passed a loud groan. That was a disastrous scenario, because even inside the transporter, we were not exactly safe and we had to take off immediately. That Unkari was our ticket out.

Ebony and the transporter were almost within my reach, but I had to go back and drag the comatose alien to the door. Ebony helped me to stuff his limp appendages into the tiny quarters of his vessel, designed for two Unkari, sealing the door behind. Through the semi-transparent skylights, we watched the flames catch up with us and envelop the ship.

I rushed to the alien, he was sprawled on the floor coughing out smoke mixed with dark-green phlegm. "Now listen to me. Unfortunately, I can kill you only once, but trust me, I will do a better job than you did with us. There will be no coming back from death once I'm done with you. Do you understand me?" The alien lifted his eyes at me, and gave me a look which I chose to interpret as an agreement. "Here is the deal. We need to get off this planet, now. You either help us, or I throw you into the fire,"

The alien gave a mortified squeal, which I chose to interpret as his refusal to be toasted.

I was getting good at Unkari.

300

"If that's something you prefer to avoid; you have a choice. You are going to pilot the transporter directly to the Earth Prime, broadcasting on all frequencies that you surrender to the Earth Nations. Do you understand me?"

The alien silently blinked at me. Ebony did not like that.

"Answer him!" she screamed and motioned her palms in his direction, threatening to torch him. Ebony was about to unravel. I considered holding her back, but decided against it. After all, who am I to tell a woman how to deal with her rage.

That had a striking effect on his collaborative spirit.

"Unkar akree."

14
VACUUM

Ebony closely watched our captive Unkari as he entered the coordinates for the flight into the transporter console. Unlike humans, Unkari often traveled in two- or four-person transporters, valuing freedom of movement. Humans opted for public transportation and cost-sharing commuting on large vessels, whether those were passenger, cargo, military, or government ships. Being an older race, the Unkari had abandoned shared commuting long ago.

303

"What are your orders regarding us?" I asked the Unkari, who had finished entering the coordinates, lifting the transporter off the surface.

"Is Lenar Unkar Varrria."

"I know you are a warrior. A soldier, that is. But what is your task on this mission?"

"Is serv Lenar Unkar."

I couldn't figure out if he was trying to be difficult or we had a legitimate language barrier. Ebony punched him.

"Miama haunnarr ammtakht!" She yelled at him. Those three words made the Unkari rapidly blink; he responded:

"Is trevl umn and umn to Lenar Unkar Leeda."

"Now we are getting somewhere! Ebony, what did you tell him?"

"I told him that I like my food on skewers."

"I see. When did you learn Unkari?"

"I started learning when we were captured. B5 has some ethnographic reports from the First Contact era. Humans and the Unkari had a brief diplomatic period, over 300 years ago. We had several cultural exchange missions set up on Earth. As a result, a few works on the syntax of the Unkari language were written, and a basic dictionary was created. I guess by now I'm fluent in conversational Unkari."

"No shit!"

"It's not that difficult given my eidetic memory. See, language is like a puzzle. My people are very good at puzzles. Our education is built around solving puzzles. Our school grade system is based not on how much we can memorize - because we are a race of eidetics, we all can memorize - but we are judged on how many creative, outside-the-box solutions to a problem we can find. So basically if I learn a few hundred words from a new language and cross-reference them to the rules of syntax and grammar..."

Ebony was interrupted by a flash of white light, that flooded everything in the transporter. Right after the flash, we heard the sound of an explosion. The front view force field collapsed and the three of us were torpedoed through the gaping hole into the vacuum of space. And then - deafening silence.

My headgear immediately flashed a "catastrophic environment failure" alert, and I tumbled like a rodent on a rubber string accelerated by the shock wave of the explosion. Trying to overcome the vertigo, I closed my eyes and tried to imagine a wide horizon and myself, firmly standing on the ground, largely to no success, because I repeatedly received new jolts from debris and secondary explosions that changed my vector and velocity. The vertigo was so strong that I could not open my eyes.

What the hell had gone wrong?

Did the alien start the self-destruction sequence?

Were we hit by an enemy ship?

Seconds later, the emotional awareness of the situation kicked in, and panic hit me like a tsunami. In order to conserve my scarce oxygen, I struggled to control my heart rate and breathing.

The only good thing in the whole situation was that, by the time of the explosion, we had already reached escape velocity and left the planet's orbit, so we were not going to burn up in the atmosphere. Or maybe this was the worst news?

Because under the present scenario, I likely was going to painfully suffocate, when my uniform ran out of the water that it used to synthesize breathable oxygen. Then, for a short period of time, the organics in my uniform would work at breaking down the CO_2, but the filters would rapidly clog with carbon sediments. I would get lightheaded.

If I got particularly lucky, I would pass out before I started suffocating.

Moments later, I still was tumbling, but at a consistent velocity; I guess I had made it far enough from the source of the explosion. I dared to open my eyes and access my life support parameters.

Crap.

The system had already processed the CO_2.

305

I had, what, ten minutes? Less so if I couldn't handle my heart rate and stop hyperventilating. I started thinking about my life. If I ever was to make peace with it, it had to be now. I saw my life laid before me in film frames, scrolls of them, all at once.

There I was, asking my grandpa why other kids in the kindergarten had mommies, and I had only him and grandma. That was because my mom had had to go to the sky when I was born, told grandpa. Then I said I wanted to be in the sky too.

There I was, at age seven or something, accompanying my grandma to a beauty salon. She had an appointment for a manicure, and I remember bursting into tears because she did not sign me up as well. A class act as she was, my grandma asked the beautician to paint my nails as well. That was it, she did not comment on it, did not talk about it, we both had our nails done - hers in a tasteful peach, and mine in bold red.

There I was, applying to the Fleet Academy. I wanted to be a pilot. By that time, I knew that being in the sky wouldn't bring my mother back, but the idea of flying was firmly ingrained in who I was. Sky was all that mattered to me.

I remember packing my suitcase for the Academy and considering if I should pack my concealer and eyeliner, but decided against it. My reasoning was that the fellow Cadets probably would not care about my dark circles. Instead, I packed a six-month supply of weight gainer supplement.

There I was, after the second year of the Academy, bulked up, with broad shoulders and not an ounce of fat, opening my test results. Ten points shy of the threshold, I was not cutting it for a pilot. It was still a high score, but not high enough for the pilot position.

I ended up in the combat operations track.

Then was Desiree's funeral. A lot of beautiful black dresses and flowers. I wanted to wear a dress as well, but did not dare, although Desiree knew, and she wouldn't have minded.

306

There I was, five years after graduating from the Academy, receiving the orders to show up in the Moroccan Fleet HQ on the demand of General Parietti. I knew the name only passingly, having no interest in military politics. I arrived in Rabat the next day and waited in the entryway, talking to the General's administrative assistant Private Garret Hur. Amazing what your memory can produce sometimes. After all these years, I remembered this random guy's name.

Private Hur showed me to the General's office.

The General was standing by the window when I walked in; I saluted. The General informed me that my file had caught his attention when he was recruiting for a new special forces unit, of which he could not tell me much due to the high clearance that I did not possess. If I was interested, I must pass the qualifying tests.

The test was aimed at discovering two things: my will to

live and my loyalty to humanity.

I scored through the roof on the first category. When it came to the second one, I thought that I scored high, likely due to a sloppy test construction. Sure I was loyal to humanity. I was willing to die for humanity if it came down to it. But I thought the test underestimated my regard for life in general. When it came down to it, I did not believe that humans had any more right to exist than other species.

Then, about three years ago, after the reassignment surgery, I called up my friends, Mike and Sater, to meet in the local bar for a beer. They didn't know yet, but I decided to tackle it head on. I had hair extensions, a blue dress and shoes on, and some basic makeup. The doctors narrowed my nose, raised the eyebrows, and removed the facial hair. Before leaving the house, I looked in the mirror and smiled. It was still me, the same me, but even more me than I used to be, if it makes sense.

I was a bit late, and the guys were sitting there, guzzling their beers and watching some game on the screen. I took a seat next to them at the bar. Sater, a perpetual charmer as he was, immediately offered me a "martini or whatever you girls are into these days," but Mike kept his gaze firmly fixed on me, and finally whispered:

"Reinsford, is that you?"

307

Sater spilled the entire pitcher of beer on the bar counter and his pants, and we started throwing napkins in the pool of beer all over the counter. Meanwhile a cute waitress, one of the new ones, walked over and helped us to mop the mess. When she leaned over the counter to reach the far end from her side, her breasts dipped in the beer puddle, and her tight white tank top was soaked with beer in that particular area.

All three watched the girl cleaning up the mess, fixated on her hard, big nipples under the wet tank top. Mike saw my reaction and pointed to Sater. They both burst out laughing. Sater concluded: "it's Reinsford alright." The awkward moment faded away. I realized I still had my friends.

The memory frames were getting clouded. My eyelids were getting heavy; I could not keep them open any more. The last conscious memory I had was amusement. I was amused at seeing the light, realizing that I was not tumbling anymore, at least that's what it felt like, because I knew that in space any movement was relative. I could not tell whether it was me approaching the light, or the light approaching me, but I knew:

This is it; this is how it happens.

The proverbial light at the end of a tunnel.

15
SHE IS A
LOONY KITE

The smell of cherry pie was the last thing I expected in the afterlife.

"Wake up, sleepy head."

A gentle woman's voice rolled through my head like an ocean tide.

"Would you like some coffee? I'll make you some. Or maybe a glass of milk?"

The voice floated in the sky like a kite. Then I saw the kite, and the kite saw me. I smiled, the kite smiled back. *What a strange kite*, I thought.

311

The kite and I floated above the waves for some time without saying a word, although I suspected that the kite did not speak because its mouth was busy sucking on a lollipop.

I realized that my toes poked holes through my socks. Don't you hate when your toes stick out of holes? The sensation was annoying, as if someone was tickling my brain with a feather.

The kite retrieved the lollipop from its mouth, dipped it in the feathers sticking out from the torn pillow and shoved it right in my mouth. Moving my head away, I pressed my lips together as tight as I could. I broke into a sweat. My entire body was shaking. I wanted to scream, but no sound came out. At first. But then, I finally managed to clear my throat and open my eyes. "Who is here?" I asked in the darkness.

"Oh, you are finally awake!" said the woman's voice, but everything around was black. "Have a glass of milk."

I felt something smooth and cold pressing against my lips. It could very well be a glass of milk, but before drinking it, I needed to know: WHAT THE HELL WAS GOING ON!

"I can't see anything. Why can't I see?"

"Your optic nerve is damaged. We can't do anything for you at the moment."

"We? Who is we? And stop sticking this thing in my mouth." I protested and realized that I could not move my hands. They were restrained behind my back. I also realized that I was on my side, on a surface that conformed to the shape of my body. That made me feel even ickier. Right now, I rather preferred the hard floor. This whole situation messed with my senses to the point of making me nauseous.

"One step at a time, sister. First, we need to get you well."

"Untie me."

"That I cannot do."

"Why?"

"Such are my orders. They know you've been using the device on your wrist and that you will try to cause problems."

"You bet my ass I will cause problems! More problems than you can imagine!"

"See! That's what I am talking about. Humans are so ... tumultuous." The last word was uttered with a dramatic flare.

"I will not tell you anything until you start explaining what is going on."

"Well, ok. As you wish. You are a prisoner of the Unkari. More so, you are a criminal. You've committed a capital offense. And you will be brought before the court. Soon. For now, you must get well. You almost died from asphyxiation."

"Yes. I remember. The ship exploded. I was tumbling in space."

"You are extremely lucky. The Unkari didn't intend to keep you alive. But they are not murderers, not like you. When they saw you on their scanners, they showed mercy."

"Who are you?"

"I am She."

"You mean, a woman?"

"Well, yes. But it is my name. My name is 'She.' I am your liaison for the trial."

Now that's a strong gender identity! I thought.

"What kind of name is that?" I asked out loud.

"It's the standard female name. Why?"

"Ok, if you say so. So you are my lawyer, is that it?"

She paused for a second as if considering the meaning of the word "lawyer."

"Hmm... Not really. A lawyer would mean that we would engage in an adversarial process. This is not what is going to happen. There is no need for such a process because the facts of your crime are well established."

"What crime?"

"What crime? Ok, I'll play your game. Let's see. You and your people invaded Unkari space with a military vessel. When the Unkari ordered your people to surrender, you opened fire. When your people were finally captured, you continually attempted to escape and kill Unkari warriors."

313

"I am a soldier. This is my job, just like interrogating me is your job."

"Your job does not remove your responsibility for your actions. However, let me finish first. The facts that I just recounted only describe the general pattern of your behavior, but do not incriminate you directly. You are guilty of murdering one Unkari warrior with exceptional cruelty. Remember? You set him on fire. I'd play you the footage of you and your fellow arsonist, captured by the transporter's security system, but you can't see it anyway. *Such a pity!*" The last sentence was said with excellent fake compassion. She continued. "That's one charge. Your second charge is that you led another warrior to commit treason. Remember? Because of your threats, the noble warrior surrendered his vessel to the Earth Nations. That we also have on record. And on top of all that, you managed to destroy an entire moon. What did you expect to happen when you exposed a highly flammable world to fire?"

"We had no time to think that far."

"By the way, it is our estimate that the moon will be on fire for several thousand years. Right now it looks like a miniature sun from space. You cannot even begin to fathom the chain reaction of events that your foolishness triggered in that entire system."

"Was it habitable?"

"Would you care?"

"Of course I would!"

"No, it was not habitable. But it was an important transportation hub for the Unkari, which is none of your business, by the way. So, does any of that have factual errors?"

"Wait, the Unkari have transportation routes in our space? This is not what we agreed to in the First Contact Memorandum!"

"I told you, it is not your business. Just answer the question. Are there errors in those facts or not?"

"No, no factual errors. But the whole thing is misinterpreted. The Unkari are preparing for a war against humans. They were testing some kind of super weapon, in their own words, 'an ultimate solution,' capable of destroying humanity. We were only gathering information. That is why we were on Erinozhan."

"Look, this may be your way of telling a story. If you want my opinion, the way you spin it does not make any difference. But I will be respectful of you, because your hours are numbered. And you better get something to eat. Who knows, it may be your last meal after all."

"Wait, I have so many questions. Where am I, who are

you, where is River?"

"No more questions. You either eat, or I leave. So what's it going to be now, Desiree Mazula?"

"Is that cherry pie I smell?"

"Yes it is. It's not bad. Try it." She pressed something to my lips that smelled like almond pastry. I realized that I was shaking with hunger. What the hell. I scooped the stuff with my lips. It had a puree consistency, resembling mashed potatoes, only with a cherry-pie flavoring.

"You Unkari are terrible cooks."

"Oh, but I am not an Unkari. I am a human. But I'm nothing like you."

16
CONTACT

Left to my own devices, I wondered if the General had figured out by now that his spying mission on Erinozhan had failed. I wondered about it more out of curiosity than out of any realistic hope for a rescue mission. Even if the Royal Moroccan Fleet had already figured out that the mission had failed, there was no way they could possibly expect anyone to survive, nor would they know where to look for the survivors. Heck, I had no idea where I was myself.

Without the B5 access, and being blind as I was, the situation was fucked.

I'm fucked. The explicit thought formed in my brain.

I know, I heard in my head.

River! Goddammit, you are alive! I straightened up on my 'bed.'

***

Some say that it was the Unkari's fault; that they lacked the "social skills," landing on Earth without prior notice. We still have no idea how they could bypass the planetary defence shield and land in the Atlantic without anyone noticing. Others speculated that the Unkari could not have passed the shield unnoticed, which meant that they had had an observation outpost in the ocean for over 300 years, before the planetary defence shield was installed. Of course, this theory stirred all the abduction believers, as a result of which Hollywood made billions on spinning old science fiction tales in the 5-D format.

One way or another, in 2275, Liberia witnessed the sight unlike anything in human history. Oddly it was my ancestor who first spotted the capsules that popped up on the Atlantic horizon. Eleven dome-like bubbles floated on the surface several hundred meters off the Liberian coast. The news spread fast. One of the domes eventually beached on the shore, where a small crowd of the most reckless headline chasers were contained by the paramilitary, while the rest of the locals rushed to their homes to prepare for the end of the world. As the dome emerged from the water, the eyewitnesses differentiated tentacles with multiple joints akin to a daddy-longlegs spider, but the size of a small condo. When the pod settled in the sand, the tentacles folded themselves above the pod in what was described later as a praying position.

The coastguard tightly surrounded the perimeter, pointing their weapons at the shored object. They speculated that the tentacles above the pod assumed a defensive position, but the orders were clear: to contain the situation until the arrival of special forces.

And so, for the ten longest minutes in human history, they had waited.

Suddenly, the pod passed a loud hissing sound, the domed lid spun about half a rotation around its axis and popped open. From the narrow opening, a tentacle emerged, holding a transparent box, slowly expanding about fifty meters towards the crowd. Then, it stopped. The observers could decipher a snake-like small tentacle separating from the main tentacle and forming a ring that held a flat golden object the size of a pizza dish. The deafening silence was broken by someone in the audience yelling of the top of his lungs:

"Voyager!"

The person was immediately apprehended by the nearest coastguard officers, the event received little attention, completely overshadowed by what was going on next.

Music flowed.

The most vibrant piece of classical music enveloped the coast. One person, however, made the connection between the "Voyager" exclamation and the classical music played by the invaders. That person was my ancestor, Dr. Otis Solarin, a professor of space history.

"They come in peace!" he yelled as loud as he could from the crowd, but the music swallowed his words. He attempted to get through the crowd to whoever was in charge of the coastguard operation. Again, the coastguard was not impressed. Dr. Solarin was apprehended just as quickly as the other enthusiast by the two solidly built coastguards, who dragged the kicking old man from the beach to the military vehicle for further detention.

Leaving the beach, Dr. Solarin heard the gun shots behind.

Then he heard a round of water splashes. He quickly counted - eleven.

***

I discovered Solarin's book in my grandpa's library when I was about fourteen years old. At first, I thought that it was a piece of fiction, like one of those alternative histories. In that manuscript, the First Contact account was told in many ways similarly, but it had significant discrepancies. The official version was that the Unkari provoked the coastguard to open fire. We were taught that both aliens and humans had weapons pointed at each other. It was from Solarin's manuscript that I found out the fact that instead of weapons, the Unkari had presented us with our own late twentieth-century Voyager's golden record that our ancestors had sent into space looking for extraterrestrial life. Dr. Solarin blamed the government for the most epic diplomatic fuck-up of all time - for opening fire on aliens who actually came with a friendly mission.

321

When the coastguard opened fire, the Unkari transporters went back under water, leaving behind the record enclosed in a transparent case, where in many Earth languages it was written: "Human lost, Unkari returned." No matter how much the marines tried to find the aliens in the Pacific, they had vanished without a trace, as if none of that ever happened.

This of course led a significant group of people, who called themselves "The Green Men Circus," to claim that the whole event was staged by the government. The Green Men Circus adepts had to eat their tin foil hats about three months after the First Contact failure. Nineteen Unkari vessels out of nowhere appeared at Titan's orbit. According to the official government narrative, NASA was observing these ships for a while when they entered the solar system.

According to the Solarin's manuscript, NASA has video footage from a satellite directed at Titan. On that footage, one second there was nothing around Titan, and then the ships started popping up from thin air, one by one, assuming a circular formation around the moon. Solarin also says that on that day, the NASA director and the president of Earth Prime mysteriously disappeared from the public eye, and the footage was hushed. About a week passed, but the ships did show any signs of activity. That was when the president finally came out of his hiding. Coincidentally, later that day the ships began transmitting a message.

322

The aliens claimed Jupiter's moon Titan to be the official embassy of the Unkari in human space. Publicly, the government hailed it as a major diplomatic victory. According to Dr. Solarin's account, politicians and the military were caught off guard and had no idea what to do - other than try to prevent mass hysteria. Although the military and the civilians put on a brave face, they still announced a Level 5 security alert, reserved for things like nuclear threats. It certainly corroborated Solarin's narrative. Meanwhile, months passed, but nothing happened.

When the riots of E.T. lovers and haters alike were taken under control, the Earth Nations transmitted a formal invitation to open diplomatic talks. The Unkari were invited to arrive with a small delegation to Reykjavik, for negotiations. Everybody wanted to know if there were Unkari ships hidden in the ocean, but the Unkari themselves were not in a hurry to reveal any of their secrets. The diplomatic relations with the Unkari lasted for about a year and were characterized by a particular bureaucratic sluggishness, equally perpetuated by both sides. Months were spent approving detailed agendas before any bilateral meeting took place.

Humanity at large was kept in the dark, only to receive public assurances that the diplomatic process was slow, but positive. Only a handful of scholars were allowed access to the Unkari camp in Reykjavik for cultural exchange, and what they revealed to the public was heavily red-taped. Dr. Solarin, however, got lucky and was invited to join the science delegation as a historian and anthropologist. The last title, Solarin joked, was mostly credited to him because he wrote a book on portrayal of aliens in fictional narratives. Although Solarin was an expert on made-up aliens, somehow it allowed the government to maintain appearances and keep Solarin's mouth shut about the Voyager's record. A year later, the Earth Nations announced a press conference on the account of the Unkari negotiations. That was when everyone found out that the Unkari requested to expand their settlements to the Milky Way galaxy in return for protection from other hostile species. Supposedly the Unkari did not reveal any details about those species, emphasizing that such information was a tradable commodity in the negotiations, although they cautioned the Earth Nations against sending any further messages into deep space.

The head of the Earth Nations announced that the parties did not reach a mutually satisfying agreement, and as a result the Unkari left the solar system and supposedly returned to their home galaxy, Sagittarius Dwarf. Later that year, that particular administration lost the elections, bringing to office an ultraconservative party that ran on species isolationism and military expansion. And so began a new chapter in human history - the era of space colonization.

***

Roughly 600 years after the Arecibo message was sent into space, and 300 years after the First Contact, humanity lives in the shadow of the great unknown harbored by the universe in its dark wrinkles of space-time. Practical space colonization required a lot more effort than anyone imagined. Even the best proxy-Earth prospects required significant terraformation steps. That was why our ancestors opted for the orbital stations model. They were versatile and mobile, and they allowed humans to colonize the nearby systems without waiting for the terraforming processes to be completed.

Today, in 2587, humans have twelve operational Orbital Colonies around the Earth Prime, six Cycler stations orbiting the sun between the Earth and Mars orbits, four Orbital Colonies around Mars, three around Ganymede, and two around Europa.

Outside of the solar system, humans colonized five nearby systems, although the terraformation of those planets is in a rudimentary stage. We have sent probes and small manned missions in hundreds of directions across the Milky Way, and among them are the ever-expanding small military outposts, keeping an eye on the ominous neighboring galaxy. In all this time, we have not met any other species more complex than a space worm. We have learned a lot about space, planetary formation, origin of species, and alternative biochemistries, but for all practical purposes, we are still alone. Our existential questions are not answered.

***

"River, are you ok?" I thought, telepathically communicating it to Ebony, who was locked up some place separately from me, but not too far away, because her range of NVC communication was limited to several hundred meters.

"I'm fine I guess. They want to prosecute us, Mazula. We are screwed!"

I received a cloud of panic transmitted with that message.

"Hang on, we will figure something out."

Ebony did not respond.

"Ebony, are you injured?"

"I am not in pain, if that's what you mean. But I can't see. They say my optic nerve is damaged."

"What are the odds."

***

About an hour later, She returned. "It is time for you to face Unkari justice," she said.

17
ISTANBUL

I couldn't see. I was hostage to an alien species, taken to receive a death sentence.

Two guards held me by my arms on both sides, and I could hear She (the name drove me nuts!) walking in front of me. I heard the doors sliding open and closed as we walked. Our footsteps were absorbed by a cushiony, track-like surface.

"How long have you been with the Unkari?" I asked her. She did not respond. "Come on, you are going to execute me, aren't you? The least you can do is to satisfy my curiosity."

"I could. But then, why would I?" She replied dispassionately.

"Why? What do you mean "why"? You say you are a human, right? Well, we have at least that much in common. How did you get here? What did they promise you to make you defect?"

"You think we have a lot in common? Let me tell you, you could have not insulted me more. You, Earth humans, are arrogant and dense. You are like babies with the fire power to destroy an entire galaxy. Why would I want to have anything in common with you?"

"Maybe so, but not everyone is this way. Ensign River, for

example. Her race is pacifist."

"And yet, here she is, a soldier and a murderer of two Unkari soldiers."

"Yeah, I see how it might look like that. But let me tell you, the Unkari are not saints either. They wanted to move in our space, we refused. And what did they do? They left, harbored resentment against humanity for 300 years, and plotted blitzkrieg."

"You think you know something, don't you." There was no question mark at the end of that one, only bone-dry bitterness.

"Then explain it to me! I know only what I was told, but maybe there is another side to the story."

"There is always another side of the story, don't you think?"

"True. But whose story is closer to the truth? For all I know, you and I may be speaking the same language, but we are far from understanding each other."

She was quiet. We stopped walking.

"You don't want to kill me without my full remorse, do you? Isn't that the purpose of the Unkari trial?"

"You may have a point there," She finally agreed. "Alright. Let me talk to the Leader."

"Leader? The Unkari pilot said he was taking us to the Leader."

"Be quiet!"

I zipped up, while She stepped aside.

"The Leader agrees that your understanding may contribute to your remorse."

"See, you might get a promotion out of it!"

"Get what?"

"Never mind. Ok, I am ready for the learning curve."

***

Later I was crying, kneeling on a beach of plastic sand facing a methane ocean with thick slow-motion waves, as if made of unset resin. I cried watching the red marble of the alien sun slowly rolling to the horizon. The Unkari evening was approaching, and I was left alone to digest what had happened. The beach was deserted, but there was no point in running. The reason why I was in such distress was that I had precisely three choices ahead of me, and all three led to my certain death. The difference between them was in how fast my death would come, and how many more humans, besides me, would have to die.

I am getting ahead of the events. I better go back and tell everything exactly how it was.

***

She directed me to a transporter, and it lightly took off in an unknown direction, once we settled in.

"What are you going to show me?"

"You will see it for yourself."

"I'm not really blind, am I?"

"We'll get to that as well. Meanwhile I need to fill in your gaps on human-Unkari relations." I was sitting in a chair of some sort, enveloped in darkness, and strapped with a safety force field, imagining She across from me (that's where her voice came from). I imagined her a young woman with an unfamiliar English accent, probably influenced by the Unkari language. I suspected that She'd been with the Unkari for a long time, maybe her entire life. From the sound of her voice, She didn't strike me as someone who'd get early "worry lines."

"First, tell me how much you know," She said.

"Well, I know maybe a fraction more compared to any other human who studied the history of the First Contact. There are a few wrinkles in the official narrative that I know not to be true. The major one is about the Voyager's Golden Record."

"How did you find out about it?"

"My family keeps the unpublished memoir of my ancestor, Dr. Solarin. He was among the Monrovia eye witnesses."

"Solarin is your relative?"

That was the first time when I registered an emotion in her voice.

"Yes. Why?"

"Well, that explains your ability to oscillate..."

"My ability to do what?"

"No, no. Forget about it. It doesn't matter. Why do you think the Voyager record is important?"

"It may or may not be important. But it may imply that the initial intent of the Unkari was peaceful."

"Your guess is right. The Unkari came to warn humans. Sending strategic information into space without any idea as to who may be coming across it ... well, it is dangerous. Humans are not ready to match any extraterrestrial civilization at war."

"Even the Unkari?"

"Especially the Unkari."

330

"Ok, if they are so powerful, why did they 'play' diplomacy with us?"

"They did not 'play.' The Unkari are patient and just. They wanted to give humans a chance." The transporter stopped, and we exited to what seemed to be a city, filled with foreign noises and chatter. "Tilt your head back and keep your eyes wide open," She commanded. I complied. I experienced sharp pain, as if punched in the eyes. I twitched in pain and grabbed my eyes with my palms. "It will get better in a minute." I heard her reassurance. "I activated your optic nerve."

"Oh my God!!!" I was yelping in pain. "This is intense! Why did you do it??"

"I needed to prevent you from using your equipment. Obstructing your vision seemed appropriate. It's just nano-saline eye drops, no big deal."

I had to sit down on the ground because the experience made me lightheaded. That was when I removed my palms from my face and saw shapes. Shapes at first, then - more clearly. My vision was returning. In a few minutes, I could make sense of my surroundings. We were obviously in an advanced city that at first glance reminded me of Earth Prime architecture. Tall buildings framed the skyline, and the streets were crowded with... people! Humans!

"What is this place?"

Awaiting for the explanation, I turned to the woman who called herself She.

Tall, with a heap of fiery red hair, She wore a slick black uniform revealing a well-trained physique. I couldn't decide if She was attractive. The word that came to my mind was "blank". Light red eyebrows, red eyelashes, extremely pale skin definitely untouched by natural sunlight, thin shapely lips that framed her small mouth - all in all, a striking appearance, but far from a heartthrob. Or maybe she just wasn't my type. But then, my captors were generally not my type anyway. "Welcome to Istanbul." She said. "I know you have many questions, but there is no one who can provide you with better answers than Otis Solarin himself."

My eyes nearly popped out of their sockets.

"Oh you must be kidding me. The man has been dead for 300 years now!"

331

"You may not be too far from the truth, Mazula. By the way, you may remove your headgear. This human reservation has perfect terrestrial climate."

18
329 YEARS AWAKE

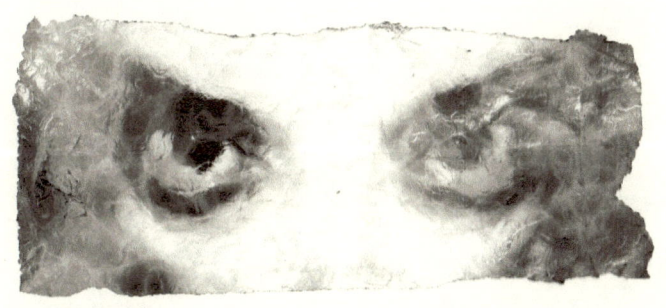

This Istanbul was nothing like the historic Istanbul I'd read about. A hodgepodge of terrestrial and alien features, it had modern architecture with many human elements: windows, balconies, skyscrapers, and doors; but it was shaped in clusters, like termite hills, with sharp peaks representing separate buildings. These individual peaks were connected by catwalks and parking zones for the air-gliding vehicles that moved in dozens of strict horizontal air lanes. Looking up to the sky, I saw a lattice of vehicles moving in orderly lanes, arranged without any visible demarcations. I immediately thought about termites travelling in strict routes that only they could understand.

335

We walked on one of the pedestrian catwalks with safety rails on both sides, and I glanced down, behind the rail. There were so many layers of catwalks below me. I could not see the ground floor; it disappeared in the lingering fog. Multiple elevators and pathways elaborately connected various pedestrian routes, creating a mindboggling maze.

"How big is this place?" I asked in complete awe.

"Six million humans live here."

That's a whole army! I thought to myself. And they are just sitting around here, prisoners in another galaxy? Another question was when and how all these people got here in the first place. "What have you done to all of these people? Are they brainwashed?"

"Not any more than you are, by your own government."

"Unkari are not their government!"

"It's just a matter of semantics. For all practical purposes, the Unkari govern this place, and they do an admirable job, if you ask me." She was unfazed.

We kept walking as more and more quirky features grabbed my attention. It was strangely familiar, and yet, very foreign, as if someone had taken my memories of human civilization, spread them out, and gone through them with scissors, randomly replacing pieces with something else. Street vendors sold big pretzel-shaped bagels sprinkled with poppy and sesame seeds, except they did not sit in the booths, but drove buggy-type vehicles that were propelled with oars! These buggies had dolly-like compartments upfront where all for-sale goodies were proudly displayed. The buggies hovered twenty centimeters above the ground.

She and I walked on the green crystalline cobblestone sidewalk, with two silent guards a few steps behind us. We came to a cross-walk and waited for the streetlight to display a "go," but instead of the green light, a spray of green powder spewed in the air from the hovering streetlight box. Across the street I noticed a couple of young men dressed in eccentric outfits, which I can't begin to describe because my attention was diverted to a pet monkey that they walked on a leash. The monkey properly heeled and waited for the command to continue walking. Once I noticed one pet monkey, I realized that they were everywhere. All kinds of primates actually: baboons, snow monkeys, chimpanzees, and others that were not like any monkeys I had seen on Earth, probably a result of selective breeding. Monkey-friendly signs were displayed at every restaurant, with water bowls and fruit baskets outside the entrances.

We crossed the busy intersection and continued walking down the pedestrian packed street. The city was enormous. It reminded me of Lagos: overcrowded and bustling with smells, sounds, and activity. Occasionally I saw people walking through the walls; other times I saw people leaping from the top floors to the ground, but instead of splattering, they slowed down and gracefully continued walking as if they merely stepped off the escalator in the mall. Not that the place was unfathomable. In fact, nothing here was out of the realm of possibility. But the probability of all these things assembled in one place was so remote, and the sights were so unique, that I had to triple-take for it to properly register in my brain.

I noticed that both men and women wore similar outfits. At least there was no apparent gender difference. Upon closer scrutiny, the outfits consisted of loose pants and tunics. This basic outfit was decorated with vibrant scarves and strands of artificial flowers.

I noticed that people intently scrutinized us when we passed by. The more I tried to understand what they thought of me, the more I felt assured that they were in fact less concerned with me, and more concerned about She and our trailing entourage. Indeed, whenever my eyes met with anyone there, I didn't see disapproval or amusement like back on Earth Prime. One thing they clearly cared about was She. I don't know what her function was in this society, but I could tell that whatever it was people knew better than to cross her path.

"They are scared of you!" I realized.

"Mind your business, Mazula," She cut me off. "By the way, we've already arrived."

337

We came to a place with an elevator attached to the side of the building. The elevator door faded away, and we stepped in. The inside walls were completely transparent, including a barely opaque floor. I have no fear of heights. I really don't. But the Unkari messed with my senses too much lately, so my brain was justified in expecting to be dropped to the ground at any point.

This mission was making me twitch, and I didn't like it.

The elevator went up twenty-seven floors and stopped. The door faded away for the second time, and we entered a dimly lit room that looked like a large high-tech cave: uneven walls had the appeal of ruggedness, and yet they were clearly purposefully designed this way.

"Hello, Desiree. It is good to finally meet you."

I heard the voice, coming seemingly from everywhere.

"Who's here?"

"I am Otis Solarin," The voice, manifested in front of us as a hologram.

The old man's eyes beamed with excitement.

"Desiree, my girl, it is an honor to meet one of my descendants. Look at you! So...strong!"

I glanced at She, who stood beside me. "You need to adjust the sensitivity settings of this simulation," I said, disregarding the hologram. But the hologram refused to be disregarded.

"Forgive me, dear, I am not a simulation. I am... I was about to say 'flesh and blood,' but there is no flesh and no blood in me, as you can see. I am confusing you. I am Otis Solarin, your great-great-grandfather."

"Ok, so you are a simulation of my great-great-grandpa," I said in a mocking tone. "So what!"

"She, tell her."

"Desiree, this is a sentient hologram. And more accurately, this is your relative's consciousness projected on a neuro-photonic matrix. Dr. Solarin is as sentient as you and me."

The self-proclaimed Solarin took me by the hand. The touch was soft, as if it was skin, but not warm. Holding my hand, he lightly tugged me towards the back of the room, where he had some unusual technology that at least in part looked organic. The corner was set up as a workstation, with a desk and a chair, and two couches arranged in an L shape in front of the desk. I followed to where I was directed and eased my weary body into the soft couch.

Solarin was fidgeting, shifting from foot to foot as he tried to find a comfortable position for his hands. "Do you still play hoverball on Earth Prime? Who won last year's championship?" Solarin was glowing with excitement. He looked like a child on Christmas morning, right before ripping the wrappings off a present.

"Stop the circus already!" I snapped. "What is this place? Who are all these humans?"

My tone seemed to put urgency in the matter, and Solarin began to talk.

"I am sorry, Lieutenant. I know how strange it all must appear to you."

"Oh, you do?"

"Certainly I do. When I arrived here, three hundred years ago, I was shocked to find out that there was a population of several million people living among the Unkari."

"Several million? And you couldn't figure out how to escape?"

"We are not prisoners. This is our home. For this generation, anyway."

"AAAAH... Stop talking in riddles! I need water. Do you have water?"

After a minute one of the guards brought a tall green glass. I ran a quick chem scan. It really was water - clean and safe to drink. I downed the entire glass in a few gulps. The emerging headache began to subside.

"Now, start talking. And no riddles."

***

"I know you have many questions, and I was told to answer them to the fullest, so we have a lot of ground to cover, and nearly not enough time. First of all, you are on Lenauri, the home planet of two Unkari dynasties: Enkri and Katu."

"Two dynasties? That's new."

"Our government did not know a lot, but whatever little they knew, they did not share with the public."

That much I already knew. Ever since the First Contact, paranoia was the only consistent characteristic in our politics. Solarin assumed a lecture mode, probably remembering his days in the university auditorium. Finally, his hands found a comfortable position, folded behind his back, and he continued.

"First of all, you need to understand something about Lenauri. This world orbits a dim star at an astonishing distance of seventy-five AUs, that is seventy-five times the distance from Sun to Earth. Lenauri orbits the star in 240.170 human years. This is one Unkari year."

"How long do they live anyway?"

"They live on average 200 years. Unkari years, that is. If you do the math, that's forty-eight million human years, but Unkari history has records of the longest-living member of the Katu dynasty who passed away at the ripe age of sixty-five million human years old."

The number was impossible to wrap my head around, but at least that explained why the Unkari negotiated with humans over the property issues that were five billion years away. From their perspective, in only two or three Unkari generations, Sagittarius Dwarf would completely lose its structural integrity and be absorbed into the Milky Way. According to Dr. Solarin, Sagittarius Dwarf completed a loop around the Milky Way every one hundred million years. For an average Unkari, that was a relatively small timescale. From their perspective, they lived in a volatile dying world. That explained a lot. It was astonishing that we didn't know about it before.

Or did we? Was the government concealing this information?

Too many questions raced through my head as I listened to Solarin's briefing. "The Unkari evolved on this planet, and although they colonized many worlds, their entire metabolism and biochemistry is firmly tied to the conditions on Lenauri. Since their species are so long-lived, even by the universe's standards, they did not develop flexible adaptive mechanisms like humans did during the course of evolution."

Solarin busily gesticulated and paced back and forth.

"What I am trying to say is that the Unkari are intimately connected to the natural cycles of Lenauri. If you keep that in mind, you will understand the nature of the Enkri and Katu dynasties. Now, you already know that the Unkari year lasts

240170 human years. How long do you think their day lasts? Don't strain yourself, dear. Lenauri's revolution period around its axis is 658 human years: 329 years of day, and 329 years of night. This cycle makes the basis of the Unkari life cycle. Lenauri is a large world, about three times the size of Earth. For 329 years, one part of the planet faces the star, while the other part is in the dark. The Unkari on the dark side hibernate, while the Unkari on the star-lit side take care of all businesses, down to foreign policy, economics, and defence. Hence the two dynasties that take shifts in running the Unkari civilization: Enkri and Katu."

"Who's in charge now?"

"Right now, it is the Enkri day. It started in 2260 and will be over very shortly, in 2589. Enkri made the official First Contact with Earth in 2275 and tried to negotiate. Enkri time is running out, Desiree. And trust me, humanity does not want to meet Katu day without firmly established diplomatic relations."

"Why?"

"Let's put it this way. Enkri and Katu have their philosophic differences when it comes to humans. There is a lot I still do not understand myself, but suffice to say, remember the old human tales about alien abductions? If you look into the history carefully, the first records of abductions can be traced to the 1930s. Do the math. Katu day started in 1931. When they awoke, they saw that humans made tremendous advances in technology and were looking at space as the next frontier. Katu knew, within their one day, they would see dramatic changes in human technology."

341

"It makes sense. From their perspective, humans could not be disregarded any more."

"Exactly. The other thing that Katu discovered when they woke up were how violent and contemptuous humans had become, how much they had increased their sheer destructive power. Observing humans from afar was not a viable option anymore. Katu needed to understand what made humans tick, how we think, the extent of our loyalty to humanity, and where our loyalties are in general. As the result of three global wars, Katu clearly believed that human loyalty was a fictional concept, and for each individual human it meant something different."

"So... are you saying... all these people here... *were abducted?*"

"This place, Istanbul, is filled with the abducted descendants of the Katu day, except it was not as nice and liveable during the Katu reign. In fact, this place had no name at all. I named it Istanbul when I arrived here. Actually, I was the first human to voluntarily go with the Unkari. When Enkri woke up, they abandoned the research carried out by Katu which relied on fresh human samples. They also tore down the barracks and built this city to give humans as close to a normal life as they could."

"Forgive me for interrupting, but what's up with all the monkeys?"

"Ah, monkeys. You will notice a lot of quirks in what the Unkari created here. Monkeys are just one of them. This is actually the result of the abandoned Katu experiments. Even I don't have access to the primate research. Supposedly it has something to do with our evolution. When Enkri awoke, they abandoned the animal research as well. All these pets are descendants of lab animals. Katu had no interest in the usual human pets, so you won't find cats or dogs here. It's all monkeys."

342

"I see."

"The rest of the oddities here are because Enkri are huge fans of human science fiction. The Unkari don't have anything like literature or movies, and at first they thought that humans were a race of pathological liars, because we constantly made up things that were not real. When I explained what fiction meant to us, that it is our drive towards excellence and achievement, all of a sudden they began reading everything they could get a hold of. Without a doubt, Enkri know our fiction better than we do. That is why you will find Unkari trying to create things that exist only in our fiction. Their technological prowess made it possible for the Unkari to make these things real."

"Sci-fi loving aliens? Ok, this may be the craziest thing I've heard so far."

"I know, I know, it is a lot to stomach at once."

"I still don't know what happened to you. What - I mean, *who* - are you now?"

"Fair enough. When I arrived here, I was sick. I had a terminal tumor, and very little time left to live. That's partly why the Unkari agreed to bring me here. They could not fix my health, but they could give me a new form of existence, a digital one."

"Ok. Let's say I believe you. What can you do, being a hologram, if you don't mind me asking?"

"I can do just about anything here."

"Aren't you are made of photons!"

"Ok, I don't know if you are ready for it. But here it goes. This whole place is a holographic projection. I - like everything else around you - am made of light."

343

19
REPRESENTATIVE

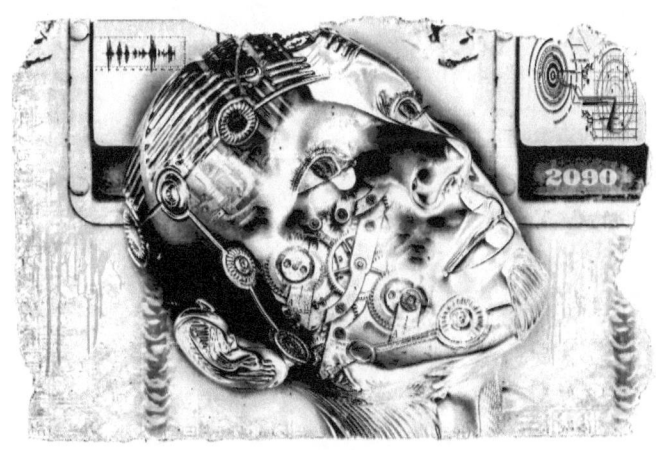

Solarin and I had been talking for over an hour when She received a ping signal. She excused herself and stepped outside, while the two guards reinforced their warning pose and fixated on us with even more intensity.

I wanted to ask Solarin how to escape, but the serious big guys peered their trained eyes at us, discouraging any funny business. In less than a minute, She returned to us and insisted that we cut the audience short because we were expected elsewhere.

I presumed that elsewhere meant my trial, and I was right.

347

The few minutes it took us to get in the elevator and outside the building, I spent recapping the situation. What was I supposed to think after talking to the hologram of my long-dead ancestor? Ok, assume there *are* two Unkari tribes: one of them likes us, and the other - not so much. One had attempted to establish diplomacy with us, whilst the other had abducted humans for centuries. And worst of all, the "good guys" were about to take a nap - one long 329-year nap. Within a year and change, humans would be facing the Katu Day, which just as well could be called Doom's Day.

The more I thought about all of it, I found myself able to understand the motives of the Katu tribe. It was logical: An up-and-coming race of short-lived, ambitious, and destructive creatures was not a perfect choice for a neighbor. Aliens must serve their own interest, just like humans do. To me, the suspicious part was Enkri's alleged affinity with humans. Could I believe in science-fiction-loving, benevolent, nearly immortal (by our standards) beings? What's so special about us? That part made no sense; and whatever made no sense bothered me.

***

After visiting with Dr. Solarin, I was directed to the transporter, and we left the reservation. The transporter walls were transparent, and with my sight returned they gave me for the first time a glimpse of the Unkari world. The red star of Lenauri was in a position of late evening, and if I did not know that a day here lasted for centuries, I would think that the darkness was about to envelope this side of the planet.

Lenauri was a frozen world, beautiful and definitely alien. Green oceans were covered with a thick layer of exotic-looking fluorescent gasses. Green-blue mountains were made of rock-hard ice. Glowing cities nestled in the valleys, peering through the thick clouds rapidly shifting above the surface. "She, are you a hologram too?" I asked.

348

"No. Otis Solarin is the only sentient hologram that the Unkari have created. In fact, the technology was designed specifically for him, as a matter of gratitude for his cooperating in the diplomatic effort. The rest of us are flesh-and-blood descendants of the humans, brought here by the Katu dynasty."

"Wait, Otis claimed that all of Istanbul was a holographic projection."

"I see. What he meant was that the entire architectural structure of everything you saw was a hologram. The living beings there are real. They are provided real nutrition. But there is no actual matter involved in building anything inside. I believe this is the compromise Enkri had to agree to with the Katu in order to prevent security breaches."

"Clever, good military thinking. If there are no actual materials in there, no weapon could be manufactured."

"Exactly."

After having an eye-opening experience at the human reservation on Lenauri, the Unkari leadership decided that I gained sufficient knowledge to fully embrace my guilt and face my death sentence. Ironically, I had died many times in those strange loops while being captured, so my brain was more preoccupied with the new reality of existential human threat rather than my own death. Being stuck 89,000 light years away from the nearest human outpost, I had no way of warning Earth about the Katu awakening.

"I still have too many questions. You can't execute me yet," I pleaded.

"One can never have too many questions. What you know is enough. Now you know that you personally, and the leadership of humanity, invaded a nation that meant you no harm. This level of understanding is sufficient."

"Wait a minute. Maybe Enkri did not mean ill, but what about Katu? They treated us like research animals, abducted us, and brought your ancestors here against their will!"

"By the same token of logic, you are personally guilty for what your ancestors did to the native populations on Earth. They also had no regard for the rights of weaker races and exploited them as they saw fit. Didn't humans move on, leaving those matters to history?"

"Don't tell me about weaker races! My home country Liberia was founded by the freed slaves who left the land of their masters! I know well what it means to live in the shadow of oppression, firmly ingrained in the psyche of generations. Only thanks to the Big Ice did the world turn to Africa for salvation..."

349

"...Big Ice?"

"That's right. You missed all of it. The Big Ice, as we call it, was the environmental disaster that turned the Earth Prime into an ice ball. The only habitable environment remained near the tropical belt. All of a sudden, our countries and our people mattered. But if you think the world leaders' attitude was sincere, you are wrong. They just needed us. They had to work with us side by side. It is a miracle that our leadership had enough courage to renegotiate the power dynamics and remain masters on their own land. Don't you see, this makes us more alike than you know. You may think you are free now, but you owe it to your ancestors, who were enslaved and brought here, to remember their history and not belittle what they have gone through just because you personally live in a refurbished, cosier version of their prison!"

I realized that I was leaning forward and clenching fists to white knuckles behind my back, as my hands were restrained. I exhaled and proceeded more calmly.

"Look, you don't even have a decent name. They might as well give you a number, or a bar code. She - what kind of name is that? This is a designation of your gender, but not of who you are."

"Hmm... I hadn't thought of it that way. Actually we do have a numerical designation as well. But don't you? You have an ID as an Earth Nations citizen, you have a military rank, various designations for property rights..."

"All true. But I also have a personal name. Reinsford was the name given to me by my mother before she died giving birth. She died for my right to bear this name. To this day, this name is important to me, and I kept it as a middle name. Desiree is the name I chose, because it represents who I really am, who I want to be. To me this name is important because it reflects my free will to be the kind of person I want to be. Mazula is my last name. It relates to my ancestors. This is my root, from which I draw strength. It reminds me of my family and everything they have been through. I must remember, otherwise I'd be adrift in this huge and lonely universe. What makes you remember?"

350

She broke eye contact. An awkward silence filled the space between us.

"You make me feel uncomfortable. I used to have all my answers in order."

"What about now?"

"I don't wish to discuss this anymore." She cut the conversation off, and I did not insist.

Whatever raw nerve I uncovered, it was up to her to deal with it.

***

The trial consisted of an Unkari panel of seven. Dressed in

green robes, they sat in a semi-circle and folded their tentacles above their heads. I suspected that it was the Unkari version of folding arms while waiting for something. She and I sat in front of the panel in a booth of transparent material that maintained human habitable conditions. After observing the panel for a while, I noticed another character, sitting separately from the panel. That Unkari was dressed in a shade of brown, wearing a headpiece adorned with an octagonal purple crystal. The character struggled to sit upright as if fighting off extreme drowsiness.

"This guy could use a cup of coffee." I pointed at the brown robe guy.

She fired off a condemning glance. "That is the Katu ambassador."

"I thought they were all asleep."

Seeing an openly hostile alien at my trial did not look promising.

"Dynasties always have representatives from the other tribe. They are sent to the other side after their birth and are raised by the opposite tribe to assume the role of an ambassador when they come of age. This is the only way to beat the Unkari metabolism and remain awake, when the rest of your dynasty is in stasis."

"Well, it doesn't look like he is doing a good job staying awake."

"Staying awake for a Katu during Enkri day is a terrible burden, and it requires additional chemical substances. If you were, however, to point it out at a public event to another Unkari, you would be considered a classless idiot."

"Duly noted, madam. Not that I am going to be invited to an Unkari reception any time soon. But what if a Katu grows up and decides not to serve as an ambassador?"

"They can't do that. First, it is an act of treason against their dynasty. Being an ambassador is an honor. This kind of honor gives the whole ambassador's kin great status and privileges. But even if they stopped being ambassadors, they could not go back to the Katu society."

"In other words, he cannot go back and cannot stay among Enkri after resigning a diplomatic rank."

"Exactly. And where would he go in the universe anyway? Without being watched over by his species while he sleeps for 329 years, his life is always in danger."

"Tough break for this guy. Speaking of bad luck, when is my trial going to start? Not that I am in a hurry."

"We are waiting for your fellow soldier. She is on her way from Istanbul."

"Oh, so she went to Istanbul as well?"

"Yes, she did. She will be here any minute. You both are required to give a remorseful speech. Collect your thoughts, you must do a good job."

"Will it help my case?"

"No."

"Oh. In that case..."

I was interrupted as guards escorted Ebony in. She stepped into the depressurizing chamber attached to our booth. Once the atmosphere in the chamber was replaced with a human-compatible one, the door slid open, and she walked in, removing her headgear.

352

"Ebony!" I fought the urge to hug her.

"I know, I am happy to see you too, Mazula. But now is not the time. I know you have met Dr. Solarin as well."

"I have. It was quite a trip."

"What a charming reunion," She snarled, sizing Ebony from head to toe.

"What's her problem?" Ebony nodded in the liaison's direction.

"You are the one with problems here," said She with cold contempt in her voice. "Mazula's offense is grave, but you are in no less trouble. So make peace with your life now, while you are still breathing."

"Hey, ladies, behave yourselves!" The small glass booth

was not a place for a cat fight. Or was it? I waved off the thought of Ebony beating the crap out of our red-head hostess as if she was a synthetic fur coat, but could not hide the smile.

"Mazula! You dirty dog!" Giggling, Ebony lightly punched me in the side with her elbow. Apparently our NVC connection had grown stronger; she received the mental image in my head.

"That is enough!" barked She, obviously perplexed as to what cheered us so much. "Prisoner, where is your liaison?"

"I am here!" The voice came from nowhere - no, more like from Ebony's pocket.

Ebony retrieved a small green crystal from her army pants pocket and placed it on the desk in front of us. From the crystal, a heap of light ushered out, arranging into a hologram of Otis Solarin." I was requested to represent Ensign Ebony River at her trial. At your service. Shall we begin?"

353

20
KATU JUSTICE

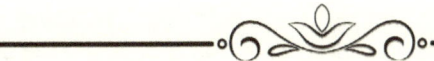

And so our trial began.

The climate-controlled chamber in which Ebony and I were kept as Unkari prisoners had a simple black matt desk and a long bench made of the same material. Our liaisons were on our sides. The prisoner chamber was situated in front of seven Enkri tribe members, and one Katu ambassador, a member of the rival tribe, whose function was to keep an eye on how the rivals did business. Humans presented the major point of contention between Enkri and Katu. Katu wanted nothing to do with us and would eliminate humanity without hesitation. It was understandable, because we occupied coveted real estate in the Milky Way. I suspected that the Katu ambassador couldn't be happier that our ship had been captured invading Unkari space on Erinozhan. This event gave him the leverage he needed in advancing an anti-humanity agenda. The caveat was that it was the Enkri day, and Enkri, for some unknown reason, did not jump on the idea of destroying humanity.

The drowsy Katu ambassador rose from his seat and announced the opening of the trial. Seven Enkri rose one by one, spraying in the air something powdery and garishly green from their tentacle orifices. *"They just swore an oath to be truthful to the facts,"* Ebony NVC'd me, sensing my confusion.

"I see you are an expert in Unkari trial procedures now," I NVC'd back, smiling.

"I did not waste my time with Dr. Solarin. Since we could pick up the speed of our conversation, I used our meeting to prepare a strategy for this trial."

"Nice. And what is my part in all of it?"

"I wish you hadn't asked me. You may not like it."

Our telepathic chatter was interrupted by new developments in the trial. By the time the judges had finished spewing colored powder, a human walked in, dressed in a full body uniform that covered his face, and took his position to the left side, between the panel and our chamber. There he made some subtle hand movements and a puddle of liquid silver hung in mid air. He inserted all his fingers in the puddle, wiggled them a bit, and then spoke.

"The Unkari interest in the trial is represented by He, Designation 11-54-87-53."

This guy must be our prosecutor, I thought.

"Who represents the interest of the human, Designation Mazula Desiree Lieutenant?"

She rose from her seat next to me and spoke:

"The interest of the human Designation Mazula Desiree Lieutenant is represented by She, Designation 65-98-75-11." After pronouncing her part, She took her seat beside me.

The prosecutor continued.

"Who represents the interest of the human Designation River Ebony Ensign?"

"The interest of the human Designation River Ebony Ensign is represented by Solarin Otis, Designation 65-99-87-65," said Otis by Ebony's side, whose hologram lightly flickered whenever I looked at him from a different angle.

The prosecutor took a long pause, "fishing" for something in his silvery puddle, and finally spoke. "Representative Solarin Otis, your designation is incorrect."

Otis had a look as if he had anticipated this turn of events.

"I plea to un-archive my file from the catalogue of deceased humans."

"On what grounds?"

"On grounds that *I am not dead,*" said Otis with a smug smile.

"Unable to verify." The prosecutor was swiping something in his liquid crystal database, sinking all ten fingers in the silver puddle hanging in front of him. "Present your evidence."

"A human, Designation Descartes, established the law that states the following: 'I think therefore I am.' According to this law, thought is a primary condition for existence, and the physical body is secondary. As it is proven by human and Unkari experience, a physical body may be replaced in part or in whole, but that does not lead to the destruction of one's thought. If a human brain is part of a human body, it may also be replaced. What constitutes the essence of a human is his consciousness, which is customarily defined as self-aware thought, irrespective of the vessel that it is contained in. During the present Enkri day, my physical body, which constituted the vessel for my consciousness, was replaced due to a terminal malfunction. The new carrier vessel, made of a neuro-photonic matrix, is a more reliable material. The difference between this procedure, and, say, the clipping of a toe nail, in essence, is only a question of scale. At this moment, the honorable Enkri panel, the honorable Katu ambassador, and the honorable Human-Unkari representative are witnessing the evidence of the self-aware thought process of a human, Designation Solarin Otis, which provides grounds for establishing the fact... that *I am not dead.* The fact that *I am not dead* testifies to the fact that my file was archived erroneously, and provides grounds for recovering my file from the archives of deceased humans of the Unkari reservation and establishing my full rights as a citizen of a second class. Lastly, once my file is recovered, I may use my privilege to serve as a representative before the honorable trial."

Otis finished his speech and took his seat by Ebony's side.

"What's going to happen next?" I NVC'd her.

"Next, they are going to vote. Don't worry, it is a mere

formality. Enkri have waited for a long time for an opportunity to re-establish Otis in his full rights, within the parameters allowed for humans, of course."

"What about Katu?"

"He will vote too, and probably will vote against it. Don't worry, his vote only counts if any of the Enkri abstain from the vote and it results in a draw."

The Unkari took a vote by spraying bright yellow pigment in the air. All seven of them were unanimous. I figured that must have been a "pro" vote. The Katu ambassador, however, sprayed a crimson red pigment. Ebony was right, he had voted against reinstating Otis in his rights. However, the total vote was overwhelmingly in Otis's favor. Next, the prosecutor began recounting a long list of our crimes. Those facts did not present anything new, so I stopped listening and turned to Ebony instead.

"Let's go back to the part that I won't like."

"Do you know about the differences in Enkri and Katu opinions on humans?"

"I do, but I have no idea what's the angle of Enkri. Their position makes no sense."

"We need to talk. After he finishes announcing our crimes, we can ask for a recess."

***

"What do you mean, I need a tumor in my brain?"

Ebony and Otis were filling me in on their plan, which evidently involved me getting a brain cancer. "It's not as bad as it sounds. I had one before," argued Otis.

"Oh yeah? And look where it got you! Cuz no offense... you are a bunch of laser beams right now."

She patiently listened. Their suggestion was just as unexpected for her as it was for me. The last thing I expected from this cold, officious, brainwashed woman was to step in and participate in planning our way around the death sentence. But, it turns out, she had her own agenda. "Desiree, you are not seeing your situation clearly. If by the end of Enkri day humans have failed to reach a diplomatic solution with the Unkari, not only will you be dead, but also I guarantee you, all of humankind will be wiped out. Not that I care about Earth Prime or any other of your colonies, but I am afraid, because of you, the Istanbul settlement on Lenauri will be wiped out as well. We are talking about six million people. If you don't do what they're suggesting, you will be guilty of no less than genocide."

"Wait a minute, Madam 'I-want-nothing-to-do-with -these-stupid-humans!' Correct me if I'm wrong, but we are prisoners here, and your job is to make sure I feel very guilty before being executed. You are standing here like a flag pole, with all your gestalt letting us know that you don't give two shits about your own race in the first place, forget about Ebony and me, two lowly, unworthy-of-your-sneeze humans. And now, if I won't allow a tumor to be implanted in my brain, I am a slaughterer of your precious six million brainwashed vegetables, living the high life in a cozy concentration camp. What exactly do you expect me to do?"

She opened her mouth to let me have it, but held it back and turned her gaze away from me. I was harsh on her, or maybe not even harsh enough. Too much was at stake, and I did not understand which side she was on, if I could trust her, and what was really going on inside her head. "Desiree, calm down, fighting is unproductive," stepped in Dr. Solarin. "There is so much you still do not understand. Just promise me to keep an open mind and listen to what I have to say." I shrugged my shoulders in defeat and sat on the bare floor of the empty, dimly-lit room we were in. The rest followed my example. Solarin began his story.

361

***

Many years ago, Unkari years, before even our solar system was formed, a group of Enkri explorers left their galaxy to study the far reaches of the universe. Their vessel entered a space-time anomaly, a fold in the fabric of the universe, and they slid into a crack that led them to an unknown region of space. The vessel was damaged, and they could not return home by the end of their waking cycle. They had no choice but to find a safe place for hibernation. Without Katu members around, they were vulnerable while in their stasis, unable to protect themselves. They landed on one planet that had similar habitable conditions compared to their homeland, and prepared to fall asleep, not knowing if they would ever wake up alive.

After the sleep cycle, the entire Enkri research team woke up unharmed, except, they found themselves in a totally different place. The planet chosen for hibernation was barren, uninhabited. That was why waking up in the middle of an alien city, buzzing with strange creatures, was so unexpected. When the Enkri woke up, the city came to an alert, and millions gathered on that square within a short period of time. It seemed as if the creatures were anticipating this moment.

Hesitant to open the stasis chambers, five Enkri waited to see what was going to happen next. That was when they saw one of the creatures stepping forward from the crowd, taking a place at a podium, and speaking through a voice amplifier. The words sounded familiar. It took a moment for the Enkri to realize that the creatures were attempting to vocalize the Unkari written language. "I have waited for this moment my entire life," said the creature in Enkri tongue, heavily laden with accent. "So had my family, who did not live to this day to see you wake up. Greeting you after your sleep cycle was a work of three of our generations.

"We found you in our neighboring system during a mining expedition. At first, we didn't know what had happened to you, but we knew once thing: we could not leave you where you were. The planet was on a collision course with a rouge asteroid. The asteroid was of an unusually large size, and we could not destroy it without scattering debris across the entire system. If we attempted to destroy it, the accelerated debris would have formed a large volatile asteroid belt that would tear apart the surface of the planet where you slept with a myriad of impacts. One way or another, you would not survive.

"We made a decision to evacuate you to our home world. Your vessel is in our orbit, and you can access it any time. We had enough time to study your language and your ship's logs to realize why you changed your course. At this point, we have almost finished updating your navigation systems. Soon you will be able to return home.

"We welcome you to our world as dear guests. However, if you decide to hurt us in any way, we have formidable means of protection that your species do not have. We weave the basic fabric of the universe. Our collective thought can skip back and forth between our choices, so that we choose the version of reality that we find most advantageous. We can go back to the moment when we made the decision to rescue you, and choose to leave you to die in your sleep."

To make their point clear, the creatures prepared a little demonstration. They brought forward a young creature of their kind, and another one, a grown-up one, who pointed a weapon at the youngster. The little one did not appear to experience any distress, and when it was ready, it signalled to the gunman to open fire. The Enkri scientists saw the little creature sprawl on the ground, with its vital liquids oozing from the fatal wound. The crowd fell silent, as if calmly waiting for something to happen. The Unkari could not believe how cruel that demonstration was. Obviously, they thought the point of the demonstration was to show that just as they were merciless with their little ones, so they would be unwavering with the outsiders.

What happened next rocked the Unkari's understanding of life and the universe as they knew it. Within a few moments of deafening silence, the bloody scene of the youngling on the ground disappeared. Instead, the Enkri saw the same small creature, alive and well, smiling and standing in front of the gunman. It was as if someone had reset reality to the previous parameters. The small creature, like before, seeming in no distress, ordered the gunman to fire.

What a ridiculous repetition of cruelty, thought the Enkri, struck to the core. Except this time, the creature quickly stepped to the side, avoiding the deadly fire.

The crowd roared in approval, throwing herbs and headpieces in the air.

***

"Otis, is there any point to this story?" I finally had to interrupt him. "I am sorry, all of this sounds like a fairy tale."

"Well, let me bring it home for you. Enkri archives hold images of numerous creatures from that planet. Would you like to see them?"

"Sure, why not."

Otis projected a holographic screen.

Click. First picture. *Click.* Second one.

Click, click, click, click, click, click.

Dozens, hundreds of them.

They were all humans.

***

I walked down the dimly lit hallway towards the trial room. My hands were restricted behind my back. We had a plan, if you could call it a plan. But it was better than nothing. Ebony sent me telepathic messages of encouragement, but I could sense that she was putting on a brave face and was not entirely confident in the outcome.

In the prisoner's chamber, we took our seats. The prosecutor walked in and accessed the liquid database. Ebony was fidgeting in her seat. The only way she could avoid looking panicked was to sit on her palms and tuck her feet under the bench. Her tension was palpable. *"Remember, you must admit your guilt and agree to a death sentence,"* she NVC'd.

364

"I doubt I can forget that," I fired back.

Meanwhile, the prosecutor completed all the formalities that resumed the trial and asked the representatives if the prisoners were ready for the guilt speech.

Ebony rose first. "Noble Enkri judges, noble Katu ambassador. I, Human Designation River Ebony Ensign, am gravely saddened with the realization of my guilt before the Unkari people. I fully accept responsibility for the death of two Holy Warriors of Lenar Unkar and am ready to accept a just and commensurate punishment. In my defence, I testify that I did not become a soldier and a killer on behalf of humans of my own free will. I had no choice. I was born on the Fourth Orbital Colony of Earth Prime to a race of reclusive and decidedly pacifist people. Never in the history of our people had we joined the military, nor committed a violent crime. Our people believe in science and the pursuit of knowledge as the ultimate virtue. For that reason, we enhance the genetic sequence of our offspring before they are born to gift them with superior mental and physical abilities.

"Many would think that the life of our race is perfect. We are sheltered from troubles and are protected by the Earth Nations like a sacred cow, providing the rest of humanity with knowledge. We never starve, rarely get sick, and live exceedingly long lives. There is only one thing that made my life miserable. My people do not allow anyone to leave the colony. My path was chosen for me before I was born. I was going to become a climatologist, a person who studies complicated weather patterns on the planets that humans colonize. My job was to sit at a monitor in my room and study terabytes of data collected by others. I would never be able to see those worlds for myself. My burden was that I wanted to choose my life for myself and become something more than I was told to be. At the age of my maturity, I took a daring step to escape my colony and asked for asylum from the Earth Prime government. I wanted to become a researcher and explorer, much like many of the noble Enkri, and to learn about the universe. However, the Earth Prime government refused to provide me asylum unless I enlisted in the military and served ten years with the Royal Moroccan Fleet.

365

"Once I escaped and created a diplomatic conflict between the Earth Nations and its protectorate, Fourth Orbital Colony, I could not simply return home as if nothing had happened. The military threatened to turn me over to my government if I refused to enlist and comply with all their requirements. If they turned me in, I was looking at capital punishment. In our justice system, capital punishment means stripping away our enhancements and blocking our ability to learn and understand. This is a cruel punishment, which never before been applied to any of my people. On the other hand, none of my people ever committed an offense as grave as I. If I did not have those abilities in the first place, I wouldn't know what I was missing. But since I was born with those abilities, it would be equal to removing a crucial body part. I would never be the same."

I looked at Ebony, and my heart thumped. I had no idea about the details of her enlistment. Poor thing, what she had to endure to earn her freedom. Ebony continued her speech.

"I had no choice but to become a killer. I was sent on a mission that I did not choose. In fact, the Erinozhan was my first field mission. The reason I was sent on this mission was because the military wanted to test my enhanced abilities in combat situations and evaluate what I was truly capable of. Plus, they knew that nobody would be looking for me. Our mission failed. Captured by the Unkari soldiers, we were subjected to various experiments that involved space-time effects. We were forced to live through our own deaths a countless number of times. We were interrogated. The hardship of this experience led us to believe that the Unkari would kill us anyway, unless we attempted to escape. We could not think any other way, because our government concealed a lot of critical information about the First Contact. I knew nothing about Enkri day and Katu day, and that humans owe it to Enkri that our race still exists."

At that point, the Katu ambassador perked up on his seat and spewed a cloud of deep blue pigment. "She, what does that mean?" I whispered in her ear.

"That was an involuntary emotional reaction. The ambassador is rather short-tempered."

"What does this emotion mean?"

"The best way I can put it is contempt."

"In conclusion, I would like to ask noble Enkri and the Katu representatives to forgive my actions. I have never murdered anyone. After much reflection, I regret it. If I could do something differently, I would. But under the circumstances, I had no choice. I ask for my sentence to be just, taking into account the facts that I have most humbly submitted."

The prosecutor nodded in approval, evidently satisfied with how the procedure was progressing.

Next, it was my turn. My speech, however, was rather short and consisted of accepting the guilt for the incriminated crimes. I also pointed out that I had operated under misinformation, and I did not know many facts about the true behavior of the Earth Nations during the First Contact era. This time, the prosecutor did not look as pleased; however, he proceeded to the next step of the trial.

The panel began voting. First, they cast the vote for Ebony's guilt. They voted on whether Ebony was guilty by spraying pigment. The first Enkri to the left voted orange [guilty].

The second voted green [abstained]. "Why would an Enkri abstain from the vote?" I asked She.

"They took an oath, remember? If the judge cannot in all truthfulness conclude that the evidence is sufficient, he must refrain from voting."

Meanwhile, the third Enkri voted orange [guilty]. Ebony was visibly distressed. Two strikes against her, and a potential for a deciding Katu vote. She could hardly breathe.

The forth Enkri voted yellow [not guilty].

"I cannot believe it!" said She, leaving me perplexed as to whether she was excited for Ebony or condemning the judge's leniency.

"Cheer up, Ebony!" Otis placed his holographic hand on her shoulder. "Two-to-one is not a bad vote so far."

However, the next vote made Otis regret his premature enthusiasm.

367

Orange [guilty].

I noticed tears swelling in the corners of Ebony's large purple eyes.

"Three to one," Ebony whispered with breathless lips.

The final two Enkri took a while before casting their votes.

"I'd like to know what goes through their heads now," I mumbled to no one in particular.

That was when the next Enkri voted:

Maroon - turquoise - navy blue - indigo blue.

I lost count of the shades.

"He is taking a recess!" exclaimed She.

"I will never learn this color language!" I exclaimed. "If this is how they spell 'recess...'" I glanced at Ebony. Her eyes looked like thick glass, still and expressionless.

"Hey, She, can we get a cup of coffee and a doughnut around here?"

"I thought you hated Unkari cooking."

"Well, I don't have many options now. Do me a favor, bring me something to eat, would you?"

"Alright. The recess will last for an hour. I guess I have time to bring you something."

"Great! Don't forget sugar and cream!"

"Don't push it, Mazula."

She exited our climate-controlled booth.

Dr. Solarin, Ebony, and I remained sitting there in silence.

"Ok, let's talk."

"What's there to say, Mazula? Do the math. Even if both Enkri vote "not guilty," we have a tie-breaker Katu vote. And we all know what *his* vote will be!"

368

"Maybe so! But Ebony, this is not the end. There is always another option! As long as we live..." I stumbled. "Otis, there is something I don't understand. If they can manipulate space-time..."

"Mazula, you really do not get it, do you? It was not them," Ebony chimed in.

"Not them?"

"It was you! You kept resetting the events every time we tried to escape."

"I did no such thing!"

Otis stepped in. "Well, you are not capable of doing it at your will, like those ancient humanoids. None of us can. But some of us have the gene. I had the gene, and so do you. Ebony here, she doesn't."

"Ok, so I am special. Can I reset reality to the moment before we left on this mission?"

"No, of course you can't!"

"Why? Would that be too easy?"

"In short, yes. Think about it. This ability could cause the end of the universe as we know it, if anyone could do it. The ancients had this ability at the higher rate, in fact, almost all of them could oscillate. But they formed a mental network that removed the ability of one individual to do it. Since right now you are a network of one, you could do it, but your ability to oscillate is underdeveloped."

"Oscillate what? I need some more information."

Ebony stepped in. "Well. This all comes down to quantum mechanics. You've heard that all particles in their natural state exist in a state of quantum superposition, until observed. What it means is that they exist simultaneously in all places at all moments in time. When they are observed, they lock into one definitive state in space and time. For a long time, we did not understand the role of the observer. We used to think that maybe it was because observation in its simplest understanding is the process of shining light on a quantum object. The process of shining light (or bombarding it with the photons, if you will) creates an illusion of observation."

"Well said, Ebony," said Otis. "You are absolutely right about the illusion of observation. What the Unkari learned from studying humans with the gene is that the nature of observation is in fact rooted in human consciousness. That is exactly right, the nature of the universe, on the most basic level, is rooted in human consciousness. Now do you understand why Katu hate us?"

369

"I suppose I do..."

"Enkri, however, well I couldn't tell you this in front of She, but I think they formed something of a cult around human consciousness. They believe that if humanoids are eradicated, the universe will dissolve into a primordial quantum state, where nothing could be defined with any degree of certainty."

"What?" I looked at Otis as if he just said the stupidest thing I'd ever heard. "They can't possibly believe such nonsense."

"You would be shocked if you saw their research. All I can say is that there are a lot of perceptional illusions that we, humans, misinterpreted until we learned more. We looked at the sun and the moon travelling across the horizon and thought that surely they revolved around the Earth. Their observation was true, but not the interpretation. Enkri research points at the fact that human consciousness alters the reality of the universe, and it scares them. They think that our consciousness 'anchors' the reality to one linear timeline, which allows a sequential, corporeal existence. I find it hard to believe, if you ask me, but then I am only a professor of space history. *Human* space history. I know when we conquered every space frontier, who did it, on which vessel, and such. None of my knowledge allows me to think of quantum mechanics at the same level as the Unkari. Ebony here, maybe she can make sense of all of this."

Ebony rubbed her tired eyes. Talking about science distracted her from the gloomy thoughts about the voting, and she welcomed this distraction. "Well, from what I understand, humans have the potential to evolve to a level of consciousness like those ancient humanoids. But right now, as a species, we are at an early stage of our evolution. What the Unkari were able to do with all that research they carried out on abducted humans is to create a certain field which amplifies the genetic ability to oscillate. This field imitates the collective consciousness that would be formed if enough humans evolved into having this ability. But even those who have the gene cannot oscillate yet. The region in our brain that is responsible for this ability is still underdeveloped. The Unkari figured out how to artificially grow the necessary neurons to form this region, but they cannot get this process under control, and eventually it kills the host. See, the brain cells necessary for developing the ability continue growing... until they become life threatening."

"Hence, the tumor," echoed Otis.

"So you agreed to implant these brain cells, that developed into a tumor, willingly?" I asked Otis.

"I did. I had nothing to lose. I had the gene. And let's face it, to study the First Contact, from the inside, is an opportunity of a lifetime for any space historian."

"Even if it would kill you?"

"So you think I am dead?"

"No, Otis, that's not what I meant."

"Well, dead or alive, I guess in my case, it's an issue of semantics. Bookworms like myself love to indulge in such wicked questions. It was too tempting to receive virtual immortality and the ability to see the future of this story. I have to admit, I wanted to know how the story ends. It's a good one."

"Yeah, it's one hell of a story, indeed," I agreed.

"Speaking frankly, I had a few more arguments that made me jump at this opportunity. First, the government was all over me. I was not allowed to speak publicly about what I knew. The university was encouraged to drop my tenure. I was headed towards the bright future of a bum who cries 'doomsday' on the street corner. On the other hand, I could live and study an alien race for centuries. Not much of a choice, if you ask me."

"Don't take it wrong, Otis, but weren't you worried about your soul?"

"Soul-Shmoul! Are you serious? Do you know much about the Solarins' legacy in history? We are the descendants of the great Tai Solarin. Have you heard of him?"

"Doesn't ring a bell." I shrugged.

"That's the problem with your generation. Three hundred years ago, our extended family remembered Tai Solarin and were proud to be related to this great man. You should look him up someday. We don't have time for African history now, but he was one of the great secular thinkers and educators in Nigeria. That's when everyone around believed that the world was created in six days."

Ebony cut our chatter short. "Hey, nice family reunion, but I may not have much time left. Mazula, you have this ability, and you will take it. And you will make the best of it to keep the two races from annihilating each other. And if, in the end, you decide you don't want to become a hologram, fine.

It's your life."

***

The trial resumed shortly after She had fed us some pastry-smelling goop. The panel returned to their seats, and the prosecutor announced that the remaining two Enkri were ready to vote.

Yellow [not guilty].

Yellow [not guilty].

Good news as it was, the vote resulted in a draw.

Ebony burst in tears. Katu's vote was going to decide her fate.

Katu rose from his seat and made some tentacle motions, which She interpreted as a request for a speech. He shook his body as if trying to shake away deep drowsiness and fatigue, and spoke in Unkari, which She translated for me. "I did not expect my vote to be deciding in your case, human Designation River. I also did not expect to learn your history. Apparently, looking the enemy in the face makes it more difficult to hate him. In your case, I realize that perhaps we have something in common: a heavy burden of responsibility placed on us at birth by virtue of merely belonging to a certain class. You were born to carry responsibility that you did not ask for and had no way of abandoning other than becoming an ally and an accomplice in an organization inherently distrustful of our species. Thus is my vote."

Katu raised a tentacle and voted.

Yellow.

Ebony looked at him in disbelief and with a huge gratitude.

She rose and spoke. *"Enticrl shumt rashti."*

Katu nodded and took his seat.

This was such a phenomenal development. I secretly began hoping that I might also get lucky. Meanwhile, the prosecutor announced the vote on my case.

First vote was orange.

Orange.

Orange.

Orange...

I stopped counting. Everyone, including Katu found me guilty.

She grabbed my hand and squeezed it hard. At that moment I wasn't sure what shocked me more, my sentence or her sympathy.

"Mazula, focus!" NVC'd Ebony. *"We have a plan, remember? This is not the end!"*

"If you say so," I fired back.

The final part of the trial was about deciding restitution for the crime.

Since Ebony was found not guilty, her troubles were over. I, however, was expected to give another speech with a proposal of restitution. The prosecutor accessed his database again and announced: "Human Designation Mazula Desiree Lieutenant, you are found guilty by a unanimous vote of Enkri panel and Katu representative. Prior to the trial, you were informed that if found guilty, your crimes amounted to a death sentence. However, you have a debt before the Unkari race. How are you going to repay it?"

373

I rose from the bench and looked at my palms. They were shaking. I clenched them behind my back and spoke. "Honorable Enkri and Katu... I... I acknowledge my guilt before the Unkari people... and accept... my death sentence." Pause. I looked over the panel, they were motionless. No emotions were sprayed in the air. Katu at that moment looked unusually attentive and sat upright with his tentacles folded above his head. "As for restitution, I believe that my death will not provide adequate compensation for my crimes."

"Good job, Desiree, you can do it!" I heard Ebony encouraging me in my head.

"I request my liaison to step in and share our plan for adequate restitution."

The room filled with various pigments. The Unkari were

debating. Finally, they decided to allow Otis to share what he had in mind.

"Honorable Enkri, honorable ambassador Katu. Allow me to express my gratitude for your kindness in reinstating my rights as a Lenauri citizen of second class. Our history goes way back to the early morning of the present Enkri day, when your representatives came ashore on the Monrovia coast. I was the witness of your kind intent and spoke about it as much as I was allowed by my government. Further, I joined the negotiations in Reykjavik and did all in my power to facilitate diplomatic relations between your and my people. I welcomed your people in my world and spent years learning your culture and trying to understand you, because I firmly believed that only through understanding one another may we build bridges.

"My loyalty to your people was repeatedly tested. When the truth of the Katu day was opened to me, I did not hold it against Enkri. For centuries, Katu abducted my people and carried out research to understand how the ancient ancestors of the human species could consciously oscillate between quantum superposition of their choices, the ability that seems to reside in the depths of human consciousness and that is completely lacking in the Unkari species. All the wrongs that Katu dynasty did to my people aside, they did isolate the genetic marker for this ability. As you remember, I volunteered to be tested. You've discovered that I belong to a rare genetic group that carries this marker.

374

"Further, you know that I volunteered to become your research subject. I dedicated my life to this cause, agreeing to implant a neuro-synaptic body in my brain that would eventually spread and disintegrate my brain. I believed that this research would move humanity forward in understanding our own origin, although the truth about it is currently unknown to them. It was Katu decision, many Unkari years ago, to seed Earth with biological material from those ancient and advanced human species to obtain a large laboratory sample and isolate this ability in the human consciousness. It was becoming apparent that only at a certain stage of evolutionary development would humans gain this ability. Previously, humans with the genetic marker could only receive an implant like I did, and like hundreds of human research subjects of the past Katu days.

"Honorable Enkri, ambassador Katu, you and I both know that humans are on the verge of their evolutionary development to be able to form naturally occurring telepathic networks, as soon as enough of them are born with a new region in the brain that is responsible for this fascinating ability. During the next Katu day, humans will make that evolutionary leap and will become a formidable threat to the Unkari race. I understand the Katu dynasty is trying to prevent their research experiment from spiralling out of control. I really do. But I appeal to the Enkri sense of moral responsibility for literally growing our race in a giant test tube and playing god with us.

"I know Enkri well enough to know that your dynasty is deeply ashamed of what your brothers from the other side of the planet have done with your discovery of an advanced peaceful species who once saved your ancestors from death at your most vulnerable moment, during your sleep cycle. Katu could not allow this fascinating ability to slip away from their hands, and whenever they took their turn in running Unkari affairs, they did everything they could to possess this power.

"It is Katu who destroyed the entire race of human ancestors. Katu are responsible for genocide. Katu are responsible for seeding the Earth. Finally, Katu are responsible for plagues and atrocities in human history, and all in order to manipulate the research sample. We all know that civil war between your tribes is imminent. We know that it will probably happen during the narrow dawn, the few Unkari hours when both dynasties are awake and sit at the High Joint Senate to handle the transfer of authority. We know that the next session of the Senate, for the first time in Unkari history, will probably result in the bloodshed."

Otis paused, but not to catch his breath. As a hologram, he did not breathe. He paused for dramatic effect. And his intent worked. Both Enkri and Katu sat in the room very quiet, emitting faint splashes of turquoise, that She interpreted for me as sadness. Otis continued. "There is a narrow window of opportunity to prevent any of this from happening. And it will slip away if you execute Lieutenant Mazula. As you know from the interrogation phase, Lieutenant Mazula has the genetic marker, like I do. However, he benefitted from 300 years of evolution, and she is almost able to oscillate without the implant. She proved it countless times, when he was captured by the Unkari soldiers, first on Erinozhan, then on the Gliese 581e research facility. Unlike me, Lieutenant Mazula can oscillate in a field that re-aligns his synaptic connections. This is the next evolutionary step. Although to be able to operate outside the field, she still requires the implant, but this is the best chance we have.

"I speak on behalf of Human Designation Mazula Desiree Lieutenant. In order to pay restitution for his crimes, Lieutenant Mazula accepts her death sentence, however, she requests to delay it. If we implant the tumor in her brain now, she will have the rest of Enkri day to work with the Earth Nations and the military, to expose them to the people, and to bring the human government to the negotiation table. We can still resolve this without extermination on a global scale. Maybe by a narrow margin, but we still can avoid the Enkri-Katu civil war and the extermination of humanity. All sides must step in and accept a sacrifice in their agendas. "Desiree Mazula volunteers her life to become a liaison between Unkari and humans. Honorable Enkri, Honorable ambassador Katu, as you can see, you have nothing to lose and all to gain."

The silence was deafening.

At that moment, I realized that She had been holding my hand all this time. *Nothing to lose.* Well put. With one small exception: one way or another, my life is over.

I was a time bomb, and now it was up to the panel to decide when it would go off.

Slowly the words and reasoning of Otis were sinking in, and I realized that avoiding a war between two galaxies at the cost of one life was not such a bad bargain. I turned to Ebony. She would not look at me, hiding two streams of tears flowing down her cheeks.

***

Enkri voted unanimously in favor of our plan, while Katu voted against. We fully anticipated it, but the most important thing was that the plan worked.

***

The tumor will kill me any time from six to eighteen months.

I am ashamed to realize I wasn't ready, even if my sacrifice would save the entire human race. Or the entire universe, for that matter. I am standing on the shore of the methane ocean, on the deserted beach, watching the fog slowly roll in and out, waiting for the surgery, when I hear quiet footsteps behind me. I turn and see ambassador Katu quickly approaching.

"Beautiful, isn't it?" he says in nearly perfect English.

"Ambassador, I did not know you spoke such good English."

"I have studied your species for a very long time."

"I see."

"I cannot allow it to happen," he says. "I am sorry." He draws a weapon from the folds of his robes and fires at me, right in the chest .

TIMELINE

286 - 615 - Enkri Day

615 - 944 - Katu Day

944 - 1273 - Enkri Day

1273 - 1602 - Katu Day

    1461 - 1463 Jeroen is abducted

1602 - 1931 - Enkri Day

    1600 - 1868 - Tokugawa Shōgunate Japan

    1882 - incident in Lebanon, Connecticut. Observance of the 'pizza slices' over the moon

    1912 - Wilfrid Voynich discovers the Voynich Manuscript

    1917 - JFK born, the incident in Portugal with Mother Mary apparition

    1930 - Voynich dies without ever deciphering the manuscript

1931-2260 - Katu Day

    1942 - battle for LA, JFK in ONI, Charleston

    1952 - DC UFO incident

    1961 - JFK's first day in office

    1962 - B-59, Cuban Missile crisis

    1969 - the missing minutes, incident on the Moon

    1986 - incident on Air Japan 1628 flight

    1998 - Riddif Ron allows Arkhipov to pass away

    2274 - Anika Borgess proposes translation of Voynichese and leaves the Fourth Orbital colony, joins the Royal Moroccan Fleet

    2275 - the First Contact

    2284 - Otis arrives on Lenauri

    2325 - Ny meets with Anika and receives information about Otis

2260-2589 - Enkri Day

2589-2918 - Katu Day

LOCAL GALACTIC GROUP:
MILKY WAY, SAGITTARIUS DWARF
AND ANDROMEDA GALAXIES

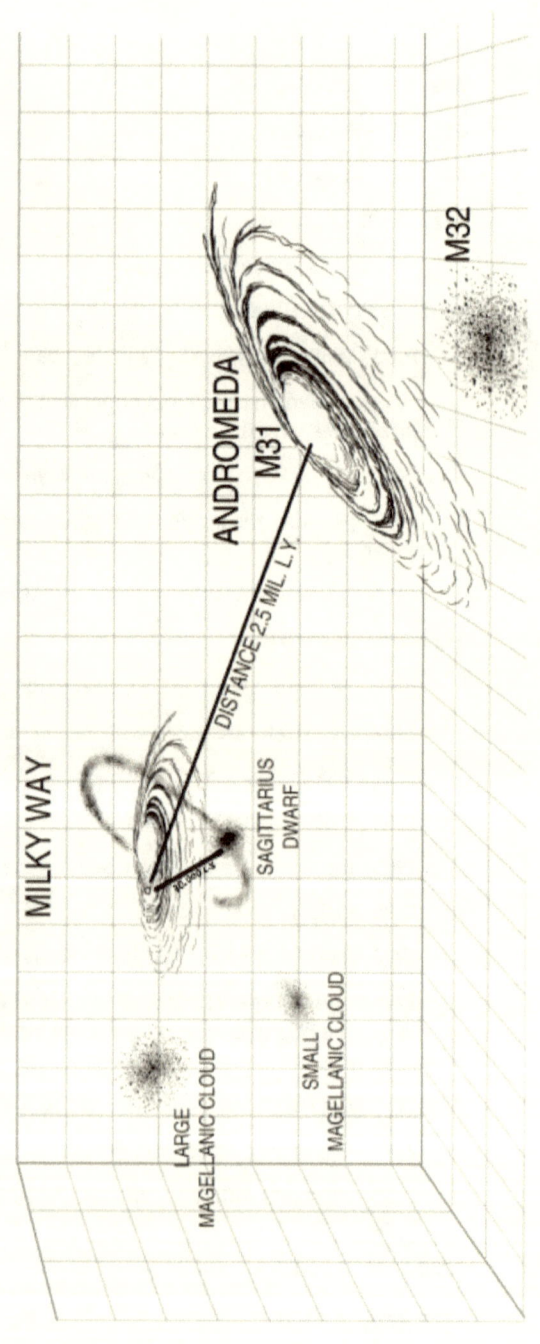

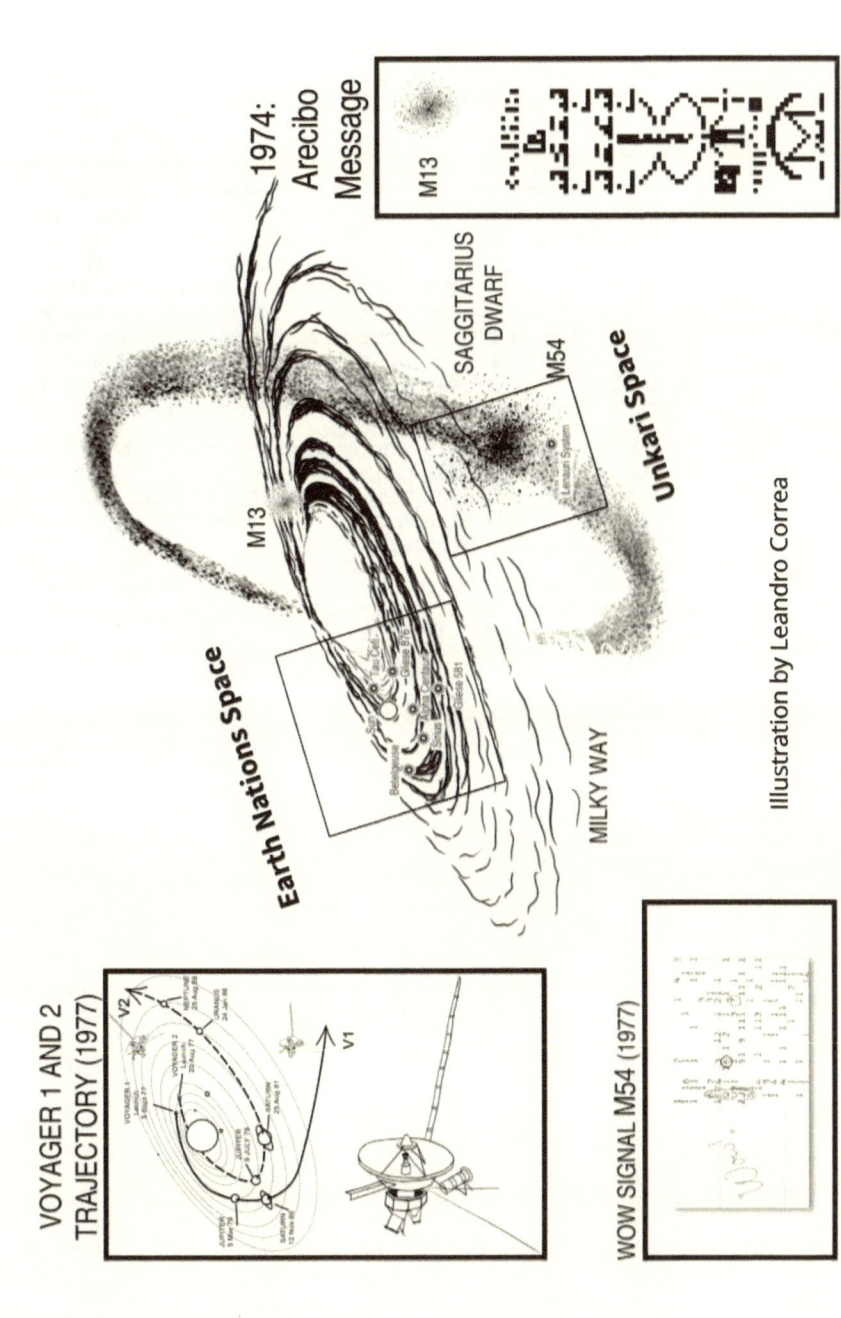

1974: Arecibo Message

M13

SAGGITARIUS DWARF

M13

M54

Earth Nations Space

Unkari Space

MILKY WAY

VOYAGER 1 AND 2 TRAJECTORY (1977)

V2

V1

WOW SIGNAL M54 (1977)

Illustration by Leandro Correa

Dear Reader!

Thank you for reading 329 Years Awake! I am beyond excited to have shared with you a universe that I've created. It is hard to believe how long it took me thinking about all these characters, their connections, and how to make the story both interesting and believable. Did it work? I really want to know your opinion! Please feel free to send me a message on any of my social media accounts, especially on @329YearsAwake on Facebook and Twitter! These accounts are created for you.

But you know what would make my heart melt? A review on Goodreads and especially on Amazon! Unfortunately without these reviews the book has no chance to succeed. Please take a minute of your time and write a quick review.

Thank you again for your time and money spent on the book. I will work hard to make my future books even better!

Sincerely yours,

Ellie

In her previous life, Ellie was a lawyer specializing in human rights. Now she writes fiction, consumes massive amounts of late night comedy and politics, collects typewriters, and lives all over the world with her spouse and a 5-yo Newfoundland dog. She lived, worked, and studied in such countries as Kosovo, Ukraine, Liberia, Albania, and the United States.

WHAT TO READ NEXT:
ELLIE'S PICKS

ELLIE MALONEY MAGAZINE

Check out Ellie's magazine **on MagCloud!** Ellie collected her exclusive fiction and professional photography in this luxury 60-page full-color magazine.

Issue #2 is coming soon! It is dedicated to 329 Years Awake, where Ellie tells about the history behind the book and opens up about exclusive subjects. She also cosplays scenes from 329 YA and photoshoots them with professional photographers.

"Lab 99", SCI-FI/COMICS

by Rujanee Mahakanjana and Christian Stanfield

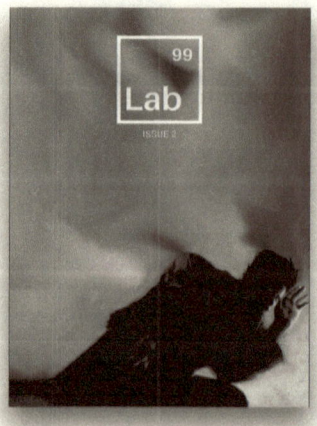

Lab 99 the comic book series follows the story of an interstellar lab that watches over our species and solar system. In the first issue, Alien (Eddie) has just returned to unexpected news after a mission on Earth. The comic book also introduces you to the backstories of the main characters in the feature film screenplay, Lab 99. Order your issue **on Patreon!**

The Three Hares & Other Memories: Poems

The Three Hares was inspired by the great Ukrainian poets, past and present, who protest against corruption, oppression, and injustice. The rest of the poems are primarily drawn from a decade of working in post-conflict countries such as Afghanistan, Kosovo and Liberia and the sense of displacement that accompanies the expat life.

Now on Amazon! Audio book is coming to Audible.com as well.

Scaffolding Magazine

Literary and art magazine featuring independent and traditionally published authors. Short fiction, artwork, fascinating editorials from around the world! Look for the issues **on Blurb.com**

ScaffoldingMag.com

Facebook/Twitter @ScaffoldingMag

"The Empty World", YA/SCI-FI

by Andrew Reeves

Fourteen-year-old Danny Ringrose's parents vanished without trace a year ago. His father a famous scientist, ridiculed for repeated attempts at cloning stones. For three years Danny has watched the mysterious building site next to his house, with its single pit hidden by a ring of cabins. Yet Danny can see the pit from his bedroom window, and he has watched the strange machinery being delivered to it, never to return, and the sombre scientist who occasionally pokes his head out, wanting nothing more than to remain unnoticed. Danny knows there is something important happening right beneath his town... beneath his house! Could it be connected to his parents' disappearance?

Now on Amazon!

www.ingramcontent.com/pod-product-compliance
Lightning Source LLC
Chambersburg PA
CBHW051318250626
47155CB00007B/2373